BONES and the DINOSAUR Mystery

A Viking Easy-to-Read

BY DAVID A. ADLER

ILLUSTRATED BY BARBARA JOHANSEN NEWMAN

VIKING

For Michael and Deborah —D. A.

"For THE guys in my life: Phil, Dave, Mike, and Ben. Gotta love 'em!" —B. J. N.

VIKING
Published by Penguin Group
Penguin Young Readers Group, 345 Hudson Street, New York, New York 10014, U.S.A.
Penguin Group (Canada), 90 Eglinton Avenue East, Suite 700, Toronto, Ontario, Canada M4V 3B2
(a division of Pearson Penguin Canada Inc.)
Penguin Books Ltd, 80 Strand, London WC2R 0RL, England
Penguin Ireland, 25 St Stephen's Green, Dublin 2, Ireland (a division of Penguin Books Ltd)
Penguin Group (Australia), 250 Camberwell Road, Camberwell, Victoria 3124, Australia
(a division of Pearson Australia Group Pty Ltd)
Penguin Books India Pvt Ltd, 11 Community Centre, Panchsheel Park, New Delhi – 110 017, India
Penguin Group (NZ), Cnr Airborne and Rosedale Roads, Albany, Auckland 1310, New Zealand
(a division of Pearson New Zealand Ltd)
Penguin Books (South Africa) (Pty) Ltd, 24 Sturdee Avenue, Rosebank, Johannesburg 2196, South Africa

Penguin Books Ltd, Registered Offices: 80 Strand, London WC2R 0RL, England

First published in 2005 by Viking, a division of Penguin Young Readers Group

3 5 7 9 10 8 6 4 2

LIBRARY OF CONGRESS CATALOGING-IN-PUBLICATION DATA
Adler, David A.
Bones and the dinosaur mystery / written by David A. Adler ;
illustrated by Barbara Johansen Newman.
p. cm.
Summary: Young Detective Jeffrey Bones investigates the disappearance of the
plastic dinosaur his grandfather just bought for him in a museum gift shop.
ISBN 0-670-06010-0 (hardcover)
[1. Lost and found possessions—Fiction. 2. Museums—Fiction. 3. Grandfathers—Fiction.
4. Dinosaurs—Fiction. 5. Mystery and detective stories.] I. Newman, Barbara Johansen, ill. II. Title.
PZ7.A2615Bof 2005
[Fic]—dc22
2004017392

Reading level 2.2

Manufactured in China

- CONTENTS -

1. Hello, Bones

"Hello, dinosaur bones.

I'm Bones, too.

I'm Detective Jeffrey Bones.

I solve mysteries."

"Hey," Grandpa called. "Look at this!"

I looked. It was a big dinosaur

with really big teeth.

I went to Grandpa and the dinosaur.

Sally was there, too.

She's Grandpa's friend.

"This is T-rex," Grandpa told me.

"When it was alive

it weighed five tons."

That's a lot of dinosaur.

I showed T-rex my detective bag.

"I've got great stuff in here," I said.

"Take a look at this."

I showed him my walkie-talkie set.

"I bet you never saw

one of these before," I said.

I walked around T-rex.

I read about him, too.

He was a meat eater.

Now that I can read,

I can find things out myself.

"Hey, Grandpa," I said

to the man standing next to me.

"Did you know T-rex

ate other dinosaurs?"

I looked up.

"Hey," I told the man.

"You're not my grandfather."

"I know that," the man said.

"Where is my grandfather?"

I asked the man.

"Where's Sally?"

"I don't know," the man said.

"I don't know either," I told him,

"but I'm a detective,

and detectives find things.

I'll find my grandfather

and Sally."

2. Little Blue T-Rex

It was easy for me

to find Grandpa and Sally.

They're old. They like to sit.

I just looked for a bench,

and there they were.

"Hey, Jeffrey," Sally said.

"Let's go to the gift shop.

We'll get a dinosaur

for you to take home."

"Oh, no," I told Sally.

"My parents say

I'm too young to have a pet."

Sally and Grandpa laughed.

"This won't be a real dinosaur,"

Grandpa said.

That's too bad, I thought.

I'd love to have a five-ton pet.

I followed the signs to the gift shop.

Grandpa and Sally followed me.

Sally picked up a large cloth dinosaur.

"I'm buying this for Michael," she said.

"He's my grandson."

Sally paid a man for it.

The man put the cloth dinosaur

in a large green bag.

Grandpa showed me a box

of small plastic dinosaurs.

"Pick one of these," he said.

I picked a blue T-rex.

Grandpa paid the man,

and he put my T-rex

in a small green bag.

I showed Sally my T-rex.

"That's so cute," Sally said.

She bought a pink plastic dinosaur

for her granddaughter Nancy.

It wasn't a T-rex.

She paid for it,

and it was put in a green bag, too.

Then she bought a dinosaur puppet

and a dinosaur oven mitt.

"I'll use this mitt when I cook," Sally said.

"Cook!" Grandpa said.

"Did you say 'cook'?

You know cooking makes me hungry."

Then Grandpa looked at me and asked,

"Aren't you hungry?"

"Yes and no," I said.

"I'm not hungry for vegetables,

but I am hungry for ice cream."

"Then we'll get ice cream," Grandpa said.

We went to the snack place.

I got a dish of strawberry ice cream.

Grandpa and Sally got cups of tea

and a piece of coffee cake to share.

The snack place was crowded,

but we found a table.

I put my green bag on the table

and ate my ice cream.

Sally put her green bags on the table.

When we were all done

with the tea, cake, and ice cream

Grandpa said, "Let's go and see

the moon rocks."

I looked at our table.

A boy and his father

were sitting there.

On the table there was ice cream

and juice, but no small green bag.

Grandpa, Sally, and I

went to the woman who sold snacks.

"Did anyone find a blue plastic T-rex

in a small green bag?" I asked.

"No," she said.

Hm, I thought.

I've got to do some detective work.

I opened my detective bag

and took out my walkie-talkies.

I gave one to Grandpa and one to Sally.

"Grandpa and I will go this way," I said.

I pointed to the tables by the windows

so Grandpa and Sally would know

which way was "this way."

"Sally, you can go the other way."

I pointed to the tables by the door.

"Please, look for my small green bag,"

I told Sally. "If you find it,

call me and Grandpa on the walkie-talkie."

Grandpa and I looked at the tables

near the window.

"Look at all these people," Grandpa said.

"People sure do get hungry

when they look at dinosaur bones."

"Hey!" I told Grandpa.

"Look over there."

A girl and her mother

were sitting at a table by the window.

On the table were salads,

cups of milk, and a small green bag.

I pushed the TALK button

on my walkie-talkie.

"Hey," I told Sally.

"I found T-rex."

Then I pointed at the small green bag.

"Hey," I said to the girl,

"what's in the bag?"

4. I Wanted T-Rex

"Oh, my," Grandpa said.

"First say hello."

So that's what I did.

"Hello," I said to the girl.

"What's in the bag?"

"It's a dinosaur," the girl said.

"I know it is," I told her.

"It's a blue plastic T-rex."

"Oh, no," she said.

"T-rex was a mean dinosaur.

T-rex was a meat eater.

I bought a plant eater."

She opened the bag

and showed me a plant eater.

I looked at the salads

the girl and her mother were eating

and knew why she wanted

a plant-eating dinosaur.

This girl and her mother

were plant eaters, too.

"Thank you," I said to the girl.

I looked up,

and there was Sally.

"This is silly," Sally said.

"We don't have to look and look

for your toy dinosaur.

We can just buy you another one."

Sally gave me my walkie-talkie.

I put the two walkie-talkies

in my detective bag.

I was happy I would get a new T-rex,

but I wasn't happy

about losing the old one.

I'm a detective.

Smart detectives find things.

Maybe, I thought,

I'm not such a smart detective!

We went to the gift shop.

I looked at all the small plastic dinosaurs.

There were lots of plant eaters,

but no T-rex dinosaurs.

I told the gift shop man,

"I want a blue T-rex."

"I'm sorry," he said.

"A small boy bought the last T-rex."

Then he looked at me.

"You're the boy who bought it."

Hey! I'm not small! I thought.

Grandpa said, "I'll buy you a different dinosaur."

But I didn't want a different dinosaur.

I wanted a T-rex.

Sally sat on a bench

and opened the bag.

She took out the large cloth dinosaur

and put it on the bench.

Then she took out

four small green bags.

In one was a pink plastic dinosaur.

In the others were a dinosaur puppet,

a dinosaur oven mitt,

and my blue plastic T-rex.

"Hey," I asked Sally.

"Where are all your small green bags?"

"In here," Sally said.

"I put the smaller bags in the big one."

Just like big fish

that eat smaller fish, I thought.

"Maybe you put my small green bag

in there, too," I said.

"Oh, my," Sally said.

"Maybe I did."

That reminded me of T-rex.

There are no more T-rex dinosaurs.

Next we saw how big animals

eat small animals.

I looked at the painting of a large fish

about to eat a smaller fish

that was about to eat an even smaller fish.

Then I looked at Sally.

Sally had a large green bag.

I smiled.

Maybe I am a good detective, I thought.

Maybe I solved the mystery

of my missing T-rex.

5. I Am a Great Detective!

Grandpa, Sally, and I
left the gift shop.
We looked at pictures
taken from outer space.
We looked at pictures of Earth
and other planets.
We looked at pictures of animals
that are disappearing.
One day soon there may be no more
whooping cranes, gray wolves,
key deer, or California condors.

I hugged my T-rex.

"I missed you," I said.

"So much has happened

since you disappeared."

"I'm sorry," Sally said.

"When I saw all these green bags

on the snack bar table,

I was afraid one would get lost."

"Well," I told Sally,

"I'm not sorry

you put my bag in yours.

You helped me prove

that I'm still a great detective."

31

Then I asked T-rex,

"You're lots of years old.

Have you ever met a better detective

than the great Jeffrey Bones?"

T-rex didn't answer.

I guess he never met

a better detective than me.

Magus to the Hermetic Order of the Golden Sprout, 12th
Dan Master of Dimac, poet, adventurer, swordsman and
concert pianist; big game hunter, Best Dressed Man of
1933; mountaineer, lone yachtsman, Shakespearian actor
and topless go-go dancer; Robert Rankin's hobbies include
passive smoking, communicating with the dead and lying
about his achievements. He lives in Sussex with his wife
and family.

Robert Rankin is the author of *Sprout Mask Replica*,
Nostradamus Ate My Hamster, *A Dog Called Demolition*,
The Garden of Unearthly Delights, *The Greatest Show Off
Earth*, *Raiders of the Lost Car Park*, *The Book of Ultimate
Truths*, *Armageddon The Musical*, *They Came and Ate Us:
Armageddon II The B Movie*, *The Suburban Book of the
Dead: Armageddon III The Remake* and the *Brentford*
quintet: *The Antipope*, *The Brentford Triangle*, *East of
Ealing*, *The Sprouts of Wrath* and *The Brentford Chainstore
Massacre*, which are all published by Corgi books. Robert
Rankin's latest novel, *The Dance of the Voodoo Handbag*, is
now available as a Doubleday hardback.

What they say about Robert Rankin:

'One of the rare guys who can always make me laugh'
Terry Pratchett

'To the top-selling ranks of humorists such as Douglas
Adams and Terry Pratchett, let us welcome Mr Rankin'
Tom Hutchinson, *The Times*

'A born writer with a taste for the occult. Robert Rankin
is to Brentford what William Faulkner was to
Yoknaptawpha County'
Time Out

'One of the finest living comic writers . . . a sort of
drinking man's H.G. Wells'
Midweek

THE MOST
AMAZING MAN
WHO EVER LIVED

Robert Rankin

CORGI BOOKS

THE MOST AMAZING MAN WHO EVER LIVED
A CORGI BOOK : 0 552 14211 5

Originally published in Great Britain by Doubleday
a division of Transworld Publishers Ltd

PRINTING HISTORY
Doubleday edition published 1995
Corgi edition published 1995
Corgi edition reprinted 1996
Corgi edition reprinted 1998

Typeset in 11/12pt Monotype Plantin by
Hewer Text Composition Services, Edinburgh.

Corgi Books are published by Transworld Publishers Ltd,
61–63 Uxbridge Road, London W5 5SA,
in Australia by Transworld Publishers (Australia) Pty Ltd,
15–25 Helles Avenue, Moorebank, NSW 2170,
and in New Zealand by Transworld Publishers (NZ) Ltd,
3 William Pickering Drive, Albany, Auckland.

Printed and bound in Great Britain by
Cox & Wyman Ltd, Reading, Berkshire.

For the most amazing man who
ever published me. All hail to
Mr Patrick Janson-Smith

1

THIS ICARUS SORT OF STUFF

'And then I shall leap from the east pier and be borne aloft by these wings.' Norman the elder made an expansive gesture which Norman the younger found most encouraging. 'Up I shall go.' The daddy's right hand described the flight path. 'Across and around.' His left hand joined in with much gusto. 'And away.' The hands flew off in the direction of France then came home to roost in the elder Norman's trouser pockets.

'Gosh,' said his son, 'and with only the aid of these.'

The daddy stroked the wings upon the garage workbench. 'The aid of these alone.'

Young Norman sighed a sigh. 'Gosh,' he said once more, 'imagine that.'

'Something to tell your school chums, eh?' The daddy nudged his son confidentially in the rib area. 'Not many of them got fathers who can fly, I'll bet.'

Young Norman shook his head. 'Not many,' he said, 'but a few.'

'*A few?*'

'Well, Blenkinsop's father claims to have mastered the Lamaist art of levitation. Charlie Huxley's brother has a pair of zero-gravity trousers and Boris Timms says he has a priestly uncle who can inflate his stomach with helium and propel himself through the sky by fa—'

His father cut him mercifully short. 'Not many got feathered wings, by the sound of it.'

Young Norman shook his head. 'Not many,' he agreed.

The elder Norman ran a loving knuckle across the feathered wings. 'Fine big wings these,' he said, gazing wistfully through the cobwebbed garage window towards the lonely sea and the sky. 'Fine big wings.'

On his way to school the next morning the boy Norman thought a lot about the conversation he'd had with his father.

Could it be, he asked himself, that the daddy has truly cracked it regarding this wing business, or is this just another of the sad flights of fancy to which the old chap has become subject of late?

The annual *Skelington Bay East Pier Man-Powered Flight Competition* always drew the holiday-makers. And the annual £1000 prize for the first successful one-thousand-foot flight always drew the town's eccentrics. But no-one was actually expected really to win the money. It was all just a bit of summertime jolly, wasn't it? Men in cardboard planes and dicky-bird costumes jumping into the sea to raise money for charity.

A bit of jolly. That was all it was.

Although it didn't *have* to be.

Norman strode on, chewing gum and bouncing a tennis ball.

It didn't *have* to be.

As it was Thursday it was Science for 3A.

Norman sat at the back of the class, that he might observe whilst remaining unobserved.

Mr Bailey bashed the blackboard with his baton. 'Boyle's law,' said he, in the voice of one who really cared about such things. 'What do we know of Boyle's law?' The eyes behind his pebbled specs searched in vain

8

for that little island of enlightenment set in the sea of vacant faces. 'Blenkinsop?'

Blenkinsop the Buddhist pulled his finger from his nose. Examining the yield he said, 'There is only one law and that is the law of dharma.'

'The law of dharma.' Mr Bailey beckoned with his baton. 'Come hither, boy, and have your trousers dusted.'

Sheltering behind Bilson's gargantuan frame, Norman leaned upon an elbow and stared out of the window. His thoughts were far from the horrors of corporal punishment. They were sailing high above with Timms' clerical uncle and a veritable flock of airborne relations. There couldn't be too much to this flying lark if you really put your mind to it. A lad of his capabilities should surely be able to figure it out.

On Friday there was Games. PE it was called.

3A's pimply personnel stood shivering in the drafty hall that springtime never reached. Those whom loving mothers had furnished with 'notes' sat grinning from the safety of the stage. Those with parents who believed in healthy exercise and team spirit shuffled in their vests and shorts and viewed the exalted ones with a healthless mixture of envy, loathing and contempt.

Mr McLaren the games teacher sprinted knees-high into the echoing hall. Clad in the regulation-issue soiled track suit and evil-smelling plimsolls, his arrival brought dread to the non-athletic noteless.

'Vaulting horse, Tompkins and Turner. At the *double*!' The order was barked out in that staccato ex-national-service voice that you don't hear much of nowadays. 'Straight line, the rest of you. Number off. Wait for . . . it. *Now*!'

'One, two, three, four,' went the quavery wavery

9

voices, to end with the big, deep 'twenty-three' of Teddy Bilson.

'And *go*!'

Number One was stubby Harry Hughes. His dash towards the towering horse was determined and courageous. His would be the only broken collar bone of the day.

Norman was unlucky Thirteen in the quivering queue. 'A man with feathered wings might soar above that vaulting horse with next to no effort at all,' he confided to the trembling Twelve.

'To paraphrase the late great Winston Churchill,' the Dozen replied, 'Give us the wings and we will finish the job.'

'*Twelve*!' screamed the martial Mr McLaren.

'God bless me,' whimpered Number Twelve, making the sign of the cross.

'With wings all things are possible,' Norman informed Number Fourteen, a big lad with a small moustache. 'All things to do with flying, anyhow.'

Number Fourteen nodded. 'Wings have their uses,' he said, 'this cannot be denied. But I am approaching fifteen years of age and beginning to take a lively interest in girls.'

Norman stroked his hairless upper-lip area. 'Further conversation with you on the subject of wings would probably be wasted then, I suppose.'

Number Fourteen nodded again. 'Isn't there a bird in South America called the Giant Condom?' he asked.

'*Thirteen*!' bawled the games teacher.

'God bless *me*!' mumbled Norman. And this gave him a sudden idea.

At 5.30 a.m. on the following Sunday, young Norman, damp with dew and ring-fingered by carrier bags, laboured to the top of Druid's Tor and stood puffing and panting to await the arrival of the new sun.

Below him Skelington Bay, holiday town of his birth, lurked in sea mist, its twin piers paddling in the tide.

Above him the sky. The big, wide-open sky.

Just waiting.

It was the 'God bless *me*' of Games that had brought young Norman here. It had recalled to him a painting he'd once seen during a force-marched school outing to the town hall.

It was one of those huge Pre-Raphaelite jobbies that municipal councils used to snap up for a song before the War, to cover the cracks in their walls. It was of angels evident at the birth of the Christ child. And the thing about these angels was that, although togged up in what appeared to be old curtains and bereft of footwear, they had, as Norman remembered quite clearly, *dirty great wings of the feathered variety growing out of their backs*.

'Fine big wings,' as his father would have said.

And the recollection of these fine big wings had set young Norman thinking.

Now, angels could fly. This was well known. But, according to the Bible, no matter how good you were while alive, your chances of becoming an angel when dead were somewhat less than zero. The old harps and wings were not doled out to the blessed the way cartoonists would have us believe. You *joined* the angels. You did not become one.

And of course you did have to be dead first.

And of course, if you were dead, then you couldn't win the man-powered flight competition and fly off with the £1000 prize.

But what say, if you could communicate with angels? Contact them, with a view to genning up on the various hints and wrinkles concerning the art of 'winging it'? Surely that would give you the supernatural edge on the opposition.

Of course it would.

And so it was to this end that Norman had spent the greater part of Saturday in the reference section of Skelington Public Library. He'd drawn a bit of a blank with the Christian tracts though. These spoke a lot about prayer and guilt and living a blameless life, but nothing about how you could get any one-on-one chit-chat with any of the feather-clad choirs eternal. In fact, the would-be aviator was just on the point of chucking the whole thing in and making off to the Wimpy Bar, when the new librarian, the one on the Job Opportunities Scheme, skulked over with a large buff-coloured book and thrust it into his hands. 'Check this out, kid,' he said. 'I think it's just what you're looking for.'

Norman eyed the book with interest.

Its title was *The Necronomicon*.

Now it is a fact well known amongst satanic circles, or wherever two or three heavy-metal fans are gathered together, that every borough library secretly possesses a copy of *The Necronomicon*. Not the original, of course, bound in the skin of a sacrificial virgin and penned in the blood of the mad Arab Abdul Alhazred. The Vatican has *that*. But most often they possess one of the forbidden Latin translations of Olaus Wormius, revised into English and published as a part-work for private subscription by Marshall Cavendish, or some such.

Of course the librarians, who have taken whatever binding oath they take during their secret initiation ceremonies, won't let you see it. They'll swear blind that it doesn't even exist.

But then they would, wouldn't they?

The new librarian on the Job Opportunities Scheme

was wearing a *Deicide* T-shirt with the legend DEAD BY DAWN* printed across the front. His name was Chris and he had lots of hair. And he'd only been working there for a day. 'Use the photocopier and go for it,' was his advice.

So Norman had done and was doing so even now.

To the early-rising passer-by, the dog-walker or poet seeking inspiration upon the misty hilltop, the youth would have presented a most disconcerting spectacle. Now stripped down to his Y-fronts and crouched within the confines of the lop-sided pentagram he'd just chalked out, his Thermos flask and sandwich box before him and a selection of anything he could find that looked remotely 'occult' spread whither and so, he clutched his photo-copies in one hand and began to make wild gestures with the other.

And to *intone*.

The way you would.

'Hail unto thee, thou Ancient Ones,' he went, as best he could, with the unbroken voice and the touch of catarrh. 'Hail unto thee, Absu Mummu Tiamet, Nar Maturu, Yog Sothoth, Nyarlathotep and the like. I conjure thee, thou fungous abnormalities too hideous for the grave's holding. Rise from your haunts of forever night and summon unto me.'

It had to be said that there was a distinct air of blasphemy about all this. And an older and wiser fellow might perhaps have thought twice before seeking to invoke the powers of darkness and taking the risk of eternal damnation, just to win the first prize in a man-powered flight competition.

But then, when you're fourteen, you do that sort of

---

* The fourth track on side one of Deicide's imaginatively titled album, *Deicide*.

13

thing. We all do. Indeed who amongst us can truly put their hand upon their heart and swear that they never once offered up a sacrifice to Satan during their teenage years?

Not many!

'Harken unto me,' the youth continued, 'Ninnghiz-hidda, lak Sakkak, Laibach, Napalm Death and Celtic Frost. Ye ghids and bogiebeasts, come serve I that standith in the five-pointed star. Deliver unto me what I request. Come bring me wings!'

Norman had decided upon the direct approach. Keep things sharp, crisp, to the point. Summon up the deep, dark denizens from out the pit-that-hath-no-bottom. Have them cough up the goods. Then back with them to from whence they came. And quick. It was all for the best.

'I summons you and constrain you by the powers of Lord Cthulhu, who is not dead but only getting his head down for a bit of shut eye. Obey my commands. Manifest. Give me Wings, Wings, Wings! I want them and I want them now. All I want is Wings!'

If there was a distinct (a very distinct) air of blasphemy about all this, then there was also the feeling that some callous spirit, with an eye for the obvious, might any moment appear before Norman, bearing a copy of Paul McCartney's latest album in its scaly paw.

'Wings!' impeached Norman. 'I command you, bring me Wings!'

It was no laughing matter really (especially the Paul McCartney gag). It was a very bad idea doing this. The birds that had been making free with the dawn chorus had gone very quiet indeed. And there was a definite chill in the air.

But Norman had started and he meant to finish. Chris had underlined for him a certain Latin incantation, which was known as *The Great Calling*. And the young magician in the Y-fronts bawled it out at the top of his voice, with a bit of the old 'What do we want? Wings! When do we want 'em? Now!' thrown in for good measure, wherever he felt it appropriate.

And then suddenly Norman stopped.

Something was stirring. Something large. Norman couldn't see it, but somehow he could sense its approach.

And then he heard it.

From far away upon that misty morn, there came a distant-flapping sound, which sounded, for all the world, like nothing less than the sound of a distant flapping.

Norman got a cold sweat on to go with his damp behind. He strained his eyes into the rising mists. The sun, now half awake, glistened upon the hedgerows and dazzled him.

He gave his ears a strain also. The flapping sound grew louder. Something was on the approach. Something monstrous.

Great wings were beating on the morning air. Great wings like those of The Giant Condom itself.

'Yes!' screamed Norman, most pleased to get such a swift return upon such a small Satanic outlay. 'I'm here. My Wings. My Wings. My Wings.'

It was overhead. It was right overhead. It had come straight to him. This was it.

'*My Wings!*'

There was a sharp, snapping sound; a moment's silence; a scream from on high. The cry of a great bird? Not as such.

Another scream and then down through the mist, at the speed of one hundred and eighty feet per second, came a cascade of wire, wood, wax, pegs, feathers—

And Norman the elder.

'Look out below,' went this unhappiest of men. 'Test-flight systems failure. Aaaaaaaagh!'

15

'Oh my God!' Norman the younger struggled to make his escape. But his left toe had somehow become intimately entangled in the crotch of his Y-fronts.

So he couldn't.

In the few seconds that remained to him on this plane of existence, young Norman had just enough time to ponder on the folly of the particular method he'd chosen to go about solving the man-powered flight problem. But not quite enough to apologize to God.

Shame really.

The sun, now fully risen, looked down upon the drying grass of Druid's Tor and viewed the broken wreckage that had once been Norman and his dad.

The old sun smiled, for, after all, it had seen this Icarus sort of stuff before and would probably come up to see it again. Some time.

A little later a party of librarians came up to hold an initiation ceremony and found the sorry remains of the two erstwhile airmen. They too mused upon man's folly.

One, by the name of Chris, who wore the robes of Initiate Novice Zero Grade, pushed aside his corkscrew hair and raised his eyes towards the heavens as if searching for a sign.

'Surely', he said, 'that would be a Roman Catholic priest I see floating up there.'

2

The most amazing man who ever lived lay soaking in his bath.

Those who personally attended to the most amazing man, who primped and pampered his person, plumped up his pillows and plucked his nasal hairs, knelt about the polished marble bath-tub in attitudes of supplication and readiness.

Theirs was to *do*. His was only to *be*.

Below, in the grand reception hall, its pink walls made gay with a priceless collection of Canalettos, Caravaggios, Carsons, Klees and Koons, servants in wigs of burnished golden wire and tasselled leotards greeted the visiting heads of state, the captains of industry, the archbishops, press barons, poets and princes.

Daily they came, these great folk, to seek the most amazing man, that he might favour them with his advice, forward a solution to some world crisis or another, bless or father children. Offer them a word. Or just a simple gesture.

In the most amazing man's nympharium, his concubines lounged upon silken cushions, sucking sherbet lemons and soaking their Lotus-feet in bowls of baby oil. Some read copies of *Hello!* magazine. Others did not.

In the kitchen, Dave the griddle chef turned a spam fritter in the frying-pan and whistled a Celtic Frost number.*

---

* Possibly 'Necromantical Screams', the last track on their classic *To Mega Therion* album.

17

In a distant room, the most amazing man's private secretary took the morning's telepathic dictation from her master and clattered away on the typewriter.

All was peace and harmony, the way that all should be.

With half-closed eyes and belly breaking surface, the most amazing man broadcast in thoughts the words, And though I am naturally touched that you have named the flagship of your new cruise line after me, I regret that I shall not be able to swing the old bottle of Bol', as I will be attending the world premier of my new movie. Yours, et cetera, et cetera.

'Kindly read that back to me, Mavis, then be so good as to pop over to the kitchen and tell Dave he's whistling that Celtic Frost number in the wrong key. Then you may take the rest of the day off.'

In the distant room, Mavis plucked the sheet of Conqueror from the Remington and read from it aloud. 'Thank you, master.' Then she said, 'You are, as ever, the nice one.'

'I am indeed.' The day's mail taken care of, the most amazing man sank lower into his bath water and sought to compose the final mathematical equation needed to complete his formula for the universal panacea and elixir of life.

And he would have had it too, if it hadn't been for the violent pounding upon his bedsit door and the howls of complaint from his landlady.

And had he not been the most amazing man who ever lived, it is probable that he would have awoken to find, that as in the very worst of comedy traditions, his amazingness was nothing more than a dream and he was very much less than amazing.

'Get out of that bed, you lazy sod, or I'll have my husband Cyril come and break down the door!'

The most amazing man who ever lived awoke with a start.

To find himself, once more in the swank West London office of his publisher.

'My sincerest apologies,' he said to this body. 'I think I must have dozed off.'

'No need to apologize.' The publisher spoke through gritted teeth. 'No need at all.'

'On the contrary, my dear fellow. I momentarily deprived you of my scintillating conversation. Quite unforgivable on my part.'

'Quite.' The publisher leaned back in his big, red-leather publisher's chair and puffed on a small cheroot. 'You were perhaps about to scintillate me with an explanation regarding the overdue delivery of your manuscript.'

The most amazing man shook his head. 'On the contrary once again. I merely dropped in to give you my monthly expense chitty and pick up a cheque. And to bring untold joy to you, by my simply being here, of course.'

'Of course.' The publisher viewed the bringer of absolutely no joy whatsoever, who dwelt hugely in the guest chair beyond his big, red-leather-topped publisher's desk. How, he asked himself, did he let this man persuade him to go on forking out great chunks of the firm's profits each month, while he worked upon his autobiography? His auto*hagiography*?

A work entitled *The Most Amazing Man Who Ever Lived*. A work of which, as yet, the publisher had not seen a solitary page.

Who *was* this man?

What was he?

He was certainly *somebody*. His physical presence alone marked him far from the madding crowd. He was large in every sense of the word: well over six feet tall and generously proportioned around and all about. He swelled from within a three-piece green plus-fours suit of hand-loomed Bolskine tweed. A red silk cravat was secured at his massive throat by a diamond pin. Exotic rings sheathed most of his prodigious fingers. A watch chain, hung with amulets and crystals, adorned his straining waistcoat.

His head was a great shaven dome. His face all beetling brows and jostling jowls. His nose was a hawk's beak. His mouth wore a merry grin.

But it was the eyes that had it. Black with white pupils they were. You didn't see eyes like that every day of the week. And the way those eyes looked at you. As if focusing not upon *your* eyes, but at some point near to the back of your head. As if they could see right into you. Most disconcerting that.

And he was doing it right now.

The publisher flicked ash from his cheroot towards the ashbowl and missed. That was what he looked like, this man.

But who *was* he?

The stories regarding him were legion. He had travelled everywhere, met everybody and done everything. Sometimes done it twice. He had crossed the Sahara desert on a unicycle to win a bet with Humphrey Bogart and swum around Cape Horn because President Truman had told him it couldn't be done. Mother Teresa referred to him as 'a sexpot' and his own grandmother gave him the credit for teaching her how to suck eggs.

He'd wowed them at Woodstock, when he upstaged Jimi Hendrix with a ukelele solo and had twice won the Summerslam at Wembley. The beasts called him brother and the brothers called him bro'. And in Fiji he was worshipped as a god.

His name was well known to the publisher, who had written it in the *pay* section of far too many cheques.

20

It was Hugo Artemis Solon Saturnicus Reginald Arthur Rune.

And he had fallen asleep once more.

'It will not do!' The publisher brought his fist hard down upon the red-leather top of his red-leather-topped publisher's desk, upending the ashbowl and jangling the telephones.

The Tallahassee Tap Dance Champion of 1934 awoke once more and enquired as to whether his cheque had been made out.

'There will be no cheque until I see words on a page. Your words.'

'I have many words,' said Hugo Rune. 'All of them profound and lots running to several syllables apiece.'

'I want the completed manuscript by the end of the week. There will be no more cheques until I receive it.'

'I'll take cash then,' said the man who shot the man who shot Liberty Valance.

'You will take yourself off to your typewriter. And *now!*' The publisher rose from his big, red-leather publisher's chair, pointing the direction to the door.

'Sit down. Sit down.' Hugo Rune fluttered his porcine pinkies and the publisher sat down. The publisher jumped up again. 'I will not sit down,' said he.

Rune cocked his head upon one side and perused the publisher. He observed a slim fellow, elegantly dressed in white cotton shirt, club tie, black blazer and grey flannels. Middle forties, neatly featured, own hair and teeth. Well-developed cerebellum.

The publisher's name was Andrew Jackson-Five. A name well known to Rune, who had seen it signed at the bottom of far too few cheques for his personal liking. And a name that the man who once *hopped* the four-minute mile could read clearly on the tag inside the publisher's shirt collar.

Rune also noticed the increased motor-neuron activity in the publisher's hypothalamus, indicating his desire to take an early lunch.

'I know a nearby eating house,' said Rune, 'that serves a most affable *bœuf en croute*, fried chicken livers with grilled pineapple, bread-and-butter pudding and banana custard. Also the griddle chef knocks out some home-brewed vodka that could strip the tiles off the nose cone of a Saturn Five. Shall we dine?'

'*No*! We shall *not* dine.' The publisher crumpled his cheroot into the ashbowl. 'I have had enough of your extravagances, Rune.'

'*Mr* Rune,' said Mr Rune. 'And I know not of which extravagances you speak.'

The publisher sank back into his chair (same one, red leather), and took up *Mr* Rune's expense chitty for the month. It was a very substantial expense chitty. It ran to twenty-three pages, closely typed. Leafing through he chose a random entry.

'Toilet paper,' he said.

'Toilet paper?' Rune buffed his watch chain with an oversized red, gingham hanky. 'You can hardly call toilet paper an expense.'

'*Monogrammed* toilet paper?'

'And why should it not be so? Are you suggesting that toilet paper which has been handmade in Japan from ground water iris, gladioli and tinted cotton flax, scented with bergamot and sassafras, then individually crafted into the shape of the sacred lotus, does not deserve to be monogrammed?'

'You have *lotus*-shaped toilet paper?' The publisher's jaw hung positively slack.

'I am Rune,' quoth Rune. 'I unscrew the inscrutable and ef at the ineffable. Do you think that I should have my bottom wiped for me with some proprietary brand of bog roll?'

'Did you say, have your bottom wiped *for* you?'

'I find your interest in my bodily functions beginning to border on the fetishistic,' said Rune. 'You're not a member of the shirt-lifting fraternity, are you by any chance?'

'*What*?' Mr Jackson-Five fell back in his chair. 'How dare you, sir!' said he.

'*Sir* is a bit more like it. And if you want to know, I flush the poo-poo all away. Unlike my good chum the Dalai Lama, whose dung used to be collected, dried, ground up and used as a sacramental host.'

'It never was.'

'It was too.'*

'That is disgusting.'

'Not nearly as disgusting as any one of a number of things I could call immediately to mind.'

'Enough,' said Mr Jackson-Five, rising once more to his feet. 'Enough, enough, enough. I am a busy man. Kindly depart at once and furnish me with your finished manuscript by no later than Friday. Goodbye.'

'Sit down,' said Rune. 'Sit down, answer your telephone, then write out my cheque.'

'My telephone is not ringing.'

'But it will. As surely as a fat lass with a cold sore will issue through your door at any moment, to tell you that your car has been wheel-clamped.'

'My car is in the car-park. Goodbye, Mr Rune. Manuscript by Friday and no later.'

'Phone,' said Rune and the telephone began to ring.

'Sheer coincidence,' said the publisher. 'Goodbye.'

'Head office,' said Rune. 'On the line, New York, the Managing Director. Urgent call, you'd best pick it up.'

---

* It was too, actually.

'Nonsense.' Mr Jackson-Five sat down and picked up the telephone receiver. 'Hello,' said he.

Words entered his ear via the transatlantic undersea cable link or the geo-stationary satellite telecommunications jobbie, or some other unlikely piece of advanced technological hocus-pocus.

'Hello, *sir*.' Mr Jackson-Five sat up very straight in his seat. 'Rune? *Mr* Rune, yes. He's with me now, sir. Do *what*, sir? But, sir, do you know how much his expenses are this month? What? Money *no* object? But, sir . . . Yes, yes, all right; at once, sir.'

'Perk up,' said Hugo Rune as Mr Jackson-Five put down the phone and took out his cheque-book. 'No sign of the fat lass with the cold sore. Make that out for cash, if you'd be so kind.'

'You would appear to have friends in very high places,' said the publisher.

'It would appear that way, yes,' replied Hugo Rune. 'But now I must away. Are you sure you will not join me for lunch?'

Mr Jackson-Five shook his head. 'The manuscript by Friday?' he asked in a tone all forlorn.

'I will have my private secretary fax it up from Skelington Bay.'

'Taking a little holiday then, are you?' The bitter edge returned to the publisher's voice.

'Rune has no time for holidays. I am going there in connection with a project I am currently engaged upon for the British government. Very hush-hush. Official Secrets Act and all that kind of thing. Regret I cannot tell you more.' Hugo Rune tapped at his hawk's-beak hooter. 'Highly classified.'

Jackson-Five buried his face in his hands. 'Go home, Mr Rune, go home.'

'Via the bank,' said Rune, whisking his cheque from

the publisher's desk and folding it into his beaver-skin wallet (a gift from Mae West). 'Goodday to you.'

'Goodday.'

And Hugo Rune took his leave.

Away across the water in the city of New York, the Managing Director of Transglobe Publishing had replaced the telephone receiver after his conversation with Mr Andrew Jackson-Five.

Now he sank back into the perfumed water of his marble bath-tub and sought once more to compose the final mathematical equation which would complete his formula for a universal panacea and elixir of life.

He was a large man and amply proportioned, and the resemblance he bore to a certain Mr Hugo Rune was so striking that one might have taken him, if not for an identical twin, then to be none other than the self-same person.

But how could this be?

For, after all, here is Hugo Rune now, entering the lift at Transglobe's British headquarters. He is entering just as a fat lass with a cold sore is leaving it. She is bound for the office of Mr Jackson-Five as it happens. And she has a sad tale to relate – about how Mr Jackson-Five's Mercedes had to be moved from the car-park to make way for Mr Hugo Rune's chauffeur-driven limousine. And how it had not only been wheel-clamped in the High Street, but now towed away to boot.

Being the great humanitarian he is, Hugo Rune will not be returning to the publisher's office to tell him, 'I told you so.'

3

'Ashes to Ashes, funk to funky,' said the Reverend Cheesefoot.

'Dust to Dust, you bastard.' His lady wife tugged at his vestments and made that kind of face that some wives do when they find their husbands stoned at quite the wrong time of the day. '*Dust* to *dust*.'

'Bless you,' said the reverend, squinting at his prayer-book. 'Dust to dust it is then.'

A warm, spring sun breathed blessings upon Skelington Church, with its picturesque Gothic bits and bobs, its topiarized yews, its fifteenth-century lich-gate, its medieval brasses, and its '*Kinky Vicar made love to my luggage*,' scandal now running to its third week in the Sunday press.

The lads of 3A, each now an avid reader of the Sunday press, were grouped untidily about the open grave, where the coffin containing the mortal remains of Norman the younger had come to take its final rest. It had come there by a rather roundabout route from the church, but the lads had enjoyed the ramble. And it was a nice day for it, at least.

Norman's dad, wheelchair-bound, with both legs in plaster, blubbed quietly into a Kleenex tissue. Norman's mum, who had run off with a double-glazing salesman five years before and left no forwarding address, sat in a bungalow a good many miles to the north, eating cheese biscuits and watching daytime television.

'Dust to Dusty Springfield,' tittered the Reverend Cheesefoot. 'Who giveth this woman to be taken in matrimony? No, I've turned over two pages there.'

'Bit of an old cliché, drunken vicars, aren't they?' whispered Boris Timms to Charlie Huxley. 'I have an uncle in the priesthood, you know. He can inflate his stomach with helium and propel himself through the air by fa—'

'I had an uncle called Aldous,' whispered Charlie. 'And *he* really knew how to get high.'

'Shut up, you two, and show some respect.' Mr Bailey dealt Timms and Huxley blows to the left earholes.

'Man that is born of woman hath but a short time to live and is filled with muesli,' went the lover of luggage.

'Muesli's not bad,' sniggered Timms. 'And . . . ouch!' he continued, as his right ear got a clouting.

Rather too near to the graveside for his own comfort, Teddy Bilson shuffled his big feet, blew a dewdrop from the end of his nose and made snivelling sounds. 'It's a crying shame, so it is,' snivelled he. 'A crying shame.'

'Death is a purely human concept,' the Buddhist Blenkinsop consoled him. 'You see consciousness, being chemical in nature, changes as its chemistry changes. The one merges into the all, the all into the one. Now, the Sufis say—'

'Shut it!' Mr Bailey leaned forward to clout Blenkinsop in the ear. Blenkinsop, however, ducked nimbly aside and Mr Bailey disappeared into the open grave. Which is another thing you don't see every day of the week.

'The Sufis say,' continued Blenkinsop, 'what goes around, comes around. Or something so near as makes no odds at all.'

Seated upon a nearby gravestone was a pale-looking youth. He was somewhat short for his height, but old for his age. His hair was red and worn in a style that used to be known as *The Beatle Cut*. He had those freckles that

27

some people with red hair have, and those unsqueezed spots that all teenage boys have. He wore a grey school uniform and a puzzled expression.

His name was Norman.

Norman the younger.

'Who is that woman holding hands with my dad?' he asked the lad in white, who stood beside him, smirking like a good'n.

'She's a librarian. She saved your dad's life. Gave him mouth-to-mouth resuscitation. In the nick of time.'

'*Him* but not *me*?'

'You were too far gone, mate. Sorry.'

'So I'm . . . you know . . . I'm—'

'Dead, mate, yes. As dead as a, well, dead as a dead boy. Yeah.'

'What a bummer.' Norman looked on as various mourners sought to hoist Mr Bailey from the open grave. He was pleased to see that none of 3A was helping.

'That suitcase-shagger is making a right holy show of my funeral,' said Norman. 'I might have hoped for a more dignified send-off.'

The lad in white smirked on. 'I thought it might give you a laugh,' said he. 'Cheer you up a bit. Bereavement can be a very traumatic time for everyone concerned, especially for the deceased.'

'I don't feel particularly deceased. In fact, I don't feel particularly much of anything really. Are you sure there hasn't been some mistake?'

'No mistake, mate. Take it from me, you look pretty dead from where I'm standing.'

'What a bummer.' Norman looked on again and watched as the Reverend Cheesefoot, leaning over to help Mr Bailey, received a kick in the trouser seat from his wife and plunged in the grave on top of him.

'Tell you what,' said the lad in white, 'if you want to

make absolutely sure, then go over to your dad and wave your hands about in front of his face. And shout a bit, if you like. He won't be able to see or hear you. But some dead folk like to do it. Get it out of their systems.'

'Do you think it would help?' Norman asked.

'Not in the least. But it makes me laugh, I can tell you.'

'Thanks a lot.' Norman tried to put his hands into his trouser pockets, but found that he could not. 'I seem to be somewhat transparent,' he said dismally. 'But who are *you* anyway? Mr Jordan, is it, or the Angel Gabriel?'

'Leave it out,' the lad in white made mirth. 'I'm your PLC.'

'Public Limited Company?'

'Post Life Counsellor. It's my job to be of comfort. To help you through your first few difficult days of readjustment. You'll find that being dead's not so bad once you've come to terms with it. You seem to be coming to terms with it rather well already, as it happens.'

'I'm just putting on a brave face,' said Norman. 'I'm really pissed off inside. And you're not being any comfort at all, if it comes to that.'

'Sorry, mate. It's my first time at doing this. They gave me a handbook, but you know how it is.'

Norman didn't, but he said, 'Yes, I know.'

'Do you want to stick around for the bit when Teddy Bilson falls into the grave and puts his foot through your coffin lid, or shall we just shove off now?'

'I think we should just shove off now.' Norman looked up at the clear blue sky, then down at the grassy ground, then up to the face of the smirker in white. And then Norman's own face fell. 'Shove off to *where*?' he managed.

'What do you mean, *where*?'

'I mean,' Norman made shaky finger-pointings, first toward the direction of where Heaven is generally supposed to be situated, then downwards to where . . .

29

'Not down *there*.' The Post Life Counsellor fell about in further hilarity. 'There's no *down there* any more. I'll explain everything to you. Well, as much as I know anyway. We'll take the lift.'

'The lift?' Norman viewed once more the clear blue sky. 'We take the lift *up*?'

'How else?'

'Well,' Norman tried to scratch his head, but couldn't, 'there's no chance of any feathered wings, I suppose?'

'Feathered wings?' The lad in white creased double. 'None at all, no mate. You really cocked up in that department.'

Norman glared bitterly towards his blubbering dad. But his blubbering dad was no longer in his wheelchair. For he too had somehow managed to fall into Norman's grave.

'Stuff it then. The lift it is.'

And the lift it was.

And a fine-looking lift it was too.

Just like those ones you used to see in big stores and underground stations. All twiddly-widdly Victorian iron-work and a big brass up-and-down-control-knob-jobbie. It looked a little out of place in the corner of the graveyard though. But then no-one could see it there, except for Norman and his PLC.

'All aboard,' said this fellow. 'Going up. Top floor: eternal life, endless bliss, harps, gowns and halos.'

'Leave it out,' said Norman.

'Please yourself.'

Norman wandered into the lift and the lad in white swung the gates shut. 'You know,' said Norman, 'you look sort of familiar. Do I know you from somewhere?'

'Took you long enough. I used to go to infants' school with you.'

'Yes, that's it. You're—'

'Jack,' said Jack. 'Jack Bradshaw.'

'Norman,' said Norman.

'Yes, I know who *you* are.'

'Oh yes. So, well, Jack, what have you been doing with yourself then?'

'I've been being dead, haven't I? Snuffed it when I was five.'

'I thought you moved away. That's what my mum said.'

'Fell off the pier and drowned, *that's* what I did.'

'What a bummer. But what a coincidence. You being my PLC.'

'Not really.' Jack cranked the big brass up-and-down-control-knob-jobbie and the lift began to rise. 'I saw your name come up in the ledger so I volunteered for the job. You're the first person that I used to know to snuff it since me, so I thought it would be nice to meet up with you again. Do you still pooh yourself when you get frightened?'

'No I do *not*. I was only five then. Do you still pick your nose and eat the bogies?'

'All the time. Doesn't everyone?'

'I suppose they do.'

The lift rose at an alarming rate of knots. And had Norman still been five, there is no doubt that he would have disgraced himself. Up and away went the lift. Through a little cloud or two, then up and up and up.

'But hold on,' said Norman. 'You're not five any more.'

'Well, nor are you.' Jack leaned close to the lift gates and spat through them. 'Look at that sucker go down. Bombs away.'

'I mean', said Norman, 'that if you died when you were five, how come you're not still five? You don't grow older in Heaven, do you?'

'I wouldn't know. I've never been to Heaven.'

'But you said—'

'I said you weren't going *down there*. Because there's no *down there* any more. I never said anything about you going to Heaven.'

'So where else is there to go? Not Purgatory? I don't want to go there. I'm not a Roman Catholic, I'm a Presbyterian.'

'What's a Presbyterian?'

'I wouldn't know. I've never been to church.'

'I reckon you're dead lucky that there's no *down there* any more. *Dead* lucky, did you get that?'

'Most amusing,' said Norman. 'Will we be there soon, wherever it is that we're going to?'

'Soon enough,' said Jack. 'Do you want to take a couple of gobs through the lift gates before we arrive?'

'Not half.'

Now, as Norman had no preconceived ideas about what he might find when he arrived at wherever it was he was bound for, what he saw when he arrived neither surprised nor disappointed him. So to speak.

Whatever it was and wherever it was, there was a lot of it about. All over the place. And it hung there, whatever it was, evidently attached to the side of something far bigger.

Whatever *that* was.

To be a little more specific, the lot of it that Norman now found himself gawping up at looked something like the outside of one of those great imposing Victorian Ministry-of-something-or-other buildings that stand around, taking up lots of space, in the Whitehall area. The ones that you never see anyone go in or out of.

In his masterwork *The Book of Ultimate Truths*, Hugo Rune explains that these buildings are, in fact, nothing more than brick façades which were knocked up at the end of the Second World War to fool visiting Germans into believing that all their bombs had missed London during the Blitz. Rune apparently learned this from his good friend Winston Churchill, who confided that they had all been erected by set builders from Pinewood Studios and were completely full of rubble.

Well, this building looked something like one of those. But there was much more of it. It went on and on and on. Tier upon tier. Row upon row of featureless windows. A great swathe of steps led towards a most imposing British Museum sort of portico.

'It's *not* Heaven, is it?' Norman scratched at his head. 'I can scratch my head again,' said he.

'Of course you can. You're all solid up here.'

'But up here is *not* Heaven.'

Jack strode off towards the steps. 'It's where you'll be working,' he called back over his shoulder.

'*Working*?' Norman chewed upon the word and then spat it back out. '*Working*? Hang about.'

'Look at it this way,' said Jack, once Norman had caught up. 'The bad news is that you're dead. But the good news is: you're in full-time, regular employment. You've me to thank for that.'

'You what?' Norman spluttered. 'But I don't want any full-time, regular employment. I'm only fourteen. I've got years left to doss about at school. Then I intend to go on and doss about at college. Get myself a degree and then doss about on the dole. You're out of touch, Jack, young people don't work any more.'

'They do here,' said Jack. 'And you don't have years to doss about at anything. You're dead, mate. Dead as a—'

'Dead boy. Yes, you told me.'

'Come on then.' They had reached the top of the big swathe of steps and now stood before a big revolve of

33

revolving doors. Jack pushed, the revolving doors re-volved, and he with them. Like you would.

Norman remained upon the threshold, making the face of great doubt. He did not like the look of this place one little bit. It wasn't Heaven and Jack might well be lying about it not being 'The Bad Place'. Perhaps he should make a run for it, take his chances elsewhere, take the lift down to earth again and escape. Haunt Druid's Tor or something. Anything would surely be better than an eternity of regular employment. No matter what form that employment would actually take.

'I'm off,' said Norman, turning to flee.

But flee he did not. At the bottom of the steps, where the lift had brought him up, there was now nothing.

And it was a serious nothing, very void-like and specked with stars. It was the kind of nothing that said, 'No way, matey.'

Norman's face of great doubt became a face of a terrible glumness. 'I don't know what I've done to deserve this,' he mumbled. But then, just for a moment, he had this crystal flash of memory. And he could see himself, in his Y-fronts, sitting in a pentagram calling out the barbarous names of unholy deities. And with this crystal flash, Norman felt that perhaps he did know *just* what he'd done to deserve this after all.

And so, very meekly, he followed Jack inside.

4

Now many miles north of Skelington Bay, but just three south of Transglobe's West London offices, there lies a little borough known as Brentford. And on this day the sun shone there, as very well it might. With tenderness it touched upon the fine slate rooftops of the elegant Victorian terraces, bringing forth the architectural splendours of the Memorial Library and the historic Butts Estate; the rich floral glories of the magnificent parks and gardens.

Ah, Brentford.

The sun entered many windows here. Those of The Flying Swan, for instance. '*That drinking man's Valhalla, where noble men take sup and speak of noble deeds.*' Here the sunlight played upon the Brylcremed head of Neville. Full-time part-time barman and now lord of his domain. What tales this man might tell, and soon perchance we'll listen when he does.

And here, The Wife's Legs Café. The sun peeps in to spy upon the fair wife here, as she, with fingers slender and nails most gorgeously manicured, adds just a touch of elder flower to an omelette in the pan. And sighs. For what? Who knows.

And down the road a piece, through double-glazed lounge window and the patio sliding door, who's this the old sun shines upon? Why, Norman's mum so it is, before the TV screen. And on the sofa. With the milkman, Mr Marsuple. Tut, tut. The old sun makes no comment and shines on.

And shines most gloriously indeed through tall arched windows of the Gothic ilk. Those of Brentford's County

35

Court. And here, in angled shafts, alive with floating motes of gold, helps set the scene for drama and excitement and intrigue to come.

The way it should.

The court is packed this day. The balcony, where sits the public, not a spare seat to be found. All tickets *sold* the night before, within The Flying Swan. By one John Vincent Omally, Dublin born and Brentford bred, whose family, so it is claimed, hold this privilege, handed down through generations, by tradition, or an old charter, or a something. And at five bob a head, who churlishly would think to argue, for a chance to view a show, the likes of which this promised so to be?

For in this town of Brentford, a town which continued to defy all national statistics and remain virtually crime-free, the occasion of a local boy coming up before the magistrate had caused a certain stir. And that this local boy should be an eighteen-year-old self-made millionaire, who had generously bestowed a great deal of largess upon the community and was now being dragged before the court upon some trifling matter, seemed nothing short of scandalous.

Especially to those who had received a share of this largess, purchased their tickets and now thronged the public gallery with their Thermos flasks, packed lunches and comfy cushions.

The courtroom was a proud affair, both dignified and venerable. With panelling of polished oak, pews of musty velvet, balustrades of burnished brass and carpets rich and red.

Beneath the town crest, with its griffins rampant above a yard of ale and the Latin motto *Non est disputandum Brentfordium Large* (there is no disputing the beer of Brentford), stood the judge's throne. And occupying this, the judge.

A short man, red of face and black of outlook. Brigadier Algenon 'Chunky' Wilberforce DSM, OTO, KY,
and so forth, fumed in a shaft of sunlight and rued the day
that hanging had been stricken from the statute books.

A stranger to the borough was this man, brought in at
the very last minute to replace Brentford's resident
magistrate, Mr Justice Glastonbury, philosopher, liber-
tine and author of the bestselling book *Don't Let the Legal
Bastards Stitch You Up: A New Age Traveller's Guide to the
British Judicial System*.

Some said that Mr Justice Glastonbury had been taken
sick at the eleventh hour, but others, who probably know
more than most, suggested that the Brigadier had been
brought in to provide that essential cheap-one-dimen-
sional-stereotypical-easy-target-comic-cliché   element
which would otherwise have been so sadly lacking.

Flanking this ogre was a clerk of the court named
Wallace and a lady in a straw hat who was knitting a
grey sock.

Around and about the courtroom sat all those people
that you find around and about courtrooms: earnest
young men in little wigs and legal attire, who move
bundles of documents from one place to another; an
efficient woman who types up all that is said onto a small
device that doesn't seem to have enough keys; people
with beards and jumpers, who make out 'social reports';
secretaries and minor officials; and this body and that.

The nation's press was represented in the person of
'Scoop' Molloy, cub reporter for *The Brentford Mercury*.

Scoop leaned against a pillar near the fire exit, puffing
on an illicit roll-up and wondering what were the chances
of anyone straining a new gag out of a court case. On the
evidence so far, not good, was his conclusion.

In 'the dock', between a brace of bobbies, stood the
defendant. A long lad in loose light linen, a crumpled

Hawaiian shirt, canvas loafers and no socks. He sported a tall turret of hair, a fine aquiline nose, a pair of gentle eyes, a smiley mouth and a noble chin that was all but made. There were points of interest to be found around and about his person, that his loose linen suit lacked for an arm being one, and that above his left eye there was a large bruise being one other. No doubt in time, these would be explained.

The long lad's name (and he *was* a *long* lad, standing head and shoulders above the boys in blue) was Cornelius Murphy.

And he was the stuff of epics.

Cornelius turned, grinned and waved an un-hand-cuffed left hand towards the balcony. This gesture was greeted by much warm applause, a whistle or two and a cry of 'Free the Brentford One'. Scoop Molloy took out his pencil and made a note of that.

Mr Justice Wilberforce, who had been leafing through the mound of papers on his venerable bench, looked up from this leafing and said, 'Silence in the bloody court,' which boded about as well as it might have been expected to do.

'Clerk,' continued his Honour, 'which is the charge sheet for this wretched villain?'

'All of them,' explained the clerk of the court.

'Damned lot of the blighters. Be here all day at this rate. Just give me the gist of it and I'll pass sentence.'

Scoop Molloy pocketed his pencil.

'It is a rather complicated case,' the clerk of the court explained. 'It began with a minor parking offence, but its implications have spread now to encompass a world-wide network of espionage, involving international crime syndicates, vast money-laundering operations, political conspiracy and a threat to destroy the economic stability of our native land.'

The magistrate cast a disparaging eye upon Cornelius Murphy. Cornelius caught it and cast it back. 'Are you responsible for all this?' asked the magistrate.

'No,' said Cornelius. 'I'm innocent.'

'Well, we'll see about that, won't we? Nature of the first charge, clerk of the court.'

'The defendant is charged that he did park his electric-blue Cadillac Eldorado on a double yellow line outside the business premises of one Wally Woods Pre-eminent Purveyor of Wet Fish to the Brentford Gentry, in or about the time of one p.m., last Thursday week.'

'That's you, isn't it?' asked the magistrate.

'Me, your Honour?' asked the clerk.

'You, Wally Woods, that's you.'

'Yes, your Honour. It is me.'

'Well, did the fellow park there or did he not?'

'He did, your Honour.'

'Then guilty as hell. Let's have him sent down.'

'Boo,' went the balcony.

'Silence,' went the magistrate.

'Excuse me,' said Cornelius Murphy, 'but I demand the right to be tried before a jury.'

'Tried before a jury?' Mr Justice Wilberforce fell back in his chair. 'Unthinkable. Justice is a matter for the professionals. Not a bunch of bally unqualified civvies. Where's your defending counsel anyway?'

'I shall be defending myself,' said Cornelius. 'I shall be exercising my right to silence and pleading rule forty-two, the fifth amendment and *Plan Nine from Outer Space*.'

'*Plan Nine from Outer Space?*' Mr Justice Wilberforce adjusted his wig. 'Do you mean the original black-and-white nineteen fifties classic, or Chris Windsor's nineteen eighty-two full-colour musical remake, *Big Flesh Eater?*'

'The original, your Honour,' said Cornelius Murphy.

'This puts an entirely new complexion on the matter. I shall bear that in mind.'

Scoop Molloy took out his pencil once more and scratched his head with it.

'Clerk of the court, read out some other charges,' said the magistrate.

'What was wrong with the first one, your Honour?'

'Didn't like it. Shan't bother with it. Next charge.'

'Huh,' said Wally.

'Careful with the "huhs" or you'll find yourself in contempt of court.'

'Nice one,' said Cornelius.

'And it's nice one, *your Honour*, to you.'

'Being in possession of an untaxed and uninsured vehicle, to wit the electric-blue Cadillac Eldorado. Refusing to show any proof of ownership and having no valid driving licence,' read Wally.

'How do you plead on that little lot?'

Cornelius shook his head and vanished momentarily beneath his hair. 'Which in particular?' he asked, when he could once more find his face.

'Refusing to show any proof of ownership,' the magistrate suggested.

'On that charge I shall be pleading Bruce Geller's nineteen seventy-six minor classic *The Savage Bees*.'

'Indeed?' Mr Justice Wilberforce stroked his chin. 'You wouldn't care to change that plea to his nineteen seventy-eight sequel, *Terror out of the Sky*, by any chance?'

'Certainly not, your Honour. The first had a credible plot and strong performances, from, amongst others, Ben Johnson. The second was strictly TV fodder.'

'Well said.' The magistrate located his little gavel and smacked the venerable bench with it. 'The refusing to show proof of ownership charge is dropped, if it ever constituted a charge at all anyway,' said he.

'Hoorah!' went the balcony.

'Shut your faces,' went the magistrate.

'I'm missing something here,' said the clerk of the court.

'Me too.' Scoop Molloy began to make what are known as copious notes.

'Why don't we call a witness for the prosecution to get the ball rolling?' asked Mr Justice Wilberforce. 'Who is conducting the case for the prosecution?'

'I am, your Honour.' A gaunt figure dressed all in black rose slowly to his feet and bowed slightly from the waist. His face was a deathly white and his black hair swept back from a widow's peak to vanish down his starched shirt collar and emerge from his left trouser cuff. His eyes looked somewhat bloodshot and his lips wore a dash of *Max Factor Midnight Red*. 'Gwynplaine D'hark QC,' said he in a Transylvanian tone.

'Quite so,' said the magistrate. 'I note that you are not throwing a shadow at all Mr D'hark. Should I find that significant?'

Gwynplaine D'hark shook his head in a slow, deliberate fashion. Scoop Molloy patted his pockets in search of a pencil sharpener.

'I wish to object, your Honour,' said Cornelius Murphy.

'On what grounds?'

'On the grounds that the prosecuting counsel is clearly one of the undead.'

'Fair point. Would you care to comment on this, Mr D'hark?'

'Not really, your Honour, no.'

'Oh, come on now, we are both on the same side after all.'

'Boo,' went the balcony.

'Shut it,' went the magistrate.

41

Gwynplaine D'hark preened his lapels. 'Your Honour's point is well taken. I would answer his request for me to comment in this fashion: by making a request of my own. May I be allowed to conduct my case out of the shafts of sunlight?'

'And why might this be?'

'Because I feel that being reduced to a pile of smouldering ashes on the carpet might inconvenience you, your Honour, prejudice the Crown's case and give the defendant the opportunity to call for a mistrial to be declared.'

'Well put, Mr D'hark.'

'Thank you, your Honour.'

'I object,' said Cornelius raising his unhandcuffed hand. 'I know of no legal precedent whereby a necrophile is allowed to conduct a prosecution case.'

'I resent the term necrophile,' said the undead Mr D'hark. 'A necrophile is a living person who makes love to corpses. I am a dead person who sucks the life blood of the living. There is a very clear distinction here and I feel that it should not go unrecognized.'

'Well put once more, Mr D'hark. Objection overruled.'

'*What?*' said Cornelius.

'Objection overruled! Certainly Mr D'hark may be a reanimated corpse who feasts upon human flesh, but he is still a Queen's Counsel and therefore qualified to conduct his case. This is England, you know, and I'll take my horsewhip to the fellow who says it's not, by Godfrey.'

'Has anyone got a Biro?' asked Scoop Molloy. 'My pencil's blunt here.'

'Please call your first witness, Mr D'hark.'

'Thank you, your Honour. I call Police Constable Kenneth Loathsome.'

'Call Police Constable Kenneth Loathsome.'

'Call Polly Scunstible Ken F. Loaf's son.'

42

'Call Pal. E. Scumdiddly Kent leftovers.'

'Forget the Biro,' said Scoop Molloy. 'That's a duff old gag, that one.'

'Are you Police Constable Kenneth Loathsome?' asked Gwynplaine D'hark QC, deceased.

'I surely am,' said the pimply Herbert in the ill-fitting uniform.

'Then kindly take this book in your left hand and repeat what is written upon this card.'

The pimply Herbert did as he was bid.

'I hereby take this oath of blood in covenant for my mortal soul that I will serve the powers of darkness and—'

'I object,' said Cornelius Murphy.

'What is it now, Mr Murphy?'

'Counsel for the prosecution is clearly leading the witness into forming a pact with his Satanic Majesty, your Honour.'

'Is this true, Mr D'hark?'

'Maybe,' said the Queen's Counsel.

'Well I take a very dim view of that sort of thing in my court. Don't let it happen again.'

'I am indebted to your Honour for drawing my attention to my breach of protocol. Might I beg to have it stricken from the court record?'

'Of course you may.'

'I object again,' said Cornelius.

'You are proving to be a most objectional young man,' said the magistrate. 'And on what grounds do you make *this* objection?'

'On the grounds of the nineteen seventy-five movie *Bug*, your Honour, directed by Jeannot Szwarc.'

'Starring?'

'Bradford Dillman, your Honour, and a fine supporting cast.'

'Quite so. Then let it remain a matter of public record

that the prosecuting counsel made an attempt to have the first witness sell his soul to Satan.'

'Damn,' said Gwynplaine D'hark, baring his pointed canines.

'I'm sure I'm missing something really obvious here,' said Scoop Molloy. 'I'll just kick myself when it all gets explained.'

'I think we have had quite enough delays,' said the magistrate. 'Kindly cross-examine your first witness, Mr D'hark.'

'Thank you, your Honour. Now, Constable Loathsome, would you please tell the court, in your own words just—'

'I'll have to stop you there, I'm afraid,' said Mr Justice Wilberforce.

'Excuse me, your Honour, but why?'

'Luncheon appointment. Little restaurant near here that serves a most affable *bœuf en croute*, fried calves liver and grilled pineapple, bread-and-butter pudding with clam sauce, and a home-brewed Vodka that could take the tar off a bargie's gumboots. Would you care to join me, Mr D'hark?'

'If it please your Honour, no. I rarely venture abroad during the hours of daylight. A pint of plasma and a liver-sausage sandwich taken in the basement will be quite sufficient. Perhaps the young constable will join *me*.'

'Quite so. Well, court adjourned until two p.m. All rise.'

'It's my job to say, *all rise*,' said the clerk of the court.

'Go on and say it then, you bally fool.'

'All rise,' said Wally and all rise they did.

'How are you doing?' asked a voice at the Murphy Kneecap.

'Hello, Tuppe,' said Cornelius, beaming down at a

44

diminutive fellow, who had the face of a cherub and the sexual appetite of Jeff Stryker. 'I didn't see you come in.'

'People don't as a rule.' Tuppe beamed up at his bestest friend and erstwhile partner in epic adventure. 'So are you winning, or what?'

'Hard to tell quite yet. The prosecuting counsel has turned out to be a bit of a surprise. But as I know something about the magistrate that he doesn't, I think it should all be over by teatime.'

'How many years do you think they'll give you?'

'No years at all. I shall be walking from this courtroom a free man, with my head held high.'

'What, higher than it is now? That's something I'd like to see. From a first-floor window, of course.'

'Truth will triumph,' said Cornelius. 'And why are you so late, by the way?'

'I had a phone call from that private detective you employed to trace your dad's whereabouts. Apparently he's done the business and tracked your old fella to the offices of Transglobe Publishing.'

'Brilliant,' said Cornelius. 'But what is he up to there?'

'Selling his autohagiography apparently. It's called *The Most Amazing Man Who Ever Lived*.'

'Yes, I suppose it would be. Anything else?'

'Indeed. The stuff you're interested in. Your private eye bugged the offices, and he says that your daddy claims to be engaged on some secret government project. Something very big and hush-hush.'

'Oh dear, oh dear,' said Cornelius.

'Yeah and he's going to—'

'I do hate to interrupt your conversation,' said the policeman who was handcuffed to Cornelius. 'But my mate and I would like to get off down to the chippy for some lunch now.'

'Oh yes, of course.'

45

'So if you don't mind, we'll just take you back to the cell, give you another roughing up, then nip off.'

'No problem,' said Cornelius. 'I'll see you later, Tuppe. Let's say three-fifteen outside The Flying Swan.'

'*Inside*,' said Tuppe. 'I'll get you a drink in.'

'Nice one. Make it a bottle of champagne on ice.'

'I will. So long, Cornelius. Be lucky.'

'I'll try.'

'So long, policeman.'

'So long, Tuppe.'

'So long.'

5

The interior of the mighty building held even less promise for Norman than had the outside. And the outside had not held very much.

Once through the revolving doors, he found himself in a large reception area, with a generous expanse of grey marble floor and much in the way of oak panelling. It lacked, however, the rays of sunlight that favoured Brentford County Court and chose to dwell in a gas-lit gloom that Norman found depressing.

There were some nicotine-coloured columns that dwindled away to an invisible ceiling far above, a row of lift doors set into a distant wall and a nearby desk with an antiquated switchboard mounted upon it. Behind this sat a lady in a straw hat knitting a grey sock.

It was not the same lady, but, as Norman had not met the first one, he was not to know this. Yet.

'Come on,' said Jack. 'Follow me.'

Norman looked up and off and around and about. 'Where are we?' he asked. 'What is this place?'

'All in good time. Follow me.'

There was another lift involved. This one rose a great many floors. Norman's spirits did not rise with it.

Then there were corridors and passageways and doors and doors and doors. At very great length Jack stopped before one of quite singular anonymity, pushed it open and announced, 'We're here.'

The room revealed sulked in that kind of half-light you find under kitchen sinks when you're trying to clear the blockage in the S-bend. It was not a large room and it was crowded.

This room suffered from a severe case of 'filing cabinet'.

There were dozens of them, shoulder to wooden shoulder, one on top of the next. Norman did not trouble himself to count just how many there were, one alone was sufficient to trouble him greatly.

And this was not a tidy room. It was to be felt that the 'order out of chaos', for which God is so famous, had not extended itself to this particular neck of the cosmic woods.

At the unbeating heart of this room, a sturdy desk offered its support to a bastion of box files. Many more of these formed towers of varying heights upon a carpet for the most part invisible beneath bundles of bound documents and discarded paper cups.

Jack closed the door, trod a wary but well-practised path between the obstacles, swept some folders from a chair and sat down upon it. 'Sit anywhere you like,' he told Norman. 'Care for a cup of tea?'

'I'd like to go home,' said the dead boy, 'if this could somehow be arranged.'

'It can't, mate. Sorry.'

Norman sat down on a stack of box files and made a glum face. There was a window in the room. But beyond was only blackness to be seen. A large sign, pasted across the window's glass, read 'DO NOT OPEN THIS WINDOW'. It did not inspire confidence.

Jack rooted around in a desk drawer. Presently a Thermos flask and two paper cups emerged into the uncertain light. Jack shook paper-clips from one cup and wiped the other upon a jacket cuff. 'So,' said he, 'what do you think of my office? Pretty fab, eh?'

'Am I supposed to work here too?'

'That's it.' Jack filled the paper-clip cup with tea and handed it to Norman. 'Sugar's already in. I needed an assistant, you see. I've got a bit behind. Well, a lot behind and I saw your name come up, so I put in to be your PLC and take you on. And so, here you are.'

'Thanks a bundle,' Norman said.

Jack grinned his grin. 'You don't seem too pleased, mate.'

'I told you. I don't want to work. I want to doss about. If I'd had the chance to win that £1,000 at the man-powered flight competition I'd have been able to have dossed about for years.'

Jack poured tea into his own paper cup and sipped from it. 'You never would have won,' said he. 'A priest wins it: inflates his stomach with helium and propels himself through the sky by fa—'

'What do you mean, a priest wins it? How can you know *that*?'

'We know everything here. It's all in the ledgers and the files. Who gets born and when. How long they live for, why they die. All that.'

Norman whistled. 'You know all *that*?'

'It's our job to know. Like when I said I put in an application to be your PLC. Do you know when I did that?'

'Last week when I died, I suppose.' Norman took a swig of tea, made an alarmed face, then spat out a paper-clip.

'Not last week,' said Jack. 'Five years ago.'

'Bummer,' said Norman. 'So whatever happened to free will?'

'You were free to do whatever you chose. It's just that we happened to know what you would choose before you chose it.'

'And so who are *you*? And what is this place? Some sort of heavenly records office?'

49

'No, no, no.' Jack gave his nose a conspiratorial finger-tap. 'We're not that. We're the best-kept secret in the history of eternity. This is *The Universal Reincarnation Company.*'

If he was waiting for applause, he didn't get any. Norman simply shrugged and asked, 'The what?'

'OK,' Jack finished up his tea. 'Another cup?'

'No thanks.'

'Please yourself.' Jack poured a second for himself. 'Are you sitting comfortably?'

'Not particularly, no.'

'Well, I'll begin anyway. It all began when God created the Heavens and the Earth.'

'Is this going to take long?' Norman asked. 'Only I—'

'Only you what?'

'Only I nothing really. Go on, God created the Heavens and the Earth.'

'He did, and it was his original intention that only *really* good people should go to Heaven when they died. The rest all went, you know.'

'To *Hell*?' Norman asked.

'We don't call it that. It was called the EDF.'

'Surprise me,' said Norman.

'Eternal Damnation Facility. You see, God gave Moses the ten commandments, right? Nine of which are reasonably easy to keep, if you put your mind to it. No killing, no stealing, no committing adultery – could be a problem that, but no big deal. But he slipped in Command Number Ten. The one about, thou shalt not covet thy neighbour's ox.'

'I can't say I've ever coveted my neighbour's ox at all,' said Norman. 'Nor his ass, come to think of it.'

'No, but I'll bet you've been jealous of his new stereo, or his computer system, or his bike or whatever. Same thing. Few people ever got past Command Number Ten, I'll tell you.'

'Where is this leading?' Norman asked.

'It all leads to here. In the book of Revelation it states the exact size of the Holy City, Heaven. It's described as a cube, twelve thousand furlongs to a side.'

'What's a furlong?' Norman asked.

'Search me, but it's not *that* big. Listen, it's all very straight forward. Hell's been closed down, and Heaven's full up. So here we all are.'

'In the Universal Reincarnation Company?'

'That's us.'

'No, hang about. Hell's been *closed down*?'

'That's it. God had second thoughts, you see. Being the all-round nice fellow that he is, he began to feel a bit guilty about all those poor souls frying in eternity simply because they'd coveted an ox.'

'Or an ass.'

'Exactly, so he closed it down.'

'Good for God,' said Norman. 'It's nice to know that I won't be going to Hell, anyway.'

'Oh, you wouldn't have been going anyhow. You had to be eighteen to get in there. It was real X-certificate stuff. No minors allowed. And I mean, babies covet rattles and stuff. Imagine all those eternally frying infants; didn't bear thinking about.'

Norman agreed that it didn't.

'Not to mention original sin.'

'Original sin?'

'I told you not to mention that.' Jack fell about in mirth. 'One of God's that. The old ones are always the best, eh?'

'If you say so.' Norman jiggled his bum about. 'No chance of a cushion I suppose.'

'None, I've got the only one and I'm keeping it. So, like I say, until the extension is completed, the URC gets on with the job.'

'I don't think you mentioned "the extension".'

'The one God's having built onto the side of Heaven to house all the millions of souls who won't now be going to Hell. Heaven's full up now, like I told you. So until the Celestial Corps of Engineers complete the extension, we have to keep right on with the job.'

'Why can't God just clap his hands and make the extension appear?' Norman asked, which seemed a reasonable question.

'That seems a reasonable question,' said Jack. 'But he can't, mate, he can't. That's not the way he does business. He likes to think about things, mull them over. Remember he's been here for ever and ever and ever. So it took him an awful long time before he got around to creating the Heavens and the Earth, didn't it?'

'I suppose it did.'

'So, until it's all finished, it's our job to keep the souls of the dead in circulation. Recycle them. When someone dies we log in their soul and then reallocate it to someone who's being born. It has presented us with a few problems, because the dead outnumber the living by thirty to one. Supply somewhat outstrips demand. There's a bit of a queue.'

'Where?' Norman asked.

'In a big ring about the sun. You see, when you die your body leaves your soul.'

'I think you'll find it's the other way around.'

'Oh no it's not. The moment you die your soul is free of your body. But your soul does not have any weight and is no longer subject to the law of gravity. So it just stays still. The Earth moves on around the sun and leaves your soul just hovering there. That's why hauntings happen on the anniversary of someone's death. The Earth has travelled right round the sun and arrived back in the same place a year later, where the soul is waiting. So if the soul wants to manifest as a ghost or whatever, it does. Most don't, of course. They just hang about in space, enjoying the sunshine and watching the planets rolling by. It's very relaxing. Quite cosmic really.'

'So what do these souls look like?'

'They don't *look* like anything. They're sort of little particles of energy. Quite powerful energy, after all they power up a human being for all of his or her life.'

'So why not simply leave all these souls to just hang about in space enjoying the sunshine until the extension gets finished? Why bother with all this paperwork?'

'Good question,' said Jack. 'Good question, mate.'

'So what's the answer then?'

'Search me, I only work here.'

'Well, I'm not going to. This is all a complete waste of time. Who's in charge? God?'

'Not here. The controller's in charge here.'

'And what does he do?'

'He controls things,' said Jack. 'It was one of his ancestors who came up with the idea. He's a big fat fellow, the controller, we call him—'

Brought up, as are all boys, upon Thomas the bloody Tank Engine, Norman was prepared to hazard a guess.

'We call him *sir*,' said Jack. 'But he won't speak to you. He doesn't speak to anyone. I've been waiting for years to get a new pencil, but no joy. But God will be at the back of it all. That's where he always is. And I have just one word to say to you about God.'

'And that is?'

'Bollocks,' said Jack.

'Steady on.' Norman covered his ears. 'He might be listening.'

'He won't be. But when I say bollocks, I do mean bollocks literally. God built man in his own image, right?

The image God had originally created himself in. And where did he put the bollocks, eh?'

'I know where he put the bollocks,' said Norman bitterly. 'And I never got a chance to give mine a proper go.'

'He put them on *the outside*, mate, that's where. Now is that a bad piece of design or what? Tenderest parts of the whole male anatomy, and does he give them a shell, or tuck them up inside your pelvis? Does he heck. He sticks them on the outside, dangling there, waiting for the knee in the groin, or the football. Says it all to me, that does.'

'Says what to you?'

Jack tapped the side of his head. 'Not on the ball.'

'Most amusing,' said Norman.

'What is?'

'Never mind. Not on the ball, you said.'

'Flawed genius. Came up with some great ideas, but let a few duff ones slip through the net. Bollocks on the outside, nipples for men, toe jam, smelly armpits, really smelly po—'

'I get the picture. You're saying that he's not quite as omnipotent as he's cracked up to be.'

'You got it, mate.'

'Well,' said Norman. 'Now I've heard the lot. Hell's closed down. Heaven's full up. The extension's not finished. And a dirty great company's been formed to reincarnate souls that don't really need reincarnating at all. And we can all put it down to God because he put the bollocks on the outside.'

'In a nutshell, right. In a *nut*-shell, geddit? No shell for the nuts. That's a good'n, isn't it?'

'A real blinder,' said Norman. 'Please show me the way out.'

'There's no way out. Look, don't knock it, mate. You've got yourself a full-time job, you should be grateful.'

'I don't know how many times I'm going to have to tell you this, but I don't want a full-time job. Especially not here.'

'There's perks,' said Jack.

'What perks?'

'Priority, when the extension's complete. We get to be first in. For our worthy labours. That's what the controller says. And it's going to be an amazing place, I've seen the brochures. I've got one here. Somewhere. Soon as it's finished, we're in.'

'How soon will it be finished?' Norman asked.

'Soon,' said Jack.

'How soon?'

'Quite soon.'

'*How* soon?'

'Couple of thousand years,' said Jack. 'But the time will fly by. We've lots to do. Lots of catching up.'

'No,' said Norman. 'No, no, no. I'm not staying. I want to float about in space and sunbathe and be cosmic. Where is the exit?'

'You can't go. Not now you've been here. It's a rule.'

'Then let me be reincarnated. I'll take my chances. I won't covet anything, just doss about.'

'Aw, come on, Norman.'

'What happened to "mate"? Really got up my nose, "mate"!'

'Stay here, you'll get to like it.'

'I won't. Get out my file, do the paperwork. Send me back to Earth.'

'Well, if it's what you really want, then I can't stop you.'

'Good, then let's be going.'

'All right. I've got a form somewhere. It's a new scheme instituted by the controller for people who don't want to work here.'

'That's me,' said Norman. 'I really don't want to work here.'

'I think you get a choice.'

'Brilliant,' said Norman. 'Then I'd like to be the lead singer in a really successful heavy-metal band. Or a Hollywood actor, I don't mind which.'

'Oh, it's not really *that* kind of choice. You see, with all the backlog of souls, the controller has extended reincarnation beyond the human species.'

'Lion then,' said Norman, who was not going to be put off by *that*. 'Or Leopard.'

'Ah,' said Jack. 'Here's the form. Take a look and tell me which one you fancy.'

Norman snatched the form away and ran his eyes up and down it. The once. The twice. And the third time. Then with a very dismal face indeed he looked up at Jack.

'So what do you fancy?' asked that fellow. 'Radish or sprout?'

6

'Radish entrecôte and boiled-sprout flambé,' said Mr Justice Wilberforce. 'Beef and broccoli. Choice of cheeses. Roly-Poly pudding. Most palatable. Damn fine port too. And Brandy. And that bally Vodka. Burn the arse out of Superman's knickers that stuff. So back to business. Are we all present and correct.'

'We are, your Honour,' said the clerk of the court.

'And I assume that we've done the "all rising" and such like, as we're all sitting down again now.'

'I presume so,' the clerk agreed.

'So, as Freddie said, "The show must go on." Mr D'hark, please continue with cross-examining your witness.'

'Ah,' Gwynplaine D'hark was dabbing his chin with a silk napkin. 'I regret that the young constable is no longer with us.'

'That, I suppose, would be some euphemism for *dead*, would it, Mr D'hark?'

'Could well mean that I suppose, your Honour.'

'Didn't like the look of the fellow anyway. Shifty eyes.'

'I object, your Honour,' said Cornelius Murphy.

'Oh, you're still with us, then. That's something, I suppose.'

Cornelius was indeed still with them. Although his appearance since he had been led away to the cells 'for lunch' had undergone a subtle change or two. He now had a fat lip to go with the bruise over his eye. And his jacket lacked for both sleeves. The policemen had undergone a subtle change or two also. One wore what the lads in the boxing fraternity refer to as 'a bloody great shiner'. The other had one arm in a sling.

'What do you object about this time, Mr Murphy?'

'That the counsel for the prosecution has clearly feasted upon the blood of Constable Loathsome and left him a dried-up little husk down in the basement.'

'An unsubstantiated allegation,' said Gwynplaine D'hark, the D'hark Destroyer. 'And a clearly libellous one. I would ask his Honour to add that charge to the list of crimes the defendant stands accused of.'

'That's the way we do justice here,' said the magistrate. 'Let the court records show that the defendant cried out to have another five years added on to whatever I deem in my leniency to award him.'

'Boo, boo, boo,' went the balcony.

'I'll second that,' said Cornelius. 'This is a hung court.'

'And bloody well hung too,' crowed his Honour.

Scoop Molloy, who had brought a dictaphone back from lunch with him, switched it off in disgust.

'So, who would you like to call next, Mr D'hark?'

'Well, if it please your Honour, I would like to skip over all the minor charges and get right down to the *meat* of this case.'

'I'll bet you would.'

'Silence, Mr Murphy, or I'll hold you in contempt.'

'The crux of this case, your Honour, rests upon the defendant's wealth and the manner in which he acquired it. I would like to call to the stand The Crazy World of Arthur Brown.'

'The Crazy World of Arthur Brown, Mr D'hark? Do you mean the nineteen sixties madcap whacko rock anarchist, chiefly remembered for the only record anyone can chiefly remember him for?'

' "Fire", your Honour? Yes, that is indeed the man.'

'Well, wheel him in, Mr D'hark, let's have a look at the bod.'

'I call The Crazy World of Arthur Brown.'

'Call the Crazy World of Arthur Brown.'

'Call Theke Raziword or R. Ferbrown.'

'Call Pal E. Scumdiddly Kent leftovers.'

'It wasn't funny the first time,' said Scoop Molloy. 'It's never funny. Never was funny. Never will be funny.'

'You are Pal E. Scumdiddly Kent leftovers?' enquired Mr Gywnplaine D'hark.

'I am Mr Arthur Brown,' said Mr Arthur Brown, 'of the accountant's firm, Brown, Urquart, Montmorency, Harris and O'Leary Erickson.'

'Which forms an acronym I believe,' said the magistrate.

'I believe so, your Honour,' said Mr D'hark. 'Apparently it gets a very cheap laugh at dinner parties.'

'And why not?'

'And why not indeed, your Honour.'

'Well, we won't wait for the laughter to die down, kindly cross-examine your witness, Mr D'hark.'

'Thank you, your Honour.' The Queen's Counsel from beyond the grave addressed the fellow in the witness box. A well-dressed, middle-aged city gent of a fellow. With a briefcase. 'Now, Mr Brown—'

'I object, your Honour,' said Cornelius. 'The witness hasn't taken the oath.'

'Stuff the oath, this is dragging on far too long. Mr D'hark, your witness please.'

'As your Honour pleases.'

'Greasy,' said Cornelius. 'Very greasy.'

'Mr Brown,' said Mr D'hark, 'your firm, I believe, deals mainly with large-scale fraud, and income-tax evasion?'

'This is the case, yes.' Very polite voice.

'And you have acquired a bona fide account of the defendant's current assets, am I correct?'

59

'I have, yes.' The smart man withdrew a slip of paper from his briefcase and passed it to Mr D'hark.

'Exhibit A,' said the Queen's Counsel. 'Might I show this to the defendant, your Honour?'

'Please do, Mr D'hark.'

'So kind, so very kind.'

'So greasy, so very greasy.'

'That's quite enough of that, Mr Murphy.'

'Pardon me, your Honour.' Cornelius accepted the slip of paper and gave it a brief perusal.

'Mr Murphy,' said the QC with the evil grin, 'would you consider this statement of your current assets to be a fair estimate regarding the extent of your wealth?'

Cornelius gave the slip of paper a less brief perusal than before. 'It looks about right, to within a million or two.'

'Would you care to read out the sum in question?'

'Well, it says here twenty-three million pounds.'

'Oooooh,' went the balcony, who had not said a thing since lunch.

'I've given a lot of it away,' said Cornelius. 'But it keeps mounting up. I'll give some more away tomorrow, if you want.'

'I'm sure that you will, Mr Murphy. But where did it all come from? That's what I want to know. We have no records to show that you have ever taken any regular employment.'

'I'm self-employed,' said Cornelius.

'Self-employed as what, exactly?'

'I'm an adventurer,' said the tall boy proudly.

'And what kind of adventurer are you?'

'An epic one. Most definitely.'

'Hoorah,' went the crowd in the balcony.

'I'll have the courtroom cleared if that rabble don't put a sock in it.'

'Murmur, murmur,' went the crowd in the balcony. Quite quietly.

'An epic adventurer?' Mr D'hark did more lapel preening. 'And where exactly do these epic adventures of yours take you to?'

'I'd prefer not to say, actually.'

'Oh, don't be coy, Mr Murphy. You left school six months ago without a job, there is no record that you have ever had a job, and here you are before us now worth twenty-three million pounds. This is no small achievement. Won't you share with us the secret of your success?'

'Would *you*?' Cornelius asked.

'*I* am not in the dock,' said Mr D'hark.

'Your Honour,' said Cornelius, 'I would like to change my plea.'

'To guilty? Well that saves a lot of time. I hereby sentence you—'

'Not to guilty, your Honour. I would like to plead William Castle's nineteen sixty-five movie *I Saw What You Did*.'

The magistrate gave this plea a moment or two's thought. 'Won't wash,' said he.

'Won't it?' Cornelius asked.

'No, it won't,' said Gwynplaine D'hark QC. 'I would like to answer Mr Murphy's plea by pleading *Dark Star* which was directed, although few seem to remember it, by John Carpenter.'

'Got it,' said Scoop Molloy.

'You bloody haven't, have you?' asked the clerk of the court.

'I have too. I looked those other movies up during the lunch-hour. I've figured it out.'

'Tell us then,' cried the balcony crowd. 'Spill the beans.'

'May I, your Honour?' asked Scoop.

'May as well,' said the magistrate. 'I'm convicting this Murphy anyhow. Man's some kind of international arms dealer or something. Short sharp shock and twenty years of it, that's what he needs.'

'*The Cars that ate Paris*' said Cornelius Murphy.

'Too late and wrong too. Say your piece, Mr Molloy.'

'It's *him*,' said Scoop. 'The magistrate. You know, whenever you see a film with a courtroom scene, the magistrate always looks vaguely familiar and you waste the rest of the film saying, "Wasn't he the bloke who was in *that* film, or *that* film, or *that* film?" Well it's this bloke, isn't it?'

'Is it?' asked the crowd.

'It is,' said the magistrate. 'Called in at the last minute to play the part of Brigadier Algenon "Chunky" Wilberforce. I've been in retirement, you see. I took the part to earn enough money to pay for my wife's hip replacement.'

'I'll buy her two new hips,' said Cornelius. 'And a set of dentures too if you want.'

'No can do, I'm afraid,' said the ex-Hollywood bit-parter. 'You're dealing with a professional here.'

'*Plan Nine from Outer Space*.' said Scoop. 'Didn't you get butchered by Tor Johnson?'

'That was me. Stung to death in *The Savage Bees*. I was the janitor.'

'You wore a beard,' said Scoop.

'False one.'

'Carried it off though. But who did you play in *Dark Star*?'

'The alien,' said the magistrate. 'But I only did the hands. Very astute of Mr D'hark though. Do you have anything to say, Mr Murphy, before I pass sentence upon you?'

'How about a fair trial?' Cornelius asked.

'Very amusing, Mr Murphy. Very satirical. But I will tell you what I'll do. I will ask you one question and if you get the answer correct you can walk from this court a free man with your head held high.'

Cornelius glanced at his wristwatch. Precisely 3.14 and a one-minute walk to The Flying Swan. 'Ask on,' said he.

'What's my name?' asked the magistrate.

'It's er . . . it's er . . .'

'Have to hurry you now.'

'It's on the tip of my tongue.'

'Is it? Anyone in the courtroom? Come on now.'

'Oh and ooh and ah,' went the balcony folk. 'What's his name? It's that bloke who was in . . . What was that picture? You know the one, he played the part of . . .'

'Can't get it, can you? Come on, Mr Murphy.'

'Give me a moment. Oh, I nearly had it then.'

'Cornelius Murphy, I find you guilty upon all counts, and I hereby sentence you to—'

'Cash Flagg,' said Cornelius Murphy.

Silence!

Pin drop!

'Wrong,' said the magistrate. 'Twenty-three years.'

'No,' said Cornelius. 'No, no, no.'

'Yes,' said the magistrate. 'Yes, yes, yes.'

'I rest my case,' said Gwynplaine D'hark QC.

'Me too,' said Arthur Brown. 'It's really heavy.'

'Briefcase gag at the end,' said Scoop Molloy. 'What a cop out.'

'Bruce Morgan,' wailed Cornelius, as he was led away to the cells. 'Charles Winthrope. Clive McMurty. Bill Seabrook . . .'

But his words vanished from the page. The court all rose and most of it went home. And justice had once more been seen to be done.

'So what *was* his name?' asked Scoop Molloy.

'Haven't the faintest idea,' said Gwynplaine D'hark. 'Would you care to take a little trip with me to the basement?'

7

'Sprout,' said Norman. 'I choose sprout.'

'*You don't?*' Jack all but fell off his chair. 'You can't be serious, mate, I mean *Norman.* I mean you can't. You just can't.'

'I can, you know. If it's a choice between working here and being a sprout, then a sprout I shall be. Where do I sign?'

'No, Norman, wait. Don't be rash.'

'Pen please,' said Norman. 'Or do you want it in blood or something?'

'No!' Jack flapped his hands about. 'You don't want to be a sprout. Really you don't.'

'I do. Sprouts doss about in the sun all day. That's the life for me.'

'Sprouts get *picked*,' said Jack. 'That's what sprouts get.'

'Comes to us all.' Norman shrugged. 'A quick pick and kaput. I can live with it. Put me down for sprout. Mark my file "*sprout until Judgement Day.*"*'

'Sprouts don't die when they're picked,' said Jack.

'Of course they do.'

'They don't, you know. Vegetables are still alive when you buy them in the shops. If they ain't rotting, they ain't dead.'

'Nonsense,' said Norman. 'You're tuning me up.'

'I'm not. You'd still be alive and fully conscious when

---

* The fourth track on side one of the Angels One Five album *Shaving the Monkey.*

you got plunged into the boiling water. You'd die in there though, once you were all cooked through. Takes about twenty minutes. Horrible way to go.'

'Vegetables don't feel pain,' said Norman.

'Oh yes they do. God didn't mention it to Adam and Eve, of course. He figured it would put them off their lunch.'

'Do they cook radishes?' Norman asked.

'Eat 'm raw, I think. Raw as in *alive*. One mouthful at a time: chomp, chomp, chomp. Bits of you would still be alive down in the stomach. Amongst the terrible gastric juices. Some bits might even survive to come out the next morning in the sh—'

'Thank you,' said Norman. 'I think I get the picture.'

'Still,' Jack had a fine grin on again, 'you do have the choice. So what will it be, the radish or the sprout?'

'What are the hours like here?' Norman asked. 'As a matter of interest.'

'Pretty good,' Jack plucked the form from Norman's fingers, crumpled it up into a ball and tossed it into a wastepaper basket. Here it came to rest amongst hundreds of other little crumpled up balls of paper, each of which had once been an identical form.

Now, had this been a movie, possibly one directed by Jeannot Szwarc or Bruce Geller, the camera would have zoomed in upon this, to register in the mind of the movie-goer that it was 'significant'. The implication being that Jack had not been altogether honest with Norman regarding the matter of Norman being the first dead boy that he had done any Post Life Counselling for.

But, as this was not (as yet), a movie, this *very* significant detail was missed altogether.

'There's recreational facilities,' said Jack. 'Ping pong and the inter-departmental five-aside-football league. And swimming in the company pool.'

'I'm thrilled beyond words,' said Norman.

'Yeah, well, you'll find something you like. You'll be OK. It's better than being a sprout, I promise you. So, shall we get started?'

'Would you mind if I just went to the toilet first?'

Jack raised the eyebrow of suspicion. 'You wouldn't be thinking of making a run for it, would you?'

'Certainly not,' Norman lied. 'There isn't anywhere to run off *to*, is there?'

'Afraid not, I suppose you could hide in a cupboard or something.'

'Would that help me?'

'No, but it would make me laugh.'

'I'll just use the lav' then, if you don't mind.'

'Good lad. Left out of the door and third door on the left.'

'Thanks.' Norman rose from his stack of boxfiles and picked his way carefully to the door.

Somewhere amidst the chaos of Jack's desk an intercom began to buzz, when the door had closed upon Norman, Jack cleared papers from it and flicked a switch.

'Bradshaw,' said he.

Words came to him via some telephonic-cable-link jobbie, but not one of sufficient interest to be worth mentioning.

'How are you progressing, Bradshaw?' asked the voice of the controller.

'No problems, sir. He'll be perfect. A right little skiver. Just what you were looking for.'

'Splendid, Bradshaw. Well, you know the drill; coax him along, tell him all he needs to know and make damn sure he doesn't find out the rest.'

'He asks a lot of questions, sir, but I know what to tell him. He's a no-mark; all he wants to do is doss about.'

'Which is all we want him to do. Nice work, Bradshaw, speak to you soon.'

'Goodbye, sir.'

Outside in the corridor Norman withdrew his ear from the door. 'A no-mark, eh?' he whispered to himself. 'Well, we'll see about that.'

In a faraway room the controller replaced his telephone receiver and sank lower into the perfumed water of his marble bath-tub. Here he sought to compose the final mathematical equation that would complete his formula for the universal panacea and elixir of life.

He was a large man, the controller. Bald of head and big of belly. And there was absolutely no doubt whatsoever as to whom he was the dead spit of.

Quite uncanny the resemblance.

'All right now?' Jack asked on Norman's return. 'Find it OK?'

'Yes thank you. So where do you want me to sit?'

'You can have *my* chair,' Jack rose from it.

Norman sat down on it. 'So what do I have to do?'

'I'll explain the procedure.' Jack did so. It was a very complicated procedure, which involved many visits to many different filing cabinets, much in the way of cross-referencing and form-filling and the use of an intricate brass Comptometerish affair, which Jack described as a Karmascope. The exact purpose of this device Jack did not elaborate upon; only to say that all the final figures gleaned from all the filing cabinet visits, cross-referencing and form-filling were to be double checked and then fed into it.

'Everything you need to know is in here,' said Jack, presenting Norman with a user's handbook the size of a telephone directory. 'All make sense to you so far?'

67

Norman yawned. 'Where will you be sitting?' he asked.

'In my new office,' said Jack. 'Upstairs. Promotion, you see.'

'My heartiest congratulations.'

'I'll pop down in an hour or so and see how you're getting on. If you need any help, push the blue button on the intercom.'

'Better make it two hours,' said Norman. 'I'd like to do a bit of tidying up first.'

'I could make it four hours if you like. Be about knocking-off time then.'

Jack made his way to the door. 'See you later,' he said.

'See you later.'

The door swung shut upon the terrible little room, leaving Norman all alone in it. Outside Jack pressed *his* ear to the door.

And heard nothing whatsoever.

No sounds of activity, of paper shuffling, of tidying up. Nothing. Exactly what he expected not to hear really.

Chuckling to himself, Jack made off towards the lift.

'Chuckle on, you sod,' whispered Norman, whose ear was pressed against the inside of the door this time. 'I'll find out just what you're up to, you see if I don't. But first things first,' said he, negotiating a route back to the desk. 'I wonder what would be the best way to break this brass machine?'

Norman sat down and sulked. 'I should have demanded a change of clothes,' he complained. 'I'm buggered if I'm going to spend the next two millennia dressed in my school uniform. But then I'm buggered if I'm going to spend the next two millennia here anyway.'

He worried at the brass machine, but it was secured to the desktop by meaty bolts. It would not be broken.

Norman leaned back in his chair, kicked boxfiles aside and put his feet up on the desk. 'I won't do anything,' he said. 'Not a stroke. They won't get any work out of me.'

Humming a tune of his own making he waggled his feet in time with its rhythm. 'I'll doss about until the roll is called up yonder, or whatever. That's what I'll do.

'No I won't. Whatever am I saying?' He removed his feet from the desk and climbed from his chair. 'That seems to be exactly what they want me to do: nothing. They want me to just doss about, know only what I'm supposed to know and not find out the rest. Well, we'll see about that.'

Norman took himself over to the nearest filing cabinet and pulled out the top drawer.

What a lot of files.

He plucked one out at random, took it back to his desk, seated himself and opened it up. 'Colin Scud,' he read. 'What kind of name is that, *Colin*?' He perused the file of Mr Scud and read aloud his details. 'Born 27 July 1949, coveted fellow toddler's blue plastic wheelbarrow at playschool (this was underlined in red ink). Infants' school.' Norman turned page after page.

'Junior school,' more pages. 'Senior school.' On and on. 'Took job in department of Social Security.' On and on. 'Interests: railways; the history of the English canal system; member of the Model Bus Federation. Never left home. Lives with his mum. And dies . . .' Norman read the date and consulted his multi-function digital watch, which was still strapped onto his wrist. 'Dies midnight the Friday after next. You poor dull bugger, Colin. How do you meet your end?'

Norman leafed through to the final page. 'Receives fatal electrical discharge whilst opening fridge door. What a bummer. Well, I wish I could help you, Colin mate, but I can't. But I'll tell you what I'll do, I'll try and find you something really red hot for your next incarnation, porno movie star or Formula One racing driver or something.'

Norman went over and pulled another file. Pulled another ten, in fact, to save all the walking back and forwards.

'Right,' said the lad. 'What do we have here? Another live-already one, and another. Wrong filing cabinet, I need the *Yet-to-be-borns*. I wonder where they're kept.'

It didn't take too long to find them. There were twenty-three filing cabinets full. Norman dragged out an armful of files and took them back to his desk.

'OK then, the yet-to-be-borns. Let's find you a good'n, Colin me old mate.'

Norman opened one up.

At random.

'Here we go, Col. A bouncing baby boy, to be born next Tuesday. Let's see if he becomes famous.' Norman flicked through to the last page of what was a very thin file. 'Oh no. He doesn't. That's very sad. Dies midnight on the Friday after next due to a short circuit in his incubator. Poor little mite. That's a real bummer. Let's find you another.'

Norman found another. 'Here's another. Little girl. That would make a change for you, Colin. Bet you'd give the train-spotting a miss. Let's see if she becomes a top fashion model or a prime minister or whatever. Oh dear, she doesn't. Dies due to electrical discharge, struck by lightning in her cot. Midnight, the Friday after next. *What is all this?*'

Norman returned to the 'live-already' files he'd pulled out. All those chronicled within came from different walks of life, had been born in different countries, in different years, had fulfilled, or failed to fulfil, different ambitions. But they all had one thing in common. They were all going to die at midnight on the Friday after next, from an electrical discharge of some kind! All of them!

'*All* of them?' Norman stumbled to the nearest filing cabinet and clawed out as many files as he could claw.

Another and another and another.

And all and all and all and all.

They all were due to die at midnight, the Friday after next.

All of them.

The old folks, the young folks and the yet-to-be-born folks.

The whole damn lot.

And all due to an 'electrical discharge'.

'No,' said Norman. 'This can't be right. It can't be right. Alphabetical order. Start at the beginning.' Norman floundered amongst the filing cabinets and began to work his way into the As.

Suddenly he said, 'Oh my dad!' Which at least meant that his surname, whatever it was, began with an A.

'Right here in the Bs,' said Norman, proving that sometimes you're right and sometimes you're wrong.

'My dad's file.' He took it back to the desk and swept all else to the floor. And his hands hovered over the file.

He turned up a corner of the cover with a quivery thumb.

But let it fall back again.

He just couldn't do it. Not look. Not see when your own father was going to die. And how. That was really horrible. You couldn't do *that*.

'Someone else,' Norman pushed the file aside. 'Someone else I know. Someone I don't care about. That bloody Mr Bailey who fell into my grave. He'll be in the Bs.'

And he was.

Norman flicked through the schoolmaster's file, boggling here and there at the science teacher's exotic sexual activities.

71

'Why the orange?' Norman asked himself.

Ah, but *here* it was. Right on the last page.

And *there* it was. Writ bold in letters big.

'Twelve midnight, Friday after next. "Short circuit in vibrating interior section of Little Miss Magic Mouth leisure facility appliance."'

Good old ELECTRICAL DISCHARGE!

'Aaaaaagh!' went Norman. 'They're all gonna die!'

8

Scoop Molloy returned from the toilet and sought out a bar stool. 'Anyone sitting on this one?' he asked.

'Yes,' said Tuppe. 'I'm sitting on it.'

'Oh sorry, I didn't see you there.'

'People don't. You're the news reporter who was at the County Court, aren't you?'

'That's me.'

They were in The Flying Swan, of course. The afternoon sun shone through different panes than had the morning sun, but the effect was the same. Simply splendid.

The saloon bar dwelt in the mellow amber tones, sunlight a-twinkle upon the burnished brass of the beer engines. There was the rise and fall of glasses, the chit-chat and merry converse of the lunch-time regulars. The sense that here was how it should be and always would be and whatever.

Ah Brentford.

'Where's my pal Cornelius?' Tuppe asked Scoop. 'He should have been here by now.'

'*Murphy!*' Scoop inadvertently ordered himself a pint of that beverage. 'The magistrate sent him down.'

'What?' went Tuppe.

'Gave him twenty-three years,' said Scoop.

'*What?*' went Tuppe.

'Well he is worth *twenty-three million quid*. I expect the magistrate was trying to be ironic, or something. Here, where have you gone?'

'I'm down here,' mumbled Tuppe, who had fallen

73

from his bar stool and now lay on the carpet with his legs in the air. 'In something of a state of shock.'

And the chit-chat and the merry converse had all died away. Twenty-three million pounds was an indecently large amount of wodge to mention in a lunch-time drinkery.

Unless, of course, it happened to be the Sultan of Brunei's poolside bar.

Which it wasn't.

'Allow me to help you up.' John Omally, drinker in residence and balcony ticket tout, hastened to aid the millionaire's friend back onto his bar stool. 'No damage done I hope.'

'No I'm fine, thank you. But this can't be right. Cornelius couldn't have lost the case.'

'He did, but it was a right conspiracy. The prosecuting counsel was a coffin dweller and the magistrate was a Hollywood bit-part player. The one who always plays magistrates in movies and you can't put a name to.'

'Not the chap out of *Plan Nine from Outer Space*?' asked Neville the full-time barlord, presenting Scoop with his pint of Murphy's.

'Yeah, that's him.'

'Played the janitor in *The Savage Bees*,' said Old Pete.

'Wore a beard in that one,' said Jim Pooley.

'He was in *Bug*,' said Norman Hartnel (not to be confused with the other Norman, who wasn't called Hartnel).

'And he played the alien's hands in *Dark Star*,' said Scoop. 'Although not a lot of people know that.'

'Kyle McKintock,' said Neville.

'Kyle McKintock,' agreed Jim Pooley, John Omally, Norman Hartnel, Old Pete and Old Pete's dog, Chips.

'I thought everyone knew that,' said Tuppe.

'Well your mate didn't, so he got sent down. But

74

twenty-three years isn't so bad. He'll be out in fifteen if he behaves himself. He'll still be a young man. Go on talk shows and be treated as a celebrity. Like that bloke who was in the great train robbery. What was his name?'

'Frank somebody, wasn't it?' asked Neville.

'Dave,' said Omally.

'It was Pete,' said Jim Pooley.

'It was never me,' said Old Pete. 'I have an alibi.'

'Didn't Roger Daltry play him in a film?' asked Neville. 'Or was that Mick Jagger?'

'I think it was Phil Collins,' said Scoop.

'Yeah that's the fellow,' said Old Pete. 'Phil Collins the great train robber. He's married to that actress now, what's her name?'

'Twiggy?' Jim suggested.

'Mary Hopkins,' said Norman Hartnel.

'No,' said Scoop. 'She married someone in the music business.'

'Phil Collins is in the music business,' said Old Pete.

'I thought you said he was a great train robber.'

'Perhaps he's married to Joan Collins then.'

'No,' said Neville. 'She was married to Norman Mailer.'

'That was Marilyn Monroe,' said Jim.

'That's her,' said Old Pete. 'She's married to Phil Collins now.'

'She's dead,' said Jim.

'Oh, dear, poor Phil, he must be devastated. Elvis passed away too, so I've heard. Not that I ever cared for him. Paul Whiteman I liked.'

'Didn't he use to play with Lew Stone's Orchestra?' asked John.

'No, that was Al Bowly. Or perhaps it was George Melly.'

'George Melly punched me in a pub once,' said Jim Pooley. 'We were arguing about Picasso.'

'No woman's worth two men fighting over,' said Old Pete wisely.

'I didn't order a pint of Murphy's,' said Scoop Molloy.

'I don't think any of this is helping much,' said Tuppe. 'I have to get Cornelius out of prison and I ought to be doing it now.'

'*I wonder what would be the best way to break your friend out of prison?*' The pitch of Omally's voice and the manner with which he delivered the line were sufficient to clear quite a fair-sized area about him at the bar.

Suddenly everyone, with the exception of John, Jim, Tuppe and Scoop, were back at their chit-chat and merry converse.

'Do you have something on your mind?' Tuppe asked.

'I do.' Omally now spoke in whispery words. 'You see my good friend Jim here and myself have not been without the occasional epic adventure in our time.'

'I've read of them,' said Tuppe. 'But I thought you blokes had retired from all that sort of thing.'

'Not a bit of it. Merely resting between engagements. And I feel that, as happy chance has brought us together this day, the least that Jim and I could do would be to rescue your unjustly imprisoned chum.'

'What?' Jim sneezed into his pint, sending froth up his nose.

'Go on,' said Tuppe.

'No, hold on,' said Jim. 'Surely this kind of business would involve illegal practices. The dynamiting of cell doors, the life-and-death fleeings from the constabulary. Things of that nature.'

'Not the way I have in mind,' said John.

'No fear for life or limb then?'

76

'The merest modicum. Jim, you're not coming across here in your true heroic form.'

'*Coming across*? What kind of talk is this? Have you taken to viewing Sony the Hedgehog or some such?'

'Fulfilling your potential then.'

'My glass is empty,' said Jim. 'Dryness of the throat inhibits my cogitation on matters which require a fullness of potential.'

'Have one on me,' said Tuppe, producing a mighty wad of high-denomination money notes. 'If you could see your way clear to releasing Cornelius, I have no doubt that he would amply reward you for your efforts.'

Omally tried to draw his eyes away from the big brown bundle, but just couldn't. 'Might *I* have the same again?' he enquired politely.

'And me,' said Scoop. 'Only different.'

'Sure thing.'

'More in this direction, Neville,' called Omally.

The full-time barlord hastened to oblige. 'I trust you are not plotting sedition in my bar, John,' said he.

'Not a bit of it. Just chatting with this wee man.'

'Word has reached my ear', said Neville, 'that Hugo Rune has returned to the neighbourhood.'

'Villain of the piece,' said Tuppe. 'My chum Cornelius will sort him out though.'

'These words are pleasing to my ears. When he does, do you think he might broach the subject of the bar bill Rune ran up here eighteen years ago. It still gives me sleepless nights.'

'I'd be happy to. So what are we drinking?'

Omally pushed his half-pint glass aside. 'Mine was a double whisky,' he said.

'Mine also,' said Pooley.

'And mine,' said Scoop.

'I'll have a triple,' said Tuppe.

'This lad has class,' said Omally. 'Triples all round it is then.'

In a private booth next to the darts board, Omally spoke in low and earnest tones. He talked of wooden horses and escape tunnels. Of the construction of kites which might bear a fellow's weight and be flown above a prison wall. Of bogus prison visitors, skilled in the arts of Pelmanism, who could memorize complicated computer entry codes and effect the premature release of a detainee by hacking into closed systems with advanced gadgetry. And of schemes diverse and intricate, understood by Omally alone, and requiring the up-front capital outlay of but a few paltry thousands of pounds.

At length, when he had finally run himself dry, he tore his eyes away from the wad which Tuppe still clutched, to discover that the three attentive listeners to whom he had been discoursing had now increased by a factor of one.

'This is fascinating stuff,' said Cornelius Murphy. 'Don't stop now, I'm loving every minute.'

9

'This is seriously appalling,' Norman gnawed upon a knuckle. 'I have to do something about this.'

But what?

'Inform somebody,' was Norman's decision.

But who?

'Jack,' said Norman. 'No, *not* Jack.'

The Controller then.

'No, not *him*.'

Who then?

'Who's asking me these questions?'

Just you. You're asking yourself.

'Well it wasn't very clear. But I'll have to speak to someone.'

Who though?

'Stop it! There's only one person who can deal with this.'

Who? Who? Tell us.

'God,' said Norman. 'I will have to speak to God.'

Cor!

'No, stuff that. I can't just go bothering *Him* no matter how bad things may appear. He knows His own business best and if He's decided to snuff out the entire population of Great Britain the Friday after next by "electrical discharge", then He won't take kindly to me asking Him what on earth He thinks He's up to. He would probably take great exception to it and smite me with a plague of boils or something.'

But then . . .

'But then,' Norman continued, 'what if he *doesn't*

79

know. I've evidently stumbled onto exactly what I was not supposed to stumble onto here, by the simple expedient of getting out of my chair and actually opening a filing cabinet. Which I was *not* expected to do.

'This is some kind of big secret. That must have been what Jack meant when he said it was *the best-kept secret in the history of eternity*. Somehow God doesn't know about this.'

It was an interesting theory. Although the route by which Norman arrived at it, and whether he would actually have arrived at it by this route, and whether it was at all correct, however he might have arrived at it, were matters for debate (or even explanation).

But it was the theory that he had arrived at, and having arrived at it, he sought to test it out.

By asking God anyway.

'And now would be as good a time as any,' said Norman, slipping through the doorway and slinking off down the corridor.

If God hung out at all in this building, he would inevitably be doing so in the penthouse suite, or whatever its URC equivalent was, on the toppermost floor.

Norman ducked along this corridor and that. All were equally drab, but mercifully so were they empty. By the time he had finally located the lift though and pressed at its button, his knees were knocking like an Eddie Floyd hit and his mouth was dry as an author's wit. (Hmm!)

There was still the possibility, and far from a remote one, that the Big G knew all about the electrical discharging and might give Norman that sound smiting for his impudence.

There was a little clunkity-click sound, a bell went ting and the lift doors opened.

Norman stepped speedily in and sought the top-floor button.

'Are you going up?' enquired a voice.

It was a deep voice. It had what is called timbre to it.

Norman nearly performed the embarrassing act which had earned him infamy when aged five.

'Ah,' said he, turning to view the owner of the voice.

He lurked in a shadowy corner. A big man, well over six feet and broad all around and about with it. He wore a white three-piece suit. White apparently being the company colour, which wasn't much of a surprise, although it did lack a certain originality.

His head was a big bald dome. His nose the beak of a hawk, set amongst a generosity of jowls and dewlaps. And he was the very *doppelgänger* of somebody not altogether unknown to some, but still completely unknown to Norman.

The voice Norman knew though, he'd earholed it coming through Jack Bradshaw's intercom.

It was the voice of the . . . Norman found strains of the TV theme tune from *Thomas the Tank Engine* springing to his lips in an involuntary nervous whistle.

The controller, for indeed it was he, viewed Norman through a pair of most alarming eyes. Dead black, with small white pupils.

'I enquired whether you were going up,' he enquired.

'All the way,' said Norman hopefully.

'To where, one might ask? And I do.'

'To the gymnasium,' Norman suggested.

'I think you had better come with me,' said the controller.

'I think I'd better get out of the lift,' said Norman.

But he could not, because the lift doors had now closed, with what is known in prison circles as the now legendary Death Cell Finality.

10

'There is a phrase currently in service,' said John Omally, as he counted and recounted the high-denomination money notes from the wad which Cornelius had insisted Tuppe pay him, in compensation for the earnings he would have accrued had he actually been able to spring the tall boy from prison by any of the implausible schemes he'd outlined. 'And this phrase is, as I understand it, "Employ a teenager today while they still know everything."'

'It's your round I think,' said Jim Pooley.

'Mine was a quadruple,' said Scoop Molloy.

'Ours shall all be *Murphy's*,' said John. 'God speed to your man, whatever he's up to.'

'What exactly *are* we up to?' asked Tuppe, as the glorious open-topped, electric-blue Cadillac Eldorado left Brentford further and further behind.

'We are heading for adventure,' replied Cornelius, holding down his hair with one hand and trying to change into a pair of trousers that had two legs to them, with the other. 'An adventure of the rock-and-roll persuasion, which is not all plot-led and dialogue-laden, as has been the case so far.'

'On the trail of your errant daddy then, is it?'

'Nope.' Cornelius flung his brutalized bags from the car. They caught a passing cyclist full in the face, precipitating a front-wheel-entanglement incident, leading to a handlebar pass-over, litter-bin encounter, Lycra shorts seam-split and paramedic call-out situation.

'What do you mean, "nope"?' asked Tuppe. 'You've had a private detective hunting down your daddy for months. And now he's found him.'

'So?' said Cornelius, with a foot down the wrong leg of his replacement trews.

'Well, he'll be up to something terrible, won't he? Something that you should stop.'

'Probably, but as we don't have the faintest idea of what this might be, I don't see what we can do about it.'

'Oh,' said Tuppe. 'Fair enough then, so what *are* we up to? Or did I already ask that?'

'We're going on holiday,' said Cornelius. 'The zip shouldn't be at the back of these trousers, should it?'

'Look out for that baker carrying the huge tray of custard pies,' said Tuppe.

Cornelius swerved around the baker, narrowly avoiding a bumper-to-bum incident, leading to tray displacement, wide area custard pie dispersal, innocent passer-by facial impact and crap slap-stick comic cliché situation.

'Holiday?' asked Tuppe.

'To Skelington Bay,' said the tall boy. 'These aren't my trousers. These are your trousers – they're up past my knees.'

'Your dad's on his way to Skelington Bay,' said Tuppe. 'Fancy you choosing *that* town. What a coincidence.'

'We shall take seaside jobs,' said Cornelius, wrestling with his groin.

'*Jobs?* What are you saying?'

'The fake magistrate has frozen my assets.'

'Sounds very painful.'

'I shall pretend I didn't hear that. But we are broke once again. The millions are no more. We're back on the road.'

'Just the way it should be. Shall I turn up the radio full blast and see what happens next?'

83

'Do it,' said Cornelius Murphy. 'I'll just pull over and pick up those two girl hitchhikers. Once I've made myself decent. Do you have a pair of scissors, or something?'

They were beautiful girls, the hitchhikers. Tanned legs, blond hair, bloom of youth on their cheeks, high-profile nipple definition in the upper T-shirt areas. An old man's dream and a young man's fancy. Political correctness? Who gives a toss?

'Can we give you a lift?' asked Cornelius.

'Sure thing,' said a slender beauty. 'We're going south.'

'Us too, hop in.'

The slender beauty and her equally slender and beauteous companion tossed their rucksacks into the back and took to hopping in.

'My name's Thelma,' said beauty number one. 'And this is my friend Louise.'

'Cornelius Murphy,' said the tall boy, battoning down his hair.

'This is some great car,' said Louise.

'We like it,' said Tuppe.

'Who said that?'

'I did.'

'Oh, I'm sorry, I didn't see you there.'

'Cornelius?' said Tuppe.

'Yes, my friend?'

'Cornelius, I would like to put in for a discontinuance of the "I didn't see you there" running gag. I fear it might seriously interfere with my sex life.'

'It's dropped as far as I'm concerned,' said the Murphy. 'We're rockin' and rollin' now.'

'I was only joking,' said Louise. 'You're very cute as it happens.'

'So,' said Tuppe, as the Cadillac sped along and left all

84

of London far behind, 'what do you ladies do with yourselves when you're not hitching rides?'

'We fly,' said Louise.

'You're air stewardesses?' Tuppe asked.

'No, we fly,' said Thelma. 'We're angels.'

'Cornelius,' whispered Tuppe, 'we've loonies on board.'

'Not real angels,' said Louise. 'We're entering the east pier man-powered flight competition at Skelington Bay.'

'Fancy that, because we're going—'

'Have to stop you there,' said Cornelius. 'Something is happening up ahead. I do hope it's not a police road-block.'

'You never did tell me how you broke out of the cell,' said Tuppe. 'I assumed, by the evidence of your person, that some degree of unpleasantness occurred.'

'There was a difference of opinion,' Cornelius explained. 'The constables held to the view that I should remain incarcerated; I, however, did not. They heard me picking the lock and lay in wait, but I had taken the precaution of removing a section of the iron bedframe, to wield in a clublike fashion, should the necessity arise.'

'Which it did.'

'A contest of martial skills ensued. The final score was Escapees 2: Constables Nil. But *something* is occurring up ahead.'

And *something* was.

They were on the A3 and the traffic was all coming to a standstill. The cause for this was not immediately apparent, but is it ever? Possibly two lanes were going into one. This usually causes motorists to go into a state of terminal idiocy and jam themselves fast. Why they do it is anyone's guess, but inevitably they do.

But then possibly it wasn't that. Possibly it had something to do with the not altogether distant pall of smoke that was rising into the otherwise clear blue sky.

'Someone's crashed,' said Cornelius. 'Which is horrid at best.'

'Should we get out and see if we can help?'

'I was going to suggest that, Tuppe. Do either of you know any first aid?' Cornelius asked the hitchhikers.

'None at all,' was the reply.

'Leave the keys in the car,' said Louise, 'then if the traffic starts to move, we'll catch you up.'

'Good idea,' Cornelius left the keys, Tuppe waved his farewells and the two struck off for the cause of the hold-up.

It wasn't too many cars ahead.

'You know what that looks like to me?' said Tuppe, viewing the wreckage.

'Go on,' said Cornelius.

'Flying saucer,' said Tuppe.

'It does though, doesn't it?'

'It does.'

And it did.

And it *was*.

It was one of those lightweight scoutship jobbies constructed, no doubt, from metals unknown upon this planet. And it bore an uncanny resemblance to the one which the US Airforce still insist is *not* housed in Hangar 27 at Muroc Air Base, Muroc Dry Lake, California.*

And here it was, crashed on the A3.

A number of folk were gathered around it. These were of the cars at the forefront of the tailback. So to speak.

There was a portly young man in a brown three-piece double-breaster. A leisurewear cultist with a lean-and-

---

* Why do they keep up the pretence? We all know it's there.

hungry look and a lady in a straw hat who stood knitting a grey sock.

Not perhaps everyone's natural choice of a welcoming committee set to greet a traveller from a distant star. But there you go.

This welcoming committee was gathered about a three-foot-sixish sort of body, decked out in a nifty-looking uniform with gold epaulettes and braided cuffs. He had a large nose fastened to a far larger head, grey in colour, Mekon in design.

The welcoming committee was shouting.

Loudly.

'Shift it!' shouted the leisurewear cultist. Making fists and bobbing up and down upon air-filled soles.

'I've got an appointment!' shouted the portly double-breaster, tapping a plump forefinger onto what the bloke who sold it to him in a pub had neglected to mention was a *fake* Rolex.

'I'm not in any hurry!' shouted the lady in the straw hat. 'But I just like shouting.'

The off-worlder was trying to get a word in edgeways. '■ΔΞW■Δ■!' he remarked.

'That's easy for you to say,' said the lady in the straw hat.

'Might we be of assistance?' asked Cornelius. 'We're plain-clothed AA men.'

'About time too,' shouted the leisurewear cultist, bouncing from toe to heel in a step-aerobic fashion and shaking his fist at the small figure with the large grey head. 'This joker nearly had my car off the road.'

'And mine,' shouted the wearer of the bogus Rolex. 'And mine's an XR3i, touring model. Top of the range.'

'So's mine,' shouted the aerobicist. 'And my air bag nearly inflated.'

'My hazard lights came on automatically.'

'So did mine.'

'My anti-lock brakes applied an independently com-puterized pull-up torque to each of my wheels. Top of the range.'

'So's mine.'

The off-worlder looked from one to the other of them. And he looked perplexed.

Cornelius looked at Tuppe.

And Tuppe looked at Cornelius.

And they both looked perplexed also.

'You're lying about having an air bag!' shouted bogus Rolex. 'Look at your front bumper. You clouted the back of this bloke's flying saucer. If you had an air bag it would have inflated.'

'I've got laser sighting,' shouted the man, who, beneath his colourful outer garments, wore a posing thong of crimson Lycra. 'Housed in my side lights, they criss-cross at an acute angle ten metres beyond the bonnet, digitally map a three-dimensional image, giving speed-to-stopping ratio, as crash tested upon dummies in the advert with that woman singing, and they declared it a no-air-bag situation.'

'What a lot of old crap,' said Tuppe.

'It's not crap, it's top of the range.'

'So's mine,' said the Rolex. 'And the metallic paint-work finish is baked on.'

'An estate agent,' said Tuppe.

'Who?' asked Cornelius.

'The bloke with the fake Rolex.'

'It's never a fake, how dare you!' The watch-wearer clutched at his wrist.

'$\Delta\Xi W\blacksquare\blacksquare\blacksquare\blacksquare\blacksquare\blacksquare oW=Z\blacksquare oo\Delta|$,' said the space pilot.

'Quite right,' said Tuppe.

'What did he say?' asked most present.

'He says that the watch has the classic oyster face, but

the numerals are in chrome and not gilt and the strap's the wrong colour.'

'His car's the wrong colour too,' sneered Leisurewear Lad. 'XR3i! That's an XR2 bog standard. He's not an estate agent, he's a sales rep from ASDA.'

'I'm not!' shrieked Bogus Rolex.

'He is,' agreed the lady in the straw hat.

'I'm bloody not!'

'You bloody are. And I should know, I'm your mother.'

'You bloody aren't!'

'I bloody am too,' the lady in the straw hat told Tuppe.

'Give him a smack,' said Tuppe. 'That sometimes helps.'

Hoot, Hoot, Hoot went the backed-up traffic, beginning to go Hoot, Hoot, Hoot.

'Zo■Z■Δ■■■W,' said the space pilot.

'What did he say?' Cornelius enquired.

'He asked if we might take him to a place of safety, before the men from *Project Grudge* and *M.J.12* arrive on the scene to drag him off for debriefing and experimentation.'

'I didn't know you spoke Venusian, Tuppe.'

'It's not Venusian, it's Romany.'

Woo, Woo, Woo, Woo, Woo, came the sound of police car sirens.

'You'd better come with us,' said Cornelius to the crashed saucerian.

'W△≡o■△■■*o*△!' said that fellow.

Cornelius, Tuppe and *The Man from Another World** jogged down the line of backed-up traffic.

Unfortunately, when they arrived at the place where the Cadillac Eldorado should have been, there wasn't even a space left waiting for them.

Thelma and Louise had nicked the car.

---

* 1958. Directed by Hal Vernon and co-starring Kyle McKintock as the small-town judge whose daughter falls in love with the alien.

11

'Let go of my ear!' wailed Norman. But the large controller* would not. He shook the dead boy all about by it.

'Where do you think you're off to?' he demanded to be told.

'I was . . . I mean . . . I . . . let go of my ear.'

'What is your name?' The plump fingers went twist, twist, twist.

'Norman!' shrieked Norman.

'Jack Bradshaw's new assistant?'

'That's me, sir, yes.'

'Then you should be at your desk, not wandering about, shouldn't you?'

'Yes, sir. Ouch.'

'But you're not.'

'No, sir. Ooooh.'

'Because you're skiving, boy, aren't you?'

'Yes,' Norman readily agreed. 'That's it, sir. I'm sorry, sir.'

'And so you should be.' The plump fingers relaxed their grip and Norman sank down hard on his bum.

'Your first day at work here and you thought you'd go walkabout.'

Norman climbed to his feet and rubbed at his fat red ear. 'I'm sorry,' he mumbled. 'Let me out of the lift, sir, and I'll get straight back to work.'

---

* He could not be referred to as *The Fat Controller* due to a possible infringement of copyright.

'I think not.' The large controller fixed Norman with a withering gaze.

'Oh dear,' said the dead boy, weakening at the knees.

'No,' said the large controller. 'If you wish to go walkabout, then walkabout you shall go. With *me*. I am on my way to inspect the relocation bays. You will accompany me.'

'Good-oh,' said Norman, without any trace of enthusiasm entering his voice.

'You will learn much.' The large controller leaned forward, stretched up and pushed the very top lift button. Way beyond Norman's reach it was. 'Much.'

'Much,' said Norman.

'Much indeed. Many are there here who have never made my acquaintance. Many who have never known the thrill of listening to me speak. You will learn much. Very much.'

The large controller peered down upon the red-haired youth. He was rubbing at his ear with one hand and picking his nose with a finger from the other.

'Or probably in your case not very much at all.'

After a space of time which was neither very long nor very short, but somewhere in between, the lift stopped suddenly with a clunk and a click and a ding of the bell.

The doors opened and Norman, who was still rubbing his ear, but no longer picking his nose (he being at the rolling, preparatory-to-flicking stage), found himself staring out at something very strange indeed.

'What is that out there?' he managed in an awestruck kind of a tone.

'The relocation bays.' The large controller strode from the lift to whatever lay beyond. 'Follow me.'

Norman dithered. He had to get out of here. Pass on his terrible knowledge about the fatal electrical dischargings to God. Or to somebody. He had to do *something*.

'Get a move on,' called the large controller.

'Coming,' said Norman.

What was out there was large and noisy. Very large and very noisy. And very brass. It was a monstrous, steam-driven, oily-smelling kind of a contrivance and there were acres of it. All in the open beneath the big black sky.

It was all burnished flywheels and ball governors and throbbing pistons and fan belts and big round glass gauges with flickering needles and pipes going every which way and bolts and rivets and bits and bobs and all sorts. It was Jules Verne meets Isambard Kingdom Brunel round at Cecil B. De Mille's house.

And there really were acres of it. It spread away, a grinding and a chugging and an emitting of small steam puffs to every direction. There were gantries and catwalks in pierced cast iron and little men in boiler-suits, of the type you normally associate with steam preservation societies, bumbled about with oil cans, greasing nipples and ragging away at things.

'What does it all do?' shouted Norman above the mechanical hubbub.

'It powers the big sky nozzles,' the large controller explained in a large voice. 'The furnaces pressure up the boilers which work the turbines that run the generators that supply the energy to the big sky nozzles.'

'What do the big sky nozzles do?' bawled Norman.

'They broadcast the frequencies that you program into your Karmascope. You have read the handbook, I trust.'

'I've been meaning to.'

'Yes, I'll bet you have.'

'Pardon?'

'Never mind. Each soul exists upon a slightly different electrical frequency. You calculate this frequency by going through the procedures that Jack explained to you. Punch it into your Karmascope, which relays it directly to one of the big sky nozzles. The big sky nozzle broadcasts the frequency, the required soul is detached from the hovering throng encircling the sun, sucked up the nozzle, reprocessed and reallocated, then spat back down to Earth to its next recipient. Are you paying attention, boy?'

Norman actually was, but his thoughts were all elsewhere.

'Something on your mind?' the large controller asked.

'Does God ever come down here himself to inspect the machinery?' Norman asked. 'Only I was hoping to say hello to Him.'

The withering gaze withered him once more. 'Follow me.'

'Yes, sir.'

Norman followed the large controller. As the big man strode on, Norman's eyes darted to the left and right in the pathetic hope that he might spy out a sign reading STAIRWAY TO HEAVEN, or a door marked GOD'S OFFICE KNOCK AND ENTER.

But he didn't.

He did come at last to a door, however. It was not the kind of door that looked as if it led to the office of God. Quite the opposite, in fact. It was a big black greasy iron door with lots of rivets and several mighty bolts.

The large controller began to draw them. One, two, three.

'What's through there?' Norman asked.

'You'll see.'

'I'm not sure I really want to.' Norman took a step back, but the large controller turned with quite remarkable speed considering his bulk and caught the lad once more by the ear.

'I ought to be getting off to work now,' squirmed Norman. 'Oh please let me go.'

With his free hand the large controller drew the final bolt and pulled upon the iron door, releasing an exhalation of fetid air. Norman fought and struggled but to no avail whatever.

'I fear', said the large controller, 'that you have done exactly what you should not have done and discovered something that you should not have discovered.'

'No,' blubbered Norman. 'Not me, sir.'

'Yes, you sir. And so regrettably I shall have to "let you go" as they say.'

'No, please wait . . . I—' But the terrible door was now open sufficiently wide to admit the passage of one medium-sized struggler with a red Beatle cut and a grey school uniform.

'Aaaaaagh!' went Norman plummeting into darkness and downwardness.

Slam went the terrible door and clunk, clunk, clunk, clunk went its mighty bolts an increasing distance above.

Echoes and darkness and oblivion and a really rotten way to end your first day at work.

Or your very existence.

Or whatever.

12

'He says he wants to speak to someone in authority,' said Tuppe to Cornelius as they sat a-puffing and a-panting in a barn. The small grey off-worlder with the large nose and the far larger head sat a-puffing and a-panting between them. But he did it in a different register and rhythm. As might well be expected.

'Someone trustworthy,' Tuppe continued. 'He says he wants to speak to Erich Von Daniken.'

'Oh right. Good idea. Have you asked him yet whether he brings us greetings from a distant star, and whether we should all lay down our nuclear weapons, live in peace with one another and share the wisdom of our benign space brothers?'

'No,' said Tuppe. 'I didn't think to. Should I ask him now?'

'No, Tuppe. You see I noticed the jack-knifed low-loader that this joker's flying saucer fell off. It had the legend DR DOVESTON'S WONDER SHOW plastered all over it. He's part of a fairground turn, Tuppe. You should have known this, you grew up with the circus.'

'Is this true?' Tuppe asked the grey-faced big-nose.

'■Δ≡o■■■Δ■o■,' the grey-faced big-nose replied. In Romany.

'He says it's not true,' said Tuppe. 'Well, some of it is. He *did* fall off the back of the low-loader, but only because he crash-landed on it first.'

'A likely story.'

'You can be a terrible cynic at times,' said Tuppe.

95

Woo, Woo, Woo, Woo, came the sound of police car sirens once again. 'We had best run again,' said Cornelius.

'I don't know why I'm running, I'm not wanted for anything.'

'You're quite right,' said Cornelius. 'You stay here with ET and I'll run on alone.'

'Stuff that,' said Tuppe.

'*■Δ■■ΔΔΔΔ,' said ET.

'He says "Stuff that too",' Tuppe explained. 'Let's all run together.'

And so run together they did.

It was a nice day for it. Nice countryside also. Wobbly wheat and dappled hedgerows. And those spinneys that might be copses but probably turn out to be thickets when you get up close to them.

Very nice.

Very agrarian. And bucolic. Agrarian and bucolic. And praedial. And agrestic. That sort of thing.

'Which way?' Tuppe asked, when they had finally done with that sort of thing and reached a road.

Cornelius was all but gone with the exhaustion. He had been carrying Tuppe on his shoulders and the little grey space man under one arm. 'Any way,' he gasped.

'■Δ ≡ ■o■WΔ=o■|,' said the little grey space man.

'He says he can hear a car coming,' said Tuppe.

'I can't hear anything.' Cornelius strained his ears. 'He can't *hear* what colour it is, I suppose.'

'■ΔW ≡ o■■W■■WΔ ≡ o■ ≡ o■ΔΔ■o■Δ∇,' said the space man.

'Red,' said Tuppe.

'Gettaway, Red!' Cornelius caught his breath and hung on to it.

The sound of an approaching vehicle reached his ears,

it appeared above the crest of a distant hill and rushed towards him. The vehicle was a car. It was a *red* car.

'Don't say lucky guess,' said Tuppe.

'I wasn't going to, I was going to say hide at the side of the road and when I give the signal get into the back seat on the passenger side.'

'$\Delta \equiv$o■WΔ■■■Δo■o■,'

'He says—'

'I don't care what he says, hide in the hedge.'

The red car sped closer and Cornelius stood with his hands raised in the middle of the road. It was a narrow road. More a country lane really. Yes, that was it, a country lane. So the car couldn't swerve around Cornelius. It being a country lane and everything. The car screeched to a halt with much blackening of tyre tread upon Tarmac. There was a loud popping sound and Cornelius looked on as the air bag, which is fitted as standard on a top-of-the-range model such as this one was, inflated, engulfing the driver in a big balloon of showroom-smelling safety fabric.

'Help, help, set me free!' shouted a most familiar voice.

'It's the man with the bogus Rolex,' said Cornelius, giving Tuppe and his new-found friend from the stars the signal they had agreed upon (secretly).

The tall boy stepped nimbly to the driver's door and pulled it open. 'Might I be of some assistance, sir?' he asked.

'Get me out of here.'

'Happy to oblige.' Cornelius took the driver by the arm and pulled as hard as he could.

Then he climbed back to his feet and returned to the car. 'I'm afraid I've ripped the sleeve off your jacket,' he apologized. 'Perhaps we share the same tailor.'

'Get me free, I'm suffocating here.'

Cornelius withdrew from his pocket a multi-function

97

Swiss Army knife. It had always puzzled him why if the Swiss were neutral they needed an army. Possibly this enemyless military body simply whiled away the hours inventing new blades for its famous knife. Or possibly *Swiss Army* was a trade name, like Ronco, or K.Tel. Or ASDA.

'Who gives a toss?' murmured the suffocating salesman. 'Just cut me free.'

Cornelius hastened to oblige. There was much ripping, much hissing and then more shouting. The Rolex-wearer issued from his automobile like a storm from a teapot. Or was it a storm *in* a teapot?

'What are you playing at? Standing in the road like that, you could have been killed.'

'I'm OK thanks,' said Cornelius. 'This car of yours can certainly pull up short when it has to. Have you got AVS* fitted as standard?'

'And a *Blaupunkt*,' said the man from ASDA.

'And leather upholstery by the look of it,' said Cornelius.

'The driver's seat is capable of twenty-three separate adjustments to mould itself to your lumber profile,' said the driver proudly.

'What anybody's or just yours?'

'Anybody's. Sit in, I'll show you how it works.'

'Cor, thanks,' said Cornelius. 'I'd really like that.'

It was the work of a moment of course. Nothing more. A door slam, a central lock (again fitted as standard), a flap aside of the shredded air bag and a twist of the ignition key (the one with the 'My other car is an XJS 3.2 MFIi' key fob).

And that was that.

Tuppe waved from the rear window.

---

* Or is it AVC or ABS or ACDC? Or who gives a toss?

The ex-driver did not wave back. He lay in the middle of the road, thrashing his legs about and weeping bitterly.

Cornelius settled himself down into the posture contouring and whistled a wistful air.*

'That's very strange indeed,' said Tuppe to the spaceman.

'What is?' Cornelius asked.

'Mavis here was just telling me—'

'Mavis?' asked Cornelius.

'Mavis,' said Tuppe. 'That's the spaceman's name.'

'That's a very strange name for a spaceman.'

'That's what *I* just said.'

'Fair enough. Hey look, we're nearly there.' The road sign up ahead, which was now passing behind as Cornelius was driving rather fast, read, SKELINGTON BAY 1 MILE. 'Where does your cosmic pal want to be dropped off?'

The spaceman spoke some more gibberish and Tuppe said—

'No, don't bother,' Cornelius told him. 'He said to drop him off near the west pier. I got it.'

'How did you get it?' Tuppe enquired.

'Because he's not speaking Romany, he's speaking Esperanto.'

'I know lots of Earth languages,' said Mavis the spaceman. 'Do you mind if I change?'

'Not a bit,' said Cornelius, shaking his head and liberally distributing his hair all about the car. 'Speak Swahili if you think it will aid your credibility.'

'No, I meant change out of my uniform. Cunningly

* Manco Capac from the Quintessence 1969 album *In Blissful Company* (which is only a collector's item if it's in the original gatefold sleeve). These things matter!

99

disguise myself as an Earth being, to avoid recognition.'

'Oh yes, please do.' Cornelius kept on driving. 'I'd like to see that.'

'Thanks, then you will. Would you mind looking away for a moment?' the spaceman asked Tuppe. 'Only I'm not wearing any underpants.'

'Oh sure.' Tuppe looked away.

There were some sounds of a struggle, then the space-man said, 'You can look back now.'

Tuppe looked back. 'Shit a brick!' said he.

'Language,' said Cornelius, glancing over his shoulder. 'Shit a bungalow!' said he.

'Pretty convincing, eh?' asked the spaceman. And it was.

Gone the three-foot-sixer with the bulbous head and nose abundance. And in his place . . .

'A sheep,' said Tuppe. 'You're a sheep.'

'No I'm not,' said the sheep. 'I'm a collie dog.'

'You're a sheep,' said Tuppe. 'Believe me. I know sheep. Not as well as I know pigs. But I do know sheep and you're one.'

'But I'm supposed to be a collie dog. Called Ben.'

'Why Ben?' Cornelius asked the sheep.

'Because collie dogs are always called Ben, it's a tradition, or an old—'

'Sheep-*dog*,' said Tuppe. 'Collies are sheep-*dogs*.'

'That's me,' said Mavis the sheep called Ben.

'No, it's not you. You're a sheep, not a sheep-*dog*.'

'But you're a very good one,' said Cornelius. 'How did you do that, by the way?'

'Do you know anything about the trans-perambulation of pseudo-cosmic anti-matter?' the sheep asked.

'Only that it's bogus sci-fi waffle.'

'It's a costume then,' the sheep reached up with its little trotters (or perhaps hooves, if sheep don't have trotters), and pulled off its head. Mavis the spaceman peeped out through the neck hole of his woolly suit. 'Do you think it will matter?' he asked. 'Sheep, sheep-dog, what's the difference?'

'Quite a lot,' said Tuppe. 'Is this your first time on Earth?'

'Certainly not. I've been here lots of times.'

'I don't think you're being altogether truthful.'

'Oh, all right then, yes it's my first time.'

'So who set you up with the sheep costume?'

'My mate Bryant. We graduated together, but he failed his pilot's licence and works in the stores now. When I told him that I'd been offered this job of flying to Earth on a secret mission, he said that he'd help me out. He organized the costume and the Earth name.'

'Ben?' asked Tuppe.

'No, *Mavis*. He said that most Earth men were called Mavis, that it was a tradition, or—'

'Stop,' said Cornelius, now stopping the car. 'It's all been very entertaining. But enough is enough. We have arrived. This I would assume is the west pier, as its brother lies in an easterly direction. Put your sheep's head back on and kindly leave the vehicle.'

'Thanks for the ride,' said Mavis, slipping on his sheep's head. 'I really appreciate it.'

'What are you doing?' Tuppe asked Cornelius. 'We can't just leave him here disguised as a sheep.'

'Why not?'

'Well, he won't get five yards.'

'I'll be OK,' said Mavis, or Ben, or whoever. 'I'll nuzzle up against someone and get taken home and fed and petted. I know the form.'

'I don't think you quite do,' said Tuppe. 'People don't treat sheep the same way as they treat dogs.'

'Don't they?'

'They do not. People may pet dogs, but they *eat* sheep.'

'*What?*'

'I'm afraid your pal Bryant has put you on a wrong'n.'

'Oh dear,' said whoever. 'Whatever shall I do?'

'Why don't you just come clean', said Cornelius, 'and own up. You're not really from outer space, are you?'

'I never said I was.'

'Oh, I think you did,' said Tuppe. 'Or at least implied it anyway.'

'That was my cover,' said a mournful whoever. 'In case I got caught. Bryant said that if the collie dog costume didn't work and saying I was an Earthman called Mavis didn't work, then I was to pretend I came from outer space and ask to be taken to Erich Von Daniken.'

Tuppe shook his little head. Cornelius sighed and drummed his fingers upon the sleek Grand Prix style steering wheel, which came as standard on this particular model. 'It would seem', said he, 'that as Tuppe observed, your pal Bryant has stitched you up. Now I can sympathize with you, but unless you tell me all of the truth then I am not prepared to help you. We are sitting here in a stolen car, this is not a good thing to be doing. So speak quickly or take your chances elsewhere.'

'I'm not from outer space,' confessed the whoever in the sheep suit.

'Aw,' said Tuppe. 'What a cop out.'

'So where are you from?' Cornelius asked.

'I'm from the same place that all the flying saucers really come from.'

'Which is outer space,' said Tuppe.

'No it's not.' The whoever pointed a trotter or a hoof or whatever towards the sea. 'It's not from outer space. It's from outta there.'

13

In space, they say, no-one can hear you scream. Norman, who had been falling and screaming for some considerable time, would, had he been asked, have been able to verify this. But as no-one was around to ask, he didn't.

'Aaaaaaaagh!' went Norman. 'Aaaaaaaagh!'

And then *Crash!* went Norman, as he ceased falling all at once and struck home at whatever he had been falling towards.

'Oh God,' went Norman. 'Oh and help.' He floundered about in a mound of debris and wondered which way 'up' had once been.

'Oh God,' went Norman again. 'I could have been killed.'

'No you couldn't,' said a voice. 'Not a second time.'

'Who said that?'

'Stay where you are and I'll put on the light.'

Norman stayed where he was.

Someone put on the light.

And Norman, blinking and twitching could now see where he was. In what looked to be (and indeed was) the bottom of an abandoned lift shaft. Wedged into a pile of mouldy papers and broken office furniture.

'Where are you?' asked Norman. 'Whoever you are.'

'I'm here!' A veritable apparition sprang up before him. Long of white hair, long of white beard, ragged of clothing and very wild of eye.

'Fuck me!' said Norman. 'It's Ben Gun.'

'No it ain't,' crowed the apparition, dancing about him. 'I'm Claude, I am.'

'Claude who?'

'Don't remember. Claude Butler perhaps. Or was that a bicycle? Claude Raines?'

'Phantom of the Opera?' Norman asked.

'Never been to the opera. Been here for years and years and years.'

'Oh dear,' said Norman. 'Years?'

'And years and years. Wasn't expecting you, though. Did you make an appointment?'

'I just dropped in,' said Norman, with ne'er a hint of humour. 'And I'd like to be shown the way out.'

'No way out. Only up and can't be climbed. Bloody big door at the top if you did and hasn't been opened for years and years—'

'And years?' Norman asked. 'Do you think you could help me out of all this rubbish? I'm stuck fast.'

'Rubbish?' The loon bobbed up and down. 'That's not rubbish, that's evidence that is. I'll have my day in court, you just see if I don't.'

'I'd like to very much,' said Norman. 'But I have important business to attend to. Please help me out.'

'Come on then.' The ancient took Norman by the shoulders and dragged him from the mouldering mound.

'Thank you very much,' said Norman. 'I didn't like that at all.'

'What did *you* do then?' asked the white-bearder. 'Clerical error was it, clerical error?'

'In a manner of speaking.' Norman dusted garbage from himself.

'Found out something you shouldn't have, I'll bet.'

'Yeah well, maybe.'

'All here,' crowed the loon. 'All the evidence. What he's been up to, what he's up to now. He dumps it all down here to taunt me. Because I found him out.'

'Who are you?' asked Norman.

'I'm Claude,' said Claude. 'Claude somebody, just keeps escaping me.'

'*What* are you then?'

'What am I? I'm the bloody controller. That's what I am.'

'*You're* the controller? I don't understand.'

'I found him out,' said the controller. 'Found out what he was up to. Caught him at it. And he got me and he threw me down here and he threw all the evidence down here on top of me and he bolted the bloody door. *Bastard*!' the ancient shouted up the shaft. 'You fat bastard! I'll get you!'

'You mean that the controller up there isn't the real controller? That you're the real controller?'

'You thick or something, sonny? What did you think I've been saying?'

'I'm sorry,' said Norman. 'I'm somewhat confused.'

'So was I. So was I. Kept seeing his name coming up again and again. Thought it was a clerical error. Tackled him over it. But he got me and he threw me down here and—'

'Yes, you said all that. But who is *he*?'

'He's a bastard, that's who he is.'

'Surely that's *what* he is.'

'Don't tell me my business, sonny. I caught him at it. I know who he is and what he is. And I've got all the evidence and—'

'You'll have your day in court?' Norman asked.

'I told you I would, didn't I?'

'What evidence have you got?'

'All this. Piles of it. And you've made a mess of it, falling into it.'

'Sorry,' said Norman. 'But I didn't fall, I was pushed.'

'Pushed by him, I'll bet.'

'Yes,' said Norman. 'Show me whatever this evidence is. Please.'

'It's all here. Dates, facts, cross-references, births and

deaths. All *his*, over and over again. There're four of him down there this very minute, you know.'

'Down where?'

'Down on the Earth, you silly fool. Four of him exactly the same. Cloned himself, he did, and just goes on and on, getting cleverer and cleverer and more dangerous every time.'

'You mean there's someone down there who somehow manages to get reincarnated as himself again and again? Is that what you're saying?'

'Not *re*incarnated, *pre*-incarnated. That's what he does. He fixed it for himself, you see. Every time he dies his soul, or one of them, seeing as he's now got four, goes back into the system and gets reallocated to himself again on his original birthdate.'

'What, reincarnates in the past?'

'*Pre*-incarnates. That's what I said. Souls can do that kind of stuff. They're not tied to physical laws. Time don't mean nothing to souls. And he found that out. Smart bugger, so he is. He just keeps getting born again and again on his original birthday. Never makes the same mistake twice, I can tell you. Knows it all, see. What's going to happen. Bastard! I'll have him though. I've got all the evidence right here, I'll have my—'

'Day in court. And quite right too.' Norman knelt down and picked up a pile of mouldy old papers. 'And all this lot refers to just one man?'

'Same man, many lifetimes though. But all the same lifetime, as far as anyone else knows. Some scam, eh? Immortality, that's what that is. Cloned himself, did I tell you that?'

'You did mention it. How did he do that?'

'Got himself born as quintuplets one time is my guess.'

'Quintuplets? But I thought you said there are *four* of him down there.'

'Four down there, that's what I said. And one up here. The bloody fake controller! Same bloke! Bastard! Don't you ever listen to what's told you, sonny?'

'I'm trying,' said Norman. 'But it's quite a lot to take in at one go. You're saying, now let me make sure that I've got all this straight, you're saying that this man preincarnates again and again on his original birthdate. And that he remembers – is this right? – all the things he'd done when he was alive the first time and so does them better the second time, better still the third time and so on and so on.'

'You've got it. Knows it all, does it all, goes everywhere, knows everyone. Always in the right place at the right time. Bastard!'

'Yeah,' said Norman. 'Bastard. But if he does *that*. If you could do *that*. Well, blimey. You'd be—'

'The most amazing man who ever lived,' said the ancient one. 'And that's not all you'd be. You'd be something more than that.'

'Which is?'

The oldster fixed Norman with a wild and glittering eye. 'You'd be the very Devil himself,' said he.

14

The most amazing man of several parts had been out of the picture for quite some time. But here he was back in it now.

Ensconced was he in the best that Skelington Bay had to offer. Far less than what he might have wished for. But the best he was going to get here.

The Skelington Bay Grande.

The *e* had been added to Grand by the new owner who felt that it gave the place a bit of class. Much in the way that putting reproduction coachlamps on your gateposts that light up when your car drives in gives the place a bit of class. Or having personalized number-plates on your mini, or making a really interesting name for your bungalow by taking the first part of your wife's first name and adding it to the first part of your first name and coming up with something like RON-DOR.

And things of that nature.

But what is 'a bit of class' anyway? Can it really be defined? Or is it like 'style' or 'good taste', a relative and unquantifiable something-or-other? Is it 'a bit of class' to have your house and your family photographed for *Hello!* magazine, as did a certain horror fiction writer who must remain forever nameless to those who do not purchase that publication?*

Or is it not?

We must draw our own conclusions.

I know I've drawn *mine*!

* James Herbert

The present owner of the Grand had drawn his, and he had added the *e*. The present owner's name was Kevin and his wife was loved as Lynne. He had retired from a successful career as an ASDA sales representative. She, from a career of equal success, as a *Dominatrix*, whose calling-card advertised that 'naughty boys get bottom marks'. They had moved from their bungalow with the lighty-up coach-lamps and were 'making a go of the Grande'.

But now the Grande was not so grand as once the Grand had been. Time and ill-attention had conspired to wear its so-proud lustre all away.

All gone its court of potted palms, where bright young things had danced till dawn and taffeta kissed court shoes in the foxtrot.

Sadly gone. The Beckstein and the Lloyd loom chairs, the standard lamps with tasselled shades, the jardinières, the mirrors in their gilded frames. All gone.

> Out with the old, they cry aloud.
> And inward with the new.
> Down with that dividing wall.
> And knock the bugger through.
>
> Bring forth the patterned carpet tiles,
> The Draylon three-piece suite.
> Raise fitted units all about,
> Cor, don't it look a treat?
> Thank you.

Hugo Rune had taken for himself the entire top floor of the Grande. When it came to having 'a bit of class', Rune had it, and then a bit more. A great deal more. And then some.

He stood now, nobly framed by the long mock-Georgian UPVC replacement window of the KEV-LYN suite, the last sunlight of the day catching the sum of his prodigious parts to perfection.

His exaggerated shadow, cast in many fashionable places, now spread over many patterned carpet tiles.

'I believe that our company is incomplete,' said Hugo Rune. 'In fact, I know this for a certainty.'

Beyond the shadow of the man, a group of well-dressed persons sat about an occasional table that failed to rise to the occasion of Rune's presence.

'We are one short,' dared one more daring than the rest.

'A foreign entity,' said Rune. 'Of no small importance in the present schema.'

'If you say so.'

Rune turned and raised a hairless eyebrow.

'If you say so, *Mr Rune*.'

'We shall begin without him. Who carries the suitcase?'

He-that-did-the-suitcase-carry rose up and offered it to Rune.

'And does it fit-to-burst with money notes as we agreed?' the great man asked.

'It does.'

The other hairless eyebrow.

'*Mr Rune*.'

The unwholesome eyes beneath the baldy brows took in the company of men. Four in number. Very well-turned out. Three of middle years and one quite young (more daring than the rest). Whitehall types. Bespoke. Shoes polished. Known to Lynne in her professional pre-retirement capacity.

Rune took the suitcase, felt its weight and tossed it to the floor. 'Out there,' he said, gesturing to some point beyond the UPVC. 'Out there. Tell me what you see.'

The young and daring one took himself over to the window. 'A clapped-out seaside town, a pair of super-annuated piers.'

'And what?'

'The sea?'

'The sea is all you see?'

'The sea, that's all.'

'That's all. You see the sea, but Rune sees more.'

'What do you see then, *Mr Rune*?'

'I see gold,' said Hugo Rune. 'Much gold. Much, much, much, much, much gold.'

'Some sunken wreck then, is it?'

'No, my dear fellow, no sunken wreck. In the sea itself is the gold.'

'I don't think I follow you there.'

'This comes as no surprise to me.' Rune joined the daring young man at the window and stood looking out at the bay. Lights were beginning to twinkle upon the twin piers. Holiday folk strolled the promenade. The sea sucked at the shoreline.

'In the water itself,' said Rune. 'A cubic mile of sea water contains, on average, $93,000,000 worth of gold and $8,500,000 worth of silver*.'

'You're kidding,' said the daring young man.

'It's absolutely true, you can look it up†.'

'I know of this,' said a middle-aged, less daring fellow, from the rear of the room. 'But then *I* went to public school, so I would.'

'I know of it *too*,' said another middle-aged fellow, who hadn't been to public school, but did know of it too. 'But no agency exists to extract this gold. If it did—'

'If it did', said Hugo Rune, 'then the man who knew of this agency and could affect such an extraction, be it only of a small proportion of the whole, would become—'

'The richest man on Earth,' said the daring young man.

---

* This is absolutely true. You can look it up.
† Told you!

'And then some,' said Hugo Rune.

'But it can't be done,' said the fellow who had been to public school.

'There is nothing that *can't* be done,' said Hugo Rune. 'Only things that haven't been done *yet*.'

The public schoolboy felt urged to ask whether Rune had got that from a Christmas cracker, but he lacked the daring so to do.

'It is a conundrum,' said Hugo Rune. 'The gold exists, we know this for a fact. The conundrum is the means by which it might be extracted. It is a conundrum. Rune solves conundrums. I think, therefore I'm right.'

'So how do you do it?' asked the daring young man.

'That is for me to know and you only to know that I know.'

'Sounds like bullshit to me,' said the public schoolboy with rare daring.

'Sounds like bullshit to me, *Mr Rune*,' said Mr Rune. 'But you are here and I am here and the suitcase full of money notes sent to me by my good friend the Prime Minister is here. So bullshit, buddy, it ain't.'

'Pardon me, Mr Rune.'

'You are pardoned. The Prime Minister and I have formed a pact in this matter. I will undertake to extract the gold and we will divvy it up between us. He will pay off the National Debt and buy back the British Empire for Her Majesty the Queen (God bless her). And *I* have plans of my own. I trust that none of you gentlemen would be so unpatriotic as to deny our dear Queen the opportunity to rule once more over an Empire on which the sun never sets.'

'Perish the thought,' said the public schoolboy.

'God save the Queen,' said the daring young man. 'You will require the services of an assistant, Mr Rune. Might I put myself forward as an applicant for the position?'

'You may,' said Rune. 'And you are hired.'

'Thank you very much, sir, now regarding my salary—'

'Don't push your luck, shorty. You may cover whatever expenses you feel require covering. And we must get to work at once. The suitcase there contains a very large amount of money. Your job will be to spend it.'

'Right.' The young man rubbed his hands together.

'You will spend it buying Skelington Bay.'

'Pardon me?'

'This town. Every shop, every house, every public utility. All. The parks, the prom and the piers. You will do it first thing tomorrow.'

'But—'

'I am Rune,' said Rune. 'And Rune will be butted no buts. Buy it all. I want the population on their bikes by Wednesday next at the latest. It is Thursday now. You have plenty of time.'

'Strewth!' said the daring young man.

'God save the Queen,' said Hugo Rune.

The stars looked down on Skelington Bay.

And—

'Enough of that!' cried Hugo Rune.

Eh? What?

'This chapter may not have been as long as I might have wished. But it is *my* chapter. And Rune does not share *his* chapter with characters in other scenes.'

Er, sorry . . .

'Sorry, *what?*'

Sorry, Mr Rune.

15

The stars looked down on Skelington Bay.

And the ocean gurgled like a happy baby in the piles beneath the old west pier.

It was nearly midnight now, the day was done with and the pubs and clubs and bayside bars were closed. The town was not quite sleeping yet, a voice or two called out in mirth, a song was sung, a whistle heard, a car horn in the distance honked farewell.

Night fishermen cast out their lines, a boy and girl walked hand in hand along the beach. A dog barked, two cats argued over something, and the vicar, turning in his sleep said, 'Handbag', and was promptly kicked from bed.

In a deck-chair at the pier's end lazed Cornelius, his long legs stretched before. Beside him Tuppe, his short legs all a dangle. Under Tuppe's deck-chair, a fellow from beneath the sea snored soundly in his somewhat matted sheep suit.

Cornelius put his hand to his head and touched certain tender places. These were places the tenderness of which had not been brought about by the truncheons of the Brentford Constabulary. These were new tender places. New and bruised from treatment Cornelius had lately received on the beach.

It had all been a dreadful misunderstanding really. And not the tall boy's fault at all. Well, it had been his fault, but it hadn't. So to speak.

It was the fellow in the sheep suit who had caused it to come about. Although he hadn't actually seen it come about. Which was why it had come about. So to speak also.

And it had come about in this fashion. The fellow in the sheep suit had told his tale to Cornelius and Tuppe. It was a fair old tale and it didn't lack for interest. It involved him coming from an undersea kingdom called Magonia, where a wise old race lived in peace and harmony with minnow and mermaid. It involved secret negotiations with surface dwellers regarding a possible exchange of advanced technology for promises that the surface dwellers would not exploit certain ocean areas. It included also a fair degree of New Age folderol, the usual sprinkling of Gaea and eco-mania, and much of what Cornelius had mentioned while sheltering in the barn, about mankind giving up its nuclear nastiness and joining a cosmic brotherhood, et cetera and et cetera.

Cornelius had listened to it all. He had nodded politely and when it finally reached the et cetera and et cetera stage, had made a humble request.

That the fellow in the sheep suit might demonstrate proof of his aquatic origins simply by walking out into the sea, holding his head beneath the water and breathing there for five minutes or so.

'And then you'll believe me?' asked the fellow in the sheep suit.

'I could hardly deny what I had witnessed with my own two eyes,' said Cornelius.

'Come on then and I'll do it.'

And so he had.

It was a really bad idea.

There hadn't been many folk upon the beach. Just a group of youths. Young farmers they happened to be. Down for the day and high upon the pleasures that come in a ring-pull can. And they could hardly deny what they had witnessed with their own, if bleary, eyes.

115

They had witnessed a tall bloke and a short bloke drive a helpless sheep to a cruel death by drowning in the sea. And they had taken out their rightful indignation at this atrocious act by gathering up pebbles and stoning the two murderers along the beach.

Breathing happily in his natural habitat, the fellow in the sheep suit had missed most of this and only after seven minutes had elapsed on his waterproof wristwatch, had he risen as a maritime Lazarus from his watery grave.

His reappearance, accompanied as it was by his cry of 'What the bloody hell is going on here?', had caused a certain panic to break out in the ranks of the stoners, who had then left off their stoning and fled howling to the nearest bayside bar.

Cornelius stretched in his deck-chair, yawned and clicked his jaw. Tuppe made little grumbling sounds beneath his breath.

'What is it?' Cornelius asked.

'Oh nothing much. I ache from head to toe and I'm not looking forward to spending the night sleeping on the end of a pier, that's all.'

'Sorry,' said Cornelius. 'But I can hardly be blamed for the local seaside landladies refusing to put up a sheep for the night.'

'I nearly had that short-sighted one going that he was a collie dog,' said Tuppe. 'Until the silly fool started going BAA, BAA.'

'Sorry,' said Cornelius. 'But I had to put him straight. He kept going BOW WOW and people were beginning to stare.'

'Your fault for the stoning we took also.'

'I accept some degree of blame for that, yes.'

'And for the fact that we can't sleep in the car? You having left the keys in it while we sought lodgings and somebody nicking it as soon as our backs were turned.'

'There is much dishonesty in the world today,' said Cornelius Murphy.

'And I'm hungry,' said Tuppe. 'Which is also your fault as you gave away the last of our money to that bloke selling *The Big Issue*.'

'He looked hungry,' said Cornelius.

'You've been a bit of a disappointment to me today,' said Tuppe.

'I'll make it up to you tomorrow though.'

'Oh yes, and how so?'

'I will earn us lots of money.'

'Oh yes, and how so, once more?'

'Promotion,' said Cornelius.

'Promotion? Promoting what, may I ask?'

'A little money-spinner of an act I intend to manage. It is called PROFESSOR TUPPE AND HIS AMAZING DANCING SHEEP.'

'Good night,' said Tuppe.

'Good night.'

16

Norman was not having a good night at the bottom of the abandoned lift shaft. 'We have to work out some plan of escape,' he told old Claude for the umpteenth time. 'When does the jailer bring the meals?'

'Jailer? Meals? Are you completely mad or is it me?'

'I don't think it's me. So what time does he bring them?'

'There aren't any meals. You don't eat here. No-one eats here or sleeps here. They *work* here. For that bastard up there. Doing his evil will, aiding and abetting him in his Machiavellian schemes. But eat and sleep? You're barking, sonny, barking.'

'But I have to get out of here. I know terrible things. I have to tell someone about them. People are going to die, millions of people.'

'People do that. All the time. By the million. Nothing new in that.'

'There's something new about the way this lot's going to die. All at once and everyone there is, as far as I can make out.'

'Bad,' said the ancient one. 'Bad that is. The bastard will be behind it, you see if he's not.'

'I'm bloody certain he is,' said Norman. 'Although I don't know how or why. But I've got to stop it happening. Which means I have to get out of here now.'

'Wish I could help you,' said the ex-controller. 'But I only experience fleeting moments of lucidity, such as the one I'm having now. Mostly I am stark staring kill-crazy. Not that you can kill dead people, of course. But you can make a really dreadful mess out of them.'

'Oh great,' said Norman. 'Just perfect.'

'There's a hole,' said the old fella.

'Where's a hole?' asked Norman.

'Up aways. Higher than the door. You can see it if you squint with your eyes.'

Norman took to squinting. 'I can't see it,' he said.

'Well, it's up there. I've seen it. Can't reach it though. Can't climb up there. Nothing to hold on to.'

'There has to be a way,' said Norman. 'There's always a way. Where there's a will there's a way.'

'And if there was a way, what would you do once you were up there?'

'I'm going to speak to God,' said Norman. 'Tell him what's going on.'

'Speak to God?' The oldster collapsed in a fit of laughter. 'You can't speak to God, no-one can speak to God.'

'Well, I have to do something.'

'Get back to Earth, that's what you must do.'

'Don't know how to,' said Norman.

'*I* do,' said the oldster. 'Reprogramme one of the big sky nozzles and shoot yourself back, that's how you'd do it.'

'Tell me how,' said Norman.

'Follow the instructions you learned from your hand-book, and—'

'Go no further,' said Norman.

'You never learned the stuff in the handbook, did you, sonny?'

'No,' said Norman. 'I didn't.'

'Never mind. I can teach you all you need to know. Take a couple of years, in between my bouts of insanity, but you'll pick it up.'

'Thanks for the offer but I don't have the time.'

'All bloody academic anyway,' said the old fella.

'Seeing as how you'd never be able to get up to that hole anyway. Whether there's a will or whether there's a way.'

'There has to be a way,' said Norman. 'There just has to.'

'Not unless you know how to fly, sonny. Not unless you know how to fly.'

'Fly.' Norman made the most dismal of all possible faces.

'Something I said?' asked old Claude.

'Something I tried to do that got me into this mess in the first place. But hang about.' Norman peered up the lift shaft and then gazed all around his miserable cell. 'That's it. Fly! That's it! That's it!'

'It is?'

'It is.' Norman put his brain into gear, engaged his mouth and showered old Claude with thoughts.

The ex-controller listened to them, then made a face of his own.

A face of horror.

'You can't do that,' he wailed. 'You can't. You just can't.'

'But I have to,' said Norman. 'It's the only way. If I could fly up to the hole, I could get out, then open up the iron door, lower a rope or something and free you too. You could work the big sky nozzle for me then. And you would be free.'

'Yes, but all my evidence. You'd burn it up.'

'Some of it, but not all.'

'Tell me what you've got in mind again, sonny. Go on say it again.'

'I fly up the shaft,' said Norman. 'Not with wings, they just wouldn't work in so small a space. But in a hot-air balloon. This paper's damp, we could glue it together like papier mâché, make a balloon, build a burner underneath and something for me to hang on to, then light up, fill with hot air and float up the shaft. It's a blinder of an idea, you have to admit it.'

'But all my evidence.'

'You'd still have all the stuff that was glued together to make the balloon. Look there's an old tin waste-paper bin here, that could serve as the burner and we could break up these bits of old chairs to burn, you'd not lose much paper.'

'How would you start the fire?' asked the oldster. 'Have a box of matches, do you?'

'Where there's a will there's a way,' said Norman.

'Yes I bet there is for you, you smartarsed little bastard.'

'Does that mean we have a deal?' Norman asked, while sticking his hand out for a shake.

'It does,' said the ex-controller shaking it vigorously.

17

The most amazing man who ever lived threw wide the Draylon curtains of the KEV-LYN suite and drew in his first breath of the new day.

And phew wot a scorcher it was.

The sun shone in through the UPVC – which was clever as it had also been seen to go down through it – and lit up the appalling apartment. A figure bundled up on the floor in blankets awoke with a start and went through the traditional, 'What, who, where am I?' routine. Then coming fully awake, arose and bowed before the man who was now his master.

'Good morning, guru,' he said. 'May I fetch you breakfast?'

Rune adjusted the sash on his monogrammed silk dressing-gown and straightened his matching cravat. 'I'll take the full Grande belly buster,' said he, 'whatever newspapers this establishment has to offer, black coffee, toast with honey, some jaffa cakes and a bottle of the finest brandy.'

'As you wish, guru.' The daring young man of the night before did not seem quite so daring now. Somewhat hollow of cheek was he and wild about the eyes. Something sinister had come to pass and something best not dwelt upon or even guessed at.

Urgh!

Rune waved the pale young man away upon his duties and settled himself down upon a Parker Knoll recliner of a hideous auburn hue. 'So much to do,' said Hugo Rune.

'But all the time in all the world to do it in. For some of us at least.'

*

'Remove the asterisk,' said Rune. 'This chapter is at an end.'

18

Something was nearly at an end at the bottom of the abandoned lift shaft.

Nearly.

'Roll that bit up,' said Norman. 'And glue it onto this bit here.'

'This bugger will never fly,' said the Ben Gun lookalike. 'Its shape's all wrong. What's it supposed to be anyhow?'

'It's a head,' said Norman. 'Hot-air balloons always look like heads nowadays. Or farm houses or hairdryers. They never look like hot-air balloons any more.'

'So whose head is this one supposed to look like?'

'Jesus,' said Norman.

'*Jesus*? That doesn't look like Jesus. If that looks like anybody then it looks like—'

'Look, OK. I don't know what Jesus really looks like. It's a representation. It's a hot-air balloon.'

'I met Jesus once,' said the ancient.

'You never did.'

'I did too. He told me this story.'

'Go on,' said Norman.

'About after he'd been crucified, when he came up to Heaven.'

'Go on,' said Norman once more.

'Yes. Well, he came up to Heaven and he was chatting with St Peter at the gates and St Peter had to go to the toilet and Jesus agreed to stand in for him for five minutes. Checking in the new arrivals.'

Norman busied himself with bits of wire and broken office furniture.

'Yes, and Jesus was standing there at the Pearly Gates and this old Jewish fellow comes up. And Jesus says, "Name?"

'And the old Jewish fellow says, "Joseph."

'And Jesus says, "Occupation."

'And the old Jewish fellow says, "Carpenter."

'And Jesus says, "Hang about, you look familiar, didn't you have a son?"

'And the old Jewish fellow says, "Yes I did, lovely boy."

'And Jesus, who is now convinced that the old chap is his dad, but wants to make absolutely sure, says, "Did your son have any distinguishing marks or scars the last time you saw him?"

'And Joseph says, "Yes, he had holes in his hands and his feet."

'And Jesus throws his arms around the old Jewish fellow and says, "Father."

'And the old Jewish fellow throws his arms about Jesus and says—'

'*Pinocchio*,' said Norman. 'Yes, I've heard it.'

'You never have?' said the ancient. 'He told it to you too?'

'Jesus never told you it,' said Norman. 'It's a really ancient gag.'

'He did too tell it to me. It's his favourite joke. That and the one about "Peter, I can see your house from up here". And of course it's ancient. He told it to me about a thousand years ago. And that's who your balloon looks like.'

'Jesus?'

'Pinocchio. You'll never get it in the air.'

'I will too. And I'll get us both out of here.'

'You bloody won't. You're barking mad, sonny. Did you hear the one about "the elephant's cloakroom ticket", by the way?'

'I'm all done here now,' said Norman, standing back to view his creation. He couldn't stand back too far, him being at the bottom of an abandoned lift shaft and everything. But he was able to get the general gist of the thing.

And a fair old thing it was too.

A touch of the Montgolfier brothers here, a hint of a Richard Branson tax dodge there, and for those with very long memories, a smidgen of the *Nimble* bread commercials up at the top end.

It looked mighty fine.

Mighty head-like and handsome.

It looked mighty like Pinocchio though.

'Told you,' said the ancient one. 'Look at that big hooter. Jesus doesn't have a big hooter like that.'

'It's a cunning innovation of my own,' said Norman proudly. 'To get *you* out. I light up the rubbish in the waste-bin, the balloon fills with hot air, I drift up the shaft to the opening. Then I untie the end of this Pinocchio's nose bit, the hot air is released, the balloon drifts down again. You tie the nose up again. The balloon re-fills with hot air and you drift up on it to join me at the hole. Now is that clever or what?'

The old boy looked at Norman, he looked at the balloon, he looked at the Pinocchio's nose and he looked back once again at Norman.

And then he grinned a fearsome grin and slapped the youth soundly on the back. 'You are a genius,' he crowed. 'A veritable genius.'

'Thank you,' said Norman. 'I do my best.'

'You certainly do. You certainly do. So go on then, sonny, light up the waste-bin. Do your stuff.'

'Ah yes,' said Norman. 'Light up the waste-bin.'

'Light it up, sonny. Light it up.'

'There must be some way of starting a fire.' Norman

rooted through his grey-flannel trouser pockets. They contained all the standard unsavoury things that four-teen-year-old boys always keep in them. But no matches. Norman considered his digital watch. He'd heard tell that if you took the battery out and crushed it, it would burst into flame. But he had tried that once, and it certainly didn't work.

Norman glanced around and about. 'Light-bulb,' he said. 'Smash the light-bulb, put something into the socket to cause a short circuit, flash bang, burst of flame.'

'Oh my word no!' The old white-bearder stepped back in alarm. 'You don't want to go messing with electricity, sonny. You really don't. Do for you that will. Souls are charged particles. You could short yourself out. You'd cease to exist completely.'

'You're joking.'

'I am not. Stay clear of electrical discharge, that's my advice to you.'

'*Electrical discharge*! Oh dear, oh dear.' Norman shook his 'Oh dearing' head. Then, 'Gunpowder,' he said. 'Make gunpowder; all the ingredients are here. Graphite out of old pencils, sulphur out of those,' Norman pointed to those certain things from which sulphur might easily be extracted. 'And saltpetre. That's potassium nitrate.' Nor-man ran his finger down the nearest wall. 'See that white powder, that's a crystalline compound, forms on bricks in conditions like this. It's all here.'

'Seems so,' the old fellow agreed. 'Where did you say you were going to get the sulphur from again? I couldn't quite see where you were pointing.'

'Er,' said Norman.

'Er indeed,' said the ex-controller.

'Now just you see here,' said Norman. 'Unless we escape from this place and get to Earth and stop what-ever is destined to happen before it does, millions of people, if not *all* people, are going to die. This is a big number. Surely you'd be prepared to overlook a bit of bullshit over where the sulphur comes from. I mean, check out the hot-air balloon. We *are* talking "fantasy" here, after all.'

'Well,' the old man shuffled his ragged footwear, 'I suppose it is remotely possible that all the ingredients to make gunpowder would be down here.'

'Of course they would.'

'But to save any embarrassment, why don't we just use this?'

'What is that?'

'It's my pocket lighter,' said the ex-controller.

19

'Did you get us anything to eat?' asked Tuppe.

'Not a lot, I'm afraid,' replied Cornelius. 'I found a couple of bob in a pay-out tray of a fruit machine. But I reinvested it. Nearly came up three bells. But not quite.'

'So we have no breakfast.'

'Not as such. Have you given any thought to the matter of our business partnership?'

'Cornelius Murphy Productions present Professor Tuppe and . . . no, not a lot,' said Tuppe. 'I asked Boris, but he wasn't keen.'

'Boris?' Cornelius asked.

'That's my name,' said the amphibious fellow in the sheep suit. 'But tell you what, do you like fish?'

'Love fish,' said Tuppe.

'Me too,' said Cornelius.

'Well, why don't I catch us the fish. You get a fire going on the beach and we'll cook up some breakfast.'

'I don't have a fishing-rod,' said Cornelius.

'I don't need a fishing-rod,' said Boris. 'Catch them in my teeth.'

'You're kidding,' said Tuppe.

'I am not. What do you favour, flounders or sea bass?'

'Anything,' said Cornelius. 'You'll want to get out of the sheep suit though, won't you?'

'Best not. Don't want anyone to see me getting back into it.'

'Well, whatever you please.'

'Righteo then, give us a lift over the parapet and I'll dive us up some brekky.'

'Good one.' Cornelius lifted Boris up and dropped him over the rail. Plop he went into the sea and sank away from view.

'He's a character and that's for sure,' said Tuppe. 'Let's get down to the beach and start a fire.'

'Oi you!' shouted a night fisherman who, with several of his burly mates, had been packing away his gear. 'We bloody saw that, you sadistic bastard.'

'Let's run to the beach,' said Cornelius. 'I like an early-morning work-out.'

'You certainly know how to fry,' said Boris somewhat later, as he munched upon a mackerel.

'How do you cook under the sea?' Tuppe asked. 'Doesn't the water put the gas out?'

'Perhaps they use the trans-perambulation of pseudo-cosmic anti-matter,' said Cornelius, tucking into a herring.

'Don't take the piss,' said Boris. 'Got you breakfast, didn't I?'

'You did,' said Cornelius. 'And we're very grateful. But what are you going to do now? You've lost your flying saucer and you've missed the secret talks you were supposed to be attending. You can't stay here and spend the rest of your life disguised as a sheep.'

'I don't see that I've got much choice,' said Boris. 'If I go back they'll throw me in jail for losing the saucer. Couldn't I just stick around with you blokes and have a few laughs?'

Cornelius looked at Tuppe.

And Tuppe looked at Cornelius.

'Of course you could,' said Tuppe.

'No he couldn't, Tuppe. He doesn't belong here. He'd

get found out eventually. He's quite a convincing sheep, I agree. But not *that* convincing and, oh come on, it's an idiot suggestion to spend your life in a sheep costume.'

'Rod Hull has a right arm that spends its life dressed as an emu,' said Tuppe. 'And it's done all right for itself.'

'You'll have to go home,' said Cornelius. 'You really will.'

'I know,' said Boris. 'But let's have a few laughs first, eh?'

'Yes,' said Cornelius. 'Let's do that.'

'So,' said Boris. 'Shall I dive back into the sea and fish us out a couple of crabs for afters?'

Cornelius looked around and about the beach. It was already starting to fill with folk. And folk with pointing fingers.

'No,' said Cornelius Murphy. 'Whatever you do, don't do that.'

By noon, a very large crowd had gathered upon the beach, drawn by the sheep-suited one.

'Fetch, Ben,' cried a little kid, tossing a stick.

'He's good with the children, isn't he, Cornelius?' said Tuppe, as Boris bounded off along the beach.

'He's drawing a lot of attention,' said the tall boy. 'You could earn us a couple of cups of tea, if you would only persuade him into a dance routine. He doesn't have to do the Moon Walk, a soft-shoe shuffle would suffice.'

'How can you even suggest such a thing, Cornelius? Boris is born of a wise old superior undersea race. To even hint at inflicting such indignity upon him is nothing less than grotesque.'

'Tuppe,' said Cornelius, 'we are broke. It is not a good thing to be broke at the seaside. At the seaside one should enjoy oneself: take in all the pleasures, make new friends, entertain these new friends.'

'What new friends?' Tuppe asked.

'Well, I was thinking of those two suntanned lovelies over there. The ones in the boob tubes and the white bikini bottoms.'

'Roll up! Roll up!' cried Tuppe.

20

Which somehow brings us to the matter of agents.

What is it about the word 'agent' that couples it so perfectly with the word 'dodgy'?

Think about the last time you encountered an 'agent'. Travel agent? Artist's agent? Literary agent? Casting agent? Secret agent?

ESTATE AGENT?

Yes, you get the picture. They can't help themselves. They are the kind of people who are drawn to careers as agents. Dodgy, that's what they are. Slippery. Lawyers are known as 'legal agents'. Then there's Advertising Agencies. Dating agencies. Satanic agencies.

So on and so forth.

Yes, you *do* get the picture.

It's a giveaway word, is agent. You know deep down in your heart that whenever you deal with an agent you are going *to get done*.

You'll try your best not to, of course. You'll work really hard at it. But you'll lose in the end, no matter. Because *they* will be up to something that *you* know nothing about. They will have what is known as a 'hidden agenda'.

And the word 'agenda' comes from the same Latin root word as does the word *agent*. That root word is *agere*, which means literally '*to do*'.

So, there you go really.

David Rodway was an estate agent. In fact, he was Skelington Bay's *only* estate agent. Which was strange, considering that Skelington Bay was such a small town. For as anyone who has ever visited an English village will have observed, the smaller the village, the more the estate agents.*

David Rodway had worked his way up to his position as the town's only estate agent. He'd worked hard. Come up the hard way. Escort agencies, time-share agencies. Born agent was David Rodway. He'd been Cardinal Richelieu in a previous incarnation. Although *he* didn't know that.

The present controller of the Universal Reincarnation Company knew it, of course.

'Good morning, sir,' said David Rodway to the wild-eyed but well-dressed young man who had entered his premises carrying the bulging suitcase. 'How might I help you?'

The wild-eyed young man put out his hand; offered a Masonic handshake; received one in return.

A brief and codified conversation ensued. Lodge details and degree hierarchies were exchanged. All appeared to be in order.

The wild-eyed young man seated himself at the estate agent's behest.† He took in his surroundings: slick little set up. Clean carpet. Chairs just comfortable enough. Computer terminal. Modern desk.‡ Greasy little baldy-headed slimeball – straightening a Rotary Club tie between the neat pinstriped collars of his Burton's shirt, jacket off, but sleeves rolled down, initialled cuff-links – behind the desk.

'My name is Stephen Craik,' said the wild-eyed young man who had once been one so daring. 'I am here in an official capacity, acting as an agent for a third party who wishes to purchase some property hereabouts.'

---

* The reason for this is unknown. But it is *not* a tradition, or an old charter, or something.

† Possibly some kind of desk?

‡ Obviously not.

134

'Indeed?' said David Rodway. 'Which particular property has captured your sponsor's interest?'

'All that you have,' said Stephen Craik. 'And all the rest as well.'

'*All?*' David Rodway jerked somewhat in his chair.

'All. All of Skelington Bay, lock, stock and barony.'

'I see.' Although internally a maelstrom of covetousness now kicked and thrashed, externally, a passive smile played lightly on the lips of Mr Rodway. '*All*, you say?'

'The lot,' replied Stephen Craik. 'Firstly every property you have on your books, for which I will pay cash, now. Then all the remaining: every shop, business, licensed premise, public utility. All.'

'All.' David Rodway had a small shake on, but not so much as to affect business. 'This is a most singular request,' said he.

'My sponsor is a most singular man.'

'Might I see the cash of which you speak?'

'Of course you may.' Stephen Craik opened the suitcase and turned it in Mr Rodway's direction. 'You might also wish to see this.'

He handed the estate agent an envelope.

The estate agent opened it and perused its contents.

'This money has been authorized by the Prime Minister,' said he, 'who is the country's Grand Lodge Master 55°–23°.'

The estate agent made a secret sign.

The wild-eyed young man made another.

'Well bugger my budgie,' said the estate agent. 'What's it all about then, eh?'

Stephen Craik gave his nose a conspiratorial tap. 'I am not permitted to say. Perhaps the Grand Lodge Master is seeking a holiday hideaway. Possibly it has something to do with the classless society he has created. I regret that I must remain mute upon the subject.'

'No problem, squire. I know where you're coming from.' Mr Rodway's fingers were doing the walking across the keyboard of his computer terminal. '*All*, you said?' said he once again.

'*All*.'

'All it is then.' The estate agent's fingers took another walk. 'My own bungalow included?'

'If it is in Skelington Bay, yes.'

'Phew,' said the estate agent. 'That won't come cheap I can tell you. I've just had these coach lamps fitted on the gateposts that light up when you drive in at night.'

'Very classy,' said Stephen Craik, wincing within.

'Very,' Mr Rodway agreed. 'I'll hate to part with DAVE-LES, but when the Grand Lodge Master plays the Bon Tempi organ, all those of the apron must dance to *The Birdie Song*, eh?'

'My sentiments entirely.'

'Cor!' said the estate agent, examining his computer screen. 'I had no idea that my bungalow would be worth *that* much.'

Stephen Craik shook his head and did a little sighing. 'Will this take long?' he asked. 'I am on a very tight schedule.'

'Not long.' Further finger walking. 'My old mum would be better off in an old folks' home anyway. Now let's see. Gosh, who'd have thought a small terraced house in this neck of the woods would be worth as much as that?'

'Any brothers or sisters?' asked Stephen Craik.

The estate agent looked up from his screen to catch a wild-eyed look which told him, 'Watch it!'

'Quite so.' He returned to his calculations. 'All done,' he said at not too great a length. 'Care to see the total?'

'Just read it out and I will pay you at once.'

'That's the way I like to do business.'

'I'll just bet it is.'

And it was.

Documents of a legal nature were drawn up with a rapidity which would have quite surprised the average house purchaser. Money changed hands. Hands were again clasped, knuckles pressed.

'A pleasure doing business with you,' said David Rodway.

'All the rest,' said Stephen Craik.

'The rest, you said?'

'I did say all the rest, yes. I want all the rest by Monday at the latest and my sponsor wants the town cleared of all of its occupants by Wednesday.'

David Rodway counted money into his wall safe. 'Can't be done,' said he, in a casual tone.

'Must be done,' said the wild-eyed young man, in a tone so far from casual, as to be positively non-casual by comparison.

'Can't be,' Mr Rodway closed his wall safe. 'Logistically impossible. We have a town here of between fifteen and twenty thousand people. Plus all the holiday-makers. You couldn't move that many people in that time. You'd need about ten thousand removal lorries. They couldn't all get down the streets, even if you could get them all here. Which you couldn't. And plenty of people would refuse to move anyway. And you can't buy municipal swimming-baths and the police station. Or the McDonald's. You and I both know who owns McDonald's.'*

'My sponsor wants all,' said the wild-eyed young man. 'And when he says all, he means all. He will be butted no buts.'

'Butted no buts, is it? Well, he'd have to be the great butter of no buts himself to pull that one off.'

* The Antichrist (allegedly).

137

The wild-eyed young man raised a knowing eyebrow.

'You don't mean—' The estate agent took on white-ness as a facial hue. 'Not—'

'*He*,' said Stephen Craik. 'As I was so informed last night.'

'The Grand High—'

'Do not speak his sacred masonic title aloud.'

'Bugger my beagle,' said the estate agent. 'And my wife's border collie dog Ben.'

'Think,' said the wild-eyed young man. 'There must be some way by which it can be done.'

'I'm trying to think,' said Mr Rodway. 'But fair dos, you walk in off the street with a proposition like this. A proposition that has *him* behind it. You're telling me you want the whole of Skelington Bay cleared by next week. Shit! That includes this shop. My livelihood!'

'I have no doubt you'll surprise yourself when you consult your computer and see how much your livelihood is worth.'

'I'm quite sure I *won't*,' said the estate agent, con-structing a figure and adding an extra zero to it for good measure. 'But I'm still telling you it can't be done. OK, offered sufficient money most people will sell up. And if the PM is behind this, then no doubt all the public bodies, town hall and what-nots can be cleared. But you won't get everyone out.'

'There has to be some way. There just has to.'

'You'd have to get them out by force,' said the estate agent. 'Evict them. That can be done, of course, but it will take time.'

'There isn't time.'

'Then you'd have to come up with something that would make them want to move of their own accord. At once.'

'Like some impending natural disaster, do you mean?'

'That sort of thing, yes. Although we're not big on natural disasters in this country.'

'A threat to health then,' said the wild-eyed young man, with his wild eyes flashing. 'A toxic-waste spill or the release of some deadly virus.'

'Now you're cooking with gas. And yes, hang about. I have the very thing.' The estate agent swung out a filing drawer from his desk and pulled from it a copy of *Property News*.

'Ever seen one of these before?' he asked the wild-eyed young man.

'Naturally. It's one of those free property papers that are pushed through people's doors. They always have headlines screaming, WHOOPIE THE RECESSION IS OVER. NOW IS THE TIME TO SELL YOUR HOUSE. And contain about as much truth as *The Weekly World News* or *The National Enquirer*.'

'No need for that kind of talk. But there's a little article in this week's, if I can find it. Ah yes. Look at this.'

MYSTERIOUS DEATH AT COLLINS' FARM. At a coroner's inquest held last week at Skelington Bay to investigate the mysterious death of local farmer Andrew Collins, evidence was put forward that he had fallen victim to the long dreaded crossover of the cattle disease *Bovine Spongiform Encephalopathy*.

'No, no, no,' said the wild-eyed one. 'BSE's no good. No-one believes it will really cross over to human beings.'

'Yes, but it has, sort of. I saw the coroner's report.'

'So one farmer dies of BSE. It's not a cause for panic exactly, is it?'

'He didn't die of BSE. He died because his tractor had repeatedly driven back and forwards over him.'

'I don't think I quite understand what you're saying.'

139

'I'm saying that the farmer never caught BSE. His *tractor* did. The disease has made the crossover but not to people. To vehicles. If you want to clear people from Skelington Bay, how better than to spread it about that this very town is the epicentre of a new and terrible plague?'

'Which is what?'

'MCD,' said the estate agent. 'Mad Car Disease.'

21

'Where is my car?' asked Cornelius Murphy.

The two tanned lovelies in the boob tubes and the white bikini bottoms looked up at him.

'I'm sorry we had to nick it,' said Thelma, for it was she.

'But we couldn't stick around and wait for the police to arrive,' explained Louise, for it was she, also.

'Ah,' said Cornelius. 'It's like that, is it? So where is my car now? I'd really like to have it back.'

'It's in the private car-park in front of the Skelington Bay Grande.' Thelma pointed towards that once-proud edifice.

'So it's probably been clamped by now. Thanks a lot.'

'It hasn't been clamped, the proprietor—'

'Kevin,' said Louise.

'Yes, Kevin, he flagged us down when we were passing and asked if we'd like to park there. Said it would give his car-park a bit of class.'

'Nice one. Keys please.'

Thelma produced the car keys. *From where?* From her shoulder-bag of course.

'Thank you,' said Cornelius. 'Did you get down here last night then?'

'No, we dossed in an abandoned farmhouse.'

'Collins' Farm,'* said Louise.

'Do you have any money?' Cornelius asked.

---

* An opportunity here for a couple of strident chords in the background music of the film version.

'No, but I see your little mate has.'

'I do,' Tuppe appeared, struggling beneath the weight of coins which filled the straw hat a lady had lent him to take up the collection. 'And where is Cornelius's car?' he asked.

Cornelius jingled the keys. 'At least we now have somewhere to sleep tonight.'

'We certainly do,' said Tuppe. 'But it's not in the car.'

'It's not?'

'It's not. Boris and I have been talent-scouted. We met this really nice fellow. He's a theatrical agent. We're going to do a Summer Season. Right here. At the Skelington Bay Grande.'

'All roads lead to the Grande then. Because that's where Thelma and Louise have parked the car.'

'That *is* handy,' said Tuppe. 'Because the agent can only get accommodation there for Boris and I. So you'll have to sleep in the car. On your own.'

'Hm,' said Cornelius. Then, turning an approving eye upon Thelma and Louise who were wildly applauding the encore of Boris the dancing sheep, he added, 'I may have to sleep in the car. But not on my own, if I can help it.'

Tuppe followed the direction of his best friend's approving eye-turn and said, 'Hm,' also. 'I think I'll have to call my agent about this and discuss the matter.'

'Perhaps over lunch,' Cornelius suggested. 'For us all.'

'Over lunch at the Grande?'

'Over lunch at the Grande.'

So lunch at the Grande it was.

'We're all together,' Tuppe told the waitress in The Manilow Bar, the 'classy' cocktail lounge of the Skelington Bay Grande. 'We are awaiting the arrival of my theatrical agent, who is booked in here.'

'D'ya wanna order sumfin while ya waitin'?'

142

'Certainly do,' said Tuppe. 'Bring us an assortment of cocktails in garish colours, with little umbrellas and sparklers in the tops. Charge them to my agent, Mr Showstein.'

'Mr *Showstein*?' Cornelius asked.

'Sammy Showstein,' said Tuppe. 'Friend to the stars.'

'Sounds about right.'

'Warrabout the sheep?' asked the waitress.

'He'll have a cocktail too. Better bring him a straw.'

'Two straws,' said Boris.

'Two straws,' said Tuppe.

'How d'ya do that?' the waitress asked.

Tuppe scratched his little head. 'Well, I suppose that instead of bringing just one straw, you bring another straw as well, and that makes two straws. Of course, you might have your own preferred method of doing it.'

'You takin' the piss?' enquired the waitress. 'I meant how d'ya make the sheep talk like that?'

'He's a ventriloquist,' said Cornelius. 'Could we also have some of those little bowls of stuff that look like budgie food.'

'Or dervs?'

'Yes, dervs will be fine, if you don't have the other.'

'You two are bleeding mad,' was the waitress's conclusion, as she tottered away on three-inch stiletto heels.

'Attractive woman,' said Cornelius. 'Very amenable.'

'Very long legs,' said Tuppe. 'That would be some kind of Playboy bunny costume she's wearing, would it?'

'More sort of Lola the Showgirl, I think.'

'We must introduce her to Mr Showstein then.'

'Yes, indeed we must. This is a most unspeakable cocktail lounge, isn't it?'

And it was. Those pink mirrors that emphasize a bad complexion. Those precarious bar stools that emphasize bottom cleavage. Those swirly-whirly carpet tiles again, which emphasize the purchaser's love of an all-through-the-hotel, coordinated-flooring effect.

Those . . .

'Here comes Mr Showstein now,' said Tuppe.

Cornelius turned and saw. 'That's not "Mr Showstein", that's "Mr Justice Wilberforce", or rather whoever played him at the County Court.'

'Kyle McKintock,' said Tuppe. 'But that's never Kyle McKintock.'

'I never said it was.'

'Mr Showstein' now caught sight of Cornelius Murphy. 'Oh dear,' he said, doing a sharp about-turn.

'No you don't,' the tall boy's long legs carried him across the cocktail lounge at an easy, loping pace. He caught the bogus magistrate by one padded shoulder of the rather dazzling suit that now encased his sturdy frame.

'Mr Murphy,' said Mr Showstein, affecting a sickly grin. 'Fancy seeing you here. I thought you were all—'

'Locked up?' Cornelius asked. 'Do come and join us please.'

'I'd really rather not. You being here somewhat complicates matters for me. I think I'd best be going. Hey now, hold on, what are you doing?'

Some call it 'frog-marching', others 'bums-rushing'. They're not quite the same, this was a bit of both. The bogus magistrate, now turned friend to the stars, found himself deposited between Thelma and Louise (who were apparently sitting down, perhaps on a sofa or something, although this had not been made clear).

'Pardon me, dear ladies,' said Mr Showstein, straightening the lapels of his dazzling suit: a sort of blue lurex with a noisy pink check.

'Are your shoes waterproof?' Thelma asked.

'I expect so, why?'

'Because that suit's a real pisser.'

'Ho, hm. Most amusing. Showstein's the name, Samuel Showstein. My card.' 'Mr Showstein' produced his card and handed it to Louise. (Probably so she might have something to say.)

'Thanks,' said Louise, which wasn't much, but it was something.

Cornelius glared down at Mr Showstein. 'You froze my assets,' he said.

There was a moment's silence. Which was tribute to the street credibility of Thelma and Louise.

'It wasn't my fault. I was hired to do it. I told you, I needed the wages to pay for my wife's hip replacement.'

'Who paid you? Who has control of my money now?'

'I mustn't say. I really mustn't.'

'You really must.' Cornelius raised a fist.

'Cornelius,' said Tuppe.

'Tuppe?' said Cornelius.

'Cornelius, I'll bet if you just gave this a moment's thought, you could narrow down the suspects in the case of your frozen assets to one single fellow. One perhaps who has a great love of money and has now acquired yours. One who wanted you locked up and out of the way so you would not interfere with whatever diabolical scheme he is presently engaged upon.'

'Isn't that *two* suspects?' asked Mr Showstein.

'No, it's just the one and Cornelius knows exactly who that one is.'

'Hugo Rune,' said Cornelius Murphy, in a tone that lacked not for bitterness.

'*I* never said that,' Mr Showstein got a serious shake on. '*I* never gave his name away. It wasn't *me*.'

'Where is he?' Cornelius waggled his fist beneath Mr Showstein's nose.

'I couldn't say. I really couldn't say.'

'Er, Cornelius.'

'Yes, Tuppe?'

'Cornelius, I don't wish to come on as Mr Smarty-pants here, but we did know that Rune was on his way to Skelington Bay, and this is the poshest hotel in Skelington Bay and Rune is a man who likes his creature comforts and—'

'Yes, OK, Tuppe. I get the picture.' Cornelius waggled his fist once more. 'What is Rune up to?' he enquired this time.

'I don't know. Honest I don't. My job was to play the part of the magistrate, get you locked away and have all your money transferred into Mr Rune's account. Mr Rune set the whole thing up, even the policemen arresting you; he hired the County Court for the trial, told the Council he was shooting a movie there.'

'But you were sending me down for twenty-three years.'

'Not really. Just for two weeks. Locked up in the cell beneath the County Court, while Mr Rune completed the project that he needed your money to help finance. He didn't want you getting in the way. But now you are going to get in the way. And I'll be blamed for it and, oh dear, oh dear.' Mr Showstein began to blubber.

Thelma offered him a Kleenex tissue.

'Does this mean my summer season with Boris is cancelled?' Tuppe asked.

Blubber and sob, went Mr Showstein.

'Was that a yes or a no?'

'It was a no,' said Cornelius. 'Mr Showstein here will see to it that all the necessary contracts are drawn up and signed. Then, if he has any wisdom at all, he will leave Skelington Bay on the first available train and flee to distant parts.'

'Yes,' blubbered Mr Showstein. 'In fact, I have the

contracts right here. Take them, I shall pack my bags at once.'

And with no further words said, Mr Showstein drew the contracts from the inner pocket of his violent suit, pressed them into Tuppe's hands, patted Boris on the head and made a most speedy departure.

The waitress, now returning with a tray of coloured cocktails watched him scurry from The Manilow. 'Wot's up wiv Mr Webley?' she asked.

'Webley?' went Tuppe.

'Yeah, that woz Clive Webley, the actor. D'n'cha recognize him? He woz in that film, wot wozzit now? *Plan Nine from Outer Space*, that woz it, got butchered by Tor Johnson. And he played the janitor in *The Savage Bees*. Wore a false beard in that'n. And—'

'Surely you're thinking of Kyle McKintock,' said Tuppe.

'Don't tork stewpid. Kyle McKintock's the bloke wot always plays the small-town magistrate. Kyle McKintock! Leave it owt!'

22

'I wonder if my surname's McKintock,' wondered the ex-controller. 'Sounds about right, doesn't it? Claude McKintock? How's the fire coming on, sonny?'

'It's coming on a treat.' Norman was warming his hands by the blazing waste-paper bin that he'd strung beneath his unlikely hot-air balloon. The balloon was filling nicely. Pinocchio's nose was rising like a stiffy.

'What are you going to hold on to then, sonny?' asked the ancient one. 'Can't hang on to the waste-bin; burn your bleeding fingers.'

'I've got all that covered. See these? Wire coat-hangers. I've twisted them all together and they form this.'

'A little trapeze.'

'A little trapeze, you've got it. Secured to the waste-bin. When the balloon starts to rise, it's onto the trapeze and up I go.'

'Where did you get those wire coat-hangers from?'

'The same place I was going to get the sulphur from.'

'I got my pocket lighter from there,' said the ancient one. 'It's a good place to look when you need something.'

'Hey, hey, hey,' cried Norman. 'We have lift off.'

And indeed they did.

Gently, gently, all majestic, bulge and rise and—

'Me first, sonny!' The ancient pushed Norman aside.

'No, me,' Norman pushed the ancient back. 'We agreed on this. I'll go up to the hole, get off and send the balloon back down to you by releasing the hot air.'

'Me first, sonny!' The ancient gave Norman a harder push.

'No,' said Norman. 'This was my idea. I go first.'

'No you don't.' The old one snatched at the trapeze as it rose between them and hoisted himself onto it.

'Get off!' Norman snatched at the old man, tried to drag him from the trapeze.

'Let go of me, sonny, you'll pull the whole caboodle to pieces.'

'Get off, it's my turn first.' Yank, pull.

'I'm on now!' Kick, elbow.

'Then get off!' Tug, tug.

'I won't!' Knee to stomach.

'You will!' Headlock, tight on. Fingers interlocked, potential submission hold that one.

'I'm not letting go!'

'Then for God's sake move over and make room for me,' cried Norman. 'My feet aren't touching the ground any more. We're going up.'

'We're going up.'

And going up they were.

The airship Pinocchio rose gracefully in the lift shaft.

Jammed together on the little trapeze, the two intrepid airmen watched the ground diminish beneath them and its little lighted area slowly shrink until it was nothing more than a tiny dot.

And then remain as a tiny dot.

And shrink no further.

'We've stopped,' said Claude the ex-controller.

'Does that mean we're there?' Norman wriggled about on the over-crowded trapeze. 'I don't see any daylight.'

'It means the fire's going out, sonny. That's what it means.'

'*What?*' Norman all but fell off his perch. 'This is all your fault. If you'd let me go all alone, I'd have whizzed straight up. Two people have weighed it down too much.'

The oldster sniffed and grunted. 'Knowing you're right

149

must be a real comfort to you, sonny. So what do you propose to do now?'

'Well, er . . .'

'Well, er . . .?'

'Er . . . Burn something! Yes, that's it. Burn something, anything that will burn. Take off your shoes, burn them.'

'I will not. Take *yours* off. Burn *them*.'

'I thought of the idea first. You take yours off.'

'No, I shan't.'

'You will.'

'I won't.'

'You will.'

'We're starting to drift back down again,' said old Claude. 'I think we'd both better take them off.'

'Pooh,' said Norman. 'What cheesy feet you've got.'

'It's not my feet that are cheesy, it's yours.'

'It bloody isn't.'

'It bloody is.'

'A vicar named Cheesefoot conducted my funeral,' said Norman miserably.

'We've stopped again,' said Claude.

'Your jacket,' said Norman.

'Your jersey,' said Claude. 'Your nasty grey school jersey.'

'My jersey,' said Norman. '*Then* your jacket.'

And so it went on from there.

The socks were the next to be tossed up into the flaming waste-bin. The removal of the socks then led to further heated debate. This, however, concluded with an agreement that they should share first prize in the cheesy-feet competition.

'I wish we could go faster,' said Norman. 'I've got to do something before all those innocent people get wiped out.'

'This will help,' said Claude, producing a grubby, crumpled piece of paper from his trouser pocket.

'A used paper hankie? I don't think so.'

'This came fluttering down to me years ago,' Claude waved the thing about. 'And I kept it. Knew it would be very valuable one day. Hung onto it I did. Knew its worth, see.'

'Then don't let me part you from it.'

'Pay attention, you little twat.'

'Who are you calling a little twat, you old fart.'

'Just listen,' said Claude. 'This is a piece of evidence.'

'Whoopie,' said Norman. 'A piece of evidence.'

The old fellow sighed. 'It's about the bastard. That bastard up there and his clones on Earth. The bastard had a son. Son of bastard. Bastard son actually. His name is Cornelius Murphy.'

'So?' asked Norman.

'So he's one of the good guys. He's the one you should seek out to help you once you're back on Earth.'

'Are you sure?'

'I'm sure I'm sure.'

'So where will I find this son of bastard?'

'I'll shoot you down to him out of one of the big sky nozzles.'

'What if he doesn't want to help me?'

'He will.'

'How do you know he will?'

'I just know it, that's all.'

'Hmmmph,' said Norman. 'So how will he be able to see me? The mourners at my funeral couldn't.'

'I'll see to that.'

'How?'

'Don't ask me all these damn fool questions, sonny, I'm the real controller, I know how the bloody process works.'

'Yeah but—'

'Yeah but what?'

'You can't even remember your own name.'

'Yes I can. It's Claude.'

'Claude what?'

'I've remembered what it is, but I'm not going to tell you.'

'Why?'

'Because you'd take the piss.'

'I would not.'

'Oh yes you would.'

'Oh no I would not.'

'Promise?'

'I promise,' said Norman.

'Cross your heart then.'

'Good God.' Norman crossed his heart.

'Its Claude mmmmmmm,' said the ex-controller.

'I don't think I quite caught the last bit,' said Norman.

'It's Claude *Buttocks*!' said Mr Claude Buttocks. 'Claude *BUTTOCKS*.'

'Claude Buttocks? What like in, clawed buttocks?' Norman fell about in mirth and nearly fell off the trapeze.

'You little bastard. You promised you wouldn't laugh.'

'I'm sorry,' Norman dabbed at his eyes. 'But I'm still only a kid. Bum jokes make me laugh.'

'Hey, look there.' The ex-controller pointed with a wizened, crooked finger. 'See it, sonny?'

By the light of the flaming waste-bin, Norman saw it. The inside of the big iron door. 'Are we nearly at the hole?' he asked.

'Yep, just a wee bit more.'

'Bung your shirt on the fire then.'

'Do what?'

'Your shirt, it's your turn.'

'No it's not, it's yours.'

152

'It bloody isn't.'

'It bloody is.'

'Aw come on. Oh!'

'Oh?'

'Oh.' Norman saw the light. A glorious bright little lozenge it was. Easily big enough to climb through. Right there in the wall opposite the door which had just passed beneath (so to speak).

'We're there!' Claude bobbed up and down and did hysterical gigglings. 'We've made it, sonny. Stop the balloon. Let's get going.'

'Right,' said Norman. 'Stop the balloon. Stop the balloon?'

'Pinocchio's hooter, like you said.'

'Pinocchio's hooter, right.' Norman gazed up. He could almost make out Pinocchio's hooter, high up on the balloon. Above the red-hot waste-bin. Completely out of reach.

'You little pillock.' Claude smote Norman in the left earhole. 'We're passing it by. Do something. Do something!'

Norman glared at Claude.

And Claude glared at Norman.

'Jump!' they agreed.

23

'It's very noisy in here,' said Mr Craik, gazing about the crowded room.

'Noisy is good', said Mr Rodway, 'for conspirators. In case you're being bugged.'

'I wouldn't know anything about bugging,' said Mr Craik. 'I work for the British government.'

'Very funny, squire, very funny. So what do you think of the place, eh?'

They were now in the Skelington Bay Grande, of course. In The Casablanca dining-suite. It was a 'theme' dining suite. Lynne had given her artistic talent its full head. Which you can take any way you want, really.

The walls were imaginatively decorated with slightly out of focus black-and-white blow-ups of Humphrey Bogart and Ingrid Bergman. And a couple that were possibly of *Plan Nine from Outer Space*. There was a less-than-grand piano, which had been given a coat of white gloss and at this sat a fat black man in a white tuxedo and dicky bow. He moved his fingers about several inches above the keyboard in time to the music-from-the-film cassette that blared from a ghetto-blaster between his spatted brogues.

The tables had nice clean tablecloths on. And an *aficionado* of the swirly-whirly carpet tile would have found much to recommend the place.

'So, what do you think, eh?' asked Mr Rodway.

'It has noise going for it,' said Mr Craik.

'And crumpet,' said Mr Rodway. 'Good place to pick up some tail, if you catch my drift. Look at those two who've just come in.'

'Where?'

'There,' Mr Rodway pointed towards a brace of beauties, who now sat several tables away, laughing and joking with a tall boy, a short boy and a sheep.

'They have a sheep with them,' Mr Craik observed.

Mr Rodway leaned over and whispered something obscene into Mr Craik's ear. Mr Craik's wild eyes took on a wilder look. 'They never do!' he said.

'I'll go over and ask them for you if you like.'

'No, please don't. We are here to discuss the fine details of your plan for clearing Skelington Bay. Particularly those regarding the financial aspects, if you catch *my* drift.'

'Surely do, squire, surely do.' The estate agent lit up a small cigar and spoke, like you do, through the smoke. 'What we have to do', he said, 'is quarantine the entire town. Spread rumours first, then some kind of official announcement, from the town hall. Fleet of trucks, brought in to move everyone out. Then close off the roads. Once they're all out, split them up, some to this town, some to that. Then tell them that Skelington Bay is going to have to remain in quarantine for ten years to be on the safe side and pay them all off.'

'I'm very impressed,' said Stephen Craik. 'You will be organizing the paying off, for an agent's fee, I suppose?'

'Good idea. It hadn't crossed my mind.'

'No, I'll bet it hadn't. But surely this could be very dangerous. Panic, riot, civil unrest. Chaos. Think of the hardship. The human misery.'

David Rodway made the face of one trying hard to imagine such things. But he couldn't quite pull it off. 'I am an estate agent,' said he, puff-puffing on his small cigar. 'The concept of human suffering has no meaning to me.'

'Good man,' said Stephen Craik. 'I was just testing. Had to be sure. Couldn't take any chances that I might be dealing with a humanitarian.'

'No danger of that, squire. You'll be wanting a receipt for the rest of the money in your suitcase, won't you?'

'I will as soon as I've spent it on something, yes.'

'But you have, squire, you have. *My shop*, remember? I'll wager that the figure I require for the purchase of my shop comes to exactly the amount you have left in your suitcase.'

'I think it well might,' said Stephen Craik. 'Minus a twenty per cent deduction to cover my own fees in this matter and all further matters to come.'

'Did I hear you say a *ten* per cent deduction?'

'I think you heard me say a fifteen per cent deduction.'

'I think I heard you loud and clear, squire. So what say we order up a bottle of bubbly to seal the deal and start the rumour spreading?'

'Sounds good to me.'

'*Waitress*!'

The waitress was serving a bottle of bubbly to the table where the tall boy, the short boy, the brace of beauties and the sheep were sitting.

'Enjoy your meal,' said Lola, tottering off.

Tuppe raised his champagne flute. 'To Boris,' he toasted.

'To Boris,' all agreed.

'Cheers, friends,' said Boris sucking on both straws.

'How *does* he do that?' asked Louise.

'He's not a real sheep,' whispered Tuppe. 'It's a bloke in a suit.'

'Aw shit!' Louise stretched forward and clouted Boris in the ear. 'I've been tickling his stomach for half an hour, no wonder he was getting so excited.'

'I'm having a great time, lads,' giggled Boris.

'I think Boris is getting a bit pissed,' said Tuppe to Cornelius.

'Well he deserves it, he's earned us lunch.'

'I don't think he's earned us quite as much as that, Cornelius. In fact, I fear that we'll be many pounds short in the bill-paying department.'

'Leave the bill to us,' said Thelma. 'Our treat for nicking your car.'

'I thought you didn't have any money,' Cornelius said.

Thelma shook her golden head. 'We don't. We're skint.'

'Then how?'

'We're professional criminals,' said Louise.

'Took it as a sixth-form subject,' said Thelma. 'Going on to do it as a degree course at university in the autumn.'

'Nice one,' said Cornelius. 'I had thought of doing that myself. But I chose to be an epic adventurer instead.'

'So what kind of crime do you specialize in?' Tuppe asked.

Thelma sipped champagne. 'Victimless mostly at the moment. Insurance frauds, small-scale stock market swindles, supermarket heists, that kind of thing.'

'We'll probably open up an agency of some sort, once we're fully qualified,' said Louise. 'But how did you come by all the money that this Hugo Rune's ripped you off for?'

'That's a long story,' said Cornelius. 'And I won't bore you with it here. But the sources from which all the wealth derived have now dried up.'

'But you'll get all your money back from this Rune somehow, won't you?'

'Probably. But I don't think I really want it back. When you can have anything you want, you soon find out that there's very little you actually *need*.'

'I'll cross that bridge when I come to it,' said Louise.

'We'd be happy to swindle you out of your money,' said Thelma. 'If you think it would help.'

'It's a deal,' said Cornelius. 'Call for some more champagne, Tuppe, while I help Boris back onto his chair.'

'*Waitress!*' called Tuppe.

The waitress was serving champagne to Mr Rodway. Mr Rodway was speaking to Mr Craik in what is known in theatrical circles (and most others, really, except possibly crop circles) as a 'stage whisper'.

'I swear it's true,' he stage-whispered. 'I read the report myself, some kind of *deadly virus* and it's spreading through the *cars* in *this neighbourhood*.'

'Not the cars everywhere then?' Mr Craik stage-whispered back.

'No, *just here*. Hasn't spread further yet. But someone should do something about it.'

'Typical that is,' Mr Craik was getting into the swing of the thing. 'Some kind of *Government cover up*, I'll bet. Some *germ warfare experiment* that went wrong.'

'I'm getting out, me,' stage-whispered Mr Rodway. 'And I'm the *estate agent*. I owe it to my wife and family.'

'Someone should demand a *statement* from the *mayor*,' s-double-ued Mr Craik. 'Be careful there, waitress, you're spilling the champagne all over the table.'

'Sorry, sir,' the waitress put down the bottle with a bang and tottered away at a brisk old pace towards the kitchen.

'Piece of cake really, isn't it?' asked Mr Rodway. 'Getting rumours started.'

'The mayor can be bought off then, I suppose?'

Mr Rodway raised his eyebrows, then lowered the one above the eye he was now winking.

'A member of your lodge?'

'How do you think he got to be mayor?'

'I feel that we shall enjoy a most lucrative business partnership,' said Mr Craik, raising his champagne glass. 'To Mad Car Disease.'

'Mad Car Disease it is. Bottoms up.'

'Where's that waitress gone?' asked Tuppe.

'This food's really good,' said Louise.

'Why did I get a plate of grass?' asked Boris. 'I wanted cod and chips like the rest of you. Hic!'

'That sleazy-looking bald bloke at the table over there's winking at us again,' said Thelma.

Louise waved to Mr Rodway. 'I think I know who'll be paying for our lunch,' she whispered to Cornelius.

'Ladies and gentlemen,' the fat black man in the white tuxedo had switched off his ghetto-blaster and was now on his feet, 'I hope you are all enjoying your lunch at The Casablanca dining-suite. As those who have dined here before, and I see a lot of familiar faces . . .' The fat black man fluttered his fingers and a lady in a straw hat fluttered hers back at him. 'As those who have dined here before will know, the Skelington Bay Grande (hot and cold running water in all rooms and fitted carpet tiles throughout) is always pleased at this time of the day to present its cabaret.'

Polite applause pattered about the dining-suite.

'And today, for the first time anywhere, we present . . .' He stooped and flicked the switch on his ghetto-blaster, a drum roll drum-rolled.

'I didn't know we were getting a floor show,' said Tuppe. 'I hope it's a stripper.'

The fat black man switched off his ghetto-blaster. 'Courtesy of Samuel Showstein Productions, I give you Professor Tuppe and his dancing sheep.'

'What?' went Tuppe, as all eyes in the room turned towards the only sheep in the room.

'Hang about, this can't be right.' Tuppe snatched up his contract. 'What's this?' He found what he was looking for almost at once, as it was all that was written in the contract. ' "Three shows a day, everyday, starting today, cheque to be made out in advance to Mr Showstein. Cheque received with thanks by Mr Showstein." Yeah, well I never signed this, so it's not legally binding.'

'Come on up now, Professor,' called the fat black white-tuxedo-wearer. 'We all want to see the woolly wonder.'

Cornelius looked at Tuppe.

And Tuppe looked at Cornelius.

'You'd better do something,' whispered the tall boy. 'One quick little song and dance before we call for the desserts tray.'

'Song and dance?' Tuppe whispered back. 'Look at Boris, he can't even walk, let alone dance.'

The little black lips of Boris's sheep mask were curled into a lopsided grin. The woolly wonder was well out of it.

'I'll handle this,' said Cornelius, rising to his feet and dusting himself down with a napkin. 'Ladies and gentlemen, I regret that Professor Tuppe's dancing sheep strained a fetlock this morning in rehearsals and will not be able to perform until this evening.'

'Aw,' went the diners, and 'shame'.

'I'm sure you're all animal lovers', said Cornelius, 'and would not wish to cause suffering to a dumb beast.' Heads nodded all around, one or two people clapped.

'Who are you calling dumb?' giggled Boris.

'Shut up,' said Tuppe, ramming a hand over his mouth.

'Thank you,' said Cornelius sitting down.

'Oi you,' said a young man, standing up. He was quite a broad-shouldered young man and fierce-looking with it.

He wore a colourful vest, shorts and trainers. And sported on his arms those crude self-inflicted tattoos that are so popular amongst juvenile offenders in remand centres.

'Are you talking to me?' Cornelius enquired.

'Yeah,' said the young man. 'Me and my mates have been watching you.'

'Yeah,' his mates agreed. They were similar-looking young men, with similar-looking tattoos. There were three of them (men that is, it was hard to count the tattoos).

'Well, nice to say hello,' said Cornelius with much politeness. 'I trust you'll catch this evening's performance.'

'We've been watching you feeding booze to that sheep.'

'Yes,' agreed the lady in the straw hat, standing up also. 'We've *all* been watching that.'

'I hate people who abuse animals,' said the young man.

'Me too,' said the lady in the straw hat. 'And I hate people who park their cars on grass verges.'

'Me too,' said someone else. 'And I hate the sound of car alarms going off in the night.'

'Me too,' agreed Thelma. 'Especially when I'm trying to get the stereo out.'

'Blokes like you ain't worth *that*,' snarled the young man, making the approved gesture. 'You need a good lesson teaching.'

'Yeah,' his mates agreed.

'There's no need for any unpleasantness,' said Cornelius, taking a firm grip upon the Thirties-revival champagne cooler. 'Let's all calm down, have a drink on me.'

'Here's one,' cried one of the young man's companions, snatching up his glass and flinging its contents towards Cornelius.

The tall boy ducked nimbly aside, taking the champagne cooler with him. Carling Black Label went all over Thelma.

'Whoops,' said Louise. 'Bad move there, she takes great exception to that kind of thing.'

'I bloody do.' Thelma leapt from her chair, climbed onto the table and launched herself at the despoiler of her boob tube.

The first young man launched himself at Cornelius.

Tuppe launched himself to a place of safety beneath the table, dragging Boris with him.

The lady in the straw hat turned round and hit her husband. 'Bloody grass-verge parker,' said she.

Cornelius brought the first young man down with the Thirties-revival champagne cooler. *Clunk*! it went against his skull.

His mates were on the move though.

Thelma decked the Black Label thrower with a fearsome blow to the groin.

Cornelius was suddenly engulfed in a firestorm of fists.

'I like a good punch up, me,' said Mr Rodway, looking on. 'Not getting involved in one, you understand, but watching the boot go in. Most exhilarating.'

'I like being trussed up and caned,' said Mr Craik. 'But then who doesn't?'

Clunk! went the Thirties-revival jobbie once again.

'Nice one,' said Mr Rodway.

'That's them over there,' said the waitress to the crowd of burly kitchen porters. 'The bald berk and the git with the crazy eyes. From wot I could get outta wot they was saying, they're Government germ warfare blokes spreading a deadly virus in this neighbour'ood.'

'Right, let's have the bastards,' agreed the burly ones.

Now violence isn't everybody's cup of corpuscle, and most of the diners weren't keen to enter into the spirit of the thing. So they made for the exit. Of course they caused a certain amount of chaos doing so. And chaos is the neighbour of violence, the live-in-lover sometimes.

'Take that,' went the lady in the straw hat, lashing out with her knitting bag.

'You kicked my Brixton briefcase,' went the black man in the white tuxedo, head-butting the wrong fellow.

'Did somebody say *briefcase*?' asked the vicar of Skelington Bay, who had been lunching with Max Clifford.

'Death to the Government plague merchants!' cried the burly kitchen porters, wading into all and sundry as they beat their righteous path.

'Stay here,' said Tuppe to Boris. 'I've got to help my friend.'

Louise was helping Cornelius and doing a good job too. She was not quite so vicious as Thelma. Well, actually, she was.

'Oooooh,' went a tattooed vest-wearer, doubling up in agony.

'Here,' said Mr Craik. 'Those burly kitchen porters are coming for *us*.'

Now who set off the fire alarm is anyone's guess (Thelma would be a good one). And fiercely ringing bells always add that bit of something and step up the action.

Tables were now being overturned and bottles thrown.

A heavy-metal fan called Chris, who had been lunching with a party of fellow librarians, cried, 'MEGADEATH!' and pummelled on a passer-by.

Tuppe bit the ankle of the vest-wearer who had Cornelius by the throat. The Reverend Cheesefoot, who was developing a passion for the lady in the straw hat's knitting bag, caught one in the ear from her Roman Catholic husband, which brought in elements of the Anglo-Irish conflict.

Cornelius *clunked*! the now-hopping vest-wearer on the head. 'Gather up the girls and the sheep,' he told Tuppe. 'And let's get out of here.'

Kevin and Lynne were returning from a trip to the ASDA superstore in the next town. The fire engine overtook them as they drove along the promenade. They followed it.

All the way home.

The fire engine had to pull up short as an electric-blue 1958 Cadillac Eldorado was leaving the private car-park at some speed. And lurching rather violently from side to side.

'There's something wrong with this car,' said Cornelius Murphy, clinging to the steering-wheel.

'Just drive,' said Tuppe. 'We'll get it fixed later.'

In the rear seat was a drunken sheep with his hooves (did we agree hooves?) about the shoulders of two bedraggled young women. 'You blokes are just great,' he giggled. 'You said we'd have some laughs. Just great. Just frigging great.'

'Get your bleeding hoof off my tit,' said Thelma. 'Or I'll punch your lights out.'

24

'Get off me. Get off me,' screamed Norman. 'I can't hold on with you clinging to my legs.'

He had his head through the hole did Norman, and one arm. But things weren't looking too hopeful.

'You need me,' crowed Claude. 'You'd better hold on.'

'I can't, you're too heavy. You're dragging me down.'

'Save your breath, sonny. Pull us through the sodding hole.'

Well, he'd got this far.

He couldn't fall back down again now.

Could he?

No. He couldn't.

Norman puffed and panted. He struggled and strained and bit by bit and inch by inch. Until at last . . .

'We did it.'

Norman gulped in air and Claude sat coughing.

But they'd done it. They really had.

They sat now upon a high gantry. The big machines that did the business for the big sky nozzles pulsed away beneath them. Rising steam puffs, oily smells, wee men in overalls.

'What now?' Norman asked between gulpings.

'Revenge,' said Claude. 'Sweet revenge.'

'All right,' said Norman. 'Let's do it.'

The two of them stood up, stretched, nursed bruised places, and considered the state of each other.

The state wasn't any too good.

They were both down to their vests and underpants.

'That's a really cakky pair of knickers,' said Norman.

'Oh yeah? Well I bet yours aren't short of skid marks.'

'Mine were clean on the day I . . .' Norman paused, made a very sad face.

Claude patted him on the shoulder. 'You're a good boy,' said he.

'I'm a *dead* boy,' said Norman, in a most mournful voice. 'And I don't like it one little bit.'

'You have things to do,' said Claude, giving him another pat. 'Great things. But things best done with clothes on. Tell you what. You lure a couple of engineers up here and I'll bop them on the head with this spanner and we'll nick their overalls and shoes. What do you say?'

'I say, where did you get the spanner from?'

'Same place as I got the pocket lighter, I suppose.'

'Fair enough.'

'That was quick,' Norman said, zipping himself into an engineer's overall. 'I never even saw you hit them with the spanner.'

'Well, I never saw you push their unconscious bodies through the hole and down the lift shaft,' said Claude, zipping himself into another.

'You missed that, did you?'

'Some bits you have to miss, sonny, when you're in a real hurry to get things moving along.'

'Which we are!'

'Which we certainly are. So let's get you to the nearest big sky nozzle and blast you back to Earth. You're going home, Norman. Going home.'

'Going home,' sighed Norman. 'Oh I do like the sound of that.'

25

Off the road and on the beach a little ways out from Skelington Bay, Cornelius drew the Cadillac to a squidily-diddly halt. 'The brakes are all fouled up,' he told Thelma. 'What did you do to this car?'

'It was all right yesterday. But ever since we left Collins' Farm it's been acting real funny. Anyway, stuff your car, Cornelius, look at the state of *me*.'

Cornelius looked at the state of Thelma. Much as a Texan might look at the State of Texas, or a Carmelite, the State of Grace.

Most approvingly.

Tousled, Thelma was, about the golden tresses; her perfect cheek-bones were lacquered with perspiration. Blue eyes showering sparks. Boob tube slightly torn. Firm young breasts rising and falling to a sensual rhythm.

Forget Texas.

Forget Grace.

'Don't stare at me like that,' said Thelma. 'Well, OK, you can if you want to.'

'I'm sorry I got you into a fight.'

'Don't be, I really enjoyed it.'

'I fear the vest-wearers may be walking with a pronounced limp for a few days.'

'And sleeping rough probably,' said Louise. 'Or two of them at least. I lifted their wallets during the fight.'

'They'll *all* be sleeping rough,' said Thelma. 'I lifted the other two.'

Cornelius shook his head at this, then gathered in his

167

wandering hair. He did not approve of such dishonesty, but considered that to take the moral highground now, might well interfere with his chances of sexual intercourse later.

Or sooner.

'Why don't we all go in for a swim and cool off?' he suggested.

'I'm for that,' Tuppe pulled off his shirt. 'How's Boris?' he asked.

'Boris has passed out on the floor,' said Louise.

'Best leave him to sleep it off then.'

'I don't think the world's quite ready for Professor Tuppe and his dancing sheep,' said Cornelius.

'I don't think *I'm* quite ready for a life on the cabaret circuit,' said Tuppe. 'If that was the Skelington Bay lunchtime crowd, then stuff the Glasgow Empire on a Saturday night.'

'What are *you* going to do?' Thelma asked Cornelius.

'About what?'

'About Mr Rune and your millions of pounds, and whatever it is that your millions of pounds are *helping* him to finance?'

'I'll get around to that,' smiled Cornelius. 'All in good time.'

'I thought you were an adventurer.'

'An *epic* adventurer. That's me.'

'Then it's your job to make things happen, not just wait for them to.'

Cornelius rose to his full height in the driver's seat and pushed his hair to the back of himself. 'I have to know what Rune is up to,' said he. 'I shall be breaking into his hotel room this evening in order to find out.'

'Oh,' said Thelma.

'Quite,' said Cornelius. 'But for now, I wish first to frolic in the waves.'

'And then?'

'And then later I hope to seduce you.'

Thelma grinned, 'Why not combine the two?' she asked. 'Right now.'

'Jolly good.'

There was jumping in the waves near Skelington Bay. Jumping and a bumping and a humping. But it wasn't gross. It was rather beautiful really. There's something about making love in the sea which sets it in a realm apart. Showers, baths and Jacuzzis have much to recommend them. Particularly the latter. And who amongst us can truly put their hand upon their heart and swear that they've never done it one hot summer's night in the Thomas the Tank Engine paddling-pool on next door's back lawn?

Not many!

But the warm waves have it every time. It's probably something primeval. Some inherited distant memory of mankind's origins. Born of the sea. Rising to the land. Returning to the watery cradle. Something like that.

Something almost spiritual.

The party of nuns on the beach who were viewing Cornelius and Thelma considered that it was probably something almost spiritual. Those who could see what Tuppe and Louise were up to in the sand dunes considered otherwise, these hitched up their skirts and fled screaming up the beach.

'That was sweet.' Cornelius and Thelma now sat in the rear seat of the Cadillac, feet upon Boris the woolly cushion, sharing a cigarette.

Tuppe and Louise were in the front seat. An exhausted Louise had fallen asleep. Tuppe was reading a copy of the day's *Skelington Bay Mercury*, which he'd found blowing along the beach.

'LUGGAGE' VICAR IN 'GRAVE' MISDEMEANOUR

Ran the headline, and beneath it:

RIOT BREAKS OUT AT LOCAL YOUTH'S FUNERAL

'They like a punch up in this neck of the woods, don't they?' said Tuppe. 'Cor look at that, poor kid.'

'What is it?' Cornelius asked. Tuppe displayed the newspaper. There was a big, blown-up photograph of Norman on the front.

'Some local boy,' said Tuppe. 'Got killed when his father fell out of the sky onto his head.'

'Are you making this up, Tuppe?'

'No, it's all here. Fourteen years of age. That's pretty tragic.'

Cornelius studied the newspaper. He looked long and hard into the face of Norman and a strange expression passed over his own.

'Whatever's the matter?' Tuppe asked. 'You look mighty strange.'

'I don't know.' Cornelius shook his head, showering the occupants of the Cadillac. 'I seemed to feel something. Or sense something. We've never met this boy, have we?'

'Nope.'

Cornelius folded the newspaper and rammed it into his trouser pocket. 'Mighty strange indeed. So what shall we do now?'

'Let's go and have a drink,' said Thelma, fishing a vest-wearer's wallet from her shoulder bag. 'I've plenty of cash.'

'Yes, I was hoping to have a word with you about that.'

'You don't approve, do you?'

'Well, it's not exactly a "victimless" crime, is it?'

'I'll tell you what,' Thelma took out the wallets and removed the cash from them, 'we'll call the money compensation for the violent interruption of our lunch. And we'll mail the wallets back to the owners' home addresses. Be a nice surprise for them after they've hitchhiked home.'

Cornelius grinned and climbed into the driver's seat. 'Wicked woman,' said he, keying the ignition.

The Cadillac shivered and the engine made a low, evil, growling sound. 'And we'll put this car into the first garage we come to. There's definitely something not altogether right about it.'

Mr Rodway's brother Clive ran the Skelington Bay Auto Agency.

He looked quite pleased to see Cornelius.

'I'll have a look at it,' he said. 'But I can't promise how soon I'll get it done.'

'You got a lot on then?' asked Tuppe.

'Didn't have until this lunchtime, but look at all those.'

The mechanic pointed to the row of smart-looking cars gleaming on his forecourt. A Porsche, a Mercedes, two BMWs. A long black limousine with the personalized number plate HR1.

'They look familiar,' said Thelma.

'They do,' said Louise. 'They were all parked in front of the Grande, when we drove the Cadillac in this morning.'

'Well they're all buggered now,' said the mechanic. 'Faulty brakes, dodgy steering, weird noises coming from the engines.'

'Curious,' said Cornelius.

'Nothing I can't handle. Stay up all night to work on them if necessary.'

'Highly commendable,' said Cornelius.

'A fine car deserves fine treatment, that's my motto.'

'And "a labourer is worthy of his hire"?' Cornelius suggested.

The mechanic wiped his hands upon his oily rag.

'I'm in no particular rush,' said Cornelius. 'If you could fix mine during the hours of daylight, while on *single time*. And notify me in advance of any expensive parts you might require, so I can have them sent to you and—'

'Yeah, I get the message,' said the mechanic.

'But I'll tell you what,' the Murphy voice took on a conspiratorial tone. 'The long black limousine with the HRl plates . . .'

'Yeah?' asked the mechanic.

'Multi-millionaire,' said Cornelius. 'Money no object at all.'

'You know him then?'

'Like I know my own father.' Cornelius winked.

The mechanic winked back. 'Cheers, mate,' said he.

26

The most amazing man who ever lived appeared once more upon the scene; soaking once more in the perfumed waters of his marble bath tub; and seeking once more the final equation to complete his formula for the universal panacea and elixir of life.

And once more came the drumming on his chamber door.

And once more came the voice of his landlady.

'Get out of that bed, you lazy sod, or I'll have my husband Cyril come and break down the door!' she cried.

Once more.

And once more he awoke with a start.

To find that he'd dozed off in his chair in the KEV-LYN suite at the Skelington Bay Grande.

'Now, where were we?' asked the most amazing man. 'Ah yes. I recall, I was asking questions and you were answering them. A curious reversal of roles. But no matter.'

Rune fixed his gaze upon a cringing fellow in a garish suit. A cringing fellow who answered to any one of a number of names. Except perhaps to that of McKintock.

'Let us recap on events,' said Rune. 'I am rudely awakened from my nap by the noise of a fire appliance. I find the hotel in an uproar. I gaze down from my window to see a certain big-haired lout and his small companion streaking away from the premises. Appalled at this circumstance I call upon you in your room and find you packing your bags, preparatory to streaking away on your own account.'

'I thought the hotel was on fire,' lied he of the garish suit. 'I was only trying to save my costumes.'

'No, no,' Rune raised a fat finger and waggled it in the air. 'This I believe to be an untruth. Murphy is here, in this town. Was here in this very hotel. I feel that you and he exchanged words. That you have spoken to him of things that you should not.'

'I never would. I never did.'

'Explain to me then his presence here.'

'I don't know. He must have broken out of the cell.'

'I think I shall have to dismiss you from my employment,' said Hugo Rune.

'Oh yes?' The man known as Showstein to some and by other names to others, could not control the look of relief which now spread across his face. 'Dismiss me from your employment?'

'Yes,' said Rune. 'Let you go, as they say.'

'Oh,' said Showstein, sighing and sweating. 'Let me go, oh my word.'

'No hard feelings,' said Rune.

'None at all,' said the man in the suit.

'I know of a company that has a vacancy for such a fellow as you. I will furnish the necessary references.'

'Why thank you, Mr Rune. Thank you very very much. What is the name of this company?'

Rune drew a derringer from the sleeve of his silk dressing-gown and pressed it to the forehead of his ex-employee. 'It's called The Universal Reincarnation Company,' he said, as he pulled the trigger. 'I'll let them know you're on your way for the interview.'

27

'Are you sitting comfortably?' asked Claude the ex-controller.

'No, I'm most certainly not.' Norman was crammed into a little bullet-shaped affair, in a kind of breech-loading affair, in one of the big sky nozzle soul-launching sort of affairs.

'Well this won't take long.' Claude worked away at another affair. It was a large version of the little brass Karmascope contrivance. It even had a computer screen. Numbers flickered across this and Claude tapped at the keyboard. He seemed to be enjoying himself.

'You never lose the old magic,' said he.

'What are you doing?' Norman asked.

'Mapping coordinates, sonny, zeroing you in on Cornelius Murphy.'

'How do you know where he is?'

'I'm working it out on the machine, don't ask so many damn fool questions.'

'Do get a move on. Someone will catch us.'

'I know exactly what I'm doing. I think.' The old boy tapped some more. 'Yes, certainly I do. Now do you remember what you have to say?'

'Of course I remember. I tell this Murphy all you've told me about his bastard of a dad and all I know about the electrical discharging and the all-round extermination of the human species next Friday.'

'And then?'

'And then let him figure out what to do about it.'

'Hm,' said old Claude. 'Doesn't sound an altogether foolproof plan when you put it like that, does it?'

'Oh do get a move on,' Norman said.

'I'm all done.' The ancient grinned. 'So I suppose it's goodbye.'

Norman peeped out at the ex-controller. 'What about you?' he asked. 'What will you do now?'

'Beat the bastard,' said Claude. 'Me up here, you down there. Between the two of us we'll beat him. All the hims of him there are.'

'You really think we can?' Norman had plenty of doubts. And he now felt a bit sad at saying goodbye to Claude. 'You *really* think we can?'

'Of course we can, sonny. Of course we can. Think positive. Do what's right.'

'I'll see you again, won't I?' Norman gave a little sniff.

'You'll see me again.'

'Look after yourself,' said Norman, getting a crinkly mouth on. 'It's been, er, good to know you.'

'Don't get drippy on me, sonny.'

'I'm not getting drippy, how dare you!'

'That's my boy.' Claude pressed a big red button. The big sky nozzle belched purple flame and a little white point of life soared off across the blackness of space, bound for planet Earth.

Claude mopped a tear from his eye. 'Good luck, Norman,' he said.

Many miles, or dimensions or whatever, down below, Skelington Bay was dressing for the evening. The lights along the promenade clicked into rainbows. Neon danced in fish-and-chip shop windows. A red-and-white-striped barber's pole revolved into nothingness.

Pavements glowed with gold. And sunset laid a molten path across the sea to shore.

Lovely stuff.

In a bar near the west pier, Cornelius brought a tray

of drinks to the table. 'Are we all up for this?' he asked.

Thelma and Louise nodded. 'As long as we get a crack at your loot once you've retrieved it.'

'And as long as I stay well clear of Rune,' said Tuppe. 'That fellow scares the breakfast from my bottom, so to speak.'

'If we all do it right then things will go without a hitch.'

'Very good,' said Tuppe. 'You almost have me convinced there.'

'Look it's simple enough. I telephoned the Grande this afternoon to confirm whether Mr Hugo Rune would be dining there tonight. They said, yes he will, in the Casablanca, which is apparently undergoing repairs. Eight o'clock, they said. Now Rune is a man who likes his fodder. He'll be settled in there for a couple of hours.'

'And to make sure of that Louise and I will be joining him,' said Thelma. 'Eager to listen to this oh so interesting man, who according to you has been everywhere and met everybody.'

'Right,' said Cornelius. 'And while he entertains you with fascinating tales, I shall break into his room and go through everything he has there. Hopefully I shall be able to find out what he's up to and what he's done with my money. I shall work as quickly as I can. If you can't keep him talking, phone up to the room, twice, three rings each time.'

'And I'll be keeping a look out for you,' said Tuppe. 'And we will communicate through these.' He proudly displayed the two-way radio sets he'd purchased with some of Thelma's wallet winnings.

Cornelius took one of the radio sets and gave it a dubious perusal. 'This isn't Watergate,' said he.

'No, but they're really good fun. We can have secret call signs. Like Blue Leader and Foxtrot Patrol.'

'It's getting on for eight,' said Cornelius. 'Let's drink up and get to it. OK?'

'OK.'

'Just one thing,' said Tuppe. 'I hate to mention it. But I feel it should be mentioned.'

'Go on.'

'Shouldn't somebody have woken Boris? We left him in the car.'

The car was up on jacks now.

And Boris was still asleep in the back.

Which was probably all for the best, as it happened.

Considering what lay in store for him.

Soon.

Cornelius, Tuppe, Thelma and Louise left the bar. Leave Boris to sleep for the night and get on with the dirty doings, had been the general consensus. Tuppe's 'mad sheep as diversionary tactic in an emergency situation' being outvoted three to one.

Two gentlemen watched the foursome's departure. Although gentlemen is not quite perhaps the word. Somewhat grazed were these two. Grazed of chin and cheek-bone. Scuffed of suit and missing of initialled cufflink.

'Interesting,' said Mr Rodway. 'The bunch from lunchtime at the Grande, conspiring to commit a felony. Should you get on the blower to the Lord High Butter of No Buts and alert him to their intentions?'

Mr Craik flashed eyes which seemed less wild now that he had been beyond the range of Rune's influence for almost all of the day. 'Play this one by ear, I think. There might well be a little profit to be turned.'

178

Mr Rodway tapped his tender nose. 'I'm with you there, squire. With you there.'

'Yore 'ere, sir,' Lola the showgirl waitress was on her evening shift. She had a bruise or two on her and one broken heel that seriously impaired her tottering, but a job's a job, and Kevin the governor had promised her a raise. 'This is yore seat.'

'My thanks,' Hugo Rune lowered his ponderous posterior onto the chair. He was clearly in high spirits (and apparently unaware that he was sharing a chapter).

'Shall I fetch ya the wine list, sir?'

'Do you have your little pad?' Rune enquired.

'Yeah, corse I 'ave.'

'Then write upon it, "Mr Rune will have what he had last night, but twice as much, as he is expecting a friend."'

'Yeah, right.' The waitress staggered away on one heel.

Rune gave his dire surroundings a careful once-over and consulted his pocket watch. 'Three, two, one,' said he.

A bit of a crash in the door area, a slip to one side, a ricochet from the sweet trolley and an old chum sat down at his side.

'Rune,' said Brigadier Algenon 'Chunky' Wilberforce. For it was none other.

'Chunky,' said Rune. Hands clasped. Knuckles pressed.

'Damn fine to see you, you old pederast.'

'Yourself also, deflowered of virgins. And some even human!'

The two enjoined hands once more. Patted backs. Fell about in mirth for no apparent reason. Called for much wine.

'How's the billet?' asked Rune.

'Mustn't grumble.' The Brigadier, for this was the real McCoy (not the now-deceased impersonator)*, plucked upon abundant mustachios, clapped hands against a bulbous belly encased within considerable tweed and clicked his military heels together. 'Shacked up with the local padre and his good lady. Man's a total loon, dips his wick in anything with a handle on the top and a pair of straps round it.'

'Better keep him clear of your wife then, what.'

The Brigadier collapsed in much humour. 'Or your toy boy, you old poo-nudger.'

'Snorter?' said Rune, pouring the wine that had been brought him.

'Stick it in the teacup and call it black pudding.'

'What the frig is going on there?' asked Thelma, settling herself down at a nearby table.

'Looks like he's got a friend with him,' said Louise. 'I think we can sit this one out for a while.'

Up on the top floor, Cornelius took out his Swiss Army knife and selected the blade with the skeleton-key attachment. Along the corridor and through a crack in the broom-cupboard door, Tuppe kept a wary eye on the staircase and a thumb on the 'speak' button of his two-way radio set.

Cornelius slotted a selection of tumbler-turners into the hollow shaft of the skeleton key and sought the keyhole in the pinkly painted door of the KEV-LYN suite.

And here he came up against his first major obstacle.

The door lacked for a keyhole.

'That can't be right.' Cornelius reached out to turn the door handle.

But now the door lacked for this also.

* Because he was now deceased. So it couldn't be him.

180

Cornelius reached his hand into his hair and scratched his head with it. Most odd. He would have to try and kick the door open. He glanced up and down the corridor.

All clear.

Cornelius drew back, raised his foot.

But did no more.

Because now the wall lacked for a door.

All gone!

'Clever,' said Cornelius. 'Very clever.' He fished the two-way radio set from his back pocket, pressed the 'speak' button and said, 'Tuppe.'

'Aaaaagh!' Tuppe collapsed amongst the mops and buckets. 'What? Who? What?'

'It's me – Cornelius.'

'Use your code name.' Tuppe sought to extricate himself from the dustpans and brushes.

'Don't be silly, it's me.'

'Could be a trick.'

'Yeah.' Cornelius viewed the wall which had so lately been a door. 'I suppose you're right.'

'So?'

'OK. What code name do you want me to use?'

'I don't know, make one up.'

'How about *Burglar* to *Lookout*?'

'No,' said Tuppe. 'That's no good. Something more exciting.'

'Look, I can't think of anything. You make something up.'

'All right, how about *Delta Force* to *Howling Commando*?'

'Fair enough. Delta Force to Howling Commando, come in please.'

'Howling Commando reading you loud and clear, Delta Force. What have you to report?'

'The bloody door has vanished and I can't find my way into the room, require assistance please, over.'

'Tough titty, Delta Force. I'm staying right here in the broom cupboard, over and out.'

'Get along here and give me a hand at once.'

'Not a chance. I said over and out and I meant it. Message ends.'

'Well, really!' Cornelius tucked the two-way radio back into his pocket. He screwed up his eyes and examined the area of wall which had lately been the door. It was a most convincing area of wall. It lacked for doorishness completely. Cornelius turned away and turned back quickly. He nonchalantly strolled a pace or two down the corridor and then jumped back. He even withdrew a shiny blade from his knife and used it mirror-fashion.

No good.

Whatever spell of protection Rune had cast over his door was unlikely to be broken by anyone possessed of less magic than himself.

'Find another way in then,' said Cornelius Murphy. 'Onto the roof, down a drainpipe, in at an open window?' The tall boy slunk off to seek a fire exit.

'Fire!' went Brigadier Wilberforce, miming the blast of an elephant gun. 'Bagged three tigers in a single day. Remember that, Rune? Three of the blighters, man-eaters all.'

'Bagged a couple of native bearers also, as I recall.' Rune poured further wine. 'And the mahout who was steering your elephant.'

'Bally fool got in the way. Those were the days though, eh? British Empire splattered all over the globe. Darkies knew their place back then, doncha know.'

A passing waiter of foreign extraction overheard this remark and made a mental note to spit in the Brigadier's soup.

'So,' said Brigadier Chunky. 'Well and good to reminisce and all that. But what's the wheeze then, Rune? Why have you called me down to this seedy resort? Prostitution conspicuous here, you know.'

'Really?' said Rune.

'Conspicuous by its bloody absence.'

Further guffaws.

'I'd like to put a bit of business your way, Chunky. Do you still run that scrap-metal yard?'

'Scrap-metal yard? How dare you, sir. Far too many unsavoury connotations. Not scrap-metal yard any more. More politically correct title. Wilberforce Associates Nice Kind Ecological Recycling Services.'

'Which is an acronym, I believe.'

'Gets a cheap laugh at dinner parties, yes.'

'But you can still "acquire" items of a metallic nature?'

'Anything you care to mention, old man. What do you have in mind? Military hardware, Scud missiles, stealth bomber?'

Rune shook his head.

'Nuclear then? Not easy to come by, but I have contacts.'

Rune shook his head once more. 'Pylons,' said he.

'Pylons? What those big eyesores that electricity board chaps who live in the town love to plague the country Johnnies with?'

'Correct.'

'Humyah. Can't see why not. Have a few ex-Desert Storm bulldozers that I "won" off Saddam, gathering dust in the old eco-friendly recycling yard. They'll get the job done. How many pylons do you want?'

'Twenty should be sufficient, with two miles of the heaviest duty cable. And a couple of radio masts.'

'Piece of pudding, when do you want 'em?'

'By next Wednesday night. Undamaged, and a team to re-erect them here.'

'Bit public, might raise an eyebrow from the locals.'

'There will be no locals. We will have this town to ourselves.'

'What *are* you up to, Rune?'

'Mum's the word on this one, Chunky.'

'With you there. No names, no pack-drill.'

'Quite.'

'And the matter of my fee?'

'How does a million pounds in pure gold sound to you?'

'It sounds good to me,' whispered Thelma to Louise.

And the sound of an electric drill being carelessly applied to the chassis of the Cadillac Eldorado awoke a sleeping sheep-suiter.

'Oh my head,' went Boris, 'Where am I?'

'Come in, Delta Force, where are you, over?'

Cornelius plucked the two-way radio from his back pocket. 'I'm up on the roof. Be quiet.'

'What are you doing on the roof?'

'I'm going to climb down a drainpipe and try to shin in through an open window.'

'Sounds very dangerous. Not the way I would have done it.'

'Oh really, and how would you have done it?'

'Well,' said Tuppe, 'I would have used one of the courtesy phones, called down to reception and asked for a bottle of champagne to be delivered at once to Mr Rune's room.'

'But the door has vanished, Tuppe.'

'Am I right in thinking that the door only vanished when you tried to break in at it?'

'Yes, I told you that.'

'Protective magic.'

184

'Yes, Tuppe, I reasoned that out for myself. Please get off the line.'

'The magic wouldn't be directed against the hotel staff,' said Tuppe. 'Only against potential intruders. So the champagne deliverer would have seen the door, used the pass key, and you could have slipped in behind them and—'

'Thank you *very* much. Kindly maintain radio silence from now on. Over and *out*.'

'Glad to be of assistance, Delta Force. Over and out.'

Cornelius stuffed the two-way radio into his pocket once more and continued to edge along the roof, with one foot in the gutter. He was a good way up. A single slip would be sufficient to ensure a fatal fall.

Nice night though.

The stars looked down. The moon hung high. The waves kissed gently. A bat flapped closely.

'Get away!' Cornelius, flapped, slipped, tumbled and fell; he grabbed, gripped, clung onto and hung.

By his fingers.

From the gutter.

'Use the courtesy phone!' muttered the dangling tall boy. 'Call for some champagne to be delivered! Nice one, Tuppe. *Oh dear!*'

It was old guttering. Cast iron. Kevin was going to have it replaced with a light-weight modern-day plastic equivalent. It was on the list of things to be done. Quite far down it though.

'Oooooooh!' went Cornelius, as the guttering came away from the wall and swung in an outwards direction. 'Oooooooh!'

Rusty, the guttering was. Old and rusty. Unsafe.

Click, click, click, it went.

Bend and snap.

'Oooooooh!' Cornelius swung down with it.

Struck the UPVC mock-Georgian window of the KEV-LYN suite.

But did not pass through it.

Well, you don't, do you? Not through double glazing. You just kind of splat against double glazing. Single glazing? Well, you'd burst through that. Like in cowboy movies.

But double glazing?

Not a chance.

'Oooooooh!' The window was open at the top. Cornelius leapt at it. Clung on. The guttering spiralled down towards the car-park. In fact, it fell directly between two young men who were walking across it and embedded itself into the Tarmac.

Mr Rodway and Mr Craik regained the composure they had momentarily lost and peered up towards the roof. They just caught sight of Cornelius, as, clinging to the window, his weight swung it inwards upon its central-pivoting jobbie and catapulted him into Rune's apartment.

'Bastard,' said Mr Rodway.

'Enterprising bastard,' said Mr Craik. 'Let us proceed inside and await further developments.'

28

Cornelius climbed dizzily to his feet.

He was in.

And that was something.

'So,' said he, clicking joints and testing for broken bones. 'To work. Let's see what we can see.'

And much there was to be seen. The suite was a confusion of maps and diagrams and textbooks.

Cornelius picked up one of the latter and scrutinized its cover. *The Science of Electrolysis*. Another. *Electroplating for Fun and Profit*. Another. *Electrokinetics*. Another. *Electrostatics*.

'A lot of electrickery,' mused the Murphy. 'What about the maps?'

The maps were all of Skelington Bay and its surrounding areas.

Some were partially shaded in. On one, the twin piers had been inked, one in red and one in blue. Lines of these colours ran from the piers and crossed the town to terminate at Druid's Tor.

Cornelius unearthed computer printouts. These appeared to catalogue the output of the National Grid. The words INSUFFICIENT POWER! had been scrawled across the bottom of them.

Then there were pages of calculations. These seemed to be concerned with multiples of cubic miles and factors of $93,000,000.

'Whatever he's up to, it's big,' was the tall boy's unenlightened conclusion. 'So where's my money?'

He peered about the room. And 'Oh,' he said suddenly. 'It would appear to be there.'

In a corner of the room stood a four-sided glass construction, with a glass top. It resembled a shower cubical. This rested upon a black base and in the middle of this base, within the four clear-glass walls, stood a little plinth. And on top of this plinth, a very large stack of high-denomination money notes.

'Strange place to store your wealth,' said Cornelius. 'Almost like an exhibit. Perhaps he likes to sit and gaze at it.'

The tall boy approached the glass cubical. It was about four feet to a side and eight in height. One side was slightly ajar, the door obviously. Cornelius swung it open and stepped in to claim his prize.

Such was not to be.

Cornelius found himself confronted by another glass wall. This, however, did not extend the full width of the cubical and the seeker after wealth was able to squeeze through the gap remaining and reach forward.

To find a further wall of glass at an acute angle blocking his way.

Cornelius stared at the stack of money. A foot or so beyond this second wall, he pressed his hand to the wall, which swung aside.

Easy-peasy.

Cornelius now found himself staring into a mirror, the stack of wealth behind him on the right-hand side. He turned. Another glass wall. He felt along it. Another opening.

Another glass wall.

Another mirror.

'There'd be a knack to this,' said Cornelius, seeking to retrace his footsteps but now somewhat confused about which way he had come in. 'I came in through the side nearest to the window.'

There seemed to be a mirror on that side.

If it *was* that side.

There seemed to be mirrors all round now.

No, there was a glass wall, and beyond it the money.

Cornelius felt his way along. Discovered an opening and squeezed through it. He reached towards the money and found his way blocked yet again.

'I am perplexed,' said Cornelius Murphy.

'What are they doing now?' asked Louise.

'Arm wrestling, by the look of it.' Thelma shook her golden head. 'Over bowls of hot soup, pathetic.'

'Got you there,' chortled Rune as Chunky sucked upon a soupy sleeve. 'That's one hundred thousand in gold you owe me.'

'Double or quits on something else?'

'On what?'

'Loudest fart,' said the Brigadier, making a strained face.

'Might we join you, ladies?'

Thelma looked up into the face of Mr Rodway.

Louise looked up into that of Mr Craik.

'No,' they agreed.

'Oh come on now, don't be stand-offish,' Mr Rodway pulled out a chair and sat down upon it. 'You girls on holiday, looking for a little fun?'

Mr Craik seated himself also. 'Or perhaps here on business?'

'Go away, you sad bastards.'

'No need to be rude,' said Mr Rodway. 'We're only trying to be friendly.'

'Would you like me to call the proprietor and have you thrown out?' Thelma asked. 'Or would you prefer to hear my friend Louise scream, "Let go of me, you pervert," at the top of her voice?'

'We could do both,' said Louise.

'Or you could shout, "Burglar in Mr Rune's suite,"' Mr Craik suggested. 'I could shout that for you, if you want.'

The burglar in Mr Rune's suite was now in a state of considerable confusion. And obvious captivity. He drummed his fists against the glassy walls of his prison. Possibly double-glazed they were.

Seemingly unbreakable anyway.

He pulled out the two-way radio set, pressed the 'speak' button and shouted '*Tuppe*' into it.

'Aaaaagh. Oh. Help. What?' came the voice of Tuppe. 'What's going on?'

'I'm stuck, I need your help.'

'Who's speaking?'

'Oh don't be so stupid, you know who it is.'

'Use your code name.'

'Delta Force!'

'Hearing you loud and clear, Delta Force. What have you to report?'

'I'm trapped in Rune's apartment. Inside the Cabinet of Dr Caligari or something. Get me out of here.'

'Do you wish me to put *Operation Call Room Service* into, er, operation, Delta Force?'

'Yes and make it quick.'

'Howling Commando signing off then. Expect me with the champagne. Lie low for now. Message ends.'

Cornelius jammed the two-way radio back into his pocket. 'Now just think calmly,' he told himself. 'If you got yourself in, you can get yourself out.'

'What exactly have you got yourself into?' enquired Mr Rodway. 'Perhaps we can help.'

Thelma offered the bald estate agent a withering glance. 'Who are *you*?' she asked.

'Businessmen.'

'Oh shit,' said Mr Craik.

'What's the problem?'

'It's Mr Rune, he's seen me. He's calling me over.'

'Well go and pass the time of day. Tell him all about our plans for the *MCD*. Impress him. I will entertain the ladies in your absence.'

'Oh shit,' said Mr Craik once more.

'Go on. Don't keep him waiting. For God's sake don't do that.'

'No, no indeed.' Mr Craik jumped up and took his leave.

'You called?' said he, a-trembling at the table of Hugo Rune.

'Who's this cove?' asked the Brigadier. 'Shifty eyes. One of your bods, Rune? Take a stick to the blighter and send him on his way.'

Hugo Rune stilled the volatile Brig with a single, though mysterioso, gesture of his left hand. 'Be seated,' said Rune to Mr Craik.

Mr Craik drew out a chair.

'Floor,' said Hugo Rune. 'And kneel with it.'

Stephen Craik knelt down.

Thelma watched this. As did Louise.

'Shit,' said Mr Rodway, watching also.

'Dining with friends?' Rune asked. 'Two ripe-looking youngsters. Who's the bald git?'

Mr Craik's wild-again eyes flashed up at Rune's shaven dome. 'That's Mr Rodway,' he ventured. 'The estate agent.'

'The born-again Cardinal, oh yes.'

'The *who*, I'm sorry?'

'Never you mind. How are you progressing with the task I set you?'

'Very well, Mr Rune. We've—'

'Not now,' said Rune, putting a fat finger to his lips. 'Later, in my suite. But why not bring your friends over to join us?'

'Oh no, I don't think—'

'At once,' said Rune. 'And please don't make me ask you twice.'

'And a couple of packets of flavoured crisps,' said Tuppe into a courtesy phone. 'And as quick as possible. It's a surprise, just let yourself in with the pass key and leave the drink by the bed. Who should you charge it to? Mr Rune's account, of course. It's a surprise by him, for someone else. Me? I'm his chauffeur, calling from the car phone. Must go now, the lights have turned green. Goodbye.' Tuppe replaced the telephone. 'Howling Commando to Delta Force,' he called into his two-way radio. 'We have a green light on *Operation Call Room Service*, lie low in your cabinet and await extraction.'

Hugo Rune stared hard into the face of Thelma who was now seated opposite him. 'You have an upper-left molar that would do well for extraction,' said he. 'Although it might be saved.'

Thelma fingered her jaw. 'How do you know that?'

Rune smiled. 'Champagne?' he asked, dipping his hand into the Thirties-revival cooler.

'Yes please, that would be nice.' Thelma looked at Louise. And Louise looked at Thelma. Both felt decidedly uncomfortable.

'You know who I am, of course,' said Rune.

Louise opened her mouth to say no. 'Yes,' she said.

'Yes, but of course you do,' Rune filled a champagne flute and handed it to Louise. She took it in uneasy fingers. Rune's large hand closed about hers.

'Ah,' said Rune, releasing it. 'Ah yes, I see.'

'What do you see?'

'I see all,' said Hugo Rune. 'And most of the rest. Do you know that if you put one grain of rice on the first square of a chessboard, two grains on the next, four on the next, eight on the next and keep on doubling, that when you reached the final square, you would end up with $2^{64}-1$ grains of rice, enough to bury England and Wales and all their population?'

'Have to be a bloody big chessboard then,' said Chunky. 'Need a white king the size of your arse, Rune.'

Hugo Rune smiled warmly upon his old chum. 'Back to your billet now,' said he. 'There's a good fellow.'

'Do us a favour, Rune, haven't even got stuck into the nosebag yet.'

Hugo Rune leaned over to the Brig. He whispered words into his ear.

The face of Chunky Wilberforce lost all of its ruddy hue. It whitened. Became albinotic, leucondermatous, eburnean.

Things of a thesaurusian nature.

'Ah, now, well, I, ah. Sorry to run and all that. But pressing business elsewhere. Say ta-ta for now then. Toodly-pip.'

And, at a speed quite unbecoming for one of his advanced years, Brigadier Algenon 'Chunky' Wilberforce made his departure.

'And so,' said Rune, forming ship-ribs with his fingers and pressing his thumbs to his forehead, 'now we are five. Unlucky number five. Who shall we lose?'

His haunting eyes fanned over the sitters. Each of whom looked extremely eager to be lost.

'You,' said Rune to Mr Rodway. 'Bald git. On your bike. Take a powder. Scram. Vamoose. Hit the road.'

'What?' This wasn't how Mr Rodway had planned

things to be. Since leaving the seaside bar, his thoughts had been moving towards the applied blackmail of Thelma and Louise. Payoffs of a sexual nature had featured in his projected evening curriculum.

Rune gazed hard at Mr Rodway. *Through* Mr Rodway.

'Yes,' said Mr Rodway, rising from his chair. 'Well, I'll keep in touch. Mr Craik will fill you in on all the details. Yes. Goodbye then.'

And, with that said, off he jolly well went. At the trot.

'Isn't this nice?' said Hugo Rune, pouring further champagne.

Thelma and Louise managed very thin smiles.

The eyes of Mr Craik looked wilder than ever.

And growing ever nearer, although not heard of for some time, the dead boy with the Beatle cut streaked on through the cosmos.

'So,' said Rune. 'I would say "isn't this pleasant", but facetiousness is not one of my failings. What exactly are you two young women up to?'

'I, er,' Louise clamped her jaws. The compulsion to answer this man's questions with only the truth was almost a physical thing.

'Come on now,' said Hugo Rune. 'Certainly I am possessed of major charisma, but your eyes have scarcely left my person since I entered the room. And I feel that you overheard every word of my conversation with dear Chunky.'

The deadly eyes turned upon Mr Craik. 'What are your thoughts concerning this?'

'I? Oh?' Mr Craik's wild eyes crossed and he fainted dead away, face down into his bowl of Brown Windsor.

'Hm,' said Rune.

'Scuze me,' said Lola, limping up to the table. 'But d'ya wanna sign fer this?'

'What is it?' Rune took the little chitty from the manicured fingers.

'It's yer bill for the champagne wot's juss bin d'livered to yer room.'

'And who ordered this?'

'Well *yew* did, dincha? The waiter said yore little kiddie was waitin' outside yer room, so 'e let 'im in.'

'*What*?' Rune rose to his impressive height and glared upon Thelma and Louise. 'So,' said he. 'All things become clear. Villainy is afoot.'

'Yew wan' me to call security for yer, or somefin?'

'Ah, no,' said Rune hastily. The mental image of the defunct Mr Showstein, now trussed up and stashed in the wardrobe, filled an area of Rune's brain that was not reserved for genius. 'I shall deal with this. *Mr Craik*.'

'*Clunk*!' went Mr Craik's chin on the table, as Rune kicked his chair from under him. And '*Clonk*!' went the back of his head on the floor (cushioned from *CRACK*! by the rich pile of the swirly-whirly carpet tiles).

'Oh my God! Aaaaagh!' Mr Craik awoke with a start. Started up in a fluster and flustered about in a panic. Louise helped him back onto his chair.

'Follow me,' cried Rune, marching from the dining-suite.

'He meant *you*!' agreed Thelma and Louise, as Mr Craik sat wondering which direction panic should now take him.

'Yes, master, coming.' Up and stumble and off.

'Time we were off.' Thelma rose to run.

'Are we just going to leave them to get caught?'

'No, we'll phone up to Rune's room from reception to warn them he's coming.'

'And then?'

'Then we get away. At the hurry-up.'

'I'm with you there.'

'OK, Cornelius. I'm with you now.'

Cornelius made and unmade fists. Flung the made ones up into his hair and beat himself on the top of his head with them. 'What did I say to you, Tuppe? What did I say to you?'

'You said, "It's a trap, don't try to follow me in."'

'And?'

Tuppe looked up at Cornelius. The two stood side by side inside the glass cubical. They were so close to the big stack of money that you would have thought they could just have reached out and touched it.

'But it seemed so simple,' said Tuppe. 'I didn't see how you could have got stuck.'

'What about *now*?'

'Oh yeah, *now* I can see how you got stuck. Clever, isn't it?'

'Ring' went the telephone. 'Ring, ring,' then nothing.

'Three rings,' said Tuppe.

'Oh dear,' said Cornelius. 'Another three coming.'

'Ring, ring, ring,' the telephone replied.

'Rune's on his way!' Tuppe began to flap his hands about. 'We have to get out of here. Do something, Cornelius, do.'

The lift containing Hugo Rune and Stephen Craik rose at a leisurely pace. Pink mirror tiles on the walls and ceiling. Understated. Classy.

Mr Craik jiggled nervously from foot to foot.

'Calm yourself,' said Hugo Rune. 'He that dares to steal from me, does so at extreme peril.'

'Shouldn't you have got some help or something?' mumbled Mr Craik. 'They might be armed.'

'*They*?' asked Rune. 'Not *he*?'

'They, he? I don't know.'

'Oh, but I think you do. It will be my beastly son and his little gnome. Time to teach them both a lesson they won't forget.'

'Whatever do you mean?' Mr Craik really didn't want to know.

'Layabouts and ne'er-do-wells,' said Rune. 'Time they took some regular employment. Settled themselves down to a bit of hard work. And I know just the company to take them on.'

'Come on, Cornelius, come on.'

'I can't come on, Tuppe, if I'd been able to come on I wouldn't have called for your help.'

'This doesn't look very good for us, does it?'

'Not very good at all, no.'

Clunk, click and ding, went the lift. Very much as another in a faraway place had done. And there was the similarity between the lift travellers. The identicality, in fact.

Hugo Rune issued from the lift with a gliding stride and a lot of green tweed. He moved as in slow motion: jowls a-rippling, ponderous, heavy, purposeful.

Deadly.

The room key in his right hand.

A large handgun in his left.

Click of key into lock.

Turn of key.

Turn of handle.

Swing open of door.

Then burst into room. All in slow motion again. The big man dropping down onto one knee, the gun held now in both hands. Two startled faces. One high, one low.

Close up of evil black eyes with hideous white pupils.

Close up of finger pulling trigger.

Bang. Bang. Bang. Bang. Bang. Bang.

Smoke.

Shattered glass.

And two new candidates for employment at The Universal Reincarnation Company.

Rune blew into the barrel of his pistol.

'Gotcha,' he said.

29

'Look on the bright side,' said Jack Bradshaw. 'You may be dead, but at least now you're in regular full-time employment.'

'I'll just charge you my time for working on the car,' said the mechanic to the breathless Thelma. 'There's no parts involved, because I can't find anything physically wrong with it.'

'Physically?' Thelma tore the cheque with the signature she had secretly forged upon it, from the chequebook she had liberated from Mr Craik whilst helping him back onto his chair, and handed it to the mechanic.

'Yeah,' said he. 'Everything's working OK. But there's something odd about this car. You take it back and good luck to you.'

'Thanks,' Thelma pulled Mr Craik's cheque card from the wallet she had also liberated. It had a £500 limit. She handed this to the mechanic. 'Fill in how much you want,' said she.

'Thanks. £500 limit. Exactly right.' The mechanic slipped off into his office to do the dirty deed.

'What now?' Louise asked.

'Drive back to the Grande, sit outside with the engine running, hope the boys have managed to get out.'

'By now they might have got out and gone.'

'Then they'd come here for the car.'

The mechanic returned with keys and card. 'Here you go,' he said.

'If our boyfriends come to pick us up here by mistake,'

said Thelma, 'would you tell them we'll be waiting in the car-park outside the Grande, please.'

'Sure, no sweat. Bye then. And take care.'

'Bye.' Thelma and Louise climbed into the Cadillac and drove away.

The mechanic put on his jacket, locked up his office and went home.

In the forecourt of his garage, the headlights of the expensive cars blinked on and their engines began to growl.

'What is this?' This growl came from the large controller. He stood before the karmascope with the computer screen. His unsavoury eyes flashed along the rows of numbers Claude had punched up onto that screen. A look of terrible rage knotted the corners of his mouth. 'The little red-haired sod. He's escaped. He's shot himself down to Earth. To Murphy!' The large controller rocked back and forwards on his great heels and roared invective towards the black dome of space that spread all around and about.

Behind a nearby chugging flywheel, Old Claude tittered to himself. 'That's only the first of your worries,' he whispered. 'I'm gonna screw you right up, you see if I don't.'

'Don't stand around,' roared Hugo Rune to Mr Craik. 'Gather up everything. Pack my bags. We are leaving at once.'

The fire-alarm bells were ringing again. The smoke from Rune's pistol had set them off.

'Get to it!' roared Rune. 'Don't just stand there like a dithering twat!'

'Yes, sir. At once, sir. But, sir?'

'What?'

'Why did you shoot that empty glass showcase to pieces, sir?'

Cornelius and Tuppe were sitting on the roof.

Cornelius had a serious shake on.

'He'd have killed us.' The tall boy's teeth went chitter-chatter-chitter, much after the fashion of the mummies on the bus.* 'He just burst into the room and shot straight at the cabinet. He'd have killed us. Killed *me*. My own father. He didn't care.'

'He's barking mad.' The teeth of Tuppe offered a castanet accompaniment. 'Did you see his eyes? Black with white pupils. What's that all about?'

Cornelius shook his shaking head. 'Something's very wrong. I could smell it in there when I was searching the place. The room smelled of him, yet it didn't.'

'Strangely I don't follow that.'

'I know the smell of my own father. It was the smell of him, but at the same time it wasn't.'

'There is only *one* Hugo Rune,' said Tuppe. 'And that one wants locking up. Go to the cops, Cornelius. Let them sort it out.'

'What, tell them how we broke into the suite, stole all this money, and were a bit peeved about being shot at while making our escape? And how *did* we make our escape, by the way?'

Tuppe managed a bit of a grin. 'It was all very straightforward. There was no trick involved.'

'Go on, tell me.'

'Well, you will recall how moments after the phone rang it occurred to you that you should use your remarkable sense of smell and sniff our way out?'

* From the classic, '*The Wheels on the Bus go Round and Round*' *and other children's favourites*, various artists (probably including Rod, Jane and Freddie).

'Yes,' said Cornelius. 'And when I suggested this to you, you were already outside the cabinet with all the money.'

'Yep. And then I went back inside and brought you out also.'

'Just tell me how,' said Cornelius.

'Hall of mirrors,' said Tuppe. 'Clever one – revolving panels, one-way mirrors, rotational floor. Clever one, but hall of mirrors all the same.'

'So?'

'Floor,' said Tuppe. 'Everyone knows that the only way to get out of a hall of mirrors is look at the floor and follow your feet. I'm somewhat nearer to the floor than you. Told you it was very straightforward. Dull really. Sorry it wasn't more clever. Thanks for helping me out of the window and up onto the roof while Rune was shooting up the cabinet. Nick-of-time stuff. Cheers.'

'Cheers to you.' Cornelius crammed the last few bundles of money into his now-very-bulging pockets. 'I suppose we'd best away. Fire-alarm's on the go once more. Off down the fire escape and farewell, Mr Rune.'

'Sounds good to me,' said Tuppe. 'What's that?' he added.

'What is what?'

'That there,' Tuppe pointed. High in the clear night sky a tiny point of light was moving. Swiftly.

'Shooting star,' said Cornelius. 'Make a wish, you saw it first.'

'Does that work then?'

'You never know, it's worth a try.'

Tuppe screwed up his face, closed his eyes and made a wish.

'Huh,' said he examining himself. 'Doesn't work.'

The tall boy had no doubt at all as to what his diminutive

202

companion had wished for. 'Probably doesn't work immediately,' he said kindly. 'Takes time.'

'Here, hang about,' said Tuppe.

'What you mean it *is* working, *now*?'

'No I mean hang about. Look at the shooting star.'

'Eh?'

'It's coming this way, Cornelius. It's getting brighter and brighter. It's coming straight at us.'

'Ooooooh!' went Norman. 'My bum's on fire. I'm burning up on re-entry. Brakes. Parachute. Help!'

'It's a comet,' croaked Tuppe. 'It's Shoemaker-Levy 9. I knew it never really hit Jupiter, we're all doomed. It's the end of the world.'

'Abandon roof,' cried Cornelius, gathering up Tuppe and preparing to flee.

'*It's going to hit us*! *IT'S GOING TO HIT US*!'

'Look at that,' said Louise pointing up through the open top. 'Is that a meteor heading for the Grande, or what?'

'I hope it's not some bugger from the Ministry of Defence test-flying my saucer,' said Boris, appearing above the back seat. 'Hello again, girls, neither of you got an aspirin by any chance, I suppose?'

Finding a suitable bit of onomatopoeia to describe a substantial explosion is always difficult. BOOM and KABOOM and all similar counterparts fall a bit short somehow.

James Joyce coined a word in *Finnegans Wake* to mean 'a symbolic thunderclap that represents the fall of Adam and Eve'.

It's a good word.

It's—
BABABADALGHARAGHTAKAMMINARRONN-
KONNBRONNTONNERRONNTUONNTHUNN-
TROVARRHOUNAWNSKAWNTOOHOOHOOR-
DENENTHURNUK.

The sound made by Norman as, in super-heated-
white-hot-soul-stuff mode, he struck the roof of the
Grande Hotel was a bit like this. But not much.

A scream of, '*WHAT A BUMMER*!' accompanied it.

And the world caved in about Murphy and Tuppe.

A pillar of flame rose up into the night sky, topped off
with a rolling mushroom of white smoke. The lads on the
night shift at the fire station were well impressed. They
had been ignoring the automatic alarm call from the
Grande. Not to be caught twice in the one day and all
that. But this was worth a bit of the old pole-sliding-tyre-
screeching-precarious-corner-taking-wrong-way-down-
the-one-way-street-macho-man-big-cock action that
they'd all joined the force for.

Cocoa cups went clatter and girlie mags were cast
aside.

'We've got a *shout*,' cried the gallant lads.

Whoomph! Crash! and Explode! and Burst into flames!
went Rune's suite as slates and laths and roof-timbers and
loft insulation (in the form of many surplus swirly-whirly
carpet tiles) and Cornelius and Tuppe and the cause of
the confusion all descended in a riotous discombobu-
lation.

'Out!' shouted Rune, grabbing Mr Craik by the scruff
of the neck and hoisting him into the corridor.

'Oooooh!' went Cornelius, crashing through the top of
the wardrobe.

'Oooooh!' went Tuppe, joining him.

'Me bum's on fire! Me *all's* on fire!' howled Norman, thrashing about amidst the chaos.

'The whole top floor's going up,' cried Thelma. 'Stay in gear, you stupid car, and stop lurching about like that.'

'Get out of the way. Get out of the way,' yelled a fire-fighter, leaning from his cab and flapping his hands at the cars in front.

The cars in front were weaving all over the road.

The cars in front had no drivers in them.

'Get us out of here, Cornelius.' Tuppe drummed on the inside of the wardrobe door. 'We'll be burned to our deaths.'

'You're all right then, not hurt?'

'Yes I'm fine thanks.'

'Glad to hear it. I'm fine too, in case you were thinking to ask.'

'I wasn't. But I'm glad you are. Get us out. Get us out.'

'Best go out the way we came in, I'll give you a lift up.'

'Thanks, I . . . *Aaaaagh*!' went Tuppe.

'What's happened? What's wrong?'

'There's a dead man in the wardrobe with us, Cornelius. It's Mr Showstein.'

'Oh God!' Cornelius put his shoulder to the wardrobe door and burst out into the flaming hell that had once been the KEV-LYN suite. 'Let's get out of here, come on.'

'I'm with you there. Oh no. Aaaaagh again.'

'What is it now? Come on, we've got to go.'

'There's a kid on fire, Cornelius. We've got to help him.'

Cornelius flapped his hands about amongst the smoke and flames. Alarming cracking sounds issued from the floor beneath him, the curtains roared; the heat was reaching critical.

'There's no-one here but us; you're hallucinating, Tuppe.'

'I'm not. He's right there.'

'Oh, oh, oh,' went Norman, hopping about and patting at his charred overall. 'Oh, oh, oh.'

'Come with us quickly,' called Tuppe.

'Eh? Hello. Are you Cornelius Murphy? Oh, oh, oh.'

'No, I'm Tuppe. Come with us before you get burned alive.'

Crash! and *Whoomph!* went falling timbers. Creak and rock, went the floor.

'Come on, Tuppe,' Cornelius snatched up the small man and made a grab at the door handle.

And the door handle vanished all away.

And then there was only wall.

'Get out of the way,' bawled the fire-fighter. 'Aw shit, what are they doing now? They're backing up. They're going to ram us.'

'Get out of this car,' ordered Hugo Rune aiming his revolver at Thelma.

'We can't get out,' wailed Tuppe. 'We're all gonna die.'

'What's the trouble?' Norman asked.

'The door's vanished,' shouted Tuppe. 'Hugo Rune's magicked it away.'

'Yes I know *that*,' shouted Cornelius.

'I wasn't talking to you, I was talking to this lad.'

'There isn't any lad.'

'Yes there is, he's here. No he's not.'

And Norman wasn't.

* * *

'Drive,' ordered Hugo Rune.

'Yes, sir,' wimped Mr Craik of the very, very, very wild eyes.

'Help!' shouted Cornelius.

Crash went further lumps of flaming roof.

'Help me too!' shouted Tuppe.

'Take the coast road,' ordered Rune. 'And slow down, there's no need to drive so fast.'

'It's not *me* driving fast, it's the car, and it doesn't want to take the coast road.'

'I don't want to die,' blubbered Tuppe, now clinging to a Murphy trouser leg. 'Do something, Cornelius, save us.'

Cornelius clawed at the wall, in search of the vanished door handle.

The flames licked up about them.

And then the floor collapsed.

Peep, Peep, Peep and Honk, went the mad cars, buffeting into the fire-engine.

'Steer this damn car, you fool,' hollered Rune as the Cadillac did a spectacular U-turn on the promenade, scattering the rubber-neckers who were flocking to the Grande.

'There you go,' said Norman, grinning in from the corridor through the now-open doorway. 'It didn't fool me and *I* managed to open it. Here, where have you gone?'

'Down here.' Tuppe still clung to the Murphy trouser leg.

Cornelius was clinging to the door handle.

And swinging wildly about.

Amongst the flames and chaos.

And everything.

'Pull us up,' called Tuppe.

'I'm trying,' called Cornelius.

'I didn't mean *you*, I meant *him*.'

'Don't start that again I . . .'

Norman tugged and Cornelius strained.

And Tuppe clung on.

And flames rushed up from beneath and out through other doorways into the corridor. And chunks of ceiling came down and UPVC windows buckled and exploded.

And the fire-engine shunted mad cars aside and ploughed into the private car-park, causing on-lookers to cheer and hotel guests, some in nought but skimpy night attire, to duck this way and that as mad cars mounted the pavements and growled after the speeding appliance.

Cornelius, Tuppe and Norman scurried down the corridor to the fire-escape, coughing smoke and gasping like good'ns.

Thelma and Louise saw Tuppe and Cornelius emerge from the blazing building and begin their rapid descent of the outside cast-iron fire-escape. They set up a bit of a cheer, but soon took to running from a rogue BMW.

Several floors down now, and relatively safe from the conflagration, Tuppe and Cornelius stopped short to catch their breath.

'Look at that lot,' gasped Tuppe, viewing the mayhem below.

'And look at that.' Cornelius pointed towards the Cadillac, skimming along the promenade road.

'It's Rune,' gagged Tuppe. 'And Boris is in the back.'

'And look at *that*!'

The Cadillac suddenly left the promenade road, banged up onto the pavement and swerved towards the entrance to the east pier.

'Apply the brakes, you oaf!' Rune thumped Mr Craik about the ear.

'I am! I am. Oh God!' The Cadillac mashed into the turnstile, smashing it aside and reducing the little ticket box to mangled matchwood, lurched onto the pier proper and tore along it.

'What's his driver think he's doing?' Tuppe clung once more to the leg of Cornelius.

'I don't think it's his driver. I think it's the car. Oh no!'

The Cadillac had been accelerating like a dragster on a Santa Pod quarter-mile. Which was exactly the length of the east pier.

The record at Santa Pod is 6.7 seconds.

Though who gives a toss who holds it.

The Cadillac was doing well over one hundred and twenty miles an hour by the time it ran out of pier.

There was no way on Earth anyone could have leapt clear and had any hope of living so to tell.

With a terrible rending of metal the Cadillac Eldorado passed through the decorative Victorian railing work and plunged down into the sea.

And cars don't, of course, explode when they hit water.

They sink.

And very fast if they're open-topped and have done the full cartwheel.

Very fast indeed.

*   *   *

Flaming bits and bobs now showered down on the fire-escapees. Fire roared above, cars growled below.

'Let's find the girls,' said Murphy. 'And let's get.'

'So there you have it,' said Jack Bradshaw, who had started earlier and now was finishing. 'What do you think then, mate?'

'I think I'll choose *sprout*,' said the dismal and deceased Mr Showstein. 'But before I commit myself, describe this controller of yours to me once again. He sounds most familiar.'

30

Cornelius Murphy woke, yawned, stretched and then went, 'Aaaaagh!'

Tuppe jumped up from the Land of Nod and went 'Aaaaagh!' too, but then he asked, '*Aaaaagh!* What?'

'*Aaaaagh!* Last night,' Cornelius explained.

'Oh yes. Aaaaagh! to *that* all right.' Tuppe rubbed at his arms and stamped his little feet. 'I'm cold.'

'Me too.' Cornelius raised himself onto his knees and strained morning dew from his hair.

He and Tuppe had slept out rough on the crest of Druid's Tor. And they had not done it alone. Around and about them lay other sleepers and other wakers. The Tor was a regular refugee camp. Thousands of people strewn across it.

And somewhere amongst them, Cornelius hoped, were Thelma and Louise.

It had not been a night of holiday fun-time at Skelington Bay. The mad cars had spread their madness through the parked ranks of their automotive brethren. At a pace. The fire-engine had been amongst the first to succumb. The fire at the Grande had gone unchecked. Much of the town that lay down wind of it was now also smouldering ruination.

Not good.

There had been panic and exodus.

Much panic, but not without some spirited resistance.

Cornelius and Tuppe had been in the thick of that, helping to raise barricades across the roads leading from the stricken town.

The cars had tried to ram these barricades, many destroying themselves in the so-doing. Much flaming wreckage. Mangled scrap. Nice big barricades now.

'This is pretty dire.' Tuppe looked down to the town below. Cars were doing chicken runs along the promenade. They weren't swerving aside at the last moment. 'The meteor did it, you know.'

'Did what?'

'That down there. The cars. There was a Stephen King movie about this meteor and big lorries coming alive.'

'Was Kyle McKintock in that one?' Cornelius asked.

'That's not funny. He was dead in the wardrobe. And Boris is probably dead too.'

'I'm sorry. But it wasn't the meteor. The word going about is that Lola the waitress overheard two scientists talking and it's a secret government germ-warfare project that's got out of control. Apparently the local estate agent invented the virus.'

'That would be the man you saved from being burnt at the stake.'

'Mr Rodway, yes. He did promise to pay me a large sum of money for saving him. But I never saw him again.'

'Perhaps he'll post it to you.'

'Yes, I'm sure he will.'

'Hey wotcha, fellas,' said Norman, ambling up. 'I've been looking everywhere for you.'

'Hello.' Tuppe grinned at the lad in the charred overalls. 'We lost you in all the confusion. Thanks for getting us out of the hotel room.'

'What are you talking about?' asked Cornelius.

'This is the lad who saved us by opening the door, Cornelius. What is the matter with you?'

'There is no lad,' said the Murphy. 'What is the matter with *you*?'

'Eh?' went Tuppe.

'He can't see me.' Norman scratched his ruddy barnet. 'That's not right. It's him I'm supposed to be talking to.'

'About what?'

'What about what?' Cornelius asked.

'I'm not asking you about what, I'm asking the lad about what.'

'It isn't funny, Tuppe. Turn it in.'

'Oh come off it, Cornelius. This is the lad who pulled us out of the burning room, who opened the door. You do remember *that*, don't you?'

'I remember something weird.'

'It was me,' said Norman.

'See?' said Tuppe.

'See what?'

'Oh no!' Tuppe took on deadly whiteshade of the face. 'Stay away from me,' he said.

'Why?' asked Cornelius.

'Not you, *him*.'

'Just stop it, will you?'

'It's in your pocket, get it out.'

'What is?' Norman asked.

'Not you, him.'

'Stop it at once,' ordered Cornelius.

'The newspaper page in your pocket. The one that made you feel strange. The one about the boy's funeral.'

'Oh that.' Cornelius dragged bundles of money from his pockets, unearthed the crumpled news-sheet, handed it to Tuppe.

'It's *you*,' whispered the small man.

'Me?' asked Cornelius.

'Him,' said Tuppe.

Norman gave the news-sheet a perusal. 'Shit, I made the front page. That handbag-humping vicar, he—'

'Then you're—'

'Dead,' said Norman. 'Dead as a dead boy. Sorry.'

213

'Then you're a—'

'Ghost I suppose. It's a real bummer, I can tell you.'

'Stone the Christians.' Tuppe sat down hard on his backside.

'Would you mind not sitting there?' Norman asked. 'That's the very place where I—'

'Aaaaagh!' went Tuppe.

'We did Aaaaagh!' said Cornelius. 'And enough is quite enough.'

'It's him. It's him.' Tuppe jumped up and down. Norman frowned. Tuppe shifted himself and jumped up and down once more.

'Thanks,' said Norman.

'Don't mention it.'

'Don't mention what?'

'Shut up, Cornelius, and listen. He's here, the—'

'Dead boy,' said Norman dismally.

'The dead boy. The one who died up here when his dad fell on top of him. The one here in the newspaper. He's here. I'm looking at him, talking to him. I swear.'

'You don't?'

'I do.' Tuppe crossed his heart and hoped not to become a dead boy. 'I swear as your bestest friend. I am not lying. He's a ghost and his name is—'

'Norman,' said Norman. 'And I'm here to help Cornelius.'

'He says his name is Norman and he's here to help *you*.'

Cornelius viewed his bestest friend. And he viewed the paleness of pallor and the earnestness of expression. 'You're serious, aren't you?' he said.

'I'm not kidding.'

Cornelius now bumped down on his bum.

'Not there please,' said Norman.

'He says, not there please,' said Tuppe.

214

'Eh?'

'That's the exact place where he, you know, er—'

'Aaaaagh!' went Cornelius, leaping up.

'Thanks,' said Norman.

'He says thanks.'

'No problem. Where is he, Tuppe?'

'He's right there.' Tuppe pointed, but Cornelius couldn't see a thing.

'I can't see a thing,' said Cornelius.

'Well he's here, I'm telling you.'

'So what does he want? What is he here to help me with?'

Norman told Tuppe and Tuppe said, 'Stopping Hugo Rune.'

'I think Hugo Rune *has* been stopped. And for all of his badness, he *was* my dad. Which doesn't make me too happy, as it happens.'

Norman spoke some more.

Tuppe said, 'Rune isn't dead.'

'Not dead? He could never have survived that crash into the sea.'

'Norman says that there's more than one Rune. That he cloned himself. How many are there of him, Norman?'

'How *many*?' asked Cornelius. 'What is this?'

'He says there are five, including the one who has taken control of The Universal Reincarnation Company.'

'*What*?'

'I think you'd better explain,' Tuppe told Norman. 'Slowly and precisely. And I will pass it on to Cornelius.'

'Fair enough,' Norman agreed. 'But you'd better tell your friend to sit down. It's a bummer of a tale and he's not going to like it.'

'He says you'd better sit down,' said Tuppe.

'But not *there*,' said Norman.

'But not *there*.'

215

And so it came to pass that Norman did speak unto Tuppe and Tuppe did speak unto Cornelius, saying all that Norman had told him. And Cornelius did drop his jaw and raise his eyebrows to what he was told. Yea verily, thus and so.

Norman told it all. Of the man-powered flight competition and his unfortunate demise. His funeral and his journey to The Universal Reincarnation Company. Of the static souls that encircled the sun and how God had put the bollocks on the outside, closed down Hell and built Heaven far too small. Of Norman's going through the filing cabinets and of the terrible disclosure that most, if not everyone, were destined to die next Friday at midnight from an electrical discharge. Of his capture by the large controller. And his meeting the real controller and all that the real controller had told him about Rune being preincarnated as himself on his original birthdate again and again. And there being five Runes, one of which was now controlling the URC.

And he spoke of the airship *Pinocchio* and the big sky nozzles and how Claude had shot him to Earth. And how something hadn't gone altogether right and he'd nearly burned up on re-entry. And how he was sorry for burning down the Skelington Bay Grande.

And everything.

'And he says, that's everything,' said Tuppe in a very small voice.

Cornelius shook his head in awe and vanished 'neath his locks.

'Big hair,' said Norman approvingly.

'I'm gobsmacked,' said Cornelius, seeking out his face. 'This is all very much *too* much. But then it makes some kind of sense. Remember when I told you that I smelt my father in the hotel room, but at the same time I didn't?'

'Strangely I don't follow that,' said Norman.

'That's what I said,' said Tuppe.

'No, it's what *I* said.' Cornelius rolled his eyes. 'But that must be it. The Rune in the hotel room wasn't the real Rune. Not my father, but one of his clones. My father's something of a nutter, I grant you, but he's not the stuff of genuine baddy-dom. Killing off the world's population isn't his game. I'm sure that must be it.'

'Could be.' Norman shrugged.

'He said it could be,' said Tuppe. 'And he shrugged when he said it.'

'Incredible. Hey, hello.'

'Hey hello?'

'Hey, hello, it's Thelma and Louise.'

'Well, hey hello to that.'

The two young women came smiling and waving. Steering their shoes between the sleepers and the wakers.

'Is this Woodstock?' Thelma asked. 'What time does Hendrix come on?'

'You OK?' Louise asked Tuppe.

'We're fine. Are you both fine?'

'We're fine.'

'Well, isn't that fine.'

'It's fine. Who's your friend?' Thelma reached to tousle Norman's hairdo. Her hand passed straight through his head.

'Aaaaagh!' went Thelma.

'We did Aaaaagh,' said Cornelius.

'But I, he—'

'He's a dead boy,' said Tuppe. 'And his name is Norman.'

'He's a *what*?'

'He has returned from beyond the grave to help Cornelius prevent Hugo Rune from wiping out the world next Friday.'

Thelma shook her golden head and stared at her

fingers. 'Things are never dull around you blokes, are they?'

They all sat down (being careful where they sat) and spoke of this and that thing and the other.

Having been introduced, Norman told Thelma and Louise everything he had just told Tuppe. Looking on, Cornelius was appalled to observe that both Thelma and Louise could see and hear the red-haired dead boy in the charred overalls.

Thelma then told her all regarding the conversation she and Louise had overheard between Rune and 'Chunky' Wilberforce, about pylons and cables and radio masts.

Cornelius chipped in with an inventory of pre-fire hotel-room contents, the maps and the printouts and the calculations and the books on electrostatics and electroplating.

And Tuppe told a story about how his father had once met Judy Garland in a London hotel and helped to put her to bed.

Norman said that this was a most interesting tale, but probably not very relevant. 'Ask Cornelius to tell us about those calculations he saw,' he told Tuppe.

Tuppe did so.

'Oh the figures,' Cornelius thought about this. 'They were to do with cubic miles and units of $93,000,000.'

'Then I know what he's up to,' said Norman. 'We did it in science with that moron Mr Bailey. It's to do with the sea. Every cubic mile of sea water contains $93,000,000 worth of gold.'

'It never does,' said Tuppe.

'It does too.'*

* It does *too*.

218

Tuppe passed this intelligence to Cornelius.

'It never does,' said the tall boy.

'Apparently it does,' said Tuppe. 'With footnotes attesting to the fact.'

'Gold from the sea?' Cornelius gave that some thought. 'But surely it can't be done. If it could be done someone would have done it by now.'

'There's nothing that can't be done,' said Norman. 'Only things that have not been done *yet*.'

'Did you get that out of a Christmas cracker?' Thelma asked.

'Yes,' said Norman. 'But think about it, it all fits together. The books Cornelius saw about electrostatics and electroplating.'

Tuppe passed this on to Cornelius.

'Go on,' said he.

'Electroplating,' said Norman. 'We did that in science. You put two electrodes into an electrolyte, a saline solution of something, and pass a current through them.'

'Yes,' said Tuppe, 'but if you wanted to draw the gold out of the sea that way you'd need a pretty monstrous pair of electrodes.'

'You would,' said Norman. 'And Cornelius saw them coloured in on the maps like he just told us. It's the twin piers.'

'The piers?'

'The piers?' Cornelius asked.

'The piers,' said Norman, pleased as a dead boy could be pleased. 'If you electrified the piers, passed a massive current through these, it might just work.'

'It wouldn't,' said Tuppe. 'The sea's too big, it would short out your power supply.'

'I'm following this from what I can hear of it,' said Cornelius. 'And there was a computer printout in Rune's room about the National Grid, and it had something like "NOT ENOUGH POWER" scrawled across the bottom.'

'But it has to be it,' said Norman. 'The deadly electrical discharge, this has to be what Rune plans to do.'

'Well, I can't see where he'd get all the energy from,' said Tuppe. 'There wouldn't be enough electrical power on Earth, he'd have to get it from somewhere else.'

'Somewhere else.' Norman ran his fingers through his Beatle cut and chewed at his bottom lip. And then he had the mother of all mental flashes. It was of billions of souls encircling the sun. Each of which was in itself an immensely powerful electrically charged particle. A particle that could be manipulated by Rune's controller *doppelgänger* with his big sky nozzles. A particle that could be wiped out for ever and ever. Used up. Snuffed out in the cause of electrical discharge.

'Oh shit!' said Norman.

'I heard that,' said Cornelius.

31

'God's teeth!' spat Hugo Rune. 'What am I doing dead? What am I doing *here*?'

The large controller stared his unliving double eye to eye. 'You're all wet,' he observed.

'You get wet when you drown. Go somewhat bonkers also. I swear that at the moment of my death I saw sheep go swimming by.'

'Perhaps it was a ship sailing by.'

'It was nothing of the sort. But I shouldn't be here. I should be being born again as myself on my original birthday. Why have you brought me up here?'

'I wished to warn you,' said the large controller. 'We have had something of a "situation" up here. As you are well aware, the success of our operation here depends on nothing ever getting done. As long as we only employ loafers, who sit around all day squeezing their spots and testing the aerodynamics of paper darts, then you and I and the other three of us are free to go on undetected, growing ever in power, until we control all.'

'This is the purpose of the exercise, yes. Absolute control of absolutely everything.'

'Well, we have come slightly unstuck,' said the large controller. 'An oaf Jack Bradshaw took on found out a good deal more than he should and has absconded with his knowledge.'

'How?' Rune asked. 'And to where?'

'Shot himself back to Earth from one of the big sky nozzles. And according to the readout on the screen, straight to our son Cornelius.'

'Shot *himself* back?'

The two Runes looked at each other.

'Buttocks,' they said.

'I will deal with Mr Buttocks,' said the large controller. 'But now we must return you to your former self on your original birthday. Conduct our affairs with a little more care next time.'

'Have no fear of that. You may expect our son's file to vanish into nothing. I shall be practising safe sex with his mother next time around.'

'Excellent, then we will continue as before. Kindly squeeze yourself into this little bullet affair and I'll blast you back into the past.'

'Rune does not squeeze himself into anything. Launch me from one of the other big sky nozzles.'

'None of the others actually works,' said the large controller. 'It's squeeze into this one or nothing, I'm afraid.'

'Outrageous.'

'But nevertheless so. Come now and I'll help ram you in.'

'Preposterous.'

But it had to be so. And with struggling and straining and effing and blinding it was finally, outrageously, preposterously so.

'Grmmph mmph bmmph,' went the Rune in the bullet-shaped affair.

'I've preprogrammed you,' said the large controller. 'I have but to push the button, so I shall.'

And so he did.

There was the necessary Whoomph!, the gush of flame and Rune was on his way.

Back on Earth and many years before, Hugo Rune awoke. He yawned and smacked his lips together. New born and eager for the nipple.

But where had the nursery ceiling gone? He appeared to be out in the open air and moving along a pace. A ride in the pram, perhaps, with dearest nanny? That was surely it.

But it wasn't. Rune became aware of a heaving and squirming against him. A most acrid stench hung over all.

Rune made to cry out 'What is this?' but found to his alarm that he was speechless. His mouth seeming no more than a rudimentary slit. He tried to strike out at the vile objects heaving around him, but discovered to his further alarm, and with a good deal of growing horror, that he possessed neither arms nor legs.

Something huge beyond proportion blotted out the sky, came down upon him, lifted him high. He saw a face. A human face, but vast, the size of a house. It was grinning. And he could see the hand that held him. Held *him*? Rune? The most amazing man who ever lived?

'Here's a real nice fat one,' said the human face. A boy's face. A grinning boy's face. His *own* face. 'Give us a number-nine hook and we'll bait it up with him.'

'*No!*' Rune wriggled and squirmed.

'He's a lively one,' said the young Hugo Rune. Six years old. The squirming Rune recalled the fishing trip. He recalled the maggot tin.

'*There's been a terrible mistake!*' screamed squirming Rune, but silently.

And then the hook went in.

'Good luck, Hugo,' said the large controller striding away towards the lift.

'He he he,' Old Claude popped his head up from behind the bullet-packing end of the big sky nozzle. 'You may have preprogrammed the bastard, you bastard, but *I* shifted a few digits about when your back was turned. One down and four to go, I reckon.'

And Claude danced a merry little dance.

The most amazing man who ever lived sank deeply into the perfumed waters of his marble bath-tub and sought once more to compose the final equation in his formula for the universal panacea and elixir of life.

And he would have done it too . . .

But for . . .

'Get out of that bedroom and do some work, you lazy good-for-nothing, or I'll have my husband bash down the door!'

The most amazing man awoke with a start.

To find a ticket inspector smiling down at him.

'So sorry to awaken you, Mr Rune, but I wonder if I might punch your ticket.'

'Where is my manservant Rizla?' this new Rune asked.

'Breakfasting in the first-class dining-car, sir.'

'I shall have to put my own hand into my pocket then.' Rune did so and fished out his first-class first-class ticket.

'First class,' said the inspector, clipping it.

'When do we arrive at Skelington Bay?' Rune enquired, returning his ticket to his poodle-skin ticket case (a present from Zsa Zsa Gabor),* and slipping this into the inner pocket of his green tweed suit.

'This train terminates at Bramfield Halt, sir. Skelington Bay is under some kind of quarantine.'

'But I might engage the services of a hackney carriage to convey me there.'

'They won't let you through the road blocks, sir, the population has been evacuated.'

* Allegedly.

224

'I am here on Downing Street business,' said Rune. 'To complete a task begun by my, er, *twin brother*. They will let *me* through.'

'As you will then, sir. I'll have a cab summoned for you as soon as we arrive.'

'Have my manservant awaken me then. Farewell.'

'Farewell, sir.'

'Well, we've not said farewell to Rune,' said Norman. 'Like I told you there're five separate versions of him in circulation, another will probably be on its way here now to replace the one that went off the pier.'

'Then *he* must be stopped,' said Cornelius. 'If he's allowed to go ahead with this he'll not only kill off everybody who's alive, he'll kill off the souls of all the dead people too.'

'That's definitely a first for anyone,' said Tuppe. 'I'm glad you can hear Norman now, Cornelius, it's so much more convenient, isn't it?'

'Ahem,' said the tall boy.

'But I don't understand why everyone will die,' said Louise.

'Electrical discharge,' said Norman. 'Rune will electrify the entire ocean. That's two thirds of the world, he'll short out the whole planet.'

'Yes, but then he'll die too.'

'Perhaps he doesn't know that,' said Tuppe.

'Perhaps if he was told,' said Cornelius. 'If I could find the right Rune. My genuine father.'

Norman shook his head. 'I don't think he'd give a damn. Remember the controller at the URC is Rune too and from what I gleaned from Jack Bradshaw, preincarnation is a secret that even God doesn't know about.'

'So what are you suggesting?'

'It's only a thought,' said Norman, 'but I reckon that Hugo Rune might be planning to overthrow God.'

'*What*?' The Murphy head went up, the Murphy hair came down.

'Well, I said it was only a thought.'

'It's a terribly bad one!'

'I agree, but the real controller told me that he thinks Rune is the very Devil himself. After all, Hell did get closed down, so what happened to all the demons and stuff? Made redundant? I don't know.'

'Does this make me Son of Satan?' Cornelius enquired. 'Should I look for a triple-six birthmark on my bonce, or something?'

'Like I said, it's only a thought.'

Cornelius climbed to his feet. 'We must act, we have enough time.'

'You must kill off all the Runes,' said Norman. 'Your dad too.'

'Get real,' said Cornelius. 'Would you kill *your* dad?'

Norman shrugged. 'Well, he killed *me*.'

'Sorry,' said Cornelius.

'I know a way,' said Tuppe.

'Oh good,' said Cornelius. 'Then I am prepared to hear it now, before I try some other way and you tell me it's not the way you would have done it.'

'Blow up the piers,' said Tuppe. 'No piers, no electrodes. No electrodes, no electrical dischargings. No patricide required. There you go.'

Bit of a silence.

'You genius,' said Norman.

'Thanks,' said Tuppe.

'It is very good,' Cornelius agreed. 'But where would you get the explosives from?'

'I know a place,' said Norman. 'I got some wire

coathangers from there a little while back. But what is that terrible noise?'

And a terrible noise it was.

Of roaring engines and bellowing loud hailers.

'It's the cars,' howled Tuppe. 'They've broken through the barricades.'

'It's not the cars,' said Cornelius, gazing over the heads of many thousands who were now leaping to their feet. 'It's military vehicles, coming along the road from London. A whole convoy.'

'Nice one,' said Tuppe. 'I was going to mention the difficulties we might encounter with the cars when we tried to blow up the piers, but I didn't want to go complicating the issue.'

'Or spoil your applause,' Norman suggested.

'Yeah well,' said Tuppe. 'But the Army will soon sort the cars out. Hoorah for the soldier boys.'

'*Attention. Attention,*' went the loud hailers atop the beefy half-tracks and armoured personnel carriers. '*This area is now under martial law.*

'*Please gather up your personal possessions and prepare to be evacuated for your own safety at once. This is an emergency situation and we are empowered to employ necessary force. Anyone attempting to remain behind on this hill, or re-enter the town will be considered a looter and shot. It's nothing personal, you understand.*'

'Bummer, bummer, bummer,' said Norman.

'Never say die,' said Cornelius. 'No offence meant. But we'll find a way to sneak back in. We've enough time. It will take more than a few soldiers at roadblocks to stop me.'

'That's him,' yelled a voice, near at hand.

Cornelius turned.

'Yeah, that's definitely him,' said another voice.

Two men were approaching in the company of many policemen.

The first man was unknown to Cornelius, the second looked vaguely familiar.

'Sorry, do I know you?' Cornelius asked.

'You bloody should!' screamed the first man. Medium height, gone somewhat to seed in middle age. Appalling 'golfing' sweater and slacks of a man-made fibre. All over smoke-blackened in appearance. 'My name is Kevin and you burned down my bloody hotel!'

'I did no such thing.' Cornelius now found himself ringed around by policemen. 'You have the wrong man.'

'No I don't, my wife and I saw you. On the roof, setting a bomb or something, then running out of the fire-exit. That little bloke was with you too.'

'You must be confusing us with someone else,' Tuppe suggested. 'Easily done.'

The second man was shaking and fuming. Cornelius noticed that his jacket lacked for a sleeve. Also that he wore what appeared at first glance to be a Rolex watch on his wrist. 'It's you. It's you,' he went.

'Do I know *you*?' Cornelius asked.

'He's my brother,' said Kevin.

'Pleased to meet you,' said Cornelius.

'You stole my car!' screamed Kevin's brother. 'Top of the range, that car. What have you done with it?'

Above the roaring of military vehicles and the bellowing of the loud hailers and the shrieking of people who now found themselves being *evacuated for their own safety* at gunpoint, the sound made by the bogus Rolex-wearer's car as it chicken-ran itself into a Volkswagen on the prom and exploded could not be heard at all.

'I can explain everything,' said Cornelius.

'What about this?' asked an officer of the law, displaying a newspaper.

Cornelius gave the front page a bit of a squint.

It was the front page of *The Brentford Mercury*.
It read:

JAIL BREAK
GALLANT POLICE OFFICERS INJURED AS
CONVICTED CRIMINAL IN £23,000,000
SCAM ESCAPES FROM CUSTODY
EXCLUSIVE BY STAR REPORTER SCOOP MOLLOY

'Nice one, Scoop,' said Cornelius. 'Thanks a lot.'

The police officer grinned. He had a tooth missing. He also had a black eye. 'Remember me?' he asked. 'From Brentford County Court?'

'Beam me up, Scotty,' said Cornelius Murphy.

Thelma and Louise, who had considered it prudent to slip away on the approach of so many policemen, looked on as Cornelius and Tuppe were led away to God knows where.

'Now that's what I call a bummer,' Norman said.

'They'll get free,' Thelma told the dead boy. 'We still have plenty of time.'

High in the cab of the leading military vehicle, a half-track of French design, English construction and sometime Iraqi ownership, sat three men. One was clad in full khaki kit, the beret of a Desert Rat perched on his red-faced head. Another was all in green tweed and commanded more than his fair share of seat. The remaining wore the remnants of a double-breasted suit and showed signs of extensive tar and feathering.

'Splendidly achieved, Chunky,' said Green-Tweeder to Red-Face. 'And my thanks for picking me up from Bramfield Halt.'

'Watched all the lunacy on the go last night from my billet at the kinky vicar's,' said Chunky Wilberforce.

229

'Presumed you were at the back of it, so phoned up the chaps at the old eco-friendly reclamation centre and had them hot-foot it over here to get the ball rolling. But what were you doing at Bramfield Halt, anyway?'

'Never mind,' said Rune.* 'And we have *you* to thank for all this, do we, Mr Rodway?'

'Er, well, I . . .' The estate agent shook a puzzled tar-spattered head. 'I suppose you do, yes.'

'And in your modesty you were making away from the town on foot, carrying nothing but that big bulging suitcase, when I spotted you and had Chunky stop to pick you up.'

'Er, well, I . . .' went Mr Rodway once more.

'Lucky that we did eh?' said Rune.

'Er, hm . . .' said Mr Rodway.

'I am pleased,' said Rune. 'Most pleased, the town cleared well ahead of schedule. I think we can bring forward the deadline. What say you, Chunky?'

'Got all the pylons you need round here,' agreed the old soldier. 'In the *restricted* zone. Have 'em sawed down for you tonight, if you wish. Get 'em up and in place by tomorrow.'

'Splendid, splendid, splendid,' said Rune, clapping his mighty hands together. 'Then I shall reschedule. Midnight tomorrow night. Quite splendid.'

And up, or wherever, at The Universal Reincarnation Company, had anyone now chosen to pull out a cabinet

* In the unlikely event that any confusion should exist as to the precise identity of this particular Rune, this Rune is the Rune who came in on the train to replace the Rune who got killed in the Cadillac and pre-incarnated as a maggot to get killed by his six-year-old self. So it's not the same Rune that Chunky dined with the previous night. Although Chunky doesn't know this. And why should he, eh?

drawer and examine the files within, that anyone would have been most surprised to observe that the expiry dates on the lives of all those listed within was no longer calculated at midnight Friday next. It was now midnight tomorrow night.

Quite *un*-splendid really.

32

Old Claude tinkered merrily away with the Karmascope affair attached to the single working big sky nozzle. He had been most pleased by the sudden appearance of the drenched Mr Rune and had attributed this sudden appearance to immediate success on the part of young Norman.

'You just keep sending the bastards up, sonny,' crowed Old Claude.

'And I'll keep sending them down as maggots, we'll soon get the job jobbed. And then I'll fix the bastard up here. You see if I don't.'

The bastard-up-here had now drawn the bolts on the unappealing door to the abandoned lift shaft. He fanned his nose against the fetor that rose from within. 'Claude,' he called. 'Dear Claude, are you down there?'

His voice echo-echoed. No reply echoed back.

'I've come to set you free,' called the large controller. 'Just say the word and I'll lower a rope.'

Echo-echo, but still no reply.

'He's got out, hasn't he?' said Jack Bradshaw.

'It is a very strong possibility, but we must make sure.'

'Do you want me to get a volunteer to go down then, sir?'

The large controller stared at Jack.

And Jack stared back at the large controller.

'Oh no,' said Jack. 'Leave me out please.'

'All in a good cause,' said the large one, snatching Jack

by the collar and hefting him through the open doorway. 'Let me know what you find.'

'Aaaaagh!' went Jack Bradshaw, heading on down.

'Aaaaagh!' went Tuppe. 'Stop hitting me with that truncheon.'

'Sorry,' replied the policeman. 'My hand slipped, I aimed at your mate.'

'Oh, that's all right then.'

'No it isn't,' Cornelius levelled a foot at the constable's kneecap.

'Ouch,' said the constable, welting the tall boy on the head.

'Ouch too,' said Cornelius.

'That's enough now,' said a superior officer (superior to what eh?). 'Shut the cell door on these two villains and let's go up to the canteen for a cup of tea.'

'Could you send down one with two sugars?' Tuppe asked.

'And some aspirins?' said Cornelius.

Slam went the cell door.

Clunk and click, the key in the lock.

Tuppe slumped down on his bottom on the floor.

Cornelius slumped down beside him.

'I'm hungry,' said Tuppe. 'We haven't had breakfast.'

'As soon as I get us out of here we'll have some.'

'Ever the optimist, you will be paying for it, with *what*?'

'Ah,' said Cornelius.

'Ah indeed,' said Tuppe. 'Trying to bribe the superior officer with all your money didn't seem to work too well, did it?'

'Easy come, easy go?' Cornelius suggested. 'Exactly where are we now, anyway?'

'Bramfield,' said Tuppe. 'Delightful little country village, five miles north of Skelington Bay. I saw the road sign while we were coming up in the police van. You had your head down, policemen were striking it with sticks, I recall.'

'Ah,' said Cornelius. 'Well delightful as it may be, I think we should be leaving it. So if you'd like to favour me with the way *you'd* do it, we'll up and out, OK?'

'I thought you'd never ask,' said Tuppe.

'*I must ask you to keep moving on,*' bellowed the loud hailer atop a military vehicle of dubious origin. '*Single file along the lanes, please. You will soon be at Bramfield where food, drink and shelter will be provided.*'

'This is inhuman.' Thelma drummed her fists on the vehicle's armoured side. 'You're driving women and children along like cattle. It's a violation of human rights. The court at Strasburg will hear about this.'

The steely snout of a machine pistol appeared through a gun port and fixed its aim on a point between Thelma's eyes. 'Just keep moving, you,' barked a voice from within.

'Leave it,' said Louise. 'You can't argue with a man who has a gun for a dick.'

Thelma spat onto the vehicle as it drove on, issuing orders through its loud hailer. She was very upset about all this.

Hugo Rune was far from upset. He sat in the lead car of the half a convoy that was not evacuating people for their own safety. His half comprised big bulldozers to the number four and superannuated, though still service-able, Sherman tanks to the number three. And his own vehicle, which made, er, eight altogether.

'About these cars on the rampage, Rune?' blustered Chunky Wilberforce. 'All very successful in clearing the town, I grant you, but how do you switch the buggers off?'

'Mr Rodway?' asked Hugo Rune. 'Your thoughts on this please.'

Mr Rodway shrugged and made a foolish grinning face. 'Wait until they run out of petrol?' he suggested.

'Sound enough thinking,' said Rune. 'But if, as you have told us, this is some infectious automotive disease, we should not wish our own wheeled conveyances to come down with the sickness.'

Mr Rodway glanced out of the slatted armoured window. 'I'll bet those tanks you have there could make a real mess of them,' he said, with no small degree of malice in his voice.

Chunky looked at Rune.

And Runc looked at Chunky.

'Gung ho, Chunky,' said Hugo Rune.

'Hello-ho,' echoed the voice of the large controller. 'What news there, Mr Bradshaw?'

'You bastard,' muttered Jack Bradshaw, which echoed quite well back up the shaft.

'Pardon?' enquired the large controller.

'The *bastard* isn't here,' called Jack. 'There's what looks like some kind of hot-air balloon down here. He must have escaped in it. Throw down a rope and hoist me out.'

'Don't seem to have one on me at the moment, Jack.' The large controller slammed shut the nasty door and secured the bolts.

'You bastard,' shrieked Jack Bradshaw. 'Let me out of here, you bastard!'

'Let me out of here,' cried Cornelius Murphy. 'Let me out, I say.' He turned back to Tuppe. 'Is that all right for you?'

'That's fine,' said Tuppe. 'The more you cry out in a

police cell, the more you'll be ignored. Just keep shouting and I'll get on with getting us out.'

'I'm innocent!' cried Cornelius. 'Let me out! Let me out!'

'Let me out!' raged Jack Bradshaw, but the large controller didn't hear him. The large controller was now back in his office. It was a palatial office. It had the lush, pile carpeting. It had that marble bath-tub. It had a wall safe.

The large controller turned the combination lock of this. 'Interference all round,' said he, in a large voice. 'Time to put a stop to all this, I think.' He opened the safe door. He crossed to his great big desk, pulled open a drawer and took out a pair of padded gloves.

He put on these padded gloves.

He returned to the wall safe.

He delved into the wall safe.

He drew out a square, black box.

It was a very very cold, square, black box. That sort of whispery white mist that rises from chest freezers rose from it. A horrid smell too.

'Hello, boys,' said the large controller, stroking the lid of the box. 'It's been a long time, hasn't it? And the big G did think you'd all been disposed of when He closed Hell down, didn't He? But I've looked after you here and now it's time to release you from your confinement and get you on the go once more.'

Murmer, murmer and evil growl, went the contents of the cold, black box.

'My sentiments entirely,' whispered the large controller. 'We enjoyed ourselves while we were running Hell, and we will enjoy ourselves again. When you and I, and the other Is that are me, are running everything. Oh what jolly good times we will have. But for now there is something you must do. My brother is proceeding with

236

his plan to take absolute control of Earth, but there's a little fly or two in the ointment and you must seek them out and wipe them out. As horribly as you please, of course. After all, you've waited oh so long, haven't you?'

Darkly growl and murmer.

'Yes, you *have*. Well, no longer. I will instruct you on who you must seek and destroy. The rest is up to you. Just get it done and quickly, you know what I mean?'

'Aw shit!' whispered Old Claude who was skulking outside the door. 'I know *just* what you mean.'

'I should have stayed with Cornelius,' said Norman to Louise. 'You know what I mean? But I went skulking off as soon as I saw those policemen. What is it about the arrival of policemen that makes you feel guilty even when you aren't?'

'Their helmets,' said Louise.

'Oh,' said Norman.

'I think we should be doing some more skulking off right now,' said Thelma. 'That's Bramfield up ahead and it looks like they've erected some kind of compound to march everyone into. I'm not having that. They'll be tattooing our wrists next; this is really all very wrong.'

'We need to get back to Skelington Bay,' said Norman. 'And we need Cornelius and his pal with us.'

'Any ideas?' Thelma asked.

'Of course,' said Norman. 'Plenty.'

'Tuppe, I'm banjoed,' said Cornelius. 'I've done plenty of screaming for help, I've been ignored aplenty and now I'm banjoed. Tuppe? Where are you Tuppe?'

'Where do you think you're off to?' asked the driver of the final Jeep in the military convoy that was chivvying along the refugee column, swerving to a halt.

'I have to take a leak behind the hedge,' said Thelma. 'Do you want to watch, or what?'

'Not really my thing,' said the driver. 'What about you, Clive?' he asked his companion.

'Oh yeah, I love all that, I'll go and watch.'

'Clive will watch,' said the driver. 'I'll wait here in the Jeep.'

'Fine,' said Thelma, clambering through a hole in the roadside hedge, closely followed by Clive.

'Do you need a wee-wee too?' the driver asked Louise.

'No, I went before I came out. That's a really sharp uniform you have there. What rank is that?'

'Oh it's not really any rank at all, I bought it from a militaria shop in Brighton. It's a genuine Second World War uniform not a fake.'

'It really suits you,' said Louise. 'I get really turned on by men in uniform.'

'Really?'

'Oh yeah,' Louise climbed into the Jeep beside the driver and began to tinker with his trouserwear.

'Golly,' said the driver.

'Yeah,' said Clive, the other side of the hedge. 'I'm into all kinds of stuff other than urolagnia. I'm an amorist, you see. I enjoy anililagnia, cataglottism, any form of deupareunia, cypripareunia—'

'Emeronaria?' Thelma asked.

'Yeah, when I'm on my own. But endytolagnia, frotteurism, lots of matutolagnia, neanirosis, sarmassotion—'

'Tachorgasmia?' Thelma asked.

'Yeah, but I prefer synorgasmia.'

'Who doesn't?'

'Yeah, right. You're a bit of a spheropygian, aren't you?'

Thelma headbutted Clive in the face and knocked him unconscious. 'You're a bit of a prat,' said she.

'Would you object if I asked to sniff your instep?' enquired the driver. 'Your shoes look ever so tight and I'm really into podoalgolagnia.'

'I'd be thrilled,' said Louise.

The driver's head went down.

Louise's knee came up.

'I think we now have use of a Jeep,' said Louise, as Thelma made her lone reappearance through the hole in the hedge. 'Where is Norman?'

'I'm back,' said Norman. 'All went according to my plan I see. Cornelius is in a police cell up ahead. I suggest we whip over there and pick him up.'

'Just like that?'

'No, we'll give him a few minutes, Tuppe appears to be "on the case" as it were. But I have a very funny feeling, as if something terribly bad is about to happen.'

'That's encouraging,' said Thelma.

'It's quite oppressive,' said Norman. 'Can't you feel it too?'

'No,' said Thelma.

'Perhaps,' Louise shivered. 'Is it getting suddenly cold, or what?'

'Or what!' said Thelma. 'Look at that.'

Dark clouds were beginning to roll across the sun-lit sky. A storm was brewing up from nowhere.

Ahead, the refugees got their heads down and hastened their pace. To where? Who knew?

'I don't like it,' said Norman. 'It's something bad.'

'Summer storm,' said Thelma, dumping the unconscious driver onto the roadside and climbing into the Jeep.

'No, it's something more than that.' Norman was in the back of the Jeep now. 'Let's get going.'

'As you wish.' Thelma revved the engine. 'Across country?' she asked.

'That's what Jeeps are for.'

And across country they now went.

'Let's go,' said Tuppe, straining open the cell door.

'How *did* you do that?' Cornelius asked.

'Boring solution yet again I'm afraid. I squeezed through the bars of the cell window and crept back into the police station and nicked the keys.'

'There really is something to be said for your boring solutions,' said Cornelius. 'They do seem to get the job done.'

'Let's away quick,' said Tuppe. 'Looks like a thunderstorm's coming.'

Crackle, crackle, went bolts of lightning.

But they weren't bolts of lightning.

'Ha ha! Ha ha!' went unsavoury demonic things, bucketing down to Earth.

'Let's run like shit,' advised Tuppe.

'What's going on out there?' asked the policemen in the canteen, springing to those oversized feet that all policemen have.

'Up this way,' called Norman. 'Knock right through that fence, I know the short cut.'

'Rock 'n' roll,' cried Thelma, steering through the fence.

Cornelius streaked past the reception desk of the police station with Tuppe under his arm and out into the village high street.

'Hang about,' called the duty sergeant. 'You can't do that. Alert, Alert!' He pushed a sort of ALERT PANIC BUTTON.

Bells began to ring.

240

'Ha ha! Ha ha!' went further demonic nasty things, bumping and careering into the high street.

'Urgh!' went Cornelius, drawing to a sudden halt. 'I don't like the look of those.'

'Halt in the name of the law!' cried various policemen, issuing from the police station.

'Run,' hollered Tuppe. 'Just run and run.'

'I'm running.' And the tall boy ran.

'Get him. Get him!' Demonic things, all black as tread and vile as a septic tank came bowling and tumbling up the high street.

'Back to the canteen, lads,' advised the superior policeman.

'Run,' instructed Tuppe. 'This would be the best thing, believe you me.'

'I'm still running.'

Black and horrid, on they came. Many and plenteous. All very bad. Dark clouds rolled across the sky. Thunder roared and lightning zigger-zagged.

'Bit of a turn in the weather,' said Tuppe. 'And I was hoping to get a tan going.'

'Oh damn!' Something hideous slammed down before them. Cornelius ducked around it, ran on.

The things came bounding after him, some on two legs, others on four. Others on six or eight.

Cornelius skidded to a halt.

'What?' asked Tuppe.

'Surrounded,' said Cornelius. 'There's some of whatever they are up ahead. And many behind.'

'Not good,' said Tuppe. 'Not good.'

'Any ideas?' Cornelius asked.

'None springs immediately to mind.'

'Then things don't look too promising.'

'Close your eyes and pray,' said Tuppe. 'There's an idea for you.'

'I think we could do with something a little more radical.'

'Better make it quick then.'

Things were closing around them. They carried with them their own darkness. It came in little dark blots, like Hell's Angels picnicking on a beach. Very worrying. Very dangerous. Very *very* bad.

These things smelled bad.

They *were* bad.

'I've run out of places to run,' said Cornelius.

'Go for places to hide,' advised Tuppe.

'There aren't any.'

And there weren't.

'Help!' cried Tuppe, as black things closed in about him and Cornelius. 'We're not supposed to end like this. Help! *Help*! *HELP*!'

33

An explosion rocked the high street, rending Tarmac towards the sky and casting paving slabs through plate-glass windows.

Shells whistled down to wreak havoc amongst the screaming, growling things that raged beyond control.

But sadly not in Bramfield.

'Renault Five at four o'clock,' bawled Chunky Wilber-force.

'I read you, Chunky.' Rune despatched a heat-seeker from the turret of his tank. The Reverend Cheesefoot's Renault took it in the boot. But not like a man.

'It's raining handbags,' Chunky observed.

But they were making steady progress. A two-man taskforce. Just like the old days for Hugo Rune VC, DSO, DSM, last man out of 'Nam and first man in at Goose Green. Though not, perhaps, for the Brig.

Chunky's military career had been forged from a different metal. During 'the second lot' he had taken command of the Army School of Art and Design's mobile camera obscura division.

This division catered to soldiers who, although keen on the uniform, 'had a thing about not getting their finger-nails all dirty from handling guns', and wished to pursue a career in battlefield art.

They worked within armoured personnel carriers, each of which had been gutted of their weaponry to provide comfortable seating for two artists with sketch pads and carried sufficient rations of paints, linseed oil and turpen-tine to remain in the field for two weeks without re-supply.

The Brigadier later went on to greater glory when he volunteered to lead the Army School of Window Dressing's armoured display window and mannequin trailer into Berlin. When under intense sniper fire he and his company, armed with little more than fifty yards of taffeta, one thousand dressmaking pins and a cardboard box full of price tags, dressed no less than twenty-three shop windows amongst the smoking rubble of the city, to raise the morale of the Allies as they marched in.

But as ABC once said, 'That was then and this is now.'

'XR GTI at twelve o'clock,' bawled Rune.

'Boom,' went a gun in Chunky's turret.

'Whoomph!' went the XR GTI—inflated air-bag and all.

But none of this was helping Cornelius.

'Help!' went he.

And 'Help!' went Tuppe, as dark and evil beasties moved in for the kill.

'Hang about,' said Norman. 'Perhaps we should have taken a right turn back there. I had no trouble just sort of locking into where Cornelius was and finding him in the police cell, but I seem to be a bit confused now. Dark all of a sudden, isn't it?'

Very dark.

And so many many refugees being force-marched into that nasty wire compound erected around the village green. That wasn't good. And this *was* England, after all.

'*No!*' declared a quite unanimous one and all. And all.

'Serious disturbance up this end,' cried a fellow in the uniform of an American marine into his army-surplus field telephone.

'Bzzt-wzzz-zzz,' received a fellow in a Russian military greatcoat, somewhere near the middle of the marching column (static from the sudden storm probably, or faulty parts).

'What did he say?' asked the fellow sitting next to the fellow in the Russian military greatcoat. He wore a Dragoon's uniform, *circa* 1848.

'Fire over their heads,' said the military-greatcoat fellow who had been dying to let off a couple of rounds.

'Good one.'

And the shots rang out.

And you just don't do that kind of thing.

And Charge!

They'd had enough, these refugees. Driven from their homes by rabid cars, camped all night upon a hilltop, hungry, tired, forced to march at gunpoint.

Quite enough!

And so they turned.

As one.

Like you would. Because this *was* England, after all.

'Back out, retreat!' Chunky's men, in their armoured cars and jeeps, now found themselves under attack. Jackboots put the foot hard down upon accelerator pedals. Wheels span, tracks churned tarmacadam.

A great battle cry rose from the throats of the refugees, like an atavistic howl. A jeep was overturned. Nasty wire netting was ripped aside and trampled underfoot.

Stirring stuff really.

And Bramfield wasn't a large village. And there were thousands and thousands of refugees. They gave chase to the retreating vehicles. They poured into the high street through side-roads, alley-ways, bridle-paths, footpaths, side-paths, cycle-paths, pedestrian-access-only paths, private-access-only decoratively paved paths which lead to bungalows with coach lamps on the gateposts that light up at night when you drive your car in. Down these, the people swarmed.

By the thousand.

And all into the high street.

Much to the surprise, it must be said, of the satanic creatures who were still in the act of falling upon Cornelius and Tuppe.

Bewildered and outnumbered (and previously lacking for description), these now rose upon great bat-like wings; called obscenities from their beaked mouths; shook scaly fists and defecated fish hooks, razor blades and copies of *Hello!* magazine* onto the raging mob beneath.

The mob, emboldened by adrenalin and sheer weight of numbers, replied with catcalls and footpath gravel.

'We had best be away,' Tuppe, on the tall boy's shoulder, called into the tall boy's ear.

And as a tattooed vest-wearer swung a waste-paper bin through the window of the village off-licence and things took a very ugly turn, Cornelius agreed that best being away was probably all for the best.

'This is bad, this is very bad.' Old Claude jigged about in a quiet and hidden corner behind the serviceable big sky nozzle. 'Those evil beasties will do for poor little Norman. The job won't get jobbed at all. Very bad it is. So very bad.'

He ceased his jigging and chewed upon a bony knuckle. 'Do something, you old fart,' he told himself. 'Help the wee boy. You're the real controller, you know how it all works, do something.'

Old Claude kicked the big sky nozzle, then hobbled about on one foot. 'Send him some help. Yes that's it, that's it. Beam him down some help. You could do that. You could work out the calculations. Take time, though,

---

* Very probably the James Herbert issue.

take time. Well, don't stand around like a dildo at a dance competition. Get to it. Get to it.'

And Old Claude got to it.

'Get to it, Chunky,' called Hugo Rune. 'Morris Minor at three o'clock.'

'Bloody crime to shoot up a Morris, doncha think, Rune?'

'Fair game,' Rune lobbed a hand grenade.

Somewhere high above God winced, but knew not why.

'All pretty much done, I think.' Chunky pulled up his Sherman tank beside that of Rune. 'Showed the blighters, eh, what?'

'You had best radio for some reinforcements to ring the town around, Chunky. Nothing in and nothing out, understood?'

'Tickety-boo.' Chunky did the business. 'Time for a snifter or two I reckon. Where do you want to set up HQ? Much of the town now gone to ruination. Shame about that hotel. Casablanca Suite, classy affair.'

'The vicarage is still standing,' Rune observed. 'Holds a commanding view of the bay.'

'Holds a lot of luggage in the basement too. But decent wine cellar.'

'Perfect then, let us repair there forthwith. I have a call or two to make, then I'll fill you in on all the details.'

'Good show, old man. Good show.'

'I'm quite lost,' puffed Cornelius, stumbling through bushes and briars.

'There's a road up ahead,' said Tuppe, clinging to the tall boy's hair. 'There's a road up ahead. And shit! There's a Jeep coming. Duck down, duck down!'

Cornelius ducked down into unspeakable country stuff.

The Jeep sped by.

'We're safe,' said Tuppe.

'I am covered in cow pooh,' said Cornelius.

'But we *are* safe, don't knock it.'

The Jeep screamed to a halt and backed up.

'We're not safe,' said Tuppe. 'Knock it as much as you want.'

The Jeep screamed to another halt.

'I can see you,' called the voice of Norman. 'Hurry up and get in.'

Cornelius and Tuppe hurried up and did so.

Thelma put the Jeep into gear once more and off they all sped together.

'Are you two all right?' Louise asked.

'I'm fine,' said Tuppe. 'The policemen duffed Cornelius up, but then they always do.'

'And I lost all my money again,' said Cornelius, 'but then *I* always do.'

'And there's the invasion of monsters from outer space going on,' said Tuppe, 'which isn't helping matters much.'

'I think we should withdraw to a place of safety for a couple of days,' Cornelius held down his hair. 'Think things through, make some kind of definite plan.'

'And get your clothes dry-cleaned,' was Norman's suggestion. 'You're covered in cow poohs by the way. You don't half hum.'

'He does, doesn't he?' Tuppe held his nose. 'But I thought we *had* a plan. Aren't we going to blow the piers up?'

'If that's the plan', Thelma called back, 'then we'd better get right onto it. I just picked up a broadcast from the Brigadier on the field radio here. He's called for his big bulldozers to be brought in, the pylons are coming down tonight.'

'Tonight?' Cornelius fell back amongst his hair. 'Then Rune's moved everything forward.'

'Forward to tomorrow night by the sound of it. And armed men now have all the roads into Skelington Bay blocked off. You can listen to it all going on, if you want.'

'I want,' Cornelius leaned forward. 'Could you stop the Jeep, Thelma, and let Tuppe and I ride in the front?'

'I am quite capable of driving, thank you.'

'I know that, I'm asking you a favour, that's all.'

'Fair enough.' Thelma swerved the Jeep to a halt. She and Louise got out, while Cornelius and Tuppe shinned over into the front seat.

'Are the back tyres OK?' Cornelius asked. 'Only they seem a bit soft.'

'We'll have a look.'

'Thanks,' Cornelius put the Jeep back into gear and tore off along the lane, 'for everything.'

'Hang about,' Norman bobbed up and down in the rear seat. 'You've left the birds behind. They don't half look angry. Stop the Jeep.'

Cornelius looked at Tuppe.

And Tuppe looked at Cornelius.

'I knew you were going to do that,' said Tuppe.

'But you didn't say anything.'

'No, because I knew *why* you were going to do it. You don't want any harm to come to them. I don't either.'

'Very touching,' said Norman, rolling his eyes. 'But if we can't stop Hugo Rune, then they're going to snuff it along with everyone else. And far be it from me to put my fourpenny worth in, but I'd say you just reduced our chances of success by a factor of two. Those girls are pretty smart.'

'Which is more than can be said for your hair-do,' said Cornelius.

'My hair-do? What, can you see me now?'

249

'I can, just. But I hope that Rune won't be able to, at all.'

Rune and Chunky were punishing the padre's port in the front garden of the vicarage. Picturesque vicarage, local stone, Georgian flat front with cozy porch. No sign of the dreaded UPVC. Rugs on oak floorboards within and ne'er a hint of a swirly-whirly carpet tile.

Cane steamer chairs were being sat upon. Hollyhocks waved at the sky, which was blue hereabouts. Bumble bees drifted, spiders dangled, honeysuckle climbed imperceptibly.

'Damn fine port,' said Chunky, pouring himself another measure. 'And damn fine tale that you've told me. Gold from the sea, eh? Who'd have thought it? Splendid wheeze. Still, can't say I quite understand the mechanics of the thing. Get the part about electroplating and using the piers as monster electrodes, get the pylons carrying the heavy-duty cables from each pier to the top of Druid's Tor. Bit baffled by the radio masts connected to the ends though. And where you're going to get all the electrical energy from.'

Rune smiled and poured port for himself, but from a different bottle. 'Many years ago', said he, 'I arrived at a theory regarding the afterlife, the nature of the soul, how things functioned on a universal level. I was quite certain that my propositions were correct, but it was necessary for me to put all to the test. And so, in the name of science and the cause of *Ultimate Truth*, I committed suicide.'

'You did *what*?' The Brig took to a fit of coughing. 'Damn me, Rune, you do talk some unmitigated drivel at times.'

'Nevertheless, that *is* what I did. My action proved entirely justified, I learned the true nature of the soul and I learned of the fallibility of God, which has all to do with 'bollocks' but I shan't bore you with that here. And I was able to infiltrate a certain *Company* and gain total control of it.'

'Haven't the foggiest idea what you're talking about, Rune.'

'But you shall. What is important for you to know now is that the present controller of this company is organizing the necessary power to energize the piers and draw the gold from the sea. But as this will be happening tomorrow night, instead of Friday night, it is imperative that he be informed of the change in schedule. So I'd like *you* to deliver a message.'

'*Me*? How dare you, sir. I'm not some bally messenger boy. Telephone the cove, speak to him yourself.'

'Regrettably that cannot be done, and I cannot deliver the message myself, I am awaiting the arrival of my brother who is flying in from America, to collect a certain item and bring it to me here.'

'Never knew you had a brother, Rune. Big fat bastard like yourself, is he?'

'Identical,' said sweetly smiling Rune. 'As are my other brothers, one of which has unaccountably gone missing, but I have mentioned this in the message you must deliver.'

'I'm not delivering any messages, I told you.'

'You'll deliver this one,' Rune handed Chunky an envelope. On it were printed the fateful words:

STRICTLY PERSONAL.
FOR THE EYES OF THE CONTROLLER
OF THE UNIVERSAL REINCARNATION
COMPANY ONLY.
BY HAND.

'Have another glass of port,' said Hugo Rune. 'It will help you on your way.'

34

'Whoa!' went Cornelius, applying the brakes.

'Oooh!' went Tuppe, disappearing onto the floor.

'Aaaagh!' went Norman, sailing over the windscreen to whack down onto the cliff-top road beyond.

'What is happening?' Tuppe struggled up and climbed onto the passenger seat.

'Up there,' Cornelius pointed. 'Circling above Skelington Bay, look at them.'

'It's the black beasties that attacked us. What *are* they, Cornelius?'

'I don't know *what* they are, but I'd hazard a guess as to who sent them after us.'

'Look at my overall,' Norman complained, as he limped back to the Jeep. 'Charred already and now torn at both knees. And look at my knees: grazed. Bloody hurts, what a bummer.'

'Sorry,' said Cornelius.

'Look at *them*,' Tuppe pointed. 'Do you know what they are?'

Norman squinted towards the circling shapes. 'They do look familiar. How do they get their wings to work like that? I was looking for a technique of that sort when my dad – aw shit, yes, they *are* familiar, there were drawings of them in *The Necronomicon*.'

'Mates of yours, Cornelius,' said Tuppe. 'You being Son of Satan and all.'

'Thanks very much. But this further complicates matters – armed guards ringing the town, cars on the rampage within, and fiends from Hell circling above.'

'Sewers,' said Norman.

'Pardon?' said Cornelius.

'Sewers. When Skelington Bay has its yearly festival, the most popular event, other than the man-powered-falling-into-the-sea competition, is the sewer tour. I've been on it, it's brilliant, we could go down a manhole and enter the town through the sewers.'

'No thank you,' said Cornelius. 'I smell bad enough as it is. There has to be another way.'

'We've got a Jeep,' said Tuppe. 'Why not disguise ourselves as soldiers and drive straight up, saying we've got an urgent message for Hugo Rune, or something?'

'Not bad. But not the way *I* would do it.'

'Oh, excuse me,' said Tuppe. 'And what way would *you* do it?'

'That way,' Cornelius pointed beyond the cliffs towards the sea. 'There's no need for us to enter the town at all. If we were to "acquire" a small boat, we could row it out to sea under cover of darkness, set the charges on the ends of the piers, light the blue touch-paper, then retire to a safe place somewhere near the horizon.'

'I like that,' said Norman. 'Do you like that, Tuppe?'

'I do indeed.'

'Are you being sarcastic?' Cornelius asked.

'Certainly not. Blowing up the piers was my idea after all.'

'Good.'

'Good.' Tuppe rubbed his little hands together. 'So, as soon as Norman has gathered all the various chemical components required for the manufacture of powerful explosives, constructed the timing trigger mechanisms, et cetera, and installed these carefully into the boat that you will have acquired, along with all the technical skills and navigational know-how necessary to row and pilot it by night, we'll be off on our way. Piece of cake, eh, lads?'

253

Cornelius took to some thoughtful head-scratching.
Norman said, 'Piece of cake.'

'Piece of cake?' asked the large controller, pushing a gilded plate across the marble top of his big swank desk.

'Piece of cake? *Piece of cake?*' Brigadier Algenon 'Chunky' Wilberforce (deceased) stamped his military footwear and made fists at the rococo ceiling. 'You murdered me, you bally bastard. Poisoned me damn port. Bloody un-British way of butchering a fellow. Cad and bounder, so you are. And how come you're *you* anyway?'

'You have a message to deliver, I believe,' said the large controller.

'Message? Message?'

'I saw your name come up on the list of today's arrivals, I assume that my brother must have, er, *sent* you.'

'Brother? Suddenly the bastard's got brothers everywhere. Murderers all. Told the fellow who brought me up in the lift that. Seems your damned brother murdered him too. Familiar looking cove the lift wallah, sure I'd seen him in a film somewhere, couldn't put a name to his face though.'

'The message.' The large controller extended a large hand.

The dead Brigadier yanked the crumpled envelope from his pocket and tossed it across the desk. 'Took the liberty of reading it. Bally bastard lied to me. Said he was moving his schedule forward from Friday night to tomorrow night. Says in the message he intends to go ahead *tonight at midnight* as soon as the pylons are in place.'

'Splendid,' said the large controller. 'I can arrange for that.'

'Says one of your brothers has gone missing too.

Drowned in the bay or somesuch, but didn't get "born again". Chap I picked up from the station's not the same chap I was chatting with the night before. Can't make head nor bloody tail of this.'

'*Not born again!*' The large controller rose largely from his chair. '*NOT BORN AGAIN?*'

'Not *pre*-incarnated, but no need to get a strop on, old thing. More than enough of you fellas to go round, I'd have thought. And bastards the lot of you.'

'It's that Claude. The old loon, he must have tampered with the big sky nozzle.'

'Still in the dark here,' said Chunky. 'And still bloody furious. What kind of an afterlife do you call this anyway? Where're the dancing girlies?'

'Shut up!'

'Damned cheek!'

'Let me think. I must have every inch of the company premises searched, stop him before he wreaks any more havoc. Punish him greatly, greatly indeed. Stay here. Don't leave this room. Eat cake. Help yourself to the drinks cabinet.'

'Dancing girlies?' enquired the defunct Brigadier.

'Dancing girlies. You just stay put until I sort this out.'

'*Big-bosomed* dancing girlies.'

Crash went the door, slamming shut on the large controller's departure.

'Don't want ones with small titties,' sulked the Brigadier, seeking out the drinks cabinet and flinging open its door.

'Waaah!' went a crazed-looking fellow, leaping from within.

'Fuck me!' croaked the Brig, collapsing on the floor. 'It's Ben Gun!'

'No-one got that the first time around. Wrong type of reader. I'm Claude, I am. Claude the real controller.'

'Nearly gave me a bally heart attack. Could have done for me.'

'Not twice. *He* did for you though, didn't he? I heard every word. Like to get your own back on him? Fix him good and proper?'

'I surely would.' The dead Brig climbed puffing to his feet.

'Then stick with me, sonny, and I'll tell you what we'll do.'

'Stick with me,' said Norman. 'I'll get it sorted.'

They were parked on the beach now. Quiet little cove sheltering beneath the cliffs. The kind of place where the Famous Five would have had an adventure involving smugglers and sandwiches.

'You get us the boat, Cornelius, and leave the rest to me.'

'Don't you think that being semi-transparent and altogether non-corporeal might present some difficulties for you? Like not being able to touch or move things, for example?'

'I opened the door of the blazing hotel room and rescued you, didn't I?'

'Yes you did.'

'Then I can organize getting the explosives together. You acquire the boat, the bigger the better, and meet me back here at exactly nine o'clock tonight. OK?'

Cornelius gave another of his thoughtful nods.

'I think you're supposed to say "piece of cake",' Tuppe told him.

'Piece of cake it is.'

'Rock 'n' roll then, chaps,' said Norman and wandered off along the beach.

'Do you think we could do something about eating now?' Tuppe asked Cornelius. 'I'm feeling faint, I am.'

'Me too, what time is it?'

'About two in the afternoon.'

'All right, let's drive along the beach, *away from Skelington Bay*, and see what we can find.'

'A fine idea.'

And Cornelius drove. The beach was flat and sandy and deserted.

The sun beamed down in a pleasing manner, waves lapped, seagulls dipped and weaved and Tuppe said, 'Look at that.'

'Look at what?'

'Out there in the sea, about thirty yards out, running along parallel with us, that's a shark's fin, isn't it?'

'Surely not here. Perhaps it's a porpoise, they used to call them pilot fish because they swam along in front of sailing ships. Or was that dolphin?'

'They don't have fins, do they? Go faster, see if it keeps up.'

Cornelius drove faster.

'It's keeping up,' said Tuppe. 'Perhaps it prefers Jeeps to sailing ships. Do you think we could entice it in and eat it?'

'Or perhaps swim out and let it eat us.'

'No thanks, keep the tyres out of the tide. Go a bit faster.'

Cornelius went a bit faster.

'It's keeping up. And it's coming nearer too.'

'It's never a shark,' said Cornelius. 'It's too angular, looks more like it's made of metal.'

'And glass. Glints in the sun, doesn't it? Strange, eh?'

'It couldn't be a submarine or something, could it? I mean . . . *Oh no!*'

'*Oh no!*' Tuppe agreed.

It rose from the waves, and it did look like metal and glass. The trim and the windscreen and the mirrors. The

257

bonnet was all covered in seaweed, but the metallic-blue finish was still visible and the big chrome bumpers, though battered, were mostly intact.

'It's the Cadillac,' Cornelius gave the accelerator pedal full wellie.

'It's coming at us, Cornelius. Faster, faster.'

'I'm going faster. But how can it do that? Cars can't run under water. They just can't.'

'*It* doesn't seem to know that. And I don't think it gives a damn. *Faster*!'

The Cadillac swung in from the tide, drawing closer and closer. Big engine the Cadillac Eldorado. Bigger than a Jeep's.

'We'll never outrun it on the straight,' Cornelius swerved up the beach. 'Might out-manoeuvre it though.' Another swerve and another.

Sand swept up in blurry cascades.

The Cadillac left the sea, surf skimming from the door seals and the radiator grille. Engine growling. Tyres churning the sand.

'You'd have thought it would have run out of petrol by now. Ouch!' Tuppe toppled to the floor as the Cadillac shunted the Jeep in the rear end, bursting the big spare water tank and making the clip-on trenching tool (which is really hard to get unless you know someone in the war-surplus circles) fall off and break.

'Faster,' shrieked Tuppe from the floor.

'It's too powerful,' called Cornelius. 'And too big. If it hits us a couple more times we'll be finished. Ooooooh!'

The Cadillac sideswiped them, tearing off a running-board and a goodly portion of side. Tuppe's side.

'Oh my goodness,' Tuppe scrambled up in his seat. 'It's had half my door off. Do something, do something.'

Cornelius swerved about in a nifty, sandy sort of U-turn. 'You do something. Anything.'

'Shoo!' called Tuppe. 'Go away. Leave us alone.'

Growl! went the Cadillac, coming about and gaining on them once more. Such a long flat beach and with the cliffs running right along, such a difficult one to escape from.

'This will make you laugh,' called Cornelius. 'According to the gauge, we're out of petrol.'

'Oh dear. Ouch!' Crash up the back end again. There goes the spare wheel. Tuppe whacked forward into the military equivalent of the glove compartment. 'Oh!' went he, then, 'Ah!'

'Ah?' Cornelius enquired.

'Yes, look, look.' Tuppe displayed his find.

Screech went brakes, Cornelius spun the Jeep to the right, the Cadillac flew by then swerved to continue pursuit.

'Hand-grenade,' said Tuppe.

'Tasty,' said Cornelius. 'You'd better let me throw it.'

'Get away, I found it.'

'Tuppe, please. It will end with one of those hand-grenade gags, throwing the pin and keeping hold of the grenade, dropping the grenade on the floor – let me do it.'

'Shan't,' said Tuppe. 'You're driving, I'm throwing. Let the Cadillac get up along side of me then I'll simply toss the grenade in and you can swerve away.'

'Having pulled the pin first.'

'What pin?'

'What pin!'

'Only joking. Oooooow!' Mash went the Cadillac into the back. 'I won't do any counting, just pull the pin and lob it in, how much time do you get anyway?'

'About ten seconds, I think.'

'You'd better do some nifty driving then. OK let's go for it.'

Cornelius swerved to the right, the Cadillac drew up

along side and began to grind against what was left of Tuppe's door.

'I hate to do this,' said Tuppe, 'as you were once such a magical car. But I'm sorry.' He pulled the pin and flung the grenade into the Cadillac. 'So long.'

'Careful!' A head bobbed up in the Cadillac's front seat, inches away from Tuppe. It was a sheep's head. It was Boris the bogus sheep's head. 'You nearly hit me with that,' he called gaily. 'What a laugh this car, eh? How are you doing, fellas?'

'Boris, it's you!'

'What?' went Cornelius.

'It's Boris in the Cadillac.'

'Then don't throw the grenade.'

'I have thrown the grenade.'

'You didn't tell me you'd thrown it.'

'Boris popped up and surprised me.'

'How many seconds ago did you—'

'*Boris*!' screamed Tuppe. 'Jump out of the car. That's a bomb I've thrown into it.'

'Eh?'

'It's a bomb. Jump! Jump!'

'Can't wait!' Cornelius swerved away and rammed on the brakes. The Cadillac shot past, leapt a small dune and then erupted in a violent gout of flame. Very forcefully and with a great deal of noise.

Cornelius threw himself across Tuppe, as shards of flaming metal rained down on the Jeep.

Boris hadn't leapt to safety.

Boris was sadly no more.

35

'Did he . . .' Tuppe asked.

'No, he didn't.'

'Then he's . . .'

'Yes, I'm afraid he is.'

'Then I . . .'

'It wasn't your fault, you didn't see him until it was too late.'

'That doesn't help. I killed him, Cornelius. I blew him up.'

'Very quick end,' said the tall boy. 'If it's any consolation, he wouldn't have felt anything.'

'It's no consolation at all. We'll have to give him a decent burial at least.'

'Do you think so?' Cornelius wasn't too keen to go looking for parts.

'I killed him, so I must bury him.'

'OK.'

They climbed from what was left of the Jeep and plodded sadly to the crest of the little dune and stared down at the horrid mess that lay beyond. The Cadillac was reduced to its blackened chassis. Little burning bits smoked here and there.

'Do you see any of him?' Tuppe asked.

Cornelius nodded. 'Over there.'

'Ah,' said Tuppe.

'And over there,' said Cornelius. 'And over there.'

'Oh dear, oh dear. I'm so sorry.'

'It wasn't your fault.'

'We don't even know anything about his family. We don't know who to tell.'

Cornelius patted his chum on the shoulder. 'I don't know what to say,' he said.

'Let's gather up his pieces.'

'Would you prefer to do it by yourself?' Cornelius asked hopefully.

'No, I'd like you to help me.'

They trudged dismally down the little dune. 'Shall I do the small pieces?' Tuppe asked.

'Whichever you prefer. You wouldn't rather I just dug the hole?'

'*No*,' said Tuppe.

'Fair enough.'

Boris wasn't overly scattered. Trotters (no hooves, sorry!), woolly tail. And the head!

The main carcass was intact. No bowels hanging out, or anything.

Cornelius stooped down, ran his hand over the scorched wool, gave the body a little pat.

'Is it safe to come out now?' the body asked. 'This *power armour** gets the job done. But I've a right headache again.'

'Tuppe!' Cornelius jumped up. Jumped up and down. 'He's alive, Tuppe. He's alive.'

'Eh, what?' The small fellow had the sheep's head in his hands and was peering into its empty husk.

'He's safe, he's alive.'

'I am,' agreed Boris, struggling out of his protective torso.

'Oh great!' Tuppe came stumbling over. He embraced Boris. 'You're alive. You're alive.'

'Leave it out,' said the Magonian. 'Don't kiss me please.'

'But you're alive!'

* Not the same Power Armour as on *Sonic Energy Authority's* legendary album *Sailors on the Sea of Fate*.

'Yes, I know I am. What is that funny noise?'

'Probably my stomach,' said Tuppe. 'It's a while since I've eaten.'

'No, not *that* funny noise. I meant *that* funny noise . . .'

And *that* funny noise wasn't really all that funny. It was more of a hideous growling noise. A hideous, mechanical growling noise.

'It's the Jeep!' Cornelius stared in horror as the mashed-about vehicle rose up over the dune, a-growling and a-roaring, the latest victim of MCD.

'Did someone say run?' Boris asked.

'Me, I think,' said Tuppe. 'Help, Cornelius.'

And the tall boy gathered up the short boy and, in the company of Boris, ran.

Hugo Rune never ran. He strode sometimes. Sauntered often. Sat mostly and slept a good deal.

Had he been sleeping now it is more than probable that his dream would have involved a marble bath-tub, perfumed water, a certain missing equation and a violent knocking upon his bedroom door.

But Rune wasn't sleeping.

He was organizing.

Something that he excelled at.

Though preferably while seated.

And thus he was seated now. Upon the mayoral throne, looted from Skelington Bay Town Hall. He wore the Mayor's cloak of office. And his chain. And his hat.

The throne was strapped onto the turret of a Sherman Tank. Rune had commandeered a loud hailer and through this he was 'organizing'.

Gathered around the tank were several hundred people. Most were clad in holiday attire, stragglers from the great forced-march, or those who had chosen to remain in hiding. All rounded up by the militia men of

Chunky's private army. A private army now under the sole command of Hugo Rune.

'This entire area is now under martial law,' called Rune. 'Your choice is this: engage in a couple of hours' work for me, or be shot as looters. Those in favour of the first option, raise your hands.' Most, but not all, hands rose upon the instant.

'I assume that the dissenters choose to be shot,' called Rune.

'You can't treat us like this,' shouted a lady in a straw hat. 'This is England after all.'

'I see, would you be so kind as to step forward, madam.'

The lady in the straw hat stepped forward from the crowd.

Rune raised a great hand towards the sky, then brought it down, forefinger angled to the hat of straw.

A dark shape dropped from on high. Bat-like wings and cruel claws. A stench of sulphur, flickering forked tongue about an eagle's beak. Talons caught hold. The lady screamed. The crowd drew back screaming and crying. Wings beat upon the air. The lady was drawn up, howling for mercy, carried high, away. Towards the sea.

'That's the third option,' called Rune. 'Have to hurry you now.'

'Hurry!' Cornelius plunged towards the cliffs, Boris plunged too. Behind them, roaring like a beast, the Jeep lurched, trailing its exhaust pipe, back tyres shredded, rims grinding.

'Ooof!' went Boris, falling flat on his face.

'Come on, my friend,' Cornelius turned, ducked, snatched up Boris, rolled to one side. The Jeep hurtled past, inches to spare, bowel-loosening stuff.

'Up the cliffs,' cried Cornelius. 'Come on, Boris, hurry.'

'Hurry, the man says.' Boris scrambled up, the Jeep

came about once more, stood, roaring and snorting like a bull. Preparing for the charge.

Cornelius gained the cliff. High cliff. Overhanging cliff. Chalk cliff. The tall boy dug in his fingers. Tried to climb. Chalk fell away. The tall boy fell with it.

'Ouch!' wailed Tuppe, as the tall boy fell on him.

Roar, Roar, Roar, went the Jeep, revving its engine.

'Give us a leg up the cliff,' implored Boris.

'I don't think this cliff can be climbed,' gasped Cornelius. 'You don't have a ray gun on you, by any chance, I suppose.'

'Ray gun,' said Boris. 'Now that's a thought.'

'Then you *do*?'

'No I don't. But it *is* a thought, isn't it?'

Roar, Roar, Roar, and then *Rush*.

Shredded tyres flailing like whips. Blue fists of exhaust smoke. Grinding metal, shuddering and shaking, snarling and shrieking. The Jeep shot forwards.

'Ooooooooooh!' Cornelius caught up Boris and Tuppe and prepared for an impossible leap.

The Jeep tore towards them. Yards were in it. Feet. Then inches. Then nothing.

Horrible contact. Mangling, rending. Destructive. Unholy.

So very, very nasty.

The concussion was such as to bring down an avalanche of cliff. Rumbling boulders and crests of chalk descended in a thunderous cascade, burying the Jeep and stifling its roars.

For ever. A big silence fell upon the now deserted beach.

'Phew,' said Tuppe. 'That was close.'

'Only inches in it,' said Cornelius.

'Thought we were done for there,' said Boris.

'What intrigues me,' said Tuppe, 'is, *how in the name of Babylon's Whore are we hovering up in the sky?*'

'Flying boots,' said Boris. 'Issued as standard to the air corps in case you have to bail out. Hang onto me now, stay within the telekinetic field.'

'Telekinetic field?' Cornelius asked, as the three drifted down towards the sand.

'Did I mention to you about the trans-perambulation of pseudo-cosmic anti-matter?'

'Once, in passing. I should have listened more carefully.'

'Still, here we are.' And the three bumped down onto solid ground.

'Thank you very much,' said Cornelius.

'Yeah,' said Tuppe. 'And then some.'

'My pleasure, lads. Lucky Cornelius mentioned ray guns, I'd quite forgotten about my boots.'

Tuppe cast frightened glances towards the big pile of fallen cliff. 'Is it safe now, do you think?'

'Let us depart in haste,' said Cornelius Murphy. 'We have much to do.'

'Can I come with you?' Boris asked. 'I don't have much to do at all, now the undersea joy-riding's finished and everything.'

'Of course you can,' said Tuppe.

'Of course he can't,' said Cornelius. 'He's not involved in any of this, we can't put him in such danger.'

'Such danger, eh?' Boris whistled. 'Well, perhaps I'll catch you blokes later. I've been thinking anyway. I may have lost my saucer, but if I can still go ahead and have my meeting, pass on the advanced technological secrets of my race, in exchange for a signed deal to leave the people of Magonia in peace, I could walk home across the sea bed. Everything will be OK.'

Tuppe opened his mouth to speak.

Cornelius didn't let him. 'I thought you'd missed your meeting,' he said.

'Yeah, but as chance would have it, I've heard that the chap I was supposed to meet is still right here.'

'*Still* right *here*?'

'Yeah, I heard it from a prawn, who got it off a whelk who'd overheard two seagulls talking about something a pigeon told them.'

'You can't argue with that kind of evidence,' said Tuppe.

'So like I say,' Boris went on, 'he's still here, so I can still have my meeting with him.'

'Who is this person?' Cornelius asked.

'Well, I shouldn't really say. After all, it is a secret. But you blokes are mates, so . . .' Boris did furtive glances to right and left. 'Your King,' he said.

'Our *King*?' asked Tuppe.

'King Hugo,' said Boris proudly. 'King Hugo Rune of England.'

> Now a King if a good King he shall be
> must give his subjects liberty.
> (Who wrote that?)

There was no hint of liberty around and about the court of King Hugo. Up on the downs that flowed inland above Skelington Bay, hundreds toiled. Blowtorch flames tongued through girders, bulldozers prised pylons from their mounts, high-tension cables snapped and whiplashed.

One after another the pylons fell, almost with the dignity of trees. But not quite. Jagged steel arms penetrated the soil, creak and crash. Chains and trucks, bulldozers and people-power. Inch by inch, yard by yard.

'Faster,' cried Rune through the loud hailer. 'We have a deadline to meet. A *deadline*.'

And someone tripped and fell. But no-one dared to

stop and lend a hand. They turned away their faces, though they could not shield their ears, as the churning wheels and steely tracks ground on their way and stifled screams. And crushed out life. Without a shred of pity.

'Faster,' Rune cried. 'One less to pull, the harder each of you must try.'

And dark shapes circled in the sky above. The clock ticked on towards the hour of four.

And most of Sussex now lacked for electrical power.

'Electrical what?'

'Like I said.'

'But he can't.'

'But he will.'

'But then he'll—'

'I know he will.'

'Then we—'

'Yes, we must.'

'More coffee, anyone?' Tuppe asked. 'More beans on toast?'

'Yes,' said Cornelius. 'Thank you.'

'But then I—' said Boris.

'You,' said Cornelius.

'And he was—'

'I know he was.'

'Then we certainly must—'

'You're quite right there.'

'Exactly what *are* you talking about?' Tuppe asked. 'And where are we, in case anyone should ask.'

'As *you* know full well,' said Cornelius. 'We are on a twenty-foot motor yacht called *The Lovely Lynne*, which Boris kindly swam round the next bay to and slipped from its moorings.'

'I don't like the swirly-whirly carpet tiles on the floor much,' said Tuppe. 'But carry on anyway.'

268

'I have just been telling Boris about "King" Hugo's plan.'

'And I have been being appalled,' said Boris. 'As King Hugo's plan will clearly lead to the extinction of my race.'

'What I want to know,' said Tuppe, 'and I am probably not alone in this, is how Hugo Rune came to make contact with your race in the first place, Boris.'

'Apparently he heard tell of our existence from a pet pigeon, who'd overheard two seagulls talking about something a whelk told them he'd got from a prawn.'

'Obvious,' said Tuppe. 'I knew there was a simple explanation.'

'He came down in a bathysphere; brought a lot of beads with him, apparently. Said he'd come in peace for all mankind.'

'In exchange for your advanced technology.'

'As soon as he realized we had it.'

'And so what were you supposed to do for him at this meeting then?'

'I was supposed to let him test drive the flying saucer.'

'Ah,' said Cornelius.

'What is "Ah"?' asked Tuppe.

'Ah is, there you have Rune's means of escape when the moment of the electrical discharging comes and zaps everyone else. Up and away.'

'Yes, but he doesn't have the saucer now.'

'I wonder who does,' said Boris, mournfully.

'Hugo,' said Hugo.

'And Hugo,' Hugo replied.

Hands were clasped, knuckles were pressed, shoulders were slapped.

One Hugo in his mayoral cloak, the other in a sharp city suit as befitted Transglobe Publishing's Managing Director. Which he was.

'Pleasant journey?' enquired Hugo One.

'Peaceful enough until we reached Gatwick. They've had a bit of a power cut there. All the radar and ground-control systems were out. Planes were bumping into each other all over the place. Most amusing to watch. I stuck around until ours ran out of fuel from all the circling, took the captain's parachute and bailed out.'

'I'd have done the same.'

'I know you would.'

The two Runes shared a laugh regarding this.

'So how is the project progressing? I see you've indentured some peasants to lend a hand. And a few old chums circling in the sky. All on schedule, by the look of things.'

'Not that you supposed it would be otherwise. You have brought the essential something I assume.'

'The flying saucer? But of course. Had a bit of trouble uncovering its whereabouts. But once I'd confirmed with the Magonian ruler that his emissary *had* been sent, it was only a matter of figuring out what had become of him. I made a few discreet calls to mutual contacts at the MoD . . .'

'And learned that the saucer had crashed and that their boffins now had it.'

'Precisely.'

'And learned *where* they had it and despatched a small task force to relieve them of it.'

'Precisely.'

'I'd have done the same.'

'I know you would.'

A chuckle shared, and evilly done.

'Then it is all systems go,' said Rune of the mayoral hat. 'The pylons will be re-erected in Skelington, with a line leading from each pier to the top of Druid's Tor. Heavy-duty cables will run along each line to terminate at the radio masts.'

'You have them?'

'They're on their way. With the power cut and the communications network destroyed, we have this area all to ourselves.'

'And at midnight?'

'At midnight our brother at The Universal Reincarnation Company throws his big switch; broadcasts an across-the-band frequency which attunes to the electrical energy-potential of every soul that hangs in a glittering ring about the sun; feeds their massed energy down through the radio masts, along the power lines and into the piers. The result: the biggest jolt this planet has had since the Creation. We will be watching from beyond the Earth's atmosphere, of course.'

'You estimate ninety-nine point nine per cent fatalities.'

'The almost complete collapse of civilization as we know it, yes.'

'Which *we* shall rebuild.'

'Oh as the richest men on Earth it will be our duty. To rebuild. And to rule, of course.'

'Of course.'

Another chuckle evilly shared. 'Roll on midnight,' said Hugo Rune. 'For tomorrow belongs to we.'

The two strode off, arms about one-another's shoulders, with talk of golden mountains springing from the sea, of slavery and concubines, power and the pleasures of its abuse. And of midnight. Always midnight.

'Midnight?' said Norman who had been dossing around unseen, earholing the entire conversation. 'Midnight *tonight*? *Midnight tonight*? *MIDNIGHT TONIGHT*! Oh dear, oh dear, oh dear, oh dear, oh dear, oh dear.'

Oh dear.

36

'What time is it?' Cornelius asked.

'Nearly nine o'clock,' said Boris. 'I can't wait to meet this dead friend of yours.'

'I can't see a thing,' said Tuppe. 'The entire coastline's in complete darkness.'

'I have pretty good night vision,' said Boris. 'But then I would, coming from a superior race and everything.'

Tuppe stuck his tongue out in the darkness.

'I saw *that*,' said Boris. 'And I can see something else.'

'Is it Norman?'

'It's a sort of three-wheeled bicycle and it's moving by itself.'

'That's Norman.' Cornelius had moored the boat as close into shore as he dared. Now he shinned over the side, dropped into the sea and waded towards the beach.

'Ahoy there,' called the voice of Norman.

'Ahoy,' Cornelius reached him in the near darkness. 'What is that you're riding on?'

'It's an ice-cream bike.'

'You have discovered a formula for creating explosives from ice-cream?'

'No, don't be silly, I've dumped the lollies.' Norman made grand gestures above the big portable-freezer affair beneath the handlebars. A selection of dangerous-looking military hardware gave off a blue-steel glint. 'I nicked a couple of mortars, some rifles and a load of grenades. Did you get a boat?'

'Certainly did.'

'Then we'd better get to it. Rune has moved everything

forward. He's going to energize the piers tonight at midnight.'

'What?'

'And he estimates that ninety-nine point nine per cent of the world's population will be killed off.'

'What?'

'And him and his brothers will be ruling the survivors. After they have returned from outer space in the flying saucer they've got hold of.'

'What?'

'Who said that "What"?' Norman asked.

'I did,' said Boris, ambling up to say hello.

'Aaaagh!' went Norman, falling off his saddle. 'It's an alien from space, grab a gun, Cornelius, shoot it.'

'He's a friend,' said the tall boy. 'He's here to help us.'

'And I'm not from space,' said Boris. 'I'm from under the sea, and it's my flying saucer Rune's got, and I want it back. Where are you, by the way? I can't see you at all.'

'I'm here,' said Norman.

'Well, pleased to meet you. My name is Boris.'

'Norman,' said Norman. 'Have you ever met Marina out of *Stingray*?'

'Let's get moving,' said Cornelius, dragging out mortars and grenades. 'If you're right, Norman, then we have less than three hours.'

'I'm right,' Norman said. 'Believe me. Please.'

'I do.'

'Is Marina the one who looks a bit like Joanna Lumley, but thankfully never speaks?' Boris asked.

'That's her, but you're being a bit harsh on Joanna, aren't you? She was voted the woman most men in the country wanted to kiss.'

'Bit old for me,' said Boris. 'But I meant it was thankful that Marina never speaks. She doesn't look too bright, does she?'

'No, I suppose not. But you've never met her, anyway?'

'No, sorry. I once met Submariner out of *Marvel Comics*.'

'You never did.'

'I did too.'

'Hurry up,' called Tuppe, from the boat. 'The tide's going out. We'll be stranded if we don't go now.'

'Hurry up,' said Old Claude to the late Chunky Wilberforce. 'We've got less than three hours to stop the bastard.'

'I'm hurrying,' puffed Chunky. 'Where are we going?'

'To the big sky nozzle, I've programmed in some help for little Norman.'

'Little who?'

'Never mind. After I've sent it down to him we'll smash up the big sky nozzle so the bastard can't tune it in to the souls and beam down their energy. Fix his whole wagon once we've reduced the big sky nozzle to scrap metal.'

'Scrap metal?' puffed Chunky. 'Now that's something I know all about.'

'Follow me.' Old Claude lead the way up a little staircase and out onto the vast roof area where the huge engines throbbed and the little men in overalls applied oil beads. The little men were two short in number now, but due to a continuity error, Jack Bradshaw had failed to find the missing pair at the bottom of the abandoned lift shaft.

These things happen.

'Call my cock a kipper!' whispered Chunky Wilberforce, espying all that spread around and about him. 'How much do you want for the lot, Claude? Name your price and if it's a fair'n, we'll do the business now.'

'Just follow me.' The old boy limped on towards the single serviceable big sky nozzle.

'What kind of help are you sending down to your little Norman?' wheezed the dead Brig.

Old Claude reached the brass Karmascope contrivance with the computer screen. 'I thought King Richard the Lionheart and a bunch of his crusaders.'

'They won't fare too well against Rune's fire power.'

'Bloody will,' crowed Claude.

'Bloody won't,' went the Brig.

'Bloody will.'

'Bloody won't,' said the voice of the large controller.

'Bloody Hell!' said Old Claude Buttocks.

'Bloody Hell!' said Norman. 'Excuse my French, but it is Bloody Hell really, isn't it?'

'It's something,' said Cornelius. They had dropped to a quiet anchor half a mile out between the piers of Skelington Bay and now sat upon the deck of *The Lovely Lynne*, gazing in awe at the town.

It was floodlit. Big ex-army generator trucks chugged away, powering arc lights that bathed the piers and promenade in a sterilized glare. The town had surely gone to Bloody Hell.

Burnt-out cars had been bulldozed into a mangled mound that ran the length of the beach. The pylons were in place, towering over the piers, shops and houses having been dynamited to make way for them. The Grande was all but gone, of course, and to the east of its gutted shell seemed nothing but a great black void all charred about the edges.

There was a good deal of noise: cables being winched into place, loud hailers barking orders, a scream and a call for mercy, the sound of a gunshot.

Bloody Hell.

'It's Bognor for me next year,' whispered Tuppe.

'Bastards,' said Norman, who was really getting into

swearing. 'I was born here. Look what they've done to my town.'

'See there,' Cornelius pointed. Two military types were dragging something along the east pier. They stopped, looked over the rail. The skulkers on *The Lovely Lynne* heard the words, 'Here's far enough.'

The military types lifted the something. Eased it over the rail. Let it fall down into the sea.

It was the body of a young woman.

The two men laughed, turned and strolled back down the pier.

Cornelius snatched up a rifle from the deck, flipped off the safety catch.

'No,' said Tuppe. 'You can't.'

'You saw what they did. I can.'

'Then you mustn't. We have to blow up these piers, we can't get involved in a gunfight. They've got tanks, remember.'

'All right,' Cornelius clicked back the safety catch. 'What we'll do is—'

'I have a plan,' said Norman.

'The way I see it—' said Boris.

'The way I'd *do* it—' said Tuppe.

'All right,' said Cornelius. 'Let's hear them all now.'

'Mine first,' said Norman.

'Mine,' said Tuppe.

'Yours, Boris,' said Cornelius.

'Right,' said Boris. 'Mine is that you lot stay here in the boat. I swim over to each pier in turn and load them up with hand-grenades. Give me twenty minutes then blast away at them with the mortars.'

'What will *you* be doing?' Cornelius asked. 'We'll wait for you to swim back here.'

'I won't be swimming back here. I'm going to find my flying saucer and radio to Magonia for reinforcements.'

'Well, that's some sort of plan. What's yours, Norman?'

'Mine's quite simple and direct. I will take two handgrenades, swim ashore, and hand one to each of the Hugo Runes. Minus the pins, of course.'

'*No!*' cried Cornelius. 'One of those Runes might be my real dad. If he is then perhaps I could still reason with him.'

Norman shook his ruddy head. 'There's no time left for reason. The two I overheard are planning to wipe out the world. If you're so certain that your dad wouldn't behave like that, then neither of them can be your dad. Right?'

Cornelius chewed upon his bottom lip. Difficult one to answer, that. And no time left for reason. 'Well, right, I suppose.'

'I am right,' Norman said.

'But it's a very dangerous plan.'

'I'm dead, Cornelius. There's no danger at all involved for me. You'll still have to blow up the piers, of course. But I think I'll be doing my bit for the good of mankind.'

'Fair enough. What about you, Tuppe?'

'Well,' said Tuppe. 'I know it was my idea to blow up the piers, but I'm having second thoughts now. We may be trying to blow up the wrong end. I think we should blow up the radio masts, then the electricity can't reach the piers.'

'Good point,' said Cornelius.

'Also,' said Tuppe, 'if Boris could simply swipe back his saucer and fly off in it, the Runes would have to abort the whole operation, having no escape craft. I don't think they'd risk the chance that they'd be amongst the point-one survivors. Not here.'

'Another good point,' said Cornelius.

'Thanks,' said Tuppe. 'So what's your plan?'

'I'm going to commit suicide,' said Cornelius Murphy.

'*What*?' went Tuppe and all.

'Well, if I can get up to The Universal Reincarnation Company, I might be able to stop the controller sending out his signal.'

'That's a terrible idea,' said Norman. 'You'd hate being dead. It's a real bummer, I can tell you. And anyway *you* don't have to go up there. I've told you all about Old Claude. He'll sort out the large controller. You see if he doesn't.'

'Well, well, well,' said the large controller. 'If it isn't Old Claude.'

'Mr Buttocks to you, you bastard.'

'Buttocks?' asked Chunky. 'Claude Buttocks? As in clawed buttocks? What a hoot, eh, Rune?'

'Enough from you,' said the large controller. 'And *you*.' He took Claude by the ear. 'You meddling old lunatic. You're in for severe chastisement.'

'Let go of my ear.' Claude wriggled like a maggot on a fish hook, which had a certain cruel irony about it. Although it was not one Claude wished to delve into. 'Let go of me, I say.'

'I shall take you apart a piece at a time, draw the nerves from your body and eat them one by one. Hell may have closed down, but I still hold the key. We'll have the place all to ourselves.'

'You don't frighten me,' said Old Claude, which wasn't altogether true.

'Muse upon it.' The large controller gave Claude's ear a very vicious twist. 'It's back to the lift shaft for you now. The little hole you crawled out of has been all plugged up. I'll call for you in a couple of hours, when my pressing business is complete.'

'You bastard.'

Twist went Claude's ear.

'Ooooooh!'

'Quite so. And where do you think you're off to, Chunky?'

'Nowhere, Rune. Perish the thought. Just wondering where the dancing girlies were, that's all.'

'You'll have your dancing girlies. But *you* . . .' Another twist of the ear and a lot of dragging away.

'No, let me go.'

'I don't think so.'

In between the big machines and over to that terrible door again. Ear held firmly in one hand, bolts drawn with the other. Then through.

'See you soon,' called the large controller.

'Aaaaaaaagh!' went the ex-one.

'So, I'm telling you, he'll take care of it.' Norman felt quite sure about this. 'Very noble thought, Cornelius. In fact, as noble as it's possible to get. But not a good idea. Trust me on this, I really know what I'm talking about.'

'I wish I could see him,' said Boris. 'Most disconcerting – this voice just kind of coming out of nowhere.'

'I'll grow on you, Boris. I did on Cornelius. And say, when you get your flying saucer back, would you take me for a ride in it?'

'Not half!'

'I think we should be getting a move on,' said Cornelius. 'What time is it now, Boris?'

Boris consulted his watch. 'Nearly nine o'clock.'

'Nearly nine o'clock? It was nearly nine o'clock when we met up with Norman.'

'No, it was nearly *ten*,' said the dead boy. 'I was late, sorry.'

'Then what time is it now?'

'Still nearly ten,' said Norman, rattling his watch against his ear.

'My watch has stopped,' said Boris. 'Luckily it's under guarantee.'

'Mine isn't,' said Norman. 'But it's stopped too.'

'So what time *is it*?'

'Listen, Cornelius,' said Tuppe. And in the distance, as if on cue, the town hall clock began to chime.

Nine . . . Ten . . . '*Eleven*!' shrieked the crew of *The Lovely Lynne*.

'Gawd,' said Norman, plucking two grenades from the deck. 'We don't have much time.'

'There's a rubber dinghy at the stern of the boat,' said Cornelius. 'Load the grenades in that. You don't want to get them wet.'

'Could I load myself in too?' Tuppe asked. 'The flaw in my plan is that I can't swim.'

'You and Norman get in,' said Boris. 'I'll swim and tow you.'

'Oh good,' said Norman. 'The flaw in my plan is that in my present condition I probably can't swim either.'

'So many plans, so many flaws,' said Cornelius. 'OK, get to it. You try for the radio masts, Tuppe. I'll start blasting away at the piers in as near to twenty minutes as I can get, counting seconds in my head.'

'Hm,' said Tuppe. 'Once more I am filled with confidence.'

'You will be very careful, won't you?'

'I'll be OK. I would like to reinstate that running gag about people not noticing me. If it's all right by you.'

'Consider it done.'

Boris tripped over Tuppe and fell straight into the dinghy. 'Sorry,' he said. 'I didn't notice you there.'

'Nice one, Cornelius,' said Tuppe.

They'd have blackened their faces, if they'd had anything to blacken them with. Cornelius suggested some of the cow pooh that was still clinging to him. No-one seemed keen.

He waved them away in the dinghy; sat down upon the deck and began to count seconds. It was all very iffy, was this.

The chances of success did not seem altogether good.

The dinghy vanished away into the shadows beneath the west pier.

Cornelius counted and counted.

After what seemed an age, but was really only three hundred and fourteen almost equal seconds, the dinghy appeared once more and set off across the bay bound for the east pier.

Something made a large splashing sound near to the boat and Cornelius lost count. 'Whatever was that?' he asked himself. 'Pilot fish perhaps?'

He began to count once more. Splash went another loud splash.

'Bugger it,' said Cornelius Murphy. 'Five hundred and eighty-two, five hundred and eighty—'

Splash went another splash. Somewhat nearer than the other two splashes had been. The dinghy had made no further appearance, Cornelius assumed correctly that Boris would be towing it ashore in the shadows beneath the east pier, to land in the blackened burnt-out area of Skelington Bay. And the tall boy began to have many second thoughts.

He shouldn't have let Tuppe go. Why had he done that? Tuppe should have stayed in the relative safety of the boat. He could have fired the mortar. Well, OK, no he couldn't have fired the mortar, but he would have been safer. And Cornelius wouldn't have just been sitting here, counting away the seconds until the end of the world, losing count every time a fish went splash. 'Seven hundred and thirty-four, seven hundred and thirty-five, oh damn. How many seconds are there in twenty minutes? Twenty times sixty. Two sixes are twelve, then you'd carry zeros.'

Mathematics had never been one of the tall boy's strong points. Nor had games or woodwork. Cornelius had his own talents – different talents that cut him out from the norm. His acute sense of smell for one. He could sniff what you had in your pockets, tell you how much loose change and of what denomination. Not that he'd found much use for this particular talent of late, although it had got him out of trouble at times.

Cornelius sniffed while he counted. Seaside towns are full of wonderful smells: the candyfloss, the hot dogs, the Lilos and beachballs and suntan lotion. Sea shells and seaweed and . . .

Ah.

Cornelius took a nose-full. The reek of sulphur had him on his back. 'What the hey?'

Something else went splash. And the boat gave a shudder. And Cornelius realized that he was no longer alone.

'OK,' said Boris as he beached the dinghy deep within the shadows of the east pier. 'We're on our own now. Good luck, Tuppe, it's been good to know you.'

'Good to know you too, Boris. If we get back together perhaps we might make a go of that dancing-sheep act.'

'Yeah, right. And even though I still can't see you, good luck, Norman.'

Two hand-grenades levitated from the dinghy.

'Neat trick,' said Boris.

'Good luck to you,' said Norman. 'And don't forget I want a ride in your flying saucer.'

'I won't.'

And with those words said the three went their separate ways.

The Magonian, the dead boy and the small man.

Bound for what, was anybody's guess.

'I know *I've* counted twenty minutes,' whispered Tuppe, as he hiked up the beach. 'And it's going to be a fair old march to Druid's Tor, a bit of an uproar wouldn't go amiss, Cornelius. What's keeping you?'

'Get back,' Cornelius Murphy brought the rifle butt down into the face of the evil winged beastie that was clambering onto *The Lovely Lynne*. The thing sank back into the waves, groaning dismally.

But another was coming up at the pointy end.

Cornelius charged along the boat, swung the rifle by the barrel, clouted the beastie into the sea.

Another screeched down at him from the roof of the cabin.

Cornelius fumbled with the rifle, trying to get it around the right way and release the safety catch. The thing hopped down and stalked along the deck towards him. Cornelius took a hasty aim and fired. No sound. No bullets in the rifle.

The thing waggled a scaly finger, blinked blood-red eyes, snapped its beak and stalked forward once more. Cornelius dropped to his knees and smashed the rifle butt down upon an eagle-clawed tootsie.

'Waaaaah!' went the beastie, hopping about.

Cornelius gave it another wallop. Side of the beak. Caught the thing off balance. It plunged into the ocean.

'Damn, damn, damn.' Cornelius snatched up the mortar. 'There isn't an instruction manual with this, I suppose.'

No, there wasn't.

'I think you just sort of aim it and drop the mortar shell down the barrel.'

Yes, that would probably be it.

'Grrrr!' went a beastie, clawing its way onto the boat. Cornelius stamped up and down on its talons and the beastie fell away.

'I'm in big trouble here.' He fumbled with the mortar tube. The boat was rocking all over the place now. Cornelius struggled to insert the shell. He only had half a dozen. And these were now rolling about dangerously.

'Grrrr!' went another something, coming up from behind.

Cornelius turned, fell backwards. The mortar shell shot down the tube, activated whatever mechanism launched these kinds of things and erupted from the killing end of the weapon with a mighty roar.

The beastie took to lurching in twisted circles. It now lacked a head.

'Urgh!' went Cornelius, booting it over the side.

Explode! went the mortar shell, striking home in the mangled car wreckage on the beach.

'Careful,' cried Tuppe, taking to his little heels.

'Alert, alert,' went loud hailers. 'Gunboat in the bay. We are under major assault. Fall into battle positions.'

'I heard that,' said Cornelius, struggling to his feet, and feeling for broken shoulder bones. 'And I don't like the sound of it one bit. Let's stick another shell in here.'

And 'Grrrrr!' went another beastie.

'Gunboats in the bay,' went suited Rune from his steamer chair in the vicarage garden. 'That's not on the curriculum, surely?'

'Chunky's blokes buggering about probably,' Rune of the Mayor's gown poured port from a separate bottle. 'Have a glass of this, brother, it will hit the spot.'

Crash, bang, wallop, went Old Claude, hitting something.

Bit of a long time falling?

Well. This may have happened a bit earlier.

Hard to say, really.

'Ouch, my bloody bum!' went Old Claude.

'Fuck me!' went Jack Bradshaw. 'It's Ben Gu—'

'Don't bother with it, sonny. It doesn't get a laugh. And who are you, for frig's sake?'

'Bradshaw. Jack Bradshaw.'

'What are you doing at the bottom of my lift shaft, Jack Bradshaw?'

'Ah,' said Jack.

'Clerical error, was it? Found out something you shouldn't?'

'Threw in my lot with a bad crowd,' was Jack's explanation.

'The bastard threw you down here, did he?'

'If you mean the controller, yes.'

'So what are you going to do about it, eh?'

'Well, actually,' said Jack, 'I was in the process of escaping.'

'Oh yes. And how?'

'I'm going to make gunpowder,' said Jack. 'Grind up these old pencils for charcoal, use the potassium nitrate that's crystallizing on the walls and get sulphur from . . . er—'

'I'll gather the sulphur for you, sonny, it's over there in the place you get the wire coat-hangers and the pocket lighter from.'

'Eh?' said Jack.

'Grrr!' went that beastie again.

'Open fire!' went men along the shoreline.

'Get away,' went Cornelius clouting the beastie in the stomach with his mortar.

'Whoosh!' went a flare, lighting up the entire area.

'Damn,' went Cornelius, well lit.

'Grrr!' went the beastie.

Clout! went the tall boy.

'Ouch!' went the beastie, falling off the boat.

'Good riddance!' went the tall boy, shaking his mortar in defiance.

Bang! went the muzzle of a Sherman tank.

Wheeeee! went its shell.

Clunk! went the shell from the tall boy's mortar, falling out onto the deck. Then whoosh it went, igniting and firing vertically into the air.

Down came the shell from the tank.

And down, came the shell from the mortar.

'Abandon ship!' cried Cornelius Murphy, leaping over the side.

37

Boris had been creeping along in the darkness at the edge of town that Bruce Springsteen used to sing about. He saw the flare as it lit up the bay. He saw the tank fire and he saw something or other occur on *The Lovely Lynne*.

And then he saw the big explosion.

And then he felt very sick inside and crept on.

Tuppe saw it too and he prayed very hard and struggled towards the Tor.

Norman didn't see it. He was lost up a back street. But as he didn't know where the Hugo Runes were, he didn't know that he was lost and going in the wrong direction. So he just continued on.

Wrongly.

'Gulp and gasp,' went Cornelius, narrowly avoiding going down for that old third time. 'I'm still alive, which is something.'

Splash! went something quite near by.

But as the flare had died away and the flaming wreckage of *The Lovely Lynne* had vanished beneath the waves, it was very dark, so Cornelius couldn't tell exactly where the splash came from. He struck out for the shore.

Bad choice.

Ding dong, Ding dong, went the chimes of the town hall clock, ringing out the half-hour.

*   *   *

'More port?' asked Rune of the mayoral cloak. 'Let me top up your glass.'

'Get a bloody move on, Jack Bradshaw,' shouted Old Claude. 'Tamp it into something and blow the wall down, come on now.'

'Ready for the final countdown here, Chunky,' said the large controller. 'I have erased all of Claude's nonsense from the Karmascope. In thirty minutes' time the old Earth will come to an end and the dawn of a new millennium will begin.'

'Any chance of a deal on the scrap metal?' Chunky enquired.

Storm clouds were gathering above Skelington Bay. Boris could hear them at it. Well, he did come from a superior race after all.

'Whoa!' said Boris, creeping from the darkness, back to the light that Brian May used to sing about. 'There's my saucer.'

And there it was, perched upon its tripod legs in the road outside the vicarage.

It looked in pretty good nick. The government boffins had evidently done repairs on it.

'Nice one,' said Boris, creeping up.

Nobody about. Up and in.

Boris scrambled up, lifted the transparent dome and dropped down inside. He rammed oversized headphones over his ears and flicked switches on the dashboard. 'Ambassador to base,' he whispered. 'Ambassador to base.'

Long silence.

Then.

'Base to Ambassador. Is that you, Mavis?'

288

'Is that *you*, Bryant?'

'Yeah it's me, how are you doing?'

'None the better for listening to you. Mavis! Sheep outfit! Erich Von bloody Daniken! You shit, Bryant!'

'Only having a laugh. No offence meant.'

'Well, much taken. Listen, we have a real emergency here.'

'Are you taking the piss now, or what?'

'No, I'm not. This is for real. King Hugo's a fraud. He's not the king of this country at all. And at exactly midnight he is going to pump trillions of volts into the sea.'

'What's a volt?' asked Bryant.

'It's a unit of electricity.'

'Like an Ohm?'

'Yes.'

'Or a Watt?'

'Yes.'

'Or an Ampere?'

'Yes, yes, yes.'

'Never heard of a Volt. What does it do?'

'It kills you. He's going to wipe out Magonia. You have to do something.'

'You *are* taking the piss. I don't blame you. Fair dos.'

'I'm *not* taking the piss. It was all a con to steal the saucer and escape. This Rune is mad. Call up the Emperor, have him do something.'

'He'll be in his bed. Get real, Mavis.'

'*Boris*! You shit.'

'Boris then.'

'Tell the Emperor. Get him to whip up something. Whack Skelington Bay with it. We have the technology. We're an advanced civilization.'

'Tidal wave,' said Bryant. 'Is that what you'd like?'

'Yes, that's it. Get him to organize a tidal wave. Smash the town with it.'

'Boris.'

'Bryant?'

'Piss off, Boris.'

The line went dead.

'No, come back. Wait. Listen.'

Not a dicky sea bird.

'I'm flying out of here,' said Boris.

'Not without these you're not.' The saucer's ignition keys dingle-dangled between the pudgy fingers of Hugo Rune. In his other hand was the deadly derringer. It was pointing right at Boris's head.

'Oh shit!' said the man from Magonia.

'Oh shit,' spluttered Cornelius, thrashing towards the shore.

He wasn't much of a swimmer.

And something bobbed up, right in his path.

'Grrrr!' went this something, lunging forward.

'Oh no!' went the tall boy, falling back.

But 'Grrrrr!' it continued to go. It meant business. It caught Cornelius by the hair and it dragged him under the water.

Ding dong, ding dong, went the town hall clock. A quarter to twelve already. Doesn't time just fly, eh?

WHOOP! WHOOP! WHOOP! WHOOP! WHOOP! WHOOP!

Cornelius came up fighting. Bright lights whizzed and turned across the bay. Boat horns did the whooping.

'What the—' Down once more into the depths.

'What the—' Chunky's chaps along the shoreline cocked their weapons, squinted into the twisting, whirling lights.

*　　*　　*

290

'What the—' Rune stood up upon the saucer's edge, gazed out across the bay. 'Oh no,' said he. 'Oh no, no, no.'

For now they could clearly be seen. The boats. Hundreds of boats. Rowing-boats, fishing smacks, trawlers and pleasure boats. Round-the-bay trippers, dinghies and coracles. And currachs and canoes and catamarans; and sailing yachts and speedboats, wherries and ferries, tugboats and tow boats and launches.

And Lilos.

And a gondola.

An irregular fleet, it was. A flotilla. A forest of masts.

An argosy.

An armada.

And a thousand folk were waving, cheering, jeering. Hooting and hollering. Raising sticks. Some bearing guns.

'Twas the folk of Skelington Bay no less. Hoorah!

Returned to retake their town. Hip, hip, hooray!

It must have required an awful lot of organization.

Probably that's why they took so long to get here.

The armada's searchlights zigzagged over the bay. The waves were growing choppy now. There was thunder in the air. A big storm was a-brewing.

Cheer! Cheer! went the town folk, letting off flares and firing shots into the sky.

Dither, dither, dither, went Chunky's troops upon the beach.

Sweep, sweep, went the searchlights.

And 'There!' cried the voice of a young woman from the leading craft, a white motor launch. 'Keep the light there. I saw him.'

'Uuuugh!' went Cornelius, breaking surface.

A claw closed about his throat.

And dragged him down and down.

'I'll get him.' The young woman dived from the motor launch, seemed to hang, as if suspended in the air, for just a moment, then arced into the blackness of the churning waves.

'More light. More light,' others cried, bringing their boats about. 'Where is she?'

Lights criss-crossed and those seconds ticked on towards twelve.

'Wah!' A great dark mass rose from the waves. Tendrils trailing.

'Shoot it!' cried many.

'No don't!' Another young woman's shout rose from the motor launch.

And the diver's head swept up through the mass, straining and hauling at it. And lo that mass was the mane of Cornelius Murphy.

'Help them out.' Hands reached, faces strained.

Up and onto the deck.

The diver clawed hair away from the tall boy's face. Pinched at his nose, put her lips to his.

Gasp and gulp and not enough seconds for all this.

'Whoa!' went Cornelius, turning his face to the side and vomiting seawater.

'Is he OK?' asked Louise.

The diver looked up and smiled. 'He'll live,' said Thelma.

And now shots rang out from the beach. The big butch lads of Chunky's private army weren't really into acts of heroism. Acts of brutality, yes. But not the 'making-a-final-stand', Rorke's Drift kind of jobbie. Oh no.

They were shooting as they ran.

Away.

'Fools!' roared Rune from the saucer top. 'Buffoons.' He pulled a golden watch from his waistcoat pocket (a present from Haille Sellaise)*, studied its face by the

* The watch, not the waistcoat pocket (the waistcoat was a gift from Rasputin).

292

lightning that now streaked across the sky. A wind was rising from seaward, twisting the pylon cables, skimming litter and debris. 'Only minutes,' cried Rune, 'and all shall be mine.' He dropped down into the saucer beside Boris. 'Fly,' said he.

'Stand back,' said Jack. 'I'm going to light the fuse, except I—'

'Use my lighter, sonny. And get a bloody move on.'

'Watch the minutes tick away,' said the large controller to Chunky.

'Nothing can stop us now.'

'Hey!' whispered Norman, who now found himself lost in the graveyard. 'Who's that I see over there?'

It was Rune – well, *a* Rune – seated in a steamer chair, in the vicarage garden. Looking as if he cared not a jot for the growing gale that decapitated hollyhocks and cast them hither and thus.

Norman pulled the pin from one of his grenades, but kept his thumb hard down on the trigger-release thingy. 'Oi, you!' he shouted.

The Rune said nothing. Glass of port in one hand, other in his lap, wind whipping every which way about him.

'What a bummer,' said Norman. 'I'd have liked him to at least have been able to hear me before I blew him up. Still, fair enough.'

Norman vaulted the low wall between the graveyard and the vicarage garden, plodded over to the Rune and glared at him, face to face. 'Can't see me, can you? Can you see this?'

Norman raised the hand-grenade, waggled it before the Rune's eyes. The Rune's eyes stared through it, as if fixed

293

upon some point at the rear of the grenade. Unpleasant habit that.

'Anyone home?' Norman leaned forward and donked the Rune on top of his great shaven head. Not hard, just enough to say 'anyone home?'

The Rune's face remained without expression. His eyes still focused on some point known only to himself. He slid gently down the steamer chair and bellyflopped into a flower-bed.

This particular Rune was dead as dead can be.

Norman stared down at the corpse.

And then he became gripped by a terrible fear.

This was a dead Rune, and the only good Rune was a dead Rune, so to speak. Except not so, because a dead Rune, a ghost Rune, could grip a dead boy by the ear and shake him all about.

Norman released the trigger-release thingy, tucked the hand-grenade into the top left waistcoat pocket of the terminated Rune.

'Go out with a bang, not a whimper,' said Norman, making off at the double.

'Make off this minute!' the living Rune demanded. 'That is an order. Get to it!'

'Shan't,' said Boris. 'You can't make me.'

'I can shoot you.'

'Won't help anything. You don't know how to fly the saucer.'

Tick tock, went the town hall clock.

'Five minutes and counting down,' said the large controller.

*   *   *

294

'Duck your head,' said Jack Bradshaw. 'There's going to be a bang.'

'*Booom*!' went the Rune in the vicarage garden, spreading bones and guts and ichor – and moving swiftly on.

'Gag and gasp,' and 'Thelma, Louise.' The tall boy's eyes were open.

'I know why you dumped us,' said Thelma. 'But we thought you could use a little help. So we brought everybody.'

Cornelius struggled up, giddy and sick. The town's folk crowding the armada of boats cheered. 'Good one,' said the tall boy. 'What's the time.'

'Four minutes to twelve,' said Louise.

'Then blast the piers. Boris has tied grenades to them. Shine the searchlights. Shoot at the grenades.'

The armada wasn't too far from the piers now. In fact, it was a bit too near to them really.

'There,' cried searchlight sweepers zeroing in.

'And there,' cried others.

'Shoot!' cried Cornelius.

'Care for a go yourself?' asked Thelma, hefting a decent-sized bazooka from the deck. 'We took a few prisoners on the way and grabbed a bit of hardware.'

'Will you marry me?' asked Cornelius, taking the bazooka and going down on one knee.

'Only if you can get the Reverend Cheesefoot to officiate.'

'*Fire*!'

The tall boy whopped the trigger, tumbled from the recoil. The bazooka shell swept over the bay and tore into the west pier.

'Booom!' went another explosion. This one at The Universal Reincarnation Company.

From the sizeable hole that now yodelled in the wall, issued Jack Bradshaw and Old Claude.

'Where are we?' asked the ancient.

'My new office,' howled Jack. 'You've blown it to pieces. My new office.'

'I didn't blow it to pieces. You blew it to pieces.'

'It's all your fault.'

'It's bloody not.'

'It bloody is.'

'You bloody will.'

'I bloody won't.'

These bloodys were being exchanged in the flying saucer.

'I don't have time for this,' said Hugo Rune, reaching down a great hand and fastening a ferocious grip upon those parts of Boris' anatomy, which, had He given just a little more thought to when He worked on the original design for males, God would have placed on the *inside*.

'Aaaaaagh!' screamed Boris. 'You dirty pervert. Unhand my anenomes.* Aaaagh!'

'Fly the saucer,' barked Rune into his ear.

'All right, I'll fly it. I'll fly it. Aaaagh!'

Booom! went the east pier.

Booom! went the west pier.

Turning, billowing, flames rising, fun-fair bits and bobs, the ghost train, the helter-skelter, countless Sony the Hedgehog video machines (good riddance), candyfloss stalls, a decorative shell shop. Deck planks. The gents' toilet.

Rolling, bursting.

Armada men and women jumping from the decks into

* Magonian slang for cobblers probably.

the storm-lashed sea. Wind hurled debris. Mushroom clouds shredded.

Lightning flash.

Thunder roar.

Struggling shapes on the wildly bucking white motor launch.

'Did we do it?' asked Louise. 'Is it done?'

Cornelius gaped into the gale. 'It's not done, the piers are still standing.'

Victorian built those piers. Take a lot more than that to have them down. Made to last. Sturdy. Solid.

'To the beach!' cried Cornelius. 'We must try to knock the pylons down – disconnect the cables. Do something.'

Two and a half minutes to twelve.

'I just knew that wouldn't work.' Tuppe was now very puffed on the crest of Druid's Tor. Very good view of the bay from up there. Even with the mighty storm and everything. 'It has to be done from up here. It really does.'

And there existed the means.

An abandoned bulldozer.

What chance that the keys might still be in the dashboard then?

With two minutes left?

'Thanks be. The keys are still in the dashboard,' said Tuppe, scrambling up. 'Only trouble is', he keyed the ignition and the engine roared, 'I won't be able to see where I'm going and work the pedals at the same time. Still where there's a will, and all that sort of stuff. Which radio mast to demolish? The one with its cables leading to the west pier, I think.'

'This pylon here.' Townsfolk from the armada, many in a most horrified state having viewed the destruction of

297

Skelington (a man with a bogus Rolex on his wrist wept over the burnt-out remnants of a car upon the beach), were gathered on the prom beside the east pier. (Handy.)

Cornelius had found a pair of sturdy bolt-cutters. 'I'll shin up this pylon,' he shouted. 'Cut the powerline. Then if we all work together we might be able to rock the pylon. Push it over.'

'Sounds about as unlikely as anything else,' said a lady in a straw hat (it was a different lady). 'But why not. We've got . . .' she had a little peep at her wristwatch, 'at least a full minute left.'

Cornelius kissed Thelma. Well, you do in times like this, when every second counts. It's a tradition, or an old charter, or the 'aaaaah' factor, or something.

'Get a move on,' Thelma told him and the tall boy was off up the pylon.

'Take it up! Take it up!' shouted Rune.

'I *am* taking it up,' winced Boris. 'You have to do a system's check. Stabilize the ionizers so as not to risk positronic overload. Don't you know anything about the trans-perambulation of pseudo-cosmic anti-matter?'

Twist! went the hand of Hugo Rune.

'All cleared for take off!' went Boris, in a very high voice.

'Gotcha!' said Norman, creeping up on the saucer. He couldn't see Boris, of course (too short), but he *could* see that big bald head.

'There's the bastard,' whispered Old Claude, spying out the big bald head bent over the screen of the big Karmascope. 'Now just you leave this to me.'

'Where did you get that three-foot-long, high-energy electric cattle prod from?' Jack Bradshaw enquired.

'Same place as the sulphur, sonny. Same place as the sulphur.'

Cornelius had made it to the top of the pylon and was edging his way towards the strange-looking ceramic-bell-sort-of-jobbie arrangement which carried the cable (like they do). The wind and the storm weren't helping. Cornelius shielded his eyes. Gazed out to sea. And then he saw something, lit momentarily upon the horizon. Another snap of lightning, and there it was once more: a thin line of white running straight across where sea met sky. Now what could that be? An early dawn? The tall boy didn't think so. He edged along and climbed across and straddled the big cable.

Roar and rev, went the big bulldozer, turning in another circle. 'There'd be a knack to this,' croaked Tuppe. 'But not one I possess.'

'I'll have you, you bastard.' The voice of Norman, not Claude.
    The dead boy leapt up onto the saucer's rim, unpinning his hand-grenade.
    'Going up!' went Boris, pulling back on the joystick.
    'Whoa!' went Norman seeking something to cling to with his spare hand.

The mechanical gubbins in the town hall clock began to clank their ratcheted wheels and hoist weights up chains and do all those things that clocks do preparatory* to striking.

The Murphy bolt-cutter bit into the cable. But there was a lot of cable and it wasn't that big a bolt-cutter.

* *Preparatory?* I ask you!

Cornelius strained, the bolt-cutter chewed, beneath him the town's folk grew restless.

A lady in a straw hat pointed out to sea. 'What is that?' she asked, viewing the line of white that Cornelius had seen.

A line of white which was now a good deal nearer.

'It's—'

Thelma stared.

Louise stared.

Everybody stared.

The lady in the straw hat said, 'That's a tidal wave, that is. Typical, isn't it? Last thing you need at a time like this is a tidal wave.'

Tidal wave! The cry went up.

It reached Cornelius.

'Oh no!' cried he, chomping away with the bolt-cutter. 'Thelma! Louise! Head for the Tor. Everyone, run for the Tor.'

Everyone ran.

'Cornelius, come on!' shouted Thelma.

'I'll catch you up. Run, just run.'

Thelma and Louise joined in the running.

'Race you to the top,' said Louise.

And on the top Tuppe's bulldozer finally got its act together and trundled towards the pylon.

But the seconds were ticking right away. Tick, tock, tick.

Crackle, crackle, crackle, came a burst of electrical discharging.

CRACKLE, CRACKLE, CRACKLE.

38

The large controller turned at the sound of this crackling.

'You!' said he, like you would. (Well, you *would*.)

'Me,' said Old Claude. 'And it's time for you to get your medicine.'

'Grab him, Jack,' said the large controller.

'*Me*?' said Jack. 'Stuff that. You threw me down the lift shaft.'

'Good boy,' said Claude, waggling the crackling cattle prod.

'Chunky, wallop that old fool, will you?'

'Bally won't,' said Chunky, folding his arms. 'Bally murdered me, you did.'

'Where are your friends when you need them, eh?' asked Old Claude.

'Right here and angry,' said the voice of another Rune. New to the afterlife, this one, wearing a suit. The Transglobe American Publishing version, newly poisoned and later exploded in the vicarage garden.

'Bravo,' said the large controller, as this Rune grabbed the ancient from behind and bear-hugged his arms to his sides.

'No,' shrieked Old Claude, as the final seconds ticked away and the cattle prod spun from his fingers to land at Jack's feet. 'Kill him, sonny. Kill them both before they kill everyone. Living and dead.'

'*What*?' went Jack.

'That's their plan,' agreed Chunky. 'Bastards, they are.'

'All in the twinkling of an eye.' The large controller

reached forward and dipped his big fat hand towards the blood-red button which is known and loved for this kind of thing.

'No!' Jack picked up the cattle prod, flicked the switch and flung himself at the large controller.

The controller caught it from behind.

Up the behind.

Right up.

'Oooooow!' he shrieked, leaping high and falling low. Fist down on the big, blood-red button.

'Zap him, sonny, zap him.'

Jack gave the prod a vicious thrust. In and up.

The large controller's mouth screamed open. Steam blew from his ears. His body quivered and shook. Jack leapt back as sparks began to fly.

Old Claude suddenly dived down his hands between his legs and did to the Rune that held him, what the other Rune had done to Boris.

This Rune took to the shrieking and the leaping high.

Old Claude struggled to the Karmascope. 'We've got to switch it off, sonny. Switch it off.'

'You won't,' screamed the Rune with the internally worn cattle prod. 'I've fixed it so you can't.'

And then there was an appropriately Hellish bang as this Rune exploded into a trillion twinkling, star-shaped shreddings and vanished into absolutely nothing.

Clunk! went the cattle prod falling onto the floor.

'Got to switch it off.' Old Claude battered away at the Karmascope. The other Rune felt this an appropriate time to slip away.

'Don't let him do it,' Old Claude told Jack. 'Give him one up the chocolate speedway with the prod. You know the form.'

'I do,' said Jack, advancing.

'No, please,' said this Rune, *backing* away.

302

'Don't like to rain on your march past,' said Chunky. 'But something's going on in the sky.'

And something truly was.

A blue light was swelling from the nose of the big sky nozzle. Fanning out.

Encompassing the heavens.

And such like.

About the sun, in a glittering ellipse, which followed the path of Earth's orbit, they sparkled. Millions and billions and trillions.

Tiny points of life. Basking in the light of sol.

Being cosmic.

Blue waves spread amongst them. Touched them. Jostled them.

Moved them.

Hurt them.

'Ouch,' they began to go. And 'Oh!' and 'Help!'

'Give the bally thing a clout!' bawled Chunky. 'Out of the way, man, scrap's my business.'

'No,' cried Rune, turning to run.

'Yes,' cried Jack, wading in with the cattle prod.

'Up,' shouted the Rune on Earth. 'Get this thing into the sky.'

'I'm trying, but something's interfering with the electric field.'

'Ouch. Oh and Help!' wailed Norman, clinging to the saucer's rim. 'Something horrible's happening to me.'

Munch, went the bolt-cutter of Cornelius Murphy.

Brum, Brum, went Tuppe's bulldozer, yards from the radio mast.

*   *   *

Rumble and roar, went the tidal wave. Rushing forward. Big tall wave. Plenty of height.

Scream and flee, went the townsfolk scrambling up Druid's Tor.

'Aaagh!' went the zillions of souls, as the blue light swept amongst them, shot around the sun in a pulsating rush and tore down towards the Earth.

'No!' cried the Rune.
  'Yes,' cried Jack.
  Zap! went the cattle prod.

Munch! went the bolt-cutter.

Brum, went the bulldozer, less than two yards in it now.

Rumble, rush and roar. The tidal wave broke over the pier ends, and tore on towards the promenade.

'Up!' cried Rune to Boris.
  'Stuff this,' cried Norman, leaping at the transparent dome and yanking it open.
  '*What*?' Rune looked up. But couldn't see a thing.
  Norman looked down. 'Surprise,' said he, dropping in the hand-grenade. 'Oh, hello, Boris.'
  'Oh,' shrieked Boris as the hand-grenade fell into his lap. 'Not another bomb.'

And then the mighty flash. Two lines of electric-blue light searing down.
  'I had best jump clear,' said Tuppe. 'But my trouser leg seems to be caught.'

'I had best climb down,' said Cornelius. 'But a tidal wave's going to hit.'

'I'd best be out of here,' said Boris, switching on his flying boots and shooting up into the sky.

Well, one out of three's not bad.

But it's not very good either.

Down came the blue light, engulfing the radio masts. Energy tore along the power lines towards the piers.

Tuppe's bulldozer struck home.

The Murphy bolt-cutter bit through the cable.

The saucer containing Rune lurched to one side and smashed into a pylon.

But nothing now could stop it.

Nothing on the face of the Earth.

The electrical discharge engulfed the power lines and pylons and hit the piers.

The tidal wave hit Skelington Bay.

39

'You're overloading the system,' said an engineer in a vest and underpants.

'You'll burn out all the fuses,' said his companion, similarly clad.

'Who are you?' asked Old Claude.

'We're the two engineers your mate Norman dropped down the lift shaft. But due to a continuity error we never got mentioned again.'

Kick, Kick, Kick, Kick, went Chunky at the Karma-scope.

'He'll damage that unit,' said the first engineer. 'And it's the only one we've managed to keep working. Can't get the parts, see. Put in chitties for them, but does anyone listen?'

'No,' said his companion. 'Last week I put in for a tube of flux, I had a two-micron downgrade on my interositor.'

'Turn it off!' yelled Old Claude. 'If you know how to, turn it off!'

'Blue button,' said the first engineer.

'*Blue button?*'

'Blue button.'

The second engineer shrugged. 'Half these fan belts want replacing,' he told Jack Bradshaw.

'Really?' said Jack.

'*Blue button? Blue button?*'

'Oil seals are going on a lot of the crank-cases too,' said the first engineer.

'*Blue button?*' shrieked Claude.

The second engineer reached past him and pressed the

blue button. 'Oil's the big issue with these old engines,' he told Jack. 'Keep your engine well lubricated and you won't go wrong.'

'I'll remember that,' said Jack.

'*Is it off*?' Old Claude flailed his arms about. 'Have you switched it off? Has it stopped?'

'Of course it's stopped. And you shouldn't have been playing with it. It's not a toy. Who are you anyway?'

'I', said Claude, with fire in his eyes, 'am the real controller. *I* am Claude Buttocks.'

The engineers looked at one another.

'Claude Buttocks,' said the first one. 'Not as in—'

40

The old sun rose above Druid's Tor. It sparkled on the dew-damp hedgerows, glittered on the grass. The sky was blue, the storm clouds gone. It looked like being a beautiful day.

The old sun looked down with some wonder. It had seen sights before. Sights a-plenty. But a sight such as this?

Not as such.

There were thousands of folk on the Tor.

Thousands.

They stood, staring down at the town.

Exhausted. Arms about one another's shoulders. Hands holding hands. Some wept. Others wrung their fingers, shook their heads and sighed.

For what the old sun saw and these people saw was something awesome, unique.

A town of two wrecked piers, fallen pylons, mangled cars and burnt-out buildings. Abandoned military vehicles. Torn-up pavements. Smashed houses. Fallen shops.

A town to inspire pity.

But then, now, a town to inspire something more.

Because here. This town. Skelington Bay. Here. Now.

Everything. All. In its smallest detail. From pebbled sandy beach to loose roof slate.

Everything.

All.

The entire town.

Was now gold-plated.

Shining like a fire in the sun.
And *that's* something you don't see every day.

41

'Where am I?' asked Tuppe.

'You're with me.'

'Oh Cornelius, it's you.'

'It's me.'

'What happened to us?'

'I don't like to think. But I think I know.'

'Then we're—'

'Dead,' said Norman, smiling from the desk in the room full of cabinets and box files. 'But look on the bright side. You may be dead, but at least you're in full-time, regular employment.'

42

Thelma and Louise looked down upon the golden town.

'They didn't make it,' said Thelma.

'No.' Louise shook her head sadly. 'But perhaps they stopped it. It all stopped.'

'And all the townsfolk survived. Which is something. But not enough.'

'We're going to miss them,' said Louise. 'Miss them very much.'

Thelma sniffed away a tear. She wasn't into sentiment. But sometimes. Sometimes. When you really do care.

Thelma put her arm about the shoulder of Louise.

And they both wept.

But the sun shone higher. And around it, only slightly chaffed and feeling all cosmic again, the zillions of souls hung in space.

Waiting.

43

'Come on, guys,' said Norman. 'It's not as bad as you think. Well, it is, but you'll get used to it. The controller's given me Jack Bradshaw's job. And now everyone's not going to die, well, it's a happy ending. Everyone likes a happy ending.'

'I don't feel dead,' said Tuppe. 'But I do feel hungry.'

'I'll show you the canteen. I'm sure there is a canteen, although I've not seen it myself.'

'I assume all the Runes are dead and gone,' said Cornelius.

'I assume so, although I lost count.'

'God will sort it out,' said Tuppe.

'Hugo Rune was my dad,' said Cornelius. 'I still can't believe what he did.'

'My dad fell out of the sky and snuffed me,' said Norman. 'Dads are not always to be trusted.'

'I never thought they were.'

'If we have to work here,' said Tuppe. 'How long for? You said it was all to do with the extension to Heaven getting completed, when is that going to happen?'

'Not long.'

'How long?'

'Well—'

'Stop it, Norman.' Old Claude appeared at the door. He looked somewhat changed: haircut, shaved chin, nice new suit. A white suit. 'That's quite enough.'

'I was going to tell them about the five-aside football,' said Norman.

'Quite enough.'

'What is this?' Cornelius asked.

'*He* knows,' said Claude, winking at Norman. 'Tell them.'

Norman smiled. 'You can go,' said he. 'I was only kidding, you don't have to stay.'

'Say again.'

'I had a word with the Big Figure,' said Claude. 'Told Him everything. About Rune and Norman and you and Tuppe. He's an all-right kind of guy, the Big Figure. Says it's bollocks on the inside the next time He creates a race.'

'I don't think I understand,' said Tuppe.

'You don't have to be dead any more,' said Norman. 'God says you can come back to life. As a favour, seeing as what you did.'

'You're joking? He didn't?'

'He did,' said Claude. 'Out the door, turn left, take the lift down.'

'No?' said Cornelius. 'I mean, thanks.'

'Thank *Him*,' said Claude.

'Thank you, sir,' said Cornelius.

'DON'T MENTION IT,' said a very big voice.

'Thanks from me too,' said Tuppe. '*Sir*, thank you.'

'HEY, TUPPE,' said the big voice, 'CAREFUL HOW YOU GO WHEN YOU GET BACK.'

'Sorry?'

'YOU'LL FIND OUT.'

'Well, thanks. I can't tell you how much thanks.' Cornelius shook Old Claude by the hand. Turned and shook Norman's hand also. 'Thanks for everything, Norman.'

'DON'T MENTION IT,' said Norman, in a very big voice of his own.

'Well, goodbye.'

Tuppe and Cornelius waved goodbye and made off through the door.

Norman sighed and put his elbows down on the desk.

'I expect you're just going to doss about again, aren't you?' asked Claude.

Norman shrugged dismally.

'Bugger off,' said Old Claude.

'Sorry, what?'

'Bugger off. Go on.'

'What do you mean?'

'I mean, Norman, that the Big Figure has given you a pardon too. I put in a good word for you. He says you can come back to life. No more incantations at dawn though, eh?'

'You mean I can be alive again?'

'That's it. Go on. Bugger off. You'll miss the lift.'

'Thank you, Claude. Thank you.' Norman threw his arms about the old fella. It was tears. It was pathos.

And why not, eh?

'Go on,' said Claude. 'And good luck.'

44

And the sun beamed down.

And if we're still into pathos.

Which I am (you can please yourself).

Down they came to Druid's Tor in rays of golden light.

'Whoa!' said Cornelius, feeling all over himself. 'I would appear to be intact.'

'Whoa!' said Norman. 'Me too.' And feeling at his face: 'My spots have all cleared up, not that I ever made a big thing about them.'

'And your hair's not so red,' said Cornelius. 'And that's a far better haircut than you had before.'

'I think it's a Tony Curtis,' said Norman, fingering his head.

'How about you, Tuppe? Are you OK?'

Cornelius turned. Looked down at Tuppe.

Looked up a bit at Tuppe.

Looked up a bit more.

'Tuppe,' said Cornelius.

'I've grown,' said Tuppe. 'God's made me tall. I'm like you, Cornelius. I'm tall. I'm not tiny any more.'

'You were never tiny to me.'

'It's them,' called Thelma. 'They're alive.'

'Hey, Tuppe,' called Louise. 'Are you looking good, or what?'

45

'We, the people of Magonia, are proud to award you this medal for bravery and noble deeds above and beyond the call of duty.' The Emperor saluted. His court saluted. The medal was pinned on. Boris beamed about the court.

'Thank you very much,' said Boris.

'Don't mention it,' said the Emperor. 'But if I ever see that bogus King Hugo again I'll have very harsh words to say to him.'

'I don't think you will,' said Boris, smiling in the direction of his good friend Bryant, who was grinding his teeth. 'I really don't think you will.'

46

The most amazing man who ever lived lay soaking in his marble bath-tub. The perfumed water rose and fell about his ample belly, as deep breaths filled his lungs and he sought to compose the final mathematical equation needed to complete his formula for the universal panacea and the elixir of life.

And he would have had it too, if it hadn't been for the violent pounding upon his bedsit door and the howls of complaint from his landlady.

'Get out of that bed, you lazy sod, or I'll have my husband Cyril come and break down the door!'

The most amazing man who ever lived awoke with a bit of a start.

He blinked his eyes. They were somewhat bloodshot, but otherwise quite normal. For this most amazing man was the original Rune, father to Cornelius and seeker after Truths of an Ultimate nature.

A Rune who had long ago disowned the evil twins of his creation. A Rune who now dedicated his life to a noble cause for the good of mankind.

The formula for the universal panacea and the elixir of life.

And he really would have had it that time.

Really.

But the banging went on at his bedsit door.

And his landlady called for Cyril.

She had a good pair of lungs on her, the landlady. Her husband's name really carried about the house. 'CY-RIL!' it went. '*CY-RIL!*'

'Cyril?' The most amazing man scratched at his shaven head. It dearly needed a shave. '*Cyril?*'

Flinging aside his wretched blanket, he sprang from his bed as one possessed, sought vellum and stylus and spoke as he wrote; with a flourish.

'CYRIL! That's it! CY as in cyanamide, the colourless soluble acid with the chemical formula H_2NCN. R being the chemical symbol for Radium. I the symbol in physics for Isospin. L the chemical symbol for the Avogadro constant, the number of atoms or molecules in a mole of a substance. That being equal to $6.022\ 52 \times 10^{23}$ per mole. The final equation. I have it. I have it!'

And he did.

THE END

SPROUT⟨P⟩LŌRE

The Now Official
RŌBERT RANKIN
Fan Club

Members Will Receive:

Four Fabulous Issues of *The Brentford Mercury*, featuring previously unpublished stories by Robert Rankin. Also containing News, Reviews, Fiction and Fun.

A Coveted Sproutlore Badge.

'Amazing Stuff!' - *Robert Rankin*.

A SELECTED LIST OF OTHER FANTASY TITLES AVAILABLE FROM CORGI BOOKS

14509 2	THE GREAT GAME 1: PAST IMPERATIVE	Dave Duncan	£5.99
14500 9	THE GREAT GAME 2: PRESENT TENSE	Dave Duncan	£5.99
13017 6	MALLOREON 1: GUARDIANS OF THE WEST	David Eddings	£5.99
12284 X	BELGARIAD 1: PAWN OF PROPHECY	David Eddings	£5.99
14252 2	THE LEGEND OF DEATHWALKER	David Gemmell	£5.99
14255 7	ECHOES OF THE GREAT SONG	David Gemmell	£5.99
14111 9	HOUSE OF TRIBES	Garry Kilworth	£4.99
14464 9	A MIDSUMMER'S NIGHTMARE	Garry Kilworth	£5.99
11804 4	DRAGONDRUMS	Anne McCaffrey	£5.99
14098 8	POWERS THAT BE	Anne McCaffrey & Elizabeth Ann Scarborough	£5.99
14386 3	MYST	Rand & Robyn Miller	£4.99
14542 4	HOGFATHER	Terry Pratchett	£5.99
13703 0	GOOD OMENS	Terry Pratchett & Neil Gaiman	£5.99
13681 6	ARMAGEDDON THE MUSICAL	Robert Rankin	£5.99
13832 0	THEY CAME AND ATE US, ARMAGEDDON II: THE B-MOVIE	Robert Rankin	£5.99
13923 8	THE SURBURBAN BOOK OF THE DEAD, ARMAGEDDON III: THE REMAKE	Robert Rankin	£5.99
13841 X	THE ANTIPOPE	Robert Rankin	£5.99
13842 8	THE BRENTFORD TRIANGLE	Robert Rankin	£5.99
13843 6	EAST OF EALING	Robert Rankin	£5.99
13844 4	THE SPROUTS OF WRATH	Robert Rankin	£5.99
14357 X	THE BRENTFORD CHAINSTORE MASSACRE	Robert Rankin	£5.99
13922 X	THE BOOK OF THE ULTIMATE TRUTHS	Robert Rankin	£4.99
13833 9	RAIDERS OF THE LOST CAR PARK	Robert Rankin	£5.99
13924 6	THE GREATEST SHOW OFF EARTH	Robert Rankin	£4.99
14212 3	THE GARDEN OF UNEARTHLY DELIGHTS	Robert Rankin	£5.99
14213 1	A DOG CALLED DEMOLITION	Robert Rankin	£5.99
14355 3	NOSTRADAMUS ATE MY HAMSTER	Robert Rankin	£5.99
14356 1	SPROUT MASK REPLICA	Robert Rankin	£5.99
14112 7	EMPIRE OF THE ANTS	Bernard Werber	£5.99